NOW I SEE YOU

A NOVEL

SHANNON WORK

ISBN: 978-1-7354353-0-5 (paperback)
ISBN: 978-1-7354353-2-9 (large print paperback)
ISBN: 978-1-7354353-1-2 (eBook)

www.shannonwork.com

"Very few of us are what we seem."

—*Agatha Christie*

CHAPTER 1

HE FOUND HE had a taste for murder and it surprised him. Who knew killing could be so cathartic, so satisfying. Besides, some people just needed killing—like when the government culled elk herds in the mountains when their numbers got unruly, usually getting rid of the weak or lame, the ones of no significance. He chose his victims carefully, as well. So really, he was doing the world a favor.

He turned up the collar of the wool overcoat, stuck his gloved hands into its pockets, and snuck sideways glances at the people passing on the sidewalk. He turned the corner onto Galena Street and was met with a blast of frigid air off the mountains. It was cold, but the wind didn't have the bite it had the day before. If what they said was true, the unusually cold spring would soon thaw. Then they would find the body.

Hiding the body so well was a mistake, but it had been his first murder and he had learned. A month later he tossed the body of his second victim just off a dirt road in the mountains where it had been found the next day.

He was the only one who knew where his first victim was and that she was dead. But they would find her soon, and when they did, the media would be all a buzz at the prospect of a serial killer among the rich and famous. Legitimate news sources and tabloids alike would descend on the mountain resort like vultures.

As he walked, he drew in a deep breath through his nose, the cold burning his sinuses. He looked up toward the mountains and marveled at their strength and majesty. Ancient stone thrust up through the earth's crust millions of years ago. He had always heard that the mountains held secrets—of ghosts and treasure, heartbreak and murder. He was like the mountains in that way. They were kindred spirits.

He stopped and watched as clouds boiled over the snowy peaks, churning up an icy wind that threatened to numb the parts of him still exposed. He thought of his victims, their last moments. Had they gone numb, grown colder and colder, finally consumed by a frigid darkness? Or were they simply there one moment then gone the next? Maybe one day he would stop, just before he was finished, and ask.

A careless bump from a passing teen snapped him from his reverie. He put his head down and continued walking, the incline making his labored breath fog in front of him.

Aspen's reputation as a playground of the rich and famous was perfect for what he wanted. One murder *here* had already grabbed the media's attention; five would set worldwide publicity off like a fire storm and firmly establish him as one of the greatest killers of all time.

It was mid-April, the spring breakers were long gone and it would be another month before the summer tourists showed up. Only a handful of people were out that afternoon. He watched as they strolled the sidewalk and crossed the street, talking and laughing. He recognized and spoke to a few.

They were locals, and they all loved Aspen. *That* he shared with them. What he didn't share were the secrets of what he had done, and what he planned to do next.

CHAPTER 2

GEORGIA GLASS LEFT Denver early that morning. The drive that would normally take three and a half hours had taken over five. The forecast had warned of light to moderate snow, but there was no mention of the near blizzard conditions she faced as she drove west through the mountains on Interstate 70.

It had been a harrowing drive. She passed multiple cars that had spun out and gotten stuck in the snow.

Once off the interstate and headed south toward Aspen, the snow had slowed and finally quit. She relaxed her hold on the wheel and took in several deep breaths, letting each out slowly before taking in the next. She finally had time to think, and let her thoughts drift as she drove the long tilted curves through the mountains.

The morning's storm, with its chaos and carnage, reminded her of the last couple of years—the drama, the fear of what might lie around the next corner. Her mother had been right when she told her she had been burning the candle at both ends for too long. She needed to decompress before it all sent her over the edge.

Georgia had spent the last few years working sixty-hour weeks at the CBS affiliate in Denver and rarely taking a day off. She couldn't remember the last time she had taken a real vacation, working holidays and weekends for as long as she could remember. But of course, the news never stops, and she reported the news.

Hosting her own weekly investigative reporting show for a national network in Los Angeles would be demanding—she knew that—but at least the hours would be more predictable. Maybe. And if she played her cards right, it would be a stepping stone to her own nightly show.

But she wouldn't think about that right now.

The movers had loaded up most of her worldly possessions in Denver and headed west the day before. They would sit in storage in Los Angeles until she got there. But first she had two months to spend in Aspen.

The uncle she'd never known hadn't been able to sell his house. He had died without a will and Georgia was his only living blood relative. Since he had spent his entire working career in law enforcement, his estate had not amounted to much—except for the house. All she had to do was pay the back taxes and closing costs, and it would be hers. She would do that with the loan she had arranged with a bank in Los Angeles. Her new job—and the salary that went with it—couldn't have happened at a better time.

Aspen was the perfect place for a second home. The question was, would she have enough time to use it? She would soon be hosting a show that would air nationwide every Sunday evening. But as her celebrity quotient increased, what better place to hide in plain sight than in a town that regularly hosted celebrities?

Plus, Colorado was her home, and she liked the idea of keeping roots there. She had been born in Colorado Springs, educated in Boulder, and until a week earlier, had worked in Denver. She loved the state and would miss it. A vacation home in the mountains would be the perfect excuse to come back often.

She would take title to the house she had inherited from the uncle she never knew. She would renovate it then decide whether she wanted to keep it or flip it. But for the next few weeks she was determined to live like she was driving—*slow and deliberate.*

Besides fixing up the house, she had nothing to do in Aspen and wasn't sure how she felt about it yet. It was too late in the year to ski, but in a few weeks the lakes would probably be thawed enough to paddle board. She made a mental note to purchase a board. For now, she would make due with trail running. It would be a nice change from running on pavement.

Her mother had urged her to use the free time to "unblock your chakras and balance your emotional energies." Whatever that meant. Her mother was so bohemian, nothing like herself, but thinking about her made Georgia smile. She had pleaded with Georgia to keep the house once it was hers—calling it "a gift from the heavens." But Georgia wasn't sure if that's what she wanted to do. She'd give herself the two months to decide.

Her car hit an ice patch—slipped to the left, breaking her train of thought. *Slow and deliberate,* she reminded herself.

It was early afternoon when she finally drove into town. She glanced at the temperature on the dashboard. The sun was out but it was still a cold thirty-seven degrees. The streets were wet but clear of snow and ice. Despite sudden gusts of wind off the mountains that rocked her car from side to side, it was a beautiful day.

She drove through town, taking it all in. The quaint buildings on Main Street, meticulously restored relics from the town's mining days, now home to upscale restaurants and stores like Gucci and Prada. There were tree-lined pedestrian malls with cobblestone paving and iron benches. Everything freshly painted and scrubbed squeaky clean like a Disney park.

The residential streets were even prettier. There were trees everywhere—dark green spruce and fir, the slick gray bark of aspen not yet in bloom. The yards covered with deep snow.

She drove slowly, glancing left and right at the Victorian-era homes in varying shades of color, their modest sizes belying the ridiculous prices they sold for. It was hard to believe that in less than 24 hours one of them would be hers.

Georgia had been to Aspen several times. As a standout on her high school ski team, then three years skiing for the University of Colorado before a particularly nasty ACL injury had ended her career early, she had made several trips for competitions.

She had vague memories of Aspen, but memories experienced and seen through the eyes of a teenager, then as a college student. Over a decade later, it was different; she was now looking at it through the eyes of an adult and was enthralled by its quaint beauty.

On the way to the hotel, she couldn't resist the urge to drive by the house she would soon inherit. She had the address on Durango Avenue already in her phone and looked down at the map as she drove. She knew it would be near the end of the street, close to the river. One more turn... two blocks... there it was. She recognized the house immediately from the photos she had gone over and over online. She pulled to a stop in front and shut off the engine.

It was a two-story Victorian in a pastel shade of blue, set on a gentle slope that angled toward the river. She sat in her car and studied the details—the high peaked gables, gingerbread moldings, a front porch that stretched the width of the house terminating in a small circular tower that rose three stories. There was peeling paint in places and a couple missing balusters, but the house was framed by tall pines and a handful of aspen trees in a setting that reminded her of something out of a fairy tale.

It was old and in obvious need of cosmetic repair, but structurally it looked solid and in good shape. But she wasn't an expert. She would keep her fingers crossed and let the contractor confirm it for her.

From the pictures online, she knew the garage wasn't in as good shape. She got out and walked around the side of the house for a quick look, her boots sinking into five or six inches of snow.

The garage was worse than she had expected. She was glad the contractor would tackle it first. The whole thing canted sharply at an odd angle, the rotting wallboards appearing to struggle under the weight of the wood shake roof.

Whether she sold the house or decided to keep it, she wanted to remodel it first. She would make a list of what needed to be done when she walked through the house with the contractor the next day. She took one last long look at the house and sighed with relief. It was a project she could handle, and something to keep her busy the next couple of months.

Back in the car, she typed the address to Hotel Jerome into her phone and was relieved to see it was only six minutes away. It wasn't even four o'clock yet, but she was exhausted. She needed a hot shower and room service.

Tomorrow would be a full day. She mentally ran through the schedule. First, breakfast and then a walk-through with her real estate agent where she would finally get to see the inside of the house. Barring any surprises, she would then sign the paperwork at the title company at eleven. Next, she'd do some shopping. During the walk-through she would make a list of what was left behind and what was still needed to fully stock the house. She had done her research and knew that furnished homes in Aspen sold faster and for higher prices than empty ones. Then she would meet with the contractor and see about getting started on the garage.

After checking in and taking a long shower, Georgia pulled on sweatpants and a favorite T-shirt. She was too tired to go out and instead decided to finish the Michael Connelly novel she had started weeks earlier, order room service, then maybe watch the evening news.

Just as she sank into the oversized chair near the window, her cell phone rang. She saw the caller ID and smiled.

"Checking up on me already?"

Eddie Jenkins was probably the friend she would miss the most in Denver, but he had promised to visit her once she'd gotten settled in Los Angeles. She planned on holding him to it.

"I tried calling a couple times but you must have been out of cell phone range. I heard about the weather. It sounds like you drove through a blizzard."

She reassured him it hadn't been as bad as he'd heard and that they'd been through much worse together. Eddie was a talented cameraman for the station, and Georgia had spent nearly every day of her six-year tenure as a special assignment reporter with him. After she was promoted to morning news anchor a few years ago, they hadn't worked directly together again but had remained close friends.

"Well I'm glad you made it okay," Eddie said. "For a while I thought I was going to have to play knight to your damsel in distress."

She laughed. "You already did that. Remember?" She could always count on Eddie to cheer her up, and she was going to miss him desperately.

Eddie had been there for her during the darkest times in her life, the bitter public breakup with TJ Williams, star linebacker with the Denver Broncos—the relationship and breakup had been a public humiliation disaster.

Then not long after the breakup, she started being stalked.

At first the police considered TJ a suspect. Georgia knew it wasn't him, he was too shallow to care she was no longer in his life. There were plenty of other girls. But the police had investigated TJ anyway, finally ruling him out when Tony Paladino had been caught.

The police called Tony an obsessed fan. She thought it was ironic a stalker would be called a "fan." How could someone who had caused her such fear be referred to in the same way as someone who had sent her a personal note telling her how she made the morning news worth getting up for, or the people who had sent random emails complimenting a particular blouse she had worn on air, or a new hairstyle. No, it didn't seem right calling Tony Paladino a "fan."

It was the exposé she had done on his father that had started it all. Georgia's report on Angelo Paladino—formerly of the Bronx, then Denver—had exposed his ties to New York's Romano crime family. It was an ambitious story for a local anchor, one that garnered her national attention that ultimately led to an Emmy and the job offer from Coastal News.

But doing the story had taken its toll.

Soon after it aired, Angelo Paladino had been murdered, along with his wife Estelle. Both shot through the head as they slept. Initially, the evidence pointed to an intruder; the house had been partially ransacked and jewelry and cash stolen. But the more the police investigated, the more it looked like a mob hit. The case was still open.

Angelo Paladino and a handful of others were long-time fixtures on the radars of both the Denver Police and the FBI, suspected of dealing in illegal gambling and loansharking, men with ties to the infamous Gambino, Genovese and Romano families.

Georgia had sought out Tony Paladino following the murder of his parents for a follow-up story. She got more than an interview, she got an infatuated admirer.

And as hard as she tried, she hadn't completely recovered from the fear of being stalked. But Eddie had been her rock. He had installed the high-tech security system and cameras outside her townhouse that helped police catch Paladino. She would be forever grateful.

They talked a little while longer—station gossip mostly—then agreed to talk again soon.

After the call, Georgia got up and checked both locks on the door, making certain they were secure. Of course they were, she had locked them immediately after the bellhop had dropped off her bags and left the room. She was pretty sure she checked them again after she had gotten out of the shower.

Stop it, she scolded herself. He was locked up—it was over. But she wondered if it would ever really be over.

She walked to the window, cranked it open and was immediately hit with a rush of cold air. The shock felt good. She shut her eyes and drew in a deep breath, smelling the hint of pine and letting her hair swirl around her. She forced the past from her mind, she wouldn't think about that now. For the moment, she was determined to put the pieces back together, make everything right with her world.

She stood at the window with her eyes closed and took in a couple more deep breaths. As hard as she tried, she couldn't shake the uneasy feeling that something sinister lurked around the corner.

CHAPTER 3

JONATHAN KRAMER WALKED with long, determined strides across the yard to the converted barn which, like a lot of the barns behind old homes in Aspen, had long ago been renovated into a garage. There were no signs of impending snow, but a brisk wind off the mountains sent him back inside to grab his coat.

He scolded himself for getting soft in his old age despite being only thirty-five. Keep it up at this rate and he'd be wearing gloves into June.

Jonathan was meeting his new client for breakfast at a small cafe a block from Hotel Jerome where he had suggested she stay the night. After breakfast he would show Georgia the house then they would head to the title company to sign the papers.

He backed his early model Range Rover out the garage and thought about the first conversation he ever had with Georgia Glass. Of course he knew who she was—the tall leggy blonde who anchored the evening news for one of the networks in Denver. He had watched her numerous times over the years. Who would have guessed she would be related to the crusty old recluse Ernest Galloway?

He'd been trying to sell Galloway's run-down house for two years, ever since the old guy had moved into a nursing home in Colorado Springs. Then the old coot up and dies, and *voilà*—enter great-grandniece Georgia Glass, instant client. He wouldn't get his normal commission but the consulting fee wasn't bad. And there was the possibility of another commission in the future if Georgia decided to sell the house.

"I never knew I had an uncle," Georgia had told him during their first conversation. "My father was his only remaining blood relative. At some point, they became estranged. My father died years ago. I only have a few memories him. But I never met his uncle."

The luck of some people, Jonathan thought. Inheriting a house from an unknown relative? Things like that didn't happen. It would be easy to be resentful, but she was too darned nice. And despite being movie star gorgeous and a successful news anchor, she had been surprisingly friendly and down to earth. Not a diva like he would have guessed.

She told him she wasn't sure yet if she would sell or keep the house, but she was excited to finally see it. He had warned her it needed renovating, but she didn't seem to care.

Jonathan parked his car on the street and walked into Miner's Cafe. She was already there. He recognized her immediately and was surprised to see she was even prettier in person.

She sat sipping a cup of coffee. A half-eaten scone sat in front of her on a small china plate.

"Ms. Glass, I'm Jonathan Kramer."

"Hi, Jonathan. Nice to finally meet you. Call me Georgia." She gestured to the chair across the marble-topped table. "Sorry I didn't wait for you to order, I couldn't resist the pastries."

"I'm impressed you could limit yourself to just one," Jonathan said smiling. "I usually get a couple to go when I'm done with breakfast."

"That's a fabulous idea. I think I'll do that. I'm so glad you suggested this place instead of the Starbucks down the street."

"Never," he said with an expression of mock horror.

"Insanely overpriced coffee and no real breakfast. Besides, the owner here is a friend of mine."

"Well kudos to the chef, this is excellent." She took another bite of the scone.

"You're early," he said. "I could have been here earlier if you'd have let me know."

She waved a dismissive hand. "No, not a problem. You'll learn I can be impatient sometimes, and I can't wait to see the inside."

"I'm glad you're excited to see it—eager buyers make my job easy. But I have to say, an eager buyer who has never set foot in a house before they buy it, makes me nervous. You're my first."

She laughed. "Well, I'm sorry for making you nervous, but I'm not really a buyer, remember? I'm inheriting it. So you're off the hook."

"Well, you're still taking ownership, even if you only have to pay the taxes and sign the papers."

"That I do," she admitted. "But I have to take title before I can sell it."

"Well I think you're going to love Aspen. My bet is that you end up keeping it."

"Maybe—you never know. Life has been crazy lately and the thought of somewhere this beautiful to escape to is appealing."

"Well, Aspen is a great place for people who can afford it," Jonathan said. "It can get crowded during the peak seasons, but the locals are friendly and there's virtually no crime. We don't even lock our doors most of the time."

Georgia's smile looked weary. "After what I've been through lately, that sounds wonderful."

Jonathan had read several tabloid reports about the breakup with her football boyfriend, and assumed that was what she was referring to. He didn't want to pry into her personal life, so he changed the subject.

"Do you ski?" he asked.

"I do."

"Well, then you'll really love it. We have some of the best skiing around. It's too late for skiing this year, but I'll give you a map of my favorite hiking trails—a couple of the lower trails are already thawed if you're interested."

"I'd love that," Georgia said. "Thank you."

Jonathan pulled a spiral-bound report out of an accordion folder and handed it to her. "The inspection report. Structurally the house is in good shape, but there's a ton of deferred maintenance. We'll go through the report as we look at the house. I want you to be comfortable with everything before signing any papers."

"I still think you're trying to talk me out of taking ownership," she teased.

"Never. But I want full transparency—no surprises. I don't want you to have any regrets later. Happy buyers are the best buyers."

She smiled and nodded. "I appreciate your honesty. Now let's get you something to eat so I can go see my house already." She signaled for the waitress.

Georgia watched him as he studied the menu. Attractive by any woman's standards. Tall, athletic build. She shook her head once and looked down at her plate. The last thing she needed was to get tangled in another questionable romance. She'd had one too many of those recently. The break up with TJ was still fresh. She wasn't ready to make that mistake again.

But even from the first phone conversation several weeks earlier, she could tell Jonathan was easygoing and sincere. It was such a relief that the agent who had been trying to sell her uncle's house, and was now helping her take title to it, wasn't one of those slick salesman types. He seemed genuinely concerned she was being too impulsive taking ownership of a house she'd never seen.

The waitress set Jonathan's food on the table and refilled his coffee cup.

Georgia took a sip of coffee then set the cup back on the table. "Thank you for helping me find a contractor."

"You got ahold of him?"

"Yes, he's meeting me at the house later this afternoon."

Jonathan finished his bite and nodded. "Karl's good. He'll be pricy, but he's worth it. Lots of A-list clients around town."

"Well, thank you again. I'm going to have him start on the garage, but we're going to walk through the rest of the house and make a list of priorities on what to remodel next."

"Maybe a fresh coat of paint on the outside."

"Definitely that," she agreed.

He ate the last bite of bacon then sopped up the remaining syrup left over from the pancakes with a bit of toast. He looked up and saw her watching him.

Georgia smiled. "The blueberry scone was excellent, but next time, I'm having what you had."

"And I didn't even offer you a bite. My mother would be appalled at my lack of manners." He wiped his easy smile with the napkin then checked his watch. "Ready? I don't want us to be rushed at the house. I want you to have plenty of time to—"

"Change my mind?" She laughed. "I'm not going to do that. But if it'll make you happy, I'll open every cabinet, go through every closet."

"That *will* make me happy," he said signaling the waitress that they were finished.

While they waited for the check, she asked him, "So how did you end up in Aspen—if you don't mind a personal question."

"I don't mind. That's the reporter in you, isn't it? Personal questions?"

"Guilty." Georgia held up her hands in surrender. "But seriously, there aren't many people who live here year-round. I'm curious how you ended up here?"

He laid his napkin on the table and sat back in his chair. "I grew up in L.A.—coincidence, I know; that's where you're headed—but we vacationed here when I was a kid. We'd stay for a week or so a couple times a year at Hotel Jerome, or Little Nell before the Jerome was renovated. I guess I got the mountains in my blood when I was young and couldn't get them out. I sold real estate for a while in California, but then one day realized I could do that anywhere, why stay in L.A.? So here I am."

"Do your parents still come to visit?"

"My father died years ago. He loved it here. He's why we would come. Skiing in the winter. Hiking and camping in the summer. Mother came some, but it was never her choice. She preferred the city—her friends, parties. She still keeps a condo here, but she doesn't get here much anymore. She's getting older and it's harder for her to travel, but she surprises me every once in a while."

"Well, it's beautiful, and I can't wait to settle in for a couple months."

"When you feel up to it, I'll introduce you to some of the locals. I have to warn you, though, they can be a quirky bunch. The tourists are one thing; they come and go, plenty of Hollywood celebrities and big business types. But the locals, those who live here year-round, or at least half the year, can be, well, you'll see."

"Now I'm intrigued."

"You should be," he said with a short laugh. "Don't get me wrong, they're good people, but some can be a little eccentric, and more than a few are leery of newcomers. They're going to welcome you with open arms once they get to know you. I promise."

"I can't wait to meet them."

The waitress set the check on the table and Jonathan got out his wallet. "This one is on me," he said. "A 'Welcome to Aspen' breakfast."

Georgia considered it a moment, then nodded. "Okay, but the next one is on me."

"Deal."

At the house, Georgia pulled to the curb and parked behind Jonathan's Range Rover. She got out and looked at the house, and felt a rush of excitement she hadn't felt since Christmas mornings as a child. But Santa Claus hadn't given her this present, Ernest Galloway had. She regretted never having met him. Although he hadn't left the house to her directly in his will—he probably never even knew she existed—she would have liked to have met the relative whose house would now be her own.

"I had the sidewalk shoveled this morning," Jonathan told her as they made their way toward the house. On the porch, he unlocked the door and handed her the key, then stepped aside so she could enter first.

"Home sweet home," she said as she stepped over the threshold.

They walked through every room. The house was just what she had expected—small but with good bones, high ceilings and worn pine floors. It smelled of dust and old wood, and she loved it.

The rooms all had an assortment of furniture left in them. Some were wonderful antiques that she would keep. Other things she would donate or throw out. She walked through it all a second time.

Her favorite room was the kitchen. Tall glass-front cabinets in desperate need of Windex hung on two walls. A window over the sink looked out to the backyard and beyond to the garage. True to her promise, Georgia went through all the cabinets and closets.

She studied the architectural details and finishes, taking mental notes on things she thought needed to be replaced and the things she hoped the builder could refurbish.

Some things would need to go, like the short partition that separated the living room from a small sitting area with a bay window that was the lower section of the tower she had seen from outside. She would ask the contractor if he could open the two spaces into one larger room. And the kitchen definitely needed new appliances. But upstairs, she was delighted to find the original claw-footed bathtub. Refinished, and with a new tile floor underneath, it would be perfect.

The house wasn't big—the living areas were downstairs and two bedrooms and a bathroom up—but it was charming. Her townhouse in Denver had been nice, but it didn't have the appeal of this little Victorian.

Even though Jonathan had the house cleaned a couple weeks before, everything was already covered in a thin layer of dust. She would clean it all again. But the house was solid, and it would be hers.

Jonathan hadn't said much as they walked through the rooms, only pointing out deficiencies noted in the inspection report. He was quiet and let her take it all in. Now he joined her at the second-floor window that looked toward downtown and the mountains beyond.

"I love it," she said. "It might sound silly, since I've never been in it before, but it already feels like home."

"Then home you are. Ready to go to sign the papers and make it official?"

CHAPTER 4

FOUR HOURS LATER Georgia was back at the house, carrying in armloads of groceries. She had also stopped at a hardware store and loaded up on new pots and pans, cooking utensils, and various other things she thought she might need to furnish the house.

Her third stop had been to Frette for bed linens and towels. She was excited to find the four-poster bed left in the house, but wasn't sure if she was up to using Uncle Ernest's old sheets and quilt.

In the kitchen she studied the avocado-colored refrigerator. It was a massive thing in the tiny kitchen, rounded in shape and bulging out into the minimal floorspace. For something so large, it had the tiniest freezer she had ever seen. Miraculously, when Jonathan had switched it on earlier, it started running, but it probably wouldn't last long. She wistfully remembered the stainless KitchenAid she sold along with the townhouse in Denver, then thought of the bright shiny new one waiting for her in the high-rise condo she'd leased in L.A. Just then the avocado monster hiccuped and the power shut off for a second before it kicked back on. She put a refrigerator at the top of the list of things still left to purchase.

Back outside as she unloaded the last box of supplies from her car, an early model gray truck pulled to the curb and parked behind her. A burly man she guessed to be in his late 40's jumped out and smiled, his white teeth in stark contrast to the dark salt and pepper beard that stuck out in every direction. He had the windburned leathery complexion of someone who spent a lot of time outdoors.

"Let me get that." He took the box from her without waiting for a reply, and stuck out his free hand the size of a bear paw, for Georgia to shake. "You must be Ms. Glass," he said pumping her hand.

Georgia smiled and nodded. "I am."

"I'm Karl Kamp. You have a garage remodel for me to look at?"

"I want to start there, but there's going to be more to do than just the garage. I'd like for you to look at the house, too."

He looked over the small wood-framed Victorian with approval. "We can get it fixed up right. In my opinion, these old houses are way better than those house-in-a-box things they're stacking together down the street." He nodded toward a three-story condominium development several blocks away.

Georgia agreed with him. "Let's get these things inside and then we'll go look at the garage."

Inside, Karl set the box on the simple oak table left by Ernest Galloway. Georgia noticed him glance around the kitchen.

"It needs a little T-L-C," she said.

"She's a fine old thing, Ms. Glass. Good bones. And we'll do everything we can to make her shine again." He shot another megawatt smile through the dark beard. "Now let's go see that garage."

Georgia nodded. His cheerfulness was contagious. She already liked Karl Kamp.

He followed her out the kitchen door and across the yard on a flagstone path that led to the garage. It was a small building, leaning to one side, and built of wood that had weathered to a silvery-gray long ago.

Georgia opened the door and was met with a gust of musty stale air. Karl pushed cobwebs aside and stepped past her into the darkness. She followed him in but stopped just inside the doorway, taking a moment for her eyes to adjust.

There were cracks between the wall boards where thin bands of dust-moted light spilled through. It smelled ancient, and somehow was colder inside than out. The whole thing looked like it could fall over any minute.

Karl slapped an interior support beam that ran from the ground to the ceiling, and stood studying the underside of the roof. There were several spots between the rotting wood shakes where daylight shone through.

"Beams look and feel solid, but the walls needs to be redone. And the whole roof's gotta be replaced."

He walked around, eyeing where the walls met the rafters, then moved aside a rake with a cracked handle and a rusted shovel that were propped against a large wooden box.

"What is it?" Georgia asked.

"Looks like an old storage box or toolbox." He ran a hand across the top and down one side. "You never know what's been left in them. Best to take a look and make sure it isn't something toxic like old paint or something that needs to be hauled out."

"Maybe it's a forgotten stash of gold from one of the old mines around here," Georgia teased.

"We should only be so lucky." He twisted the rusted latch, pushed up the lid and jumped back—"Holy mother of God."

Georgia could see around his broad shoulders just enough to glance at what was inside—a stiletto heel—still on someone's foot.

CHAPTER 5

DETECTIVE JACK MARTIN stepped out of the Airstream trailer and gazed past the trees to the surrounding mountains. He drew in and released a long breath, soaking in the view and listening to the deep whoosh of the wind through the pines.

He didn't particularly like the mountains. He could appreciate their beauty, but they were too solitary. He needed the distraction of people, not anyone in particular, just people. Out here he was trapped, alone with his memories.

He would move soon—back to Houston or New Orleans, maybe to Denver if he didn't want to pull the trailer that far.

He took a couple steps and sat down in a folding chair, setting a Shiner and a case file on the flimsy card table in front of him. He ran his fingers through a mop of wavy dark hair sprinkled with gray that he never could completely tame and had long ago lost interest in trying to.

A couple nearby chipmunks raised their heads to look at him then went about their business. Not wanting to open the file yet, he took a couple long draws on the beer and reflected on the past year.

The first nine months in Aspen had been pretty much what he had expected. Aside from investigating the occasional domestic violence case or stolen bicycle, there wasn't much for a detective in Aspen to do. That's why he was puzzled when soon after he was hired, the department promoted a local patrol officer, Luke McCray, to junior detective.

It was ludicrous for such a small department to employ two detectives when there wasn't enough work to keep even one busy. But it didn't take long to read the writing on the wall. Luke McCray was to be groomed for *the* detective position, and Jack was there to do the grooming.

Instead of getting angry, Jack went along with it. He realized his employment options following the incident in Houston were limited. He was just glad to finally have a reason to get out of bed in the morning, and wouldn't worry about the day he didn't until the time came. He'd figure something out then, he always did.

Jack took another long swallow of his Shiner and looked toward the mountains already cast in late-day purple shadows. An eagle fought the winds overhead, its sudden screech sending several chipmunks chirping and scurrying into the shadows of the forest. It was too vast, too empty. He needed to lose himself in a crowd.

But he was here now. Small town in the mountains. His job might not be what he had wanted, but he was content. And he was grateful for the amicable—for the most part—working relationship with his boss. When Jack had arrived in Aspen, the other officers in the department had quickly let him know Police Chief Carl Rogan wasn't known for his patience.

Jack got along with Rogan, but Rogan had been on a terror the last couple months, ever since the disappearance of Rachel Winston. Things got worse when a second woman, German model Greta Moss, was murdered just a month later.

Now Rogan's frequent rants and demand for answers had nearly everyone in the department on edge. With his stellar career at the Bureau before being pushed into an early retirement, and since he was the chief detective and closest in rank,

Jack was designated the unofficial department go-between—a job he knew he could handle, but didn't relish.

It had been two months since Rachel Winston's kidnapping, and nearly one since the murder of Greta Moss. It seemed the department wasn't making any progress in the investigations which had Chief Rogan furious, and Jack frustrated.

"If we don't figure out something on one of these cases soon, the town's going to have both our heads," Rogan barked at him every few days. He was reluctantly beginning to agree with his boss.

Jack took another drink, set the bottle aside, then opened the case file on the table. He flipped through pages of interviews and notes and stopped at a picture of Rachel Winston. The photograph had been taken at the party at her parents' house the night she disappeared. She was wearing a short pink dress that looked like it was covered in lace the same color pink as the fabric underneath. She was tall in her high-heeled shoes. He checked the file; her height was listed at five feet nine. From the stories told by family and friends, he gathered she had a strong personality—loud and outgoing—no shrinking violet. Not the usual target for an abduction.

She was a beautiful twenty-three-year-old who should be enjoying the prime of her life. Instead, she was missing, and so far, they still didn't have a clue as to what happened to her. Their biggest clue was a single tan high-heeled shoe found next to the Winstons' driveway. It was confirmed Rachel had been wearing the shoe—along with its mate—during the party.

The soil around the shoe had been disturbed, indicating a possible struggle. And since a review of webcam images taken from cameras set up throughout town didn't show any signs of Rachel that night, Jack believed she had been abducted from the party. It would have been nice if *anyone* in town had an actual CCTV surveillance system, he thought, but this was

Aspen he reminded himself, not Houston. He'd have to settle for sorting through webcam images uploaded for tourists.

Jack rifled through the pile of paper and pulled out the guest list from the party. He was grateful it had been a small affair and he wasn't dealing with reams of names. He was convinced that somebody who had been at the Winston's that night knew or heard something that was the key to figuring out what happened, even if they didn't realize it. There would be a nugget of information, a comment in passing, something that someone considered unimportant, that would in fact lead to a break in the case. As a result, he had questioned and re-questioned the Winstons and their guests. He had talked to everyone who had been in contact with Rachel the night she disappeared.

He had questioned the staff of the catering company, the DJ, even the Winstons' housekeeper who had been there that night to help. He had questioned them all repeatedly, but they had offered no useful information—not yet.

Jack kept an extra copy of the guest list in the small spiral notebook he carried with him and would often look up one or another for an impromptu interview. He checked out everyone thoroughly, and so far he didn't have a single credible lead.

Rachel had disappeared from her parents' home but no one saw her leave the grounds of the estate. The last one to see her was the housekeeper cleaning up after the party. The only information Jack got out of the interviews was what Rachel had been wearing when she disappeared—the pink lace dress and tan-colored high-heeled shoes.

Next, Jack went back over all the notes in his file on Greta Moss's murder, now nearly a month old. She had been abducted sometime after having lunch with a group of friends, and reported missing when she hadn't shown up for their planned dinner. Her body had been found the next morning, the expensive Hermes scarf used to strangle her still wrapped around her neck. The alibis of her friends all checked out and there hadn't been any new leads in the case in almost two weeks. The media had gone so far as to name her killer the "Hermes Strangler."

Jack shut the folder and drummed his fingers on the top of it. Greta's murder was exactly a month after Rachel's disappearance. For a town with no crime, Jack's gut told him the cases were somehow related.

Bits and pieces of Rogan's frequent tirades about the department not being able to produce a single credible suspect rolled around in his head. But he didn't need Rogan to remind him. The two unsolved cases plagued Jack Martin like an itch he couldn't scratch. But his instincts he had relied on for years were buzzing. And although it didn't appear so—to Rogan or anyone else—Jack knew he was closing in on *something*.

He leaned the chair back onto two legs, took a drink and dragged his free hand down his face. He couldn't put his finger on it yet, but it was a gut feeling that had served him well in the past. He just needed to work the interviews again, dig a little deeper.

Jack felt his cell phone vibrate, dropped the chair back down to all four legs, and pulled it from his pocket. The caller ID showed it was dispatch.

"Yeah." He listened for a few moments. "I'm on my way." He took the steps into the trailer in two strides, pulled a beat-up jacket off the back of the couch, and left without bothering to lock the door.

On the way he hit the speed dial on his phone.

A voice grumbled over the line, "Chief Rogan."

"Chief, it's Jack. We've got a body."

CHAPTER 6

AFTER SHE AND Karl found the body, Georgia had run back to the house for her cell phone and called the police. She couldn't bring herself to go back out to the garage, and instead stood at the front curb watching for the police, an ambulance, anyone.

As a reporter, she had seen plenty of bodies—victims of car accidents, murders—but she'd never seen one this up close, and never one in her own backyard.

The body had been dumped head first into the wooden trunk. She had seen parts of a woman's leg and a shoe—a nude stiletto heel. There was something else, farther down—a flash of color. Then she caught a glimpse of what she imagined were hands, but she hadn't let herself look close enough to be sure.

Georgia felt sick to her stomach but was distracted by the sound of an approaching siren. A police car turned the corner and raced toward her. It screeched to a halt at the curb. When the siren was turned off, she could hear another coming in the distance.

Georgia directed the officer around the side of the house to the garage and went back inside. She wanted to sit in one of the chairs and cry, but she wasn't going to let herself do that. There was too much to do.

She began methodically putting the groceries away. Cold items into the refrigerator, frozen into the freezer. For a moment, she stood still, staring at nothing. Even in her hazy state she realized she was battling the effects of shock. Keep going. Keep moving.

Who was dead in the garage? What happened? Why was she left here? The questions swirled. With renewed determination, she redirected her focus to next unpacking the items from the hardware store. Georgia knew the police would want to speak with her, but she needed to get herself together first.

After several minutes she couldn't stand it. She cracked open the blinds covering the window overlooking the back yard. Karl was talking to two policemen. Inside the garage, strobes of light flashed. She knew from experience it was a police photographer. She closed the blinds and leaned on the counter, bracing her hands on either side of the sink. She jumped at the sound of the doorbell.

Detectives Jack Martin and Luke McCray stood on the front porch. The initial description of the body led them to believe the victim was Rachel Winston. The dress and shoes matched what she had been wearing the night she went missing. And although they wouldn't know for sure until they got the body back to the morgue, both men agreed the search for Rachel Winston was probably over.

Jack looked back toward the street and watched a couple cars slide by. A handful of onlookers had stopped to mingle on the sidewalk.

He turned to Luke. "We need to get this body identified ASAP and let the Winstons know if it's their daughter before they hear about this from someone else."

Luke nodded.

The door opened. Jack held up his badge and spoke first. "Ma'am, I'm Detective Jack Martin with the Aspen Police Department and this is Detective Luke McCray. May we come in and ask you a few questions?"

"Of course." She opened the door wide and stepped aside to let them in.

Jack studied her. She looked shaken but lucid. She hadn't fallen apart like a lot of people would after finding a body. He and Luke would compare their impressions of her later.

Jack pulled a small notebook from a pocket of his jacket. "We've got a few questions if that's alright, then we'll get out of your way."

"Sure," she said. "I'll help however I can."

"How long have you lived here?" Jack asked.

"Since this morning."

He looked up at her with raised eyebrows. "This morning?"

"Yes, just this morning."

She told him the details about inheriting the house and the timeline of events that led up to finding the body.

He took notes as she talked, then looked up. "But you've never been in the house until today?"

"That's correct. You can verify it with Jonathan Kramer, my real estate agent."

He wrote the name down in his notebook. Kramer had been a guest at the Winstons the night Rachel went missing. Jack had interviewed him a couple times already. Now he would question him about his client who moved into a house and found a body, all on the same day.

He asked Georgia a few more questions— if either she or Karl had touched anything inside the garage, if she had any idea how the body had gotten there. He didn't expect her to know much and she hadn't, not having been in town even a day yet.

Satisfied, Jack flipped his notepad shut and shoved it back into his pocket. "That should do it for now, Ms. Glass."

They walked to the front door. On the porch, Jack turned back and handed her his card. "We'll have to secure the scene until the guys are done processing it. That'll probably be some-time tomorrow. Then you can proceed with any remodel work you were planning to do. But word is already getting out about a body being found here. You'll probably get some curiosity seekers. Feel free to call me directly if you have any trouble."

"I will, detective. Thank you."

"We'll need to talk to you again," he said stepping off the porch. "So let us know before you leave town."

"I will."

"In the meantime," he added, "keep your doors locked."

CHAPTER 7

"WE WERE GUESTS the night their daughter went missing," Thomas Murphy said over the top of his newspaper to his wife June. "Now that she has been found dead, I think paying them a brief visit to express our condolences would be the decent thing to do."

But June Murphy wasn't having any of it. "We've suffered enough inconvenience and public humiliation from the repeat police interrogations as a result of that capricious girl's disappearance," she said. "I'll send the Winstons a card."

The Murphys had been interviewed by Detective Jack Martin at least three times since the night of the party, two times more than what June Murphy had thought was necessary.

Like the rest of Aspen, the Murphys had heard the dreadful news that Rachel's body had been found. It was undoubtedly the most salacious story to hit Aspen since Tom and June had moved there six years earlier after Tom was forced into an early retirement from his position as Chief of Staff at Mount Belvedere Hospital in Manhattan—just one of many infractions June would never let him forget.

They had visited Aspen several times in the early years of their marriage. Tom liked the mountains and didn't miss the city. June liked being around the rich and famous, never missing an opportunity to let everyone know that she was June Fairchild of *the* Manhattan Fairchilds. Tom knew that June had been a welcome addition to several local Aspen charity boards where she was applauded for her organizational skills and admired for her deep pockets, but not her likability.

"A card is too impersonal," Tom said.

June ignored his comment. "That detective is going to use the discovery of her body as an excuse to inflict yet another round of interrogation on us. You just watch."

Tom didn't respond, pretending to read his newspaper. While Rachel was missing, he knew Walter and Harriet would hold out hope that she was still alive. They must be reeling with the discovery of her body, he thought. But he wouldn't dare pay a condolence call and risk suffering the wrath of his bridezilla. He would make do watching the news account on television that evening.

"She always was quite a tart, don't you think," June had remarked on more than one occasion while Rachel was missing, more as a statement than a question, almost daring her husband to disagree.

Tom was not about to tell his wife what he really thought—that June was jealous of any woman she thought he might find attractive. And he *had* found Rachel Winston attractive, as he was sure most men did. Pity she was now dead.

Still pretending to read the newspaper, Tom glanced at his wife with concealed disgust. Fifty-eight years old, June Fairchild Murphy was not an attractive woman by anyone's standards—short-cropped gray hair with an ashen complexion to match. Medium height, her width nearly equaling her girth, she exuded an air of pomposity that most thought didn't suit her appearance.

Thirty-five years earlier, she had been more attractive—not beautiful, just more attractive. Tom often wondered if he had known how she would turn out, would he have married her anyway. Even though she came with a Fairchild trust fund, he wasn't sure. He wasn't convinced his wife's wealth had been worth the years of suffering her scorching temper. Soon after their wedding, the shy retiring heiress had sprouted a devil's tongue that lashed him regularly at every perceived infraction, of which there were many.

Tom looked at his watch and saw it was ten o'clock. He reached for the remote and found the Denver news station they regularly watched. They had just started the intro—the music playing as photos of the lead anchors and weatherman rolled across the screen.

"I wonder what happened to that Georgia Glass," June remarked. "She was much better than this new girl—all looks and no talent, this one. You would think Denver was a big enough market to find someone more qualified."

Tom didn't say anything; no sense in spawning jealous suspicions. He had made that mistake plenty of times before. He didn't tell June about the rumors he'd heard, that Georgia Glass was buying a vacation home in Aspen and that she was moving to Coastal News with her own weekend show. He wouldn't tell June any of it.

They sat in silence as they watched the night's lead story: "Rachel Winston had been in Aspen, staying with her parents the night of her disappearance…"

When the story was over, June snatched the remote from the coffee table and switched off the television. "That's enough of the Winstons," she said tossing the remote back down. "I'm going to bed."

"Goodnight, sweetheart." Tom hoped he sounded like he cared. "I think I'll stay up and finish the news." He picked up the remote and turned the television back on. "I heard a storm might be coming late next week. I want to watch the weather."

"Do whatever you want. I don't care. That Winston story reminded me how much I miss my scarf. All you had to do was put it with my purse on the front table with all the other purses. I told you I got it in Paris the year after I graduated from college. I'll never be able to replace it. I still don't understand how you managed to lose it."

He didn't reply. The story of the murdered daughter of friends of theirs reminded June of her lost scarf? Tom despised his wife.

"You knew how much I loved it. It was Hermes." At the stairs she turned back, thinking. "Two murders in Aspen. What are the odds they're *not* related? It *has* to be the same killer."

Tom still didn't say anything.

"You know," June continued, drumming her fingers on the oak banister, "that model was strangled with a scarf. The news stories after the murder were all calling her killer the Hermes Strangler."

Tom stared at the television, pretending not to hear.

"Wouldn't it be something if my Hermes turned up wrapped around Rachel Winston's neck. *That* would be just my luck." With one last huff she started up the stairs.

Thomas Murphy sat silent, his teeth clenched.

CHAPTER 8

GEORGIA GLANCED OUT the front window. The dim light from street lamps cast eerie shadows across patches of snow that seemed to claw at her. She shut the blinds and went through the house checking that all the doors and windows were locked, then busied herself unpacking and cleaning, trying to take her mind off the afternoon's events and the dozens of onlookers and media that came and went throughout the afternoon.

Detective Martin had stationed a marked patrol officer at the front curb. The cruiser left before dark, but only after all the onlookers were gone.

Finding the body had been a shock, but the investigative reporter in her was curious and wanted answers. But she would think about that later.

She settled into the living room sofa with a book she had brought from Denver. She looked at the book's cover—a sinister illustration of a deserted highway in shades of gray and black. If only she had grabbed a romance novel instead.

She sighed and opened the book, read the first few paragraphs several times before giving up. The body haunted her. Leaving the book on the coffee table, she headed upstairs for a hot bath.

Thirty minutes later she had dressed in her favorite pajamas and was ready for bed. It had been a long day and the only thing she wanted was a good night's sleep.

She pulled back the covers but hesitated. She had left her cell phone downstairs on the kitchen table, and although she wasn't expecting any texts or calls, she wanted it nearby. She would also double-check that all the doors and windows were locked, even though she already knew they were.

As she walked into the kitchen, a text pinged her phone. She reached out for it but her hand froze short. She stared down at the thumbnail picture on the screen and felt her heart beat heavy in her chest. With the phone still on the table, she touched the picture and enlarged it.

The photograph was of a woman, taken from a distance. It was dark and grainy, obviously taken from a distance and cropped. A woman standing at a window, several floors above where the photographer had been. The building... it looked familiar. And the woman? Georgia squinted—it was her.

Her mind raced as she stared at the picture. The hotel. She remembered opening the window. Someone had been standing across the street. She grabbed the phone from the table and checked the number. It wasn't one in her contact list. And she knew that when the police checked it, they would come up empty-handed like they had before.

How could this be? Had Tony Paladino followed her from Denver? But he couldn't have; he was in jail. Or was he?

Her hands shook as she scrolled through her contacts list.

"Denver Police Department."

Within a couple minutes she was connected to the detective on duty. The officer remembered her case.

"Did Tony Paladino get out of jail?" Georgia asked.

"Paladino? You haven't heard?"

There was a sudden lump in her throat. "No."

"Tony Paladino killed a prison guard a couple days ago. He was moved to a maximum security facility outside of Pueblo."

"So he's not out?"

"He won't be getting out anytime soon, I can assure you of that."

"But could you double-check for me? I got another text tonight with a photograph, just like before."

"There's no way it was Paladino, but if you hold on a minute, I'll confirm it for you."

She waited on hold for what seemed like an eternity.

"No ma'am, he's locked up tight as a drum. You might contact Detective Thurmond in the morning since he was the lead investigator on your case. I imagine he'll tell you the stalking trial is now on the back burner while the prosecutor's office gets the murder charges sorted out. But you don't need to worry. Tony Paladino's going to be locked up for a very long time."

She couldn't get the image of the dark squatty Paladino out of her mind. Thirty-something, jet-black hair and soulless eyes that seemed to see nothing, yet everything, at the same time. She shuttered.

She remembered how he had lunged at her after the judge denied bail and ordered him to remain behind bars declaring him a flight risk. As two bailiffs hauled him out of the court-room, Paladino had screamed obscenities at her, accused her of lying and vowed to get revenge.

"Has he changed his story?" Georgia asked the detective on duty.

"Not to my knowledge."

She could hear him typing at a computer.

"It says here he still claims he never stalked you, that you guys were friends but you turned on him."

"He still says I'm lying about the harassment?"

"Tries to," the officer said. "But I'm looking through the file and it's going to be hard for him to argue with the footage from your security camera and then being caught with a cell phone with your pictures on it."

"And caught with a switchblade knife," Georgia said quietly. She would be forever grateful to Eddie for setting up the security system at her townhouse. Paladino had been caught on camera outside her home trying to get in, and carrying an iPhone with dozens of pictures of her downloaded from the internet. He even had one set as his phone's wallpaper. It was a photograph from a story about her in *Denver Life* magazine that Georgia's mother had deemed *racy*.

"Ms. Glass," the officer began, "it's normal for a victim to worry about a stalker getting out and doing it all over again, but after murdering a guard in the county prison, Tony Paladino isn't going anywhere. I suggest you contact the local police where you are and report this new incident."

Georgia thanked him and hung up. She studied the picture of her dark silhouette in the third-floor window of Hotel Jerome. If Tony Paladino didn't send it, then who did?

She opened the blinds in the kitchen just enough to see the dark outline of the garage. Although she had been told an officer would be stationed there overnight, it was too dark to see if anyone was really there. She didn't dare risk opening the door and going to look.

She found the card Detective Martin had given her and dialed his number.

Within minutes, a uniformed officer knocked on her back door.

"Good evening, Ms. Glass, I'm Officer Bobby McDonald." He swung his middle-aged paunch around to point in the direction of the garage. "I'm watching the crime scene tonight.

Detective Jack Martin asked that I check in with you. You have an incident to report?"

Georgia showed him the picture and told him about Tony Paladino.

"And he's still locked up?" he asked her.

"Yes. I just confirmed it with the Denver Police Department." Georgia told him about Paladino murdering a guard and being moved to the state prison outside Pueblo.

The officer's eyebrows lifted. He looked back down at the photograph on her phone and thought a moment. "My two cents is that Paladino guy has found someone on the outside to continue his dirty work."

Georgia nodded. That's what she was afraid of.

He held her phone, still studying the image. "We need a copy of this picture, and a screen shot showing the number it came from. Send it to Detective Jack Martin. I'll give you his email address."

She held up the card. "I've already got it."

He handed the phone to her. "I'll call in for extra drive-bys tonight, to keep a close eye on your place. And I'll be out back at the garage. Come get me if you need anything."

After he left, Georgia bolted the deadlock on the back door then double-checked the front door was locked. In bed, she pulled the covers up to her chin and forced herself to switch off the lamp. The fear of being stalked had flooded back.

Could this be someone working for Tony Paladino? Would he follow through on his threat for revenge?

She remembered the hate in his eyes, and the last words he hollered at her from across the courtroom.

You're gonna regret this.

CHAPTER 9

HE KNEW IT was inevitable someone would find Rachel's body when the old house on Durango Avenue sold. It had been two months since her disappearance, and although he didn't know how much he would enjoy the swirl of speculation about whether she had suffered the same fate as Greta Moss, it was time for her body to be found.

After he had killed Rachel, he walked the streets every day looking for the perfect second victim. It had taken only a week—too soon—but he could wait.

It had been a cold, frigid afternoon when he saw Greta Moss duck into Lauren's Boutique on Main Street. He followed her in and pretended to shop as he watched her try on then purchase a long shearling coat. He made sure to be the next customer at the register, made small talk with the owner of the boutique, coaxing Moss's identity from the old man.

When it was time, he took her, and was surprised at how easy it had been. She was the perfect second victim. Rachel's disappearance had gotten attention from a smattering of media outlets, but nothing like the interest the murder of an international model had garnered.

The media coverage exploded when Greta's body was found. He smiled as he imagined the hysteria that would ensue when he killed his third victim, then his fourth and fifth. He'd be an international celebrity. The thought of tabloids and internet websites around the world all reporting his story was almost too good to imagine.

But finding the perfect third victim had taken more time. He only had a week left and was about to give up when she showed up in town with nary a clue as to what nightmare awaited her. She'd be the perfect one to die.

He was smart, smarter than just about anyone he knew. What made him angry was that no one appreciated it. But he would outwit the Aspen police, that was a given; then who knew, maybe he would continue his spree somewhere else, keep the fun going.

He reached for the remote and wielded it like a sword, clicking on the television and sat back for the evening news.

As he had expected, the lead story was introduced and a photograph of Rachel Winston flashed across the screen. The reporter spoke of Aspen's shock and horror at the revelation of a second murder. A grin spread across his face.

If they only knew how exciting it was about to get.

CHAPTER 10

A HALF-HOUR BEFORE the scheduled press conference, Jack was in Chief Carl Rogan's office with Detective Luke McCray. Rogan had briefed them on what he was going to tell the press—and what he wasn't.

Rogan told them he wasn't going to reveal the cause of death. "We don't need amateur sleuths in the media or the public making premature connections between the two murders before we have time to investigate the possibility ourselves. If the public jumps to the conclusion that we're dealing with a serial killer, the hysteria will make our lives miserable. And if the media gets wind of a possible serial killer... well, then all hell's going to break loose."

Jack was glad Rogan had taken his advice and agreed to his strategy. The less the public knew the better. They would feed out just enough information to help with the investigation—no more, no less.

Jack looked over at Luke, the junior detective hanging on every word the chief said. He was a good kid, hadn't complained when Jack asked him to come in early. They had been at work since daybreak, combing through the case files and devouring every detail.

Done with the briefing, Rogan glanced at his cell phone. "Time to face the jackals. And there'll probably be more of them than usual." He shut the file in front of him and stood up. "Let's go."

The tiny briefing room was filled to capacity with reporters and a couple camera crews. Jack and Luke stood near the door at the back and listened as reporters fired questions at Rogan after his brief statement.

"How was Rachel Winston murdered?"

Questions and answers went back and forth for several minutes. Then the question came that Jack knew was inevitable, the one he knew Rogan had hoped to avoid.

A woman's hand shot up. She was sitting in the front row.

"Liz Kelly, from *The National Tattler*. Do you think this murder is related to the murder of Greta Moss? Is this the work of a serial killer? The Hermes Strangler?"

Rogan hesitated. "It's early in our investigation and we aren't prepared to rule anything out, but we have no direct evidence to support that theory at this time."

He immediately pointed to another reporter who had a hand raised, but was interrupted by the woman in the front row.

"Greta Moss was kidnapped and strangled. Was Rachel Winston strangled—"

"As I mentioned before," Rogan interrupted, "we aren't yet in the position to reveal the cause of death, and there's no—I repeat, *no*, verifiable evidence at this time that indicates the recent murders are related."

Jack Martin overheard a reporter in the back whisper to a colleague. "Maybe not verifiable *yet*. There's more to this than he's letting on. This is Aspen for God's sake. Playground of the rich and famous. Kevin Costner and Jack Nicholson live here. A second murder? This story's going to be huge."

Rogan thanked the reporters for coming and assured them his office would keep them abreast of any new developments.

Jack was still standing along the back wall when Rogan walked out of the room. Their eyes met. Both men knew what the other was thinking.

This case was about to explode.

CHAPTER 11

GEORGIA WOKE EARLY Wednesday morning, disappointed she hadn't slept well the first night in her house, but how could she? The day before seemed like a nightmare, but she knew it wasn't.

A body found in her garage.

Another text.

She got out of bed and wrapped herself in her favorite chenille robe. Downstairs she opened the blinds over the kitchen window and looked toward the garage. She didn't see Officer McDonald but assumed he was there; his patrol car was still parked where she could just make out the front bumper.

The sun hadn't yet crested the horizon but was already casting long rays that streaked the sky in deep shades of orange and pink. Sunrises and sunsets in the mountains were beautiful. She would miss them.

She stood at the window, thinking about the day before. The body. The text. She remembered back to the first time she had come home and realized someone had been inside her townhouse in Denver. It had been a late night at work not long after she was promoted from morning to evening news anchor. She had walked in and laid her purse on the kitchen counter. Something immediately felt off. It was then she noticed small things out of place—her stack of unopened mail in the kitchen, framed photographs on a side table in the living room, even her makeup on her bathroom counter appeared to have been rearranged. Nothing had been broken or destroyed, but it was like someone had walked through the house, picking up her things then laying them back down slightly askew or at odd angles.

The police hadn't taken it seriously until the second time it happened. Again Georgia noticed things rearranged, but then she saw the photograph. It had been taken earlier that evening as she had walked from her car into the television station. It had been printed out on a sheet of copy paper and left on her bathroom counter.

Immediately after that, Georgia had all her locks changed and Eddie had installed the security system. As far as she knew, her stalker never got back into her house, but the photographs kept coming. At first they were mailed to her, then one day she got her first text—no words, just a picture, grainy and taken from a distance while she worked out at the gym. Then she got another. It didn't matter that he wasn't getting into the townhouse any longer, he seemed to be everywhere she went.

Whenever she was at home, whatever the time of day, she kept all the doors and windows locked with the curtains closed tight. She even stopped running after she had received a text with a picture of her running in Cherry Creek Park.

She changed her cell phone number, but somehow he got the new one. The police had traced the calls and texts numerous times, but they were all made from pre-paid burner phones, and rarely from the same one.

For six months the police were unable to find her stalker. "You're a public figure, Georgia," Detective Mark Thurmond had told her. "It could be someone you know or it could be a total stranger. Sometimes these guys get bored and go away on their own. We can hope for that, but in the meantime, know that we are working hard on the case. It's just a matter of time before we find out who it is."

The detective's assurances hadn't comforted her. As hard as the police worked the case, Tony Paladino wasn't caught until he was recorded lurking outside her townhouse on one of the surveillance cameras Eddie had installed for her.

Tony had claimed he was only trying to find Georgia to ask her for a date, that her number had changed and he couldn't get ahold of her. But that didn't explain all the pictures he had of her on his phone, or the knife he carried in his pocket. Or the fact that once Paladino was caught, the stalking had stopped—at least until now.

Georgia kept telling herself there was no need to worry about Tony anymore. He was locked behind bars. He couldn't get to her. Or could he?

She saw movement across the yard out of the corner of her eye. It startled her, but she was relieved to see it was Officer McDonald who had spent the night behind her garage.

He walked around the side of the garage and stepped inside, two other men following him. The garage was small, and the whole thing looked like it was about to fall over on the men inside. She wondered how much longer it would take them to process the crime scene then release it to her. It would be a relief when they were gone and she could have Karl Kamp start the renovation. She didn't want anything left that reminded her of the body they found inside.

She made a pot of coffee, took a mug of it upstairs and sat down on the bed. As she did almost every morning, Georgia flipped open her laptop and turned it on to check the news. She used her cell phone as an internet hotspot since her WIFI wouldn't be hooked up until later that day.

Checking the first website, she frowned when she saw the lead story about the discovery of Rachel Winston's body—including a picture of her own small blue house. She should have expected it.

"Billionaire's daughter found murdered in Aspen."

Georgia clicked on another news page. "Walter Winston's daughter found dead."

If these were the headlines on legitimate news websites, she could only imagine what the tabloids were reporting. She held her breath and clicked—

"Heiress Butchered in Aspen." She couldn't help but read the first couple paragraphs that recounted what little information the police had revealed in the case so far. At the third paragraph, Georgia winced when she saw her own name. She took a deep breath and kept reading.

"The body was found outside a home recently purchased by Georgia Glass, television news anchor and former girlfriend of Denver Broncos star linebacker TJ Williams."

Georgia shut her laptop and tossed it onto the bed. Just then her cell phone rang. She picked it up and glanced at the number.

"Mother," she answered in as cheerful a voice as she could muster. "How was the writers' conference in Arizona?"

"Hot. I spent most of the time sweatin' like a hooker in church. How are you, baby?"

Joni Glass was a sixty-year-old widow fond of flowing skirts, Birkenstocks, and singing to Bob Dylan ballads. She wrote romance novels, the kind with sex scenes that Georgia still couldn't read without cringing.

"Mother, are you having wine again for breakfast?" Georgia teased.

"No, honey, I'm not. But that's a fabulous suggestion."

Georgia loved her mother, a carefree spirit so unlike herself. She didn't want to tell her about the body in the garage, but knew she had to. The story was all over the news, and it would only be a matter of time before she found out on her own. Besides, if there was anyone in Georgia's life who would help her get over it, it was Joni Glass, eternal optimist and lover of life.

Georgia told her mother about the body, and if Joni was upset, she didn't let on. "Well I can't say that I'm that surprised," she responded. "Anything associated with crazy Ernest Galloway was bound to come with some surprises.

At first, Joni had been surprised at Georgia's unexpected inheritance, then ecstatic when she considered keeping it. She let it be known she hoped her daughter's move to Los Angeles would be short, and that she'd return home to Colorado permanently as soon as she came to her senses.

"He's been out of the house for two years—"

"Doesn't matter. Karma. People can pollute a place the same as a smokestack. But now you're gonna infuse that house with *your* karma—*good* karma."

Georgia smiled. She pictured her mother sitting in her large wicker chair overflowing with tattered pillows in the small sunroom just off the back of the house. She remembered when her father had built the sunroom for her years ago. Her mother had always said it was where she "danced with the muses," which had confused Georgia as a child since she never saw her mother dance in the room, only write, and only with colored pencils on long yellow pads.

They talked a while longer, Joni gushing on how wonderful the latest writers' conference had been. Georgia couldn't remember her mother ever attending one that hadn't been *wonderful*.

When she clicked off her phone, Georgia vowed to never go more than a week without calling her mother. Always her greatest cheerleader, Joni kept her grounded, and never failed to refocus her attention on the positive aspects of life.

She didn't tell her mother about the text she got the night before. The news of the body was enough for one call. Besides, Georgia was tired of worrying about Tony Paladino, and didn't want to think about him for a while.

Georgia dressed in jeans and a simple cashmere sweater, slipped on a pair of well-worn loafers and pulled her hair back into a ponytail. It was the first full day in her new house, and there was a lot she wanted to get done, so she dressed for unpacking boxes and organizing closets.

The first box she tackled was full of books that she unloaded onto the built-in shelves in the small downstairs sitting area. From another box she removed several framed photographs and placed them among the books on the shelves. There were a couple of her and her mother, one with her father when she was just a girl, and one of her and Eddie with a few of their friends from the station.

When she had packed it all up in Denver, she had carefully edited which ones made it into the boxes bound for Aspen or Los Angeles. Gone were the pictures of her and TJ. Their romance had been a whirlwind at first, parties and media events. A past Lombardi winner and frequent Pro Bowler, he was often in the news for his wild antics and flamboyant personality. When they had started dating, Georgia found herself in unchartered territory—on the pages of tabloids.

A relationship that had started out fun and exciting turned sour after the first year. The last few months they were together, Georgia started suspecting he hadn't lost his eye for other women. Her suspicions were confirmed one afternoon at the grocery store when she thumbed through a tabloid while standing in line.

There it was, a picture of a drunk TJ with not one but two scantily clad women leaving a nightclub in New Orleans late one night after a game at the Superdome. The headline across the top of the page read: "TJ Williams is no Saint."

It was the only time Georgia could remember her mother saying, "I told you so."

But that was history. The betrayal hurt, but Georgia had moved on. It was another time in her life she was grateful for Eddie's friendship, although he, like her mother, had discouraged the relationship from the start. She should have listened to them.

Thirty minutes later, as she was breaking down the empty boxes, the doorbell rang. She was apprehensive as she walked to the door. It would be either the police, a technician to set up her cable and WIFI, or someone from the media wanting information for a story.

She opened the door and was relieved to see a man in a shirt embroidered with the AT&T logo.

An hour later, with the technician finished and gone, Georgia sat down in the living room and clicked on the television. She surfed the channels until she found one of the national all-news stations.

She heard, "… murder in Aspen…," and watched. The report included a couple quotes from the Aspen Police Chief. It didn't seem they had much to go on yet. But from experience, she knew they would withhold certain information during the early stages of an investigation.

When the segment ended, she turned off the television and sat staring at the black screen. The investigative reporter in her kicked in again. Her mind swirled with questions and theories.

Two murders. Could there be two killers? In Aspen?

Probably the work of a single killer.

Who could the killer be?

Why were the victims murdered?

Why was one of the victims found here?

Georgia remembered Jonathan mentioning that crime in

Aspen was almost unheard of—until recently anyway. She wanted to verify that herself and made a mental note to check current and historical crime rates. But online research would be limited since Aspen was a small town. She searched the internet and found a local history museum and library, jotting the telephone number down on a notepad. They should have old newspaper articles, she thought, maybe even old police records stored there. She called the museum and made an appointment for later that morning.

Deep in thought, she was startled by another firm knock, this time at the back door. Officer McDonald informed her they had finished their on-site investigation and were releasing the crime scene—her garage—back to her. She thanked him, stepped out onto the small back porch and watched as another officer removed the yellow crime scene tape.

Her mind wandered back to the different possibilities—*who, what* and *why?*

From her experience covering crime in Denver, she knew the murderer probably knew the victims, but maybe not. She also knew the murderer would likely be a male, but that wasn't for sure either.

From the beginning, even as a fledgling journalist, she had been interested in the psychology behind the crimes she reported. She had always wanted to study them and delve deeper. Now, with a few weeks on her hands before the new job, she decided it would be a good time.

She stepped inside just in time to catch a glimpse through the living room window of a rusted white van crawl past the house, its driver cloaked in a dark hoodie.

CHAPTER 12

GEORGIA WAS SITTING at her kitchen table when her cell phone rang. It was almost noon.

"I'm sorry I couldn't call sooner," Jonathan said. "I had a closing on a condo at eight then a showing of a mountainside estate at ten. When I heard the news about the body last night, it was too late to call you, but I thought about you all morning. It had to have been such a shock."

With no other friends in town, Georgia welcomed Jonathan's concern. "It was. Did you happen to see the press conference this morning?"

"No, I was out, but my assistant Margie saw it and gave me the highlights."

Georgia closed her laptop and pushed it to the center of the table. "I've been thinking about the murders all morning."

"There's almost no crime in Aspen, now two women killed in two months?"

"I don't think they're random," she said. "It's too coincidental. My guess is that they're related."

"From what I was told about the press conference, it doesn't sound like the police know anything yet."

Georgia drained the last of her coffee and shook her head. "I've covered crime for years, the police almost always withhold certain information, and I think they're holding something back now. I'm hoping that since the body was found here—at my house, they might answer a couple questions from me."

"I thought you were on a temporary hiatus from work until you start your new job," Jonathan said with a quick laugh. "It sounds to me like you're investigating."

Georgia got up and refilled her coffee cup. It was the fifth one that morning. "I guess old habits are hard to break," she admitted. "But I feel terrible for the Winstons—Rachel's parents. Do you know them?"

"I've known them for years—wonderful people. I sold them the land they built their house on."

Georgia sighed. "I obviously don't know them, but I found their daughter's body and I'm having a hard time with it. Do you think I could meet them? Just an introduction and a quick visit sometime when it's convenient?"

Jonathan hesitated. "I'll talk to them." Georgia sensed a hint of resignation in his voice. "They might not be up to visitors for a while. They really withdrew after Rachel's disappearance."

"That's understandable. But if you wouldn't mind asking, I'd really appreciate it."

"Sure," Jonathan said. "I'll be in touch."

For nearly thirty minutes, Jonathan sat at his desk trying to sort through emails but found it impossible to concentrate. The intercom on his desk phone buzzed, a welcomed interruption.

"Mr. Kramer, Bridget Ferrari is here to see you."

Jonathan let out a long sigh. "Thank you, Margie. Send her in."

Bridget was the third wife of Carlo Ferrari, a long-time summer resident of Aspen. Four years earlier, Carlo had sold his private equity group in Silicon Valley and moved to Aspen permanently. He was in Aspen a year when he opened Ferrari's Cigar Bar & Lounge to huge fanfare.

Bridget was forty-one. Carlo was fifty-nine. When they married, Carlo had loved Bridget, and Bridget had loved Carlo's money. By all outward appearances, the couple seemed happy. But Jonathan knew better, he'd deflected too many romantic passes from Bridget to think their marriage was a happy one.

When Bridget swooped into his office, Jonathan could tell immediately that something was wrong. Gone was the exaggerated greeting with kisses on both cheeks. She walked in with a sullen expression and dropped into a chair across from his desk.

Despite her mood, she looked stunning in a lilac-colored mohair sweater that stopped just below her waist. Tall boots were pulled on over tight black pants. Her long black hair was pulled back in a sleek ponytail that fell down the middle of her back.

"Hello, Bridget," Jonathan said, ignoring her obvious distress. Bridget was known for her dramatics, but like most people—most men at least—Jonathan overlooked the annoying personality flaw because she was just so damn gorgeous.

"It's horrible, Jonathan. Horrible what happened to Rachel Winston," she began. "I feel terrible for Walter and Harriet. I do. But this is going to be trouble for all of us."

Jonathan frowned. "What do you mean? And who's 'all of us'?"

"All of us," Bridget said exasperated. "All of us at that damned party. This is going to get that detective hot to trot and he's going to harass us all again."

"Bridget, it's a murder investigation. Of course they're going to talk to those of us who were at the Winstons that night. They're going to interview a lot of people."

"Well it's going to look bad."

"*Look bad?* For heaven's sake, Bridget. They've got a body now. Who cares if it looks bad?"

"I do," she said. "And Carlo will. He's put over half of what he made from selling his company into that damned cigar bar. It was an idiot thing to do, but he did it. And he did it not knowing a thing about how to run it. Bad publicity is the *last* thing he needs."

"You think the investigation is going to hurt Carlo's business?" Jonathan could hear the cynicism in his own voice but didn't care. Everyone knew Bridget was shallow, but this was reaching a new low. The Winstons were friends of the Ferraris. Now their daughter was dead and Bridget showed no sign of sympathy, but instead was worried how it would hurt Carlo's business. She should offer at least of hint of concern for Walter and Harriet, even if it was fake. It grated on him.

"Of course it will hurt business. If people start thinking one of us could have murdered her, it's going to kill what little business he has left."

Jonathan had been a regular at Carlo's lounge when it first opened. It was smart to patronize the businesses of potential clients, but he rarely went anymore. Both the cigars and alcohol were overpriced. He preferred the bar and atmosphere at Republic Humidor and Lounge, but he wouldn't mention that to Bridget.

"Listen, I know you're worried about Carlo and the business, but us being at the Winstons the night Rachel disappeared isn't going to keep someone from going to Ferrari's." Although he could think of at least a dozen other reasons that *would* keep someone from going there.

Bridget rose from the chair in a huff. "Maybe you're right. I'll worry about that later," she said. Then she smiled at him. "See, I knew I'd feel better if I talked to you. I bet you haven't eaten yet. I'm hungry. Take me to lunch."

"I wish I could," Jonathan replied, "but I've been out all

morning and really need to get some things done. I was going to skip lunch." He said it delicately, trying not to offend her.

"All you do is work," she said. "I'm not taking 'no' for an answer."

"I—"

She cut him off. "Let's go. I've been wanting to try the new place on Mill Street."

He knew when to give in, and knew enough not to insult her. Bridget could hold a vicious grudge.

"Alright," he said and forced a grin. "I've been wanting to try the new place, too."

Outside, Bridget wound her arm through his, locking them together.

Jonathan gestured toward their entwined arms. "I don't think the investigation is going to start rumors, but *this* might."

"Let them talk. I'm sick of this town and everyone in it— except for you, of course."

They turned the corner onto Mill Street. The restaurant was a couple blocks further.

She pulled his arm in closer. "I heard about your new client. You have to tell me all about her." When Jonathan didn't respond, Bridget rolled her eyes. "Don't give me any client confidentiality BS, Jonathan. I've heard the rumors. I know Georgia Glass bought a house in town, and I assume you're the one who helped her."

Jonathan hesitated telling her, but decided there was no sense in keeping it a secret. If Bridget was snooping around, determined to find something out, he knew she would stick her nose where it didn't belong and dog the rumor to death until she found out what she wanted. If Jonathan didn't tell her, she'd find out anyway.

"I did help her," he admitted.

"I knew it!" she exclaimed. "Well, Carlo thinks if he can

get her into the lounge he can use the publicity to drum up some business." Bridget rolled her eyes again. "So tell me about her. She's beautiful—in that sort of made-up television way, if that's what you like."

Jonathan shook his head and laughed. "I'll introduce you. You'd like her."

"I'm sure I would dislike her *immensely*," Bridget said tugging his elbow in closer. "But I want you to give up all the dirt on her anyway."

CHAPTER 13

BRENDA PAWLOSKI WAS not what most people would expect the Chief Archivist at the Aspen Historical Library and Museum to look like. Medium height with a lean athletic build and auburn hair that curled down her back. An avid hiker and skier, she looked younger than her 42 years.

But it was her knowledge of Colorado's history that made her a popular speaker at local conventions and business conferences. Brenda was known for regaling even the dullest of audiences with stories of outlaws, lost mines and buried treasure in the Rockies.

She was a widow; her husband Michael had been killed in Fallujah, and she had never remarried. The handful of dates she had gone on since his death had been unsatisfying, and left her despondent. She still missed Michael desperately. Although it had been years since his death the pain she felt was still raw.

Well-meaning family and friends encouraged her to let go of the past, to move on. But how could she? Her life's work was to honor the past. She had received her master's degree in history from the University of Colorado at Boulder, and as an archivist, history was her job. So her love of history justified clinging to her memories, or at least that's what she told herself.

When she heard that Rachel Winston's body had been found, her heart ached for Walter and Harriet. The Winstons were valued benefactors of the museum. She knew them well.

She imagined the death of their daughter felt much like the loss of her beloved Michael. Both having been cut down in the prime of their lives way too young.

The news of Rachel's death had consumed her thoughts for most of the morning. She had been at work for nearly an hour, but hadn't gotten anything done except sort through a handful of emails.

Crockett, Brenda's chocolate lab mix laying at her feet, barked, jolting her from her thoughts. Susan Taylor, Brenda's assistant, appeared at the door and offered a quick tentative rub to the excited dog.

"Did you hear they found Rachel Winston's body?" Susan asked, breathless as she snatched the television remote and perched herself on the corner of Brenda's desk.

"I did."

Susan pointed the remote toward a small television. "They're holding a news conference in a few minutes. We have to turn it on."

Several minutes after the press conference had ended, the museum phone rang. Susan jumped off the desk and went to answer it.

A couple minutes later she returned with a stunned look on her face.

"What is it, Susan? You look like a guppy looking for food."

"That was Georgia Glass—the television reporter—TJ Williams's old girlfriend." Susan looked at Brenda with an impatient wide-eyed expression imploring her to remember.

"Was she the one on the cover of *The National Tattler*— after the break up?"

Susan nodded, resembling the bobblehead Hello Kitty mounted to her dash. "That was her," she said. "Georgia Glass."

Brenda waited a moment for more information, but Susan stood there, eyes still bulging in disbelief.

"Well... what did she want?" Brenda asked.

Susan pawed at her hair, tucking an unruly strand behind an ear. "She's coming today—here."

CHAPTER 14

IMMEDIATELY FOLLOWING THE press conference, Jack Martin and Luke McCray had taken all the files on the Winston and Moss cases, stacked them on a table in a small conference room, and began methodically combing through them again for any important detail that might have been overlooked.

They listened to the 911 call from Harriet Winston reporting Rachel's disappearance, and the call from Georgia Glass after her body was found. They magnified and scoured through photographs taken at the party. Together they went back through the testimonies of every witness who had been a guest that night.

They spent the same amount of time scrutinizing the details regarding Greta Moss's murder. They had an autopsy report in the Moss case and went back through the findings one by one. The cause of death was strangulation, a Hermes scarf was still knotted around her neck when a couple hikers found her the morning after she had gone missing. Bruises and scrapes on the body were superficial and found to have occurred post-mortem. Test results on the soil particles removed from the body indicated the killer had dragged her across the gravel near the highway where she had been found.

After several hours, Jack shoved the pile of papers and reports toward the center of the table and rubbed his eyes with his palms.

"That's it," he said. "We need the Winston autopsy. When did Lester say we'd have it?"

Luke took advantage of the break to stand up and stretch. "Tomorrow morning."

"When the autopsy is complete, they'll release the body. I'm sure the family is already making funeral plans. Find out when that will be. Everyone who was at their house that night will be at the funeral. I want to assemble them somewhere secure afterwards and interview them again one by one."

"To check for any inconsistencies in their stories?"

Jack nodded. "With all of them in the same place, if there *are* any discrepancies, we can get to the bottom of it right then and there."

They had caught a break on timing. Had the party been held later in the spring, more of the Winstons' friends would likely have been back in residence from winter homes in Florida or Texas. It hadn't been a big party. Jack felt they were fortunate to be dealing with a limited number of guests.

Jack looked at the list again. There had been twenty-one invited guests at the Winston's that night. Add six more to account for the caterers, the DJ, and the Winstons' housekeeper, and that was twenty-seven—thirty-one total counting members of the family, minus Rachel. All of them had been questioned before, but Jack was determined to question them again now that they had a body.

"We're going to have them go over their stories again—one by one." Jack gestured toward the stacks of files and reports. "We've spent enough time on this for now."

Luke McCray took the cue they were finished and leaned back in his chair, crossed his arms behind his head. "So what's next, boss?"

"We're going to line them up and see who cracks. Someone on that list knows something about what happened to Rachel Winston."

CHAPTER 15

PARKER RANDOLPH STOOD at the window in his high-rise office and watched the traffic crawl by on the freeway below. The cars were bumper to bumper even though it was only midday.

He lifted his gaze and looked west toward the Pacific Ocean. He could just make out the coastline, a hazy gray blur in the distance, and longed to escape to his parents' weekend house in Malibu. But his schedule at the network ensured his visits to the beach were few and far between.

He drew in a deep breath and imagined the smell of salt and the sound of waves. He imagined sitting and reading for hours, reclined in a chair propped in the sand, only taking breaks to surf or to walk the beach. He would sleep with the windows open, the ocean breeze wafting through the gauzy curtains of the guest bedroom.

When he wasn't surfing or reading, he would write. It was at the house in Malibu, during the summer between his junior and senior years at Stanford, where he had written his first novel.

Stored on a flash drive and hidden away in a desk in his condo, he had kept the novel a secret. He knew his father would dismiss it as a whim, then tell him to get his head out of the clouds and his feet out of the sand and get back to work.

He turned his attention back to the snarled traffic below,

back to the belching exhaust engulfing his urban prison. *The son of a media baron.* He felt the weight of expectation, shook his head, and turned back to his desk.

Malcolm Randolph liked to tell people, "Twenty-five years ago I bought a failing television station that was in a death spiral. Everyone thought I was crazy. But little by little, we changed formats, cut expenses, beefed up talent, and here we are today."

Coastal News Corporation was a nationally televised news channel headquartered in Los Angeles and with Malcolm Randolph at the helm, had become a phenomenal success and made Randolph a billionaire. Courted by businessmen and politicians across the globe, Randolph was admired for his business acumen and meteoric success.

Parker had joined his father's company soon after graduating from Stanford Business School. Groomed as Malcolm's eventual successor, Parker was placed on the management fast-track at Coastal despite his own misgivings. "I'm not wired for it like you, Dad," he had insisted on numerous occasions during the twelve years he had worked for the network. Malcolm consistently dismissed his son's doubts. "You're a Randolph. You graduated the top of your class at Stanford. You were born to head this company."

Parker didn't want to hurt his father, but he wasn't going to live his life for him either, and knew he couldn't carry on the charade much longer. It was easier when he had started, years ago. The news business still had a modicum of integrity—at least he thought so. He would never be comfortable at the network. He had tried, had given it twelve years of his life. He didn't want to give it any more.

The office door swung open and Malcolm Randolph loomed in the doorway. Parker took in a deep breath, expecting a new assignment or other directive from his father.

"Parker, I need you to go to Aspen and talk to Georgia Glass. It was a mistake to let her take so much time off before she reports to work."

"She'll be here June first." Parker ticked off the weeks in his head. "That's less than six weeks away."

Malcolm gave him a dismissive wave. "We've got the gubernatorial race with all the accusations of corruption heating up, the DeLorenzo murder trial about to start, the insider trading scandal at Apex Financial… There's too much that she could be capitalizing on right now. We need her here. I want you to fly to Aspen and see if you can talk her into coming in early."

Parker frowned. "And this doesn't have anything to do with the murders in Aspen?"

"The Winston girl's murder?"

The Randolphs and the Winstons had been acquainted for decades, running in the same billionaires' circle of private country clubs and charity galas.

"And Greta Moss—the model," Parker said.

"It has nothing to do with that. It's business. You've got to consider how things affect the bottom line." Malcolm hesitated a moment. "But if there *is* a serial killer murdering beautiful women in Aspen, that's another reason to get her out of there. Use that angle if you have to."

"Angle?" Parker was sick of the games. Running a media company and reporting the news had come full circle from the days of yellow journalism under the helm of William Randolph Hearst. The irony of the shared name not escaping him.

"Fear," his father said. "Fear's the angle. Use it. Just get her here. Although…" He stopped, and put a finger to his pursed lips then wagged it at Parker. "Maybe she could get some information on the murders first—for a news segment. If she doesn't want to start early—which I hope she does— then mention the murders as a possible story segment. She might be able to dig something up. But first, try to get her here early."

Parker remembered the hours of tape he had reviewed before Georgia was hired. She was relentless in the way she conducted her interviews, refusing to accept half-truths and cryptic answers, dogging interviewees until they folded under the pressure or were left speechless. She always got what she wanted, a characteristic that reminded Parker of his father.

Coastal's research team had found that Georgia appealed to a wide demographic. His father had attributed her charms to her Midwestern roots. "She's no East or West Coast diva," he had said before hiring her. "She should appeal to our middle-class viewers—draw more in."

It was always about ratings. His father's attraction to Georgia was fueled by how she could affect Coastal's bottom line. Parker didn't fault him for it, it was the way he had always been. And who knows, Parker thought, he might see Georgia as a kindred spirit—both coming from modest beginnings, clawing their way to the top with a ruthless determination to succeed.

But for some reason, Parker found he liked her. Underneath the hard-driving veneer, she had been approachable, even friendly. And it didn't hurt that she was gorgeous—wavy blonde hair, tan legs that stretched on for days under the short skirts she wore on air.

Parker was tired of working at Coastal, and was tempted to tell his father then and there that he wouldn't go to Aspen, that he was quitting the family business to write novels on the beach. But the thought of a day in the Rocky Mountains—with Georgia—made him reconsider. He had waited this long to tell his father he wanted to quit, he could wait a little longer.

Parker looked at his father and nodded. "I'll call the hanger and schedule one of the planes."

CHAPTER 16

"IS THIS THE work of a serial killer? The Hermes Strangler?"

There it was. The question had his heart pounding and he loved his new moniker—the Hermes Strangler. He leaned forward, breathing shallow and fast, waiting to hear the response. Finally they were going to take notice of him and he would get the notoriety he deserved.

But the police chief's disregard for the question had infuriated him. How dare they dismiss the brilliance of his crimes?

Soon after, he had hatched his plan. It would be impossible for them to ignore him. His genius would be obvious to everyone, and everyone would be talking about it. The story would go viral nationally—no, *internationally.*

It was fate on that cold, wet day when he had found the scrapbook, a forgotten relic stuffed with newspaper clippings that had yellowed with time, lying out of sight on a top shelf in the vacant house. At the time he had been disappointed, he had been hunting for something more valuable—a left-behind stash of money or old coins. He didn't realize then how valuable the scrapbook would be, or how it would change his life.

Any other time, he probably would have tossed it aside with the trash. But something kept him from throwing it out. Maybe he was triggered by voyeuristic tendencies. Perusing through an old personal scrapbook wouldn't be the same as peeping into windows of unsuspecting college coeds, or snooping through the personal belongings of roommates, but it was compelling nonetheless. Maybe it was boredom and the dreadful weather that made him take it. He would be housebound the rest of the day and might as well flip through it before tossing it out. Maybe he took it for the simple reason that he *could,* so why not? He was glad he did.

He flipped through the dusty old scrapbook again, but knew all the details by heart. He knew how killer Gerald Ray Toomey had chosen each of his five victims in Aspen in the 1950's. He knew how they were murdered and where their bodies had been dumped. He knew where Toomey had lived and where he was finally caught. Like a religious pilgrimage, he had visited all the locations.

He closed the book and placed both hands palm down on the cracked leather cover, remembering the first time he had gone through it. The first several pages were nothing exciting—newspaper accounts of petty theft cases, minor incidents of vandalism, a couple arrests. Accompanying the stories was the occasional picture of stern-faced lawmen. The same grim face on all of them had amused him. Whether the picture was of an officer escorting a suspect to jail or court, or a picture of one of them receiving an award, they all wore the same idiotic face, refusing to display any emotion for the camera.

The articles, most from *The Mountaineer,* Aspen's weekly newspaper during the 1950's, were of little interest to him. The pictures were only mildly amusing because of their dated clothes and grim faces. He glanced over the pages but dismissed the stories.

About a quarter of the way through he was about to toss the whole thing aside when a headline leapt from the page. It was from the front page of *The Mountaineer,* February 28,

1957. "Body of Missing Girl Found." A subheading added "Strangling Suspected, Scarf Still Knotted Around Neck."

Now this is more like it, he had thought. He consumed the article and learned the girl, Mary Lampshire, the eighteen-year-old daughter of a local dry goods merchant, had been missing for a week when she was last seen walking home from her father's store.

He turned the page. The next clipping was from *The Denver Post* which obviously deemed the murder of the girl newsworthy, even if it was in the sleepy mountain town nearly 200 miles away.

The story contained much of the same information but also included a photograph. It was of the same grim-faced group of lawmen he'd seen earlier in the scrapbook, but this time they were standing over a gaping hole in the ground, snow and hay thrown off to the sides and behind them. It was obvious the body had been found there but had already been removed.

Too bad, he thought, a good grisly shot of the corpse would have made the grainy old black and white photograph much more interesting.

The next several pages were local stories on the investigation. From what he could tell, the police were baffled and didn't have any leads.

It wasn't until several pages later that a second story reached out and grabbed him by the throat.

"Second Girl Missing, Feared Dead" the headline screamed. He read and found out she had disappeared March 25, 1957. There were a variety of stories on the investigation of the second missing girl in both *The Mountaineer* and *The Denver Post*. And although a body had not been found in the case of the second missing girl, many of the stories speculated as to whether or not the two cases were connected in some way.

Several pages later, when confronted with the headlines "Second Body Found" and "Third Girl Goes Missing," he realized with delight that Aspen had once had a bona fide serial killer.

He pored over the articles one after the other. He read about Toomey's fourth murder, then his fifth. What began as curiosity quickly became full-blown obsession. He devoured every detail about the missing girls, about finding their bodies, and eventually, the arrest of Gerald Ray Toomey.

The articles on Toomey were what fascinated him the most. Toomey's troubled past—no father on record, a mother who had been a prostitute (who he thought was an older sister until he discovered the truth as a teenager), older siblings in and out of jail. His childhood spent living with an abusive alcoholic grandmother.

The pictures of Toomey, though grainy and aged a deep yellow, showed a handsome young man, probably early-30's. Medium height with dark hair that nearly reached his shirt collar, worn longer than the prevailing style of time. His clothes were more relaxed and casual than the uptight lawmen posing for pictures with him for the newspaper. Toomey looked every inch the star that fascinated the media and the public until he was put to death in 1961 in Colorado's gas chamber.

Stuffed in the scrapbook were stories not only from *The Mountaineer* and *The Denver Post*, but from across the country. *The Houston Post*, the *St. Louis Post-Dispatch*, and even *The New York Times*. Toomey had become a celebrity, but he had made mistakes, been careless, and had gotten caught.

For several months, living vicariously through the titillating details of Toomey's life and crimes he uncovered through the scrapbook, then his further research online and at the local museum, was enough to satisfy his fascination. Then one day it wasn't.

Rachel Winston was the perfect first victim. The daughter of Walter and Harriet Winston; the couple was among Aspen's wealthiest permanent residents. Walter had made his billion-dollar fortune years earlier through his venture capital firm that had struck gold funding some of Silicon Valley's early start-ups. They kept a house in Aspen for years, but as soon as Rachel had followed her older sister Sophie off to college, Walter and Harriet moved to Aspen as year-round residents.

Rachel's fate had been sealed at the party her parents held at their palatial mountain home for Sophie and her husband. They had been married a month earlier.

It was a spur of the moment decision. He saw Rachel stumble through the large empty foyer spilling champagne from a crystal flute then snatch a multi-colored silk scarf from an assortment of purses piled on a table near the front door. He watched unnoticed in an adjoining room as she draped the scarf over her shoulders, then held it aloft, swinging it one side then the other, admiring herself in the large mirror over the table. It was then that the idea came to him.

Later that night she had stepped outside, presumably for fresh mountain air to help clear away a looming hangover. She wasn't seen again until her body was found in the garage of the vacant house on Durango Avenue.

Efforts by police to find Rachel had intensified after the discovery of Greta Moss's body a month later. He congratu-lated himself on choosing another perfect victim. Moss was a famous model of German descent who regularly vacationed in Aspen. She went missing exactly a month after Rachel Winston. Her body had been discovered by a couple early morning hikers. She had been strangled—an expensive Hermes scarf still twisted around her neck.

The stars were aligning. With the perfect third victim, the media frenzy would reach a crescendo that would seal his destiny. After his fourth and fifth murders, he would go down in history as one of the greatest and most elusive serial killers of all time.

CHAPTER 17

"THERE SHE IS," Jack Martin said, getting out of the truck when Georgia pulled to the curb behind them. As he walked toward her, she tucked a folder under her arm and shut the car door.

"Hello, detectives. I didn't know you were coming. I hope you haven't been waiting long."

"We just got here," Jack said falling in step beside her on the sidewalk. Luke followed close behind.

At the front door, Georgia fumbled through her purse for her keys.

"Let me get that for you," Luke said reaching for the folder about to slip from under her arm.

The detectives followed her into the kitchen. Luke set the folder on the table and Georgia immediately laid her purse on top of it. It was obvious she didn't want them to see what it was.

"Are you working?" Jack asked. She looked confused and he gestured to the folder under her purse. "I thought you were between jobs. It looks like you're working."

"Oh that," Georgia replied. "That's just some personal research I'm doing on the side—not job related. Well, not *officially*, anyway. Have a seat. I'm going to make a pitcher of iced tea. Could I get either of you a glass?"

Jack accepted the offer. Although Luke passed on the tea,

he couldn't resist taking one of the cookies she placed on a plate and set on the table.

She looked tired, or nervous, Jack wasn't sure. He got right to the point. "Detective McCray and I read the report on the text you received last night and we wanted to ask you a few questions."

"Alright," she said with a slow nod.

She was tired, Jack concluded, but that would be understandable. As if finding a body on her property wasn't enough; the same day she had been contacted by a possible stalker. He decided she was holding up well, under the circumstances.

After she and Karl Kamp found the body, he and Luke had run background checks on them that revealed she was a high-profile news anchor—no surprise there since almost everyone in Colorado already knew who she was. But they also learned more about her break up with TJ Williams, and read about Tony Paladino, now in maximum security for murdering a prison guard.

Jack watched her move about the kitchen, unsure and slow. He could almost see the great weight setting on her shoulders. He felt a sudden pang of concern for her, but for the life of him didn't know why. He never let a case get personal. A good investigator kept emotions out of it. He approached every case objectively, logically. Emotions only got in the way.

"Tell me about the previous stalking case," Jack said. "I've got the police report from Denver, but I want to hear *your* side of the story. Start from the beginning."

Jack took notes as Georgia spent several minutes telling him what had happened—the news story she had done on Angelo Paladino and his ties to the mafia in New York, Angelo and Estelle's murder, seeking out Tony for a follow-up story, and Tony becoming an obsessed fan. She told him about the texts with photographs, and Paladino's arrest.

As Georgia talked, she studied her hands, fingers splayed across the table top. When she finished, she looked up at Jack, determination in her eyes.

"If it is Tony again, I'm not going to let him get to me this time. I'm scared, I'll admit that, but I'm not going to let it consume my life again like it did in Denver. I'm tired of jumping at the sound of someone shutting a car door or bumping into someone in a grocery store aisle. I'm done with all that."

She might look tired, but after talking with her a few minutes, Jack was impressed by her resilience. She was holding up a lot better than he would have expected.

"It's possible Tony Paladino has help on the outside," Jack told her. "It's also possible we could be dealing with a copycat." Georgia frowned and he continued. "I don't know much about copycat criminals, but it could be someone who knows about Paladino and what he's done. Anyone could google 'Georgia Glass' and find plenty of information on your case."

She nodded, thinking, then got up from the table, took the pitcher of tea from the counter and refilled their glasses and sat back down.

"They released the garage to me earlier this morning," she said. "Did they find anything else?"

They hadn't, but Jack didn't want to admit it. He wanted to give her answers, give Chief Rogan and the Winston and Moss families answers. But he didn't have any yet and it bothered him. "Unfortunately we can't disclose any additional information at this time," he said.

"Well I'm glad they're done. My contractor can start the renovation. I'll be glad to get my car off the street."

"We're done with the garage," Jack said. "But we need to talk to you about your house."

"My house?"

"Since the body was found on the property, and the house

was vacant for an extended period of time, we'd like to conduct a brief search. To be thorough."

Georgia frowned. "I don't understand. What would you be looking for?"

"Anything out of the ordinary. It's routine. It would exhaust the on-site investigation, and you would have the reassurance of knowing the entire property had been thoroughly searched."

"And there wouldn't be any more surprises." Georgia circled the rim of her glass with a finger, then looked back at him and nodded. "Okay, you can search it."

Jack turned to Luke. "Call in and let them know the search is a go."

Luke nodded, then excused himself and stepped outside.

"The search will be thorough, but I'll make sure they put everything back the way it was. You won't know they were ever here," Jack said. "Then you can put all this behind you."

"Thank you, detective. But I've got a favor to ask in return."

He looked at her, wondering what she could want.

"I did some research online and at the local historical library regarding crime in Aspen, and I came across some interesting articles. There was a serial killer in the 1950's—Gerald Ray Toomey. He strangled five girls, all with scarves. The murders were exactly one month apart from each other. I'd like to get a copy of the old police records to fill in some of the gaps on what I've found out about the cases."

Jack wasn't sure why, but the name Gerald Ray Toomey sounded familiar. He was intrigued. He had heard stories about shoot-outs on the streets of Aspen during its mining days over a hundred years earlier, but when he started work at the department, he had been told violent crime was virtually non-existent. At least until the recent murders.

"Why do you want the files?" he asked.

"Curiosity. There are similarities to the recent murders and I wanted to research it further, compare them."

The police hadn't revealed Rachel's cause of death, but it was public knowledge that Greta Moss had been strangled with a scarf. Jack knew Georgia wasn't aware of the connection between the two cases, but he reminded himself that she *was* an investigative reporter. He wasn't too proud to want to hear her theories.

Jack shook his head. "I don't know. Old case files are sealed and archived."

"These are sixty-year-old cases and they're solved. What would it hurt to let me take a look at them?"

He thought about it a moment longer, he didn't like the idea of handing police records over to a civilian but didn't see any harm in having her take a look. Nobody had probably opened those old files since they were sealed up decades ago. Besides, he was intrigued and would like to take a peek at them himself. "I can probably arrange it," he said and stood up.

"Great. Thank you." Georgia followed him to the front door.

On the porch, he turned back. "You saw the press conference this morning?"

"I did."

"Then you heard the chief of police say there was no evidence linking the Winston and Moss murders. We still don't know if we're dealing with one murderer or two. You're probably wasting your time researching some old serial killer looking for a connection."

Before she replied, Georgia took in a long breath and let it out slow. "Detective, I saw Rachel Winston's body." When he didn't say anything, she added—"I saw the scarf."

CHAPTER 18

AFTER THE DETECTIVES left, Georgia took the articles she had photocopied at the museum out of the folder. She had gone through archived newspaper accounts of violent crime and been surprised by the near lack of it in recent history. Aside from the string of murders committed by Gerald Ray Toomey in the 1950's, Aspen hadn't seen any real violence since its wild mining days of the 1880's and 90's. But the Toomey murders intrigued her. Five women murdered, all strangled with scarves. Georgia had copied all the articles on the Toomey murders she and Brenda Pawloski, the museum's director, had found in the archives.

She spread the articles across the table, pulling out the ones she wanted to start with and scanning the headlines. *Horror in Aspen Continues. Fifth Victim Found.* But before she read them, there was something she needed to do first.

Georgia clicked on her cell phone and rifled through her contacts until she found the one she was looking for.

"Detective Mark Thurmond."

The voice was familiar to her, and oddly comforting for some reason. Georgia told him about the latest text. He was quiet while she talked, taking it all in.

"There are two likely scenarios," he said when she was done. "Either Tony Paladino has someone on the outside who's now doing his dirty work, or you've got yourself a copycat stalker."

Detective Thurmond was the second one to bring up the possibility of a copycat. Detective Martin had suggested it earlier. She hadn't considered the possibility of a copycat stalker, but suddenly realized the implication for her research in the current murder cases. The similarities between the current cases and the Toomey murders in the 50's had intrigued her, but could the current killer be a copycat?

Detective Thurmond was still talking. "I'll check into it. We'll find out if this has anything to do with Paladino. In the meantime, be extra careful. Wherever you are, be aware of your surroundings. Don't put yourself in a vulnerable situation."

Sitting at the table, Georgia glanced through the kitchen window at the waning daylight and it dawned on her that anyone outside in the shadows would be able to see in. As they continued their conversation, she went through the house and shut all the blinds. The vulnerability she felt before Tony Paladino was arrested was back.

"I'll contact the Aspen police," Detective Thurmond told her. "I'll fill them in on the details of Tony Paladino and the prior stalking case, and warn them about the gravity of your situation."

Georgia then called Eddie Jenkins. It was late, but he answered after the first ring.

"How are the mountains, blondie? I hope good because Denver misses you."

She managed a weary smile. It was nice to hear his voice. "And you? You miss me, too, I hope."

"It's been a whole forty-eight hours. I'm practically going through withdrawals."

"Good," she said. "Then it's mutual. Hey—seriously, though—I have a favor to ask."

"Sure," he said. "Shoot."

She told him about the text she had received with the photo taken at Hotel Jerome. "The cameras you installed at the townhouse were the reason the police caught Tony Paladino. I can't believe I'm saying this, but I think I need a security system here, too."

"I thought people in Aspen didn't even lock their doors. You want everything? Even cameras?"

"I think I need them."

"I think you do, too. I'm glad you called me. I'm scheduled to be at the station through the weekend, but how about Monday?"

"That'll be perfect," she said. "Thank you, Eddie. I hope you know how much I appreciate it."

"No reason to get all mushy. Besides, wait till you get my bill."

She laughed and they talked a while longer.

They had been friends for years, with only one spat—more of a misunderstanding than anything—in all that time. As often happens when a man and woman work closely together, one person becomes attracted to the other. In their case it was Eddie who had been attracted to Georgia and had professed his feelings one awkward and unfortunate evening they found themselves marooned in the boonies with a flat tire.

Although she had turned him down as tactfully as she knew how, by the time the wrecker dispatched by the station had shown up to fix the tire, things had gone from really awkward to contentious. Georgia wasn't sure their relationship would recover, but thankfully Eddie had gotten over the rebuff and they had remained friends, growing even closer over the years.

After she hung up, she turned her attention back to the articles fanned across the kitchen table. She read for over an hour, making notes in a spiral notebook. The more she read about Gerald Ray Toomey and his murders, the more intrigued she became. She made notes on Toomey's five victims—all young single women living in Aspen at the time of their death. All five had been strangled, each found with a scarf still wound around their neck. Georgia made notes on the timing of the murders and realized the victims had been killed a month apart. She remembered the two recent murders had also been committed a month apart.

The similarities between the murders in the 1950's and the recent two were compelling. Coincidence? She was starting to think not.

She read articles about the investigation, several quoting her uncle, Ernest Galloway. Georgia found it eerie to read quotes from her distant uncle in the very house he lived in at the time. She kept reading. There were reports about Toomey's arrest, and an interview he had given after being convicted. Ernest Galloway was identified as the arresting officer.

The more she read, the more questions she had, but it was late and she decided to call it a night. She stacked the articles she had read in one pile, and the few she still hadn't in another.

After a quick clean of the kitchen, she double-checked that the doors were locked and headed upstairs to bed, turning off lights as she went. She would be cautious, but vowed not to let fear consume her ever again. As she closed her bedroom curtains, she thought she caught a glimpse of a shadow disappear behind a pine tree across the street.

CHAPTER 19

MARK THURMOND CRACKED the window just enough to slip his badge to the officer stationed at the guard house. The sky was dumping freezing rain and he didn't want to get soaked.

"Detective Mark Thurmond. Denver PD," he said.

The officer scanned a list of names on a computer monitor, studied the badge, then looked back at Mark. Finally he handed back the badge, nodded, and opened the gate.

Mark parked his car, grabbed his umbrella and took the sidewalk to the entrance of the prison holding Tony Paladino. Through the rain he could see rows of towering chain-link fence topped with spiraling razor wire and cameras. Two expansive open yards were punctuated by concrete guard towers that rose from the ground and loomed over the prison.

Mark's gaze shifted from the guard towers to the concrete walls of the buildings beyond, where some of the state's worst criminals were waiting for their day in court.

Initially Paladino was incarcerated in a county prison to await his stalking trial, but his mob ties and a prison scuffle resulting in a dead guard had landed him in maximum security outside Pueblo. Paladino had been in the state detention center for three days, but Mark wanted to lay eyes on him to verify he was really there.

The phone call from Georgia Glass had reawakened the

animosity he felt toward Paladino. He had arrested plenty of hardened criminals in his career, but none quite as remorseless or cold-hearted.

He had been trying to lock up Paladino for years—money laundering, illegal gambling—but nothing had stuck. With the help of his mob-connected father, Paladino always managed to shirk the charges with a sneer and a smartass comment to the arresting officers.

His latest arrest was for stalking Georgia. Fortunately, her security system had sent her a text notification when movement was detected at her back door. Caught on camera, Paladino had made his way through a back gate and onto the back patio. He was recorded trying to get in through the door then a couple windows. When he found them locked, he left, but not before his image had been digitally recorded. Georgia had sent the video clip to the police and it proved the break in the case they needed.

Mark had been working on the Angelo and Estelle Paladino murder case and Georgia's stalking case at the same time. When Tony was arrested for stalking Georgia, he thought it was an eerie coincidence that the victims of first case were the parents of the perpetrator in the latter.

He was frustrated the murder case had gone cold. But arresting the stalker of a popular local celebrity had been a public relations victory for the department. While the other detectives in the department had cheered the arrest, Mark wasn't satisfied the case had been thoroughly investigated and closed. He voiced his reservations to his boss in the department and the assistant prosecutor assigned to the case. Both had turned a deaf ear.

Now, several weeks later and two hundred miles away, Georgia was again being stalked. Mark didn't believe in coincidences. He also didn't like cases he couldn't tie into a neat bow and file away. The latest stalking incident had him troubled.

In the prison reception area, Mark shook the water off his umbrella and presented his badge again. When the guard on duty was satisfied with his identity, Mark was buzzed in and led through a maze of concrete corridors to a small windowless room that immediately seemed to close in on him.

In the center of the room, a square metal table was bolted to the floor. Two metal chairs were bolted to the floor on opposite sides of it. A camera was perched high in a corner near a concrete ceiling.

He realized he couldn't tell north from south, east from west. He knew the prison—like Supermax nearby—had been designed so that inmates would never know their location in the facility. The design was an effective way to deter escape.

He waited for what felt like an eternity, struck by the near absolute silence. The quiet was pierced only by the occasional rolling of heavy steel doors in the corridor separating different sections of the building.

Typically he would request to have whoever he was questioning already in the room. There was something about being left alone that increased a prisoner's urge to talk once Mark got there. But he didn't have that luxury today. He needed answers from Paladino, and he needed them now.

He checked his cell phone. It had been six minutes. Finally he heard shuffling and clanking metal. Tony Paladino was escorted into the room by two armed guards. He was dressed in an orange jumpsuit with chains looped around his waist and shackled to his hands and feet.

Paladino dropped into a chair across the table, the guards taking opposite corners of the room like silent sentry posts.

Paladino looked cocky, a smug expression on his face like he had somewhere else to be. Mark noticed he had lost weight, but was still paunchy around the middle. He chalked it up to prison rations which he was sure were nothing like Del Frisco's where Paladino regularly dined on fifty-dollar steaks before being incarcerated.

"How's the new place treating you, Tony?" Mark asked glancing around the room.

"How do you think?"

"It's clean—quiet. Doesn't look too bad."

Paladino blew out air. "There's more than four hundred of us in this freakin place, but I never see anybody but these stooges," he said gesturing toward the guards. "Out of the cell for one lousy hour a day and the food's for crap. *That's* how I'm doin."

"Sorry to hear that, Tony."

Paladino rolled his eyes and slouched back in his chair. "Yeah, sure you are."

Mark wanted to get to the point of his visit and get out of there. "Someone sent Georgia Glass an anonymous text with a picture of her taken without her knowledge. Sounds like your old MO. Did you have anything to do with it?"

Paladino's eyebrows shot up. He took a moment before he answered. "No, I didn't. But I didn't have nothing to do with it the first time. I told you guys a million times—I was at her house because I just wanted to ask her on a date." A slow grin spread across his face. "So Georgia's got herself a stalker again. How fitting."

Mark thought Paladino looked genuinely surprised by the news of Georgia's recent text. "This latest incident happened two days ago. Did you have anything to do with it?"

"I already told you no. Even if I *had* stalked her before—which I *didn't*—how would I stalk her now?" He held up his shackled wrists and shook them, rattling the chains.

"You've got friends."

Paladino nodded and laughed, exposing a chipped tooth. "That I do, but in case you haven't noticed, I've got more pressing issues at the moment than wasting my time with Georgia Glass. Besides, I'm a model prisoner in here. That guard in county came at me first, it wasn't my fault. I'm not causing anybody any trouble. When acquitted, I'll be outta here."

"You're not going anywhere, Paladino, and you know it. And since you don't have anything better to do, I think you've found some way of still harassing Georgia Glass."

Paladino sat forward in his chair, the smirk gone. "Why would I bother?"

"Revenge. And to keep yourself relevant—at least in your own mind. But you're *not* relevant, Paladino. Look at you."

Tony Paladino was a narcissistic criminal capable of despicable crimes, but Mark knew he wasn't stupid. He wanted to hit him where it hurt—his ego.

The two men sat in silence, staring at each other.

Mark broke the standoff and spoke first. "I'm done with you today, but I'm not finished with you. I'll be back."

Paladino leaned back in his chair. "It's like you said—I don't have anything better to do, right? Maybe I'm behind it, maybe I'm not. I guess you'll have to figure it out." He crossed his arms in front of him and stared at Mark with unblinking eyes, the smirk back.

It was typical cat and mouse, but Mark wasn't going to play the game. He stood up and motioned to the guards that he was finished talking.

"See you around, Paladino."

"I look forward to it."

Outside, the weather was trying to clear. It had stopped raining and scattered rays of noon sun reflected off the snow-capped Rockies. The brisk air was redolent of pine and wet spring grass.

In the parking lot, Mark stood at his car taking in the disparate landscape of mountains and concrete and considered the near absurdity of it all. The majestic beauty of the Rockies—an unlikely backdrop to the stark ugliness of the prison wrapped in razor wire.

He was glad Tony Paladino was denied the pleasure of the view.

He drove the winding two-lane road that led back to the interstate. The three-hour drive from Denver had been worth it. With over thirty years of experience interrogating suspects—sorting the lies from the truth—Mark had developed a keen sense as to whether someone was lying.

Seeing Paladino's reactions in person was revealing, but also raised more questions than were answered. He was now sure Tony Paladino wasn't stalking Georgia and probably never did. He was back to square one, and realized he had no idea who the stalker was.

He had never feared for Georgia Glass's safety more than he did at that moment.

CHAPTER 20

TWICE THE DAY before, Parker Randolph had picked up his phone to call Georgia Glass, and twice he had clicked it off before hitting the dial button.

He sat drumming his desk with a pencil and attempted self-analysis. Why was he procrastinating calling her? Butterflies? That was ridiculous. He could see how Georgia might intimidate some people—but she had been nothing but friendly with him.

Guilt? Maybe. He was going to ask her to cut a vacation short and start work early—at a company he hated working for. Why would anyone leave the Rocky Mountains for the cutthroat world of broadcast news? He wanted to trade places with her, or warn her, not coax her into starting work early.

But Georgia wasn't like him, she actually *wanted* the job, he reminded himself. She was more like his father, the type that seemed fueled by chaos—a life driven by ambition and accomplishment. She might actually welcome the offer to come in early. He'd call her today, but there was something he needed to do first.

Parker hit speed dial on his phone.

"Yes?" Malcolm Randolph answered.

Always efficient, never wasting time on a greeting or small talk.

"Dad, it's Parker."

"I was just about to call you. Have you spoken to Georgia Glass about coming in early?"

"No, there's something I'd like to talk to you about first."

There was a hesitation at the other end of the line. "Sure, what is it?"

"Not over the phone. Can I buy you lunch today? We can discuss it then."

Parker heard the clicking of a keyboard and knew his father was checking his schedule.

"It looks like I'm free. How about twelve-thirty at the Polo Lounge? I'll have the car meet us downstairs at twelve-fifteen."

"That sounds great. I'll meet you in the lobby." Leave it to his father to set the agenda even when someone else extends the invitation. Parker loved his father, but was completely exasperated by him at times, too.

At exactly 12:30 the car dropped them off in front of the restaurant and Parker followed his father inside.

"Welcome back, Mr. Randolph. Your table is ready." The maître d' had been expecting them.

As usual the Polo Lounge was filled with some of the city's most influential people. Parker recognized the faces of studio heads and actors. A prominent politician and one of the city's wealthiest businessmen were huddled at a corner table deep in discussion.

On the way to their table, Malcolm stopped several times to greet people he knew. When they had finally been seated, Malcolm turned to his son and got right to point. "Okay, Parker, what did you want to talk to me about?"

Parker was nervous. "I'm not happy working at Coastal, Dad. And we both know I'm not cut out for it."

"What do you want to do?" If Malcolm was angry, he didn't show it.

"My dream has always been to write novels. I want to live at the beach and be a full-time writer."

Malcolm frowned, the first sign of emotion Parker detected.

When Parker was done talking, Malcolm took a long drink of gin and tonic and set the crystal glass back on the table. "There's no money in writing. You'll never make anywhere near what you're used to making at the network."

"I know that."

"Even if you were to write a bestseller—which I have no doubt you're probably capable of—the odds of succeeding are infinitely lower than if you stay on and eventually take the helm at Coastal."

"I understand—"

"And you realize that even though I'll let you live at the Malibu house temporarily, I won't subsidize this—no work, no paycheck."

"I wouldn't expect anything else. I've got a couple freelance writing projects in mind and have already talked to my friend who's the editor of *Outside* magazine."

A waiter appeared with two large steak salads. Sensing the tension, he set them delicately on the table and inquired if there was anything else they needed. Malcolm shook his head and dismissed him with a wave of his hand. Then he studied his son without saying a word.

After a moment he nodded, picked up his fork and began digging into his salad. "Alright. So when does this Ernest Hemingway adventure of yours begin?"

Parker hadn't realized he was holding his breath and let out a sigh of relief. "I'll wrap up the projects I'm currently working on, and I'll go to Aspen and try to convince Georgia Glass to start work early."

Malcolm had just finished a bite. "Do that right away," he said, stabbing the air in front of him with his fork.

"I've scheduled a flight for Sunday."

"Have you told your mother about your writing plans?"

"No, not yet."

"Well do that immediately. She's been worried about you. Thinks maybe you have cancer or something and aren't telling her."

They spent the rest of lunch talking about the stock market and the scandals surrounding the upcoming gubernatorial election. Parker was relieved it didn't appear his father was going to hold a grudge.

After they finished eating, and while the waiter cleared the table, both men sat back and studied each other. Many people considered them strikingly similar in appearance, but no one who knew them would say they were anything alike in temperament.

On the sidewalk outside, Malcolm put a hand on Parker's shoulder. "You're a damn fine executive, Parker. And you would have made a hell of a network boss. But good executives are easy to find, and good sons aren't." His father shook his head. "I still believe you were born for this, and if you change your mind about this writing thing, you can come back."

"Thanks, Dad."

Malcolm checked his watch as the car pulled to the curb. "I've got an appointment downtown. You don't mind getting an Uber back to the office, do you?"

Parker looked at his father with a mixture of hurt and relief. How, when faced with the news his only child was leaving the family company, Malcolm Randolph could jump right back into the mode of business as usual.

Parker shook his head. "No, Dad. I don't mind."

Malcolm opened the car door and stepped in. "When you get back to the office, call Georgia Glass ASAP, but call your mother first." With that, his father pulled the car door shut and motioned to the driver. The dark Lincoln pulled away from the curb and sped away.

Parker opened the Uber app on his phone. As he waited, his thoughts turned again to Georgia. He would be honest, tell her he was quitting his job at the network and why. If she decided to start early—fine. But he wouldn't be luring her into an environment he detested under false pretenses.

Back at the office, Parker strolled through the cavernous Coastal News lobby, his footsteps echoing off the marble floor. He greeted the receptionist by name. Just as he was about to open the glass door that led into the suite of executive offices, something caught his eye.

A stack of magazines was fanned out on a large glass coffee table. He walked over and picked up the one on top. It was the most recent issue of *The National Tattler*. There was a picture of Rachel Winston on the cover. He read the headline: "Murder in the Mountains."

CHAPTER 21

"CAN YOU BELIEVE Georgia Glass was *here* yesterday?" Susan Taylor buzzed about the museum not getting a thing done to prepare for the school tour later that day. "Would it have been rude to ask for an autograph? Probably would have been rude. But wasn't she beautiful?"

Brenda Pawloski sat at her desk deep in thought, Crockett tethered and sleeping at her feet. Something about Georgia Glass's visit had been unsettling. Together they had researched and copied articles on past violent crimes in Aspen—of which there were very few. But the similarities Georgia had pointed out between the recent murders and ones committed in a short spree sixty years ago had Brenda disturbed. She didn't mention it to Georgia, but something in the articles had triggered a vague memory, something Brenda knew she needed to remember but couldn't put a finger on.

"Wasn't she?" Susan insisted again.

Brenda looked up at her frustrated. "What?"

"Wasn't she beautiful?"

"Who?"

Susan stuck a hand on her hip and frowned. "Georgia Glass," she screeched. "Brenda, where *are* you?"

Brenda pinched her lips together and let out a deep sigh. "Yes, she was beautiful. But Susan, we don't have time for that right now. We've got a million things to do before the kids get here this afternoon. Could you please help me and get something done? Walk Crockett for me or something."

Brenda saw Susan visibly deflate. She unleashed the dog then turned and left her office. Brenda immediately regretted being short. She massaged her temples trying to coax the clouded memory from her mind.

She wished she could cancel the school tour and skip the presentation she was scheduled to give that evening at a conference for rural water board directors—whatever that was.

With the turmoil over the recent murders—and now realizing the similarities of the murders to ones committed over sixty years earlier—how could she possibly focus on extolling the fascinating cataclysmic geological events occurring billions of years ago that ultimately formed the Rocky Mountains to a bunch of conference-goers.

She wanted to research Gerald Ray Toomey and his crimes. To find out as much as she could about Toomey, but also research the victims and what Aspen was like in the 50's.

A night at home with her computer and the internet sounded more appealing than lecturing to a bunch of middle-aged bureaucrats. But, aware of her own obsessive compulsive tendencies, she knew the distraction would probably do her good.

Although she had given the same geological presentation at least a half a dozen times before, she decided to go over it one more time before the lecture that night.

She jostled the mouse to wake her computer, and for nearly twenty minutes methodically clicked through page after page of her PowerPoint presentation. There were slides on Colorado's prehistoric ecosystems, slides on various ice ages and tropical oceans, slides on how the ancient layers of earth rose to form the mountains. Brenda stared at the screen but saw none of it.

Then she remembered.

CHAPTER 22

HE WAS DISTURBED by a sense of foreboding—a feeling of dread he couldn't shake. The trip to the museum had been a mistake, he knew that now, but it was too late. He was angry with himself for being careless.

In his defense, he hadn't known that he would follow in the footsteps of Gerald Ray Toomey, imitating his murders, but making them brilliant, creating a media frenzy that far surpassed the attention Toomey got in the 1950's. How could he have possibly known all those months ago?

He had gone out of curiosity. He'd read everything again and again in the scrapbook; Gerald Ray Toomey fascinated him and he wanted to know more.

That museum woman—Barbara or Brenda something—had seen what he was looking at on the computer—a headline blaring Toomey's name, the story accompanied by a giant mugshot. Nosy Barbara–Brenda had come up from behind to offer help at just the wrong time.

He thought about her, remembering what she looked like—long auburn hair, hazel eyes, pretty in a natural kind of way. He had overheard her talking on the telephone about some lecture she would be giving. She sounded smart. But her intelligence was a liability.

Going to the library might have been his mistake, but *she* would have to pay for it.

If the police or some over-zealous reporter went sniffing around the museum, they might find out someone had done research on Toomey or his murders. Although it had been months ago, nosy Barbara–Brenda might remember there *had* been someone. Or maybe she would remember on her own, even before the police or media questioned her. He couldn't take that chance.

She might not remember his name, but she would remember his face.

He wouldn't let that happen.

CHAPTER 23

LATE THAT AFTERNOON, Georgia pulled to the curb in front of a large rambling home with cream-colored siding and a dozen windows all the same size except for one, a stained glass window in an unusual starburst pattern set high in the front gable. She double-checked the address Jonathan Kramer had given her an hour earlier.

Georgia had called him to ask a favor. "Jonathan, I'm sorry to bother you at work. I know you thought that when I closed on my house you were rid of me, but I have another request. "

"You don't need to apologize," he said without any hint of being annoyed by her call. "Call me anytime. What can I help you with?"

"I'm looking into the Rachel Winston and Greta Moss murders—nothing formal, just my own curiosity and peace of mind, and I'd like to talk to someone who knows about personality disorders. I was thinking about calling the police department to see if there's a psychologist or psychiatrist they work with in town, but they might consider me media and be hesitant to help, so I thought I would check with you first."

"You're supposed to be on vacation," he said with a chuckle. "You're between jobs, right?"

"I am, but I'm not busy and I'd really like to know what happened. I thought I would start with motives. Kind of 'get in the mind of the murderer' thing. I know it sounds crazy—"

"It doesn't—it sounds intriguing."

"Okay, good." Georgia laughed. "I wouldn't want you to think I was nuts."

"Not nuts," Jonathan said. "Maybe a workaholic though."

"Guilty as charged," Georgia said, relieved. "But maybe a little nuts, too. But we'll keep that between you and me."

"Deal. And as a matter of fact, I *do* know a psychiatrist. I sold him his house several years ago. It was actually an old boarding house that had been renovated—very cool. His name is Thomas Murphy—Dr. Thomas Murphy. He's retired now but was a bigwig at one of the large hospitals in New York. If he can't help you, he'd know someone who could."

"Oh, that's perfect."

"He and his wife, June, were guests at the Winstons the night Rachel went missing. He'd probably do whatever he could to help you. Let me call him and see if I can set something up."

Jonathan had called her back within five minutes. "Tom said he'd be happy to talk to you anytime and that he was free now if you wanted to run by."

Georgia got out of the car and hesitated a moment. It was mid-afternoon and clouds had rolled in, chilling the wind and cloaking the mountains in a gray veil. She turned up the collar to her jacket as she walked up the sidewalk.

"Hello. I'm Dr. Thomas Murphy. I'm a big fan of yours." He was handsome. Tall and lean, dark hair graying at the temples. His voice was deep. He extended his hand for her to shake.

"Thank you," Georgia said. She was surprised to find his handshake cold and clammy.

"Please come in."

"Thank you for visiting with me. I won't take up much of you time."

Georgia felt his eyes on her as she stepped into the foyer

and he shut the door behind them. The small entry suddenly seemed to close in on her.

"This way." He gestured with his arm then followed her into a large room that opened to the backyard. It was beautiful, and a welcome surprise after the small dark entry. The ceilings were high and the room flooded with natural light from the windows looking out onto a long flagstone porch. It was furnished in contemporary mountain style with clean lines mixed with a few rustic pieces. One entire wall was floor-to-ceiling bookshelves. Georgia had to restrain herself from heading straight over and snooping to see what the doctor had on his shelves.

He must have noticed her looking. "I have a weakness for books," he said. "A room large enough to accommodate all of them was at the top of my wants list when June and I were house hunting. I *almost* got them all in here. Our home was an old boarding house and this room was the dining hall."

"It's quite a house," Georgia said, looking around the cavernous room then back to what were easily a couple thousand books. "And quite a collection. Do you read anything in particular, or a little bit of everything?"

"My interests are eclectic. History and architecture. Travel books. Books from museums I've visited around the world." He let her take it all in. "Help yourself," he said gesturing toward them. "Have a look."

Georgia stepped slowly along the wall, reading the titles as she went. There were books on Europe and Asia, Colorado and the Rocky Mountains. Art books from the Louvre, the Smithsonian, the Frick Museum in New York. Biographies and history books. She continued to scan until her gaze fell on *Helter Skelter*, a book about the Manson Family. She stopped. Next to it was a book on Bonnie and Clyde. Then *In Cold Blood* by Truman Capote. She glanced at the next few books and felt her pulse quicken. The entire row was books on murder.

"I have an extensive collection of mysteries and true crime." He let that sink in before he continued. "Jonathan probably told you that I'm a psychiatrist—forensic psychiatrist actually, or at least I was before I got mired in hospital administration. I'm retired now but I still research some and publish the occasional article in a medical journal. So when Jonathan called and told me you wanted to talk to someone regarding personality disorders, I thought I could help."

Georgia turned her back to the books. "Thank you for seeing me."

"What specifically were you wanting to know?"

He gestured for her to take a seat on the sofa then sat in a facing chair.

"I'm interested in the psychology of murder—and more specifically copycat murders." She wanted to ask him about copycat stalkers as well, but didn't. She decided that would be a subject for another day. "What would motivate them? How would law enforcement profile them?"

He looked intrigued. "It's an interesting subject. The term 'copycat' was first used in association with criminal behavior over fifty years ago, but there hasn't been a lot of research on the subject."

"I wonder why?"

"Probably because knowing whether or not a crime is perpetrated by one criminal imitating another is really not that useful to law enforcement in solving the crime. It may be an actual copycat, but often times it's not—even when it looks like it is."

Georgia sat on the edge of the sofa and frowned. "So, even if the police *know* a murder was committed imitating a previous one, that information wouldn't be of any help to them?"

"Not much. A copycat criminal can have any number of motives. This makes it difficult to profile to any degree that is useful to law enforcement. And furthermore, the only way to determine if a crime was a *true* copycat is to catch the perpetrator and ask them why they did it. But even then, you're relying on a criminal to tell you the truth."

"So it's hard to determine whether or not a crime could be a copycat. But if it's known that it was, what would some of the possible motivations be?"

"The motives could be the same as ones that provoke any criminal." His scrutinizing stare made her uncomfortable. "Jonathan mentioned your research was regarding the Winston and Moss cases. Do you believe one was a copycat of the other?"

"No, not of each other, but of five previous murders." She hesitated, not sure how much of her research she was ready to reveal.

"What previous murders?"

Georgia decided she wanted as much help from Dr. Murphy as she could get, and despite her reluctance, explained the similarities she had uncovered between the current murders and those committed by Gerald Ray Toomey decades earlier.

"It's a hunch," Georgia said. "The similarities are compelling and I think it's highly likely the killer had some knowledge of Toomey's murders when he killed Rachel and Greta."

"You've already concluded the murderer is male. From my understanding, there was no evidence of sexual assault. Do you think it's possible the murderer is a woman?"

"It's possible, but I don't think it's probable. I've been an investigative reporter for over ten years. I'm not a criminologist or a profiler, but I've learned a few things. It may sound crazy, but I believe someone learned of the Toomey murders and decided to go on their own killing spree. The similarities in the crimes point to a copycat killer. The fact that there are two victims, and the nature of those victims—young, attractive—leads me to believe it was a man who murdered them."

"You're probably right," he said. "But don't jump to any definitive conclusions this early. There are no standards when it comes to murder—or murderers."

She nodded in agreement. "Could I run another theory by you?"

"Of course. You've piqued my interest."

He smiled flashing large white incisors, and for a brief moment she felt like Little Red Riding Hood to the Big Bad Wolf. She knew she was being ridiculous. He was a doctor, *and* a friend of Jonathan's.

She cleared her throat. "I don't know about Greta Moss, but I think Rachel knew her murderer."

She waited for a response.

"Why do you think so?"

"She disappeared from the reception at her parent's house. I believe she was abducted sometime during the party or right after since she was found still wearing the clothes she had on that night. If she had gone for a late-night walk she would have put on something more comfortable—at least changed out of stiletto heels. And it was cold that night. If she had gone to town, she would have taken a jacket, but there wasn't one with her body.

Dr. Murphy nodded. Georgia couldn't tell if he agreed with her, thought she was crazy, or had already come to the same conclusion.

She continued. "If her abductor had been a stranger, she would have resisted—screamed, fought back. With all the people on the property that night, it's unlikely someone could have taken her against her will without being seen or heard, so I think she was taken by someone she knew—and probably trusted."

"You've put a lot of thought into your theory."

"I have, Dr. Murphy. Do you think there's merit to it? Or am I way off base?"

"First of all, call me Tom." He walked over to a desk tucked in a corner of the room and grabbed an accordion folder from under a closed laptop. "Second, no, I don't think you're way off base. In fact, I had already come to a lot of the same conclusions you have. And I'll admit, the theory of a copycat killer is very intriguing."

Georgia took the folder he handed her and scanned its contents.

"Light reading," he said. "A handful of reports and articles on psychiatric criminology. Nothing referring to copycat crimes, but now that I know what you're looking for, I'm sure I can find you something."

"Thank you," Georgia said, still flipping through the folder.

"It's what I could put my hands on quickly, but it's enough to get you started. I know I've got a few more things stashed away somewhere that will be of interest to you. If it's alright, I'll get them to you later."

"That'll be perfect. Thank you again, Dr.—"

"Ah, ah," he held up a hand in protest.

"Tom," she corrected. "You've been very helpful and I really appreciate you taking the time to talk with me."

"I've thought a lot about the crimes as well," he said. "Walter and Harriet are good friends of ours."

"That's right. Jonathan told me you and your wife were guests of Winstons that night. So do you have any theories on who might have abducted Rachel? Or why?"

"I've gone over it in my head a dozen times. I think it was an edge-sitter."

"An edge-sitter?" She had never heard the term.

"In forensic psychiatry, there's a small percentage of the population that we unscientifically classify as 'edge-sitters.' These are people who live their life teetering on the edge between normal behavior and psychotic. On the outside, they appear as normal as you and me. If they were walking down the street, nothing about them would make you look twice."

"What causes them to snap?"

"Any number of things. The possibilities are endless—trauma, rejection, stress. I think whoever murdered Rachel was someone who looks like you or me, but secretly has the tendency to strike if confronted with just the right stimuli."

She would google 'edge-sitter' to find out more.

He followed closely behind as she walked to the door. Georgia reached for the doorknob but he grabbed it first, startling her.

"Let me get that for you."

"Thank you," she said, the uneasy feeling washing over her again.

"I'll get you more information that might be helpful to your research, then let's talk again. I'm working on my own theories, but I'm very interested in yours as well."

He opened the door and Georgia stepped out onto the porch.

"Have you talked with the police about any of this?" she asked.

"About Rachel Winston's abduction? Yes. They interviewed all of us who were at the party that night."

"Have you discussed your profiling theories with them?"

"No. I've kept my opinions on the murderer to myself... until I shared them with you today." He flashed a wolf's grin again.

Back in her car, Georgia locked the doors. Something about meeting Thomas Murphy had been unsettling. She dismissed it as nerves coupled with exhaustion. It had been a grueling three days in Aspen.

CHAPTER 24

GEORGIA WOKE THE next morning to the sound of splitting wood. Pulling on her robe, she headed downstairs.

In the kitchen, she started the coffee maker then peeked through the blinds. Two men with crowbars were plying the worn siding off the old garage. She recognized one as Karl Kamp and forgot that he had told her he would start demolition as soon as the police were finished with the garage. Karl was wearing the same set of overalls and tattered baseball cap he'd worn the day she met him. The man helping him—not much older than a boy—was tall and thin, dressed in a plaid shirt and jeans so big that they seemed to teeter on the verge of dropping to the ground. It was cold outside, but neither wore a jacket.

When the coffee was ready, Georgia poured herself a cup and sat down at the table to read one or two more of the articles Dr. Murphy had given her before she got dressed. She pulled the top article from the pile and began to read. The title was *Studies in Profiling*.

As she had the night before, she took notes as she read, writing down anything that she found interesting or that might be of use. The night before, she had filled multiple pages with notes and statistics on past cases, personality traits, and theories—anything that might have a remote chance of helping her investigate the murders.

She had decided that, once she was confident she knew enough to talk intelligently on the subject, she would call Detectives Martin and McCray and request a meeting. She hoped they would regard her more as an interested citizen than as a reporter.

When she was done going through what Dr. Murphy had given her, Georgia googled *copycat murders* and kept reading.

She read that many criminologists credited Jack the Ripper with the birth of the copycat killer. The extensive newspaper coverage of his murders in London in 1888 had incited a series of similar crimes.

Another article on a mass killing hit closer to home. It was about the massacre in an Aurora, Colorado theater several years ago. As she read, Georgia thought of her high school classmate who had been gunned down at the theater while out with her husband. Both were slain by a deranged killer acting out his version of the role of the Joker at a premiere of the latest Batman movie. Following the rampage in Aurora, there had been a spate of copycat incidents at theaters around the country.

There were other, more notorious copycat murders. She read how John Hinckley, who shot Ronald Reagan in 1981, pointed to the movie *Taxi Driver* and its star, Robert De Niro, as his inspiration for attempting to assassinate the president.

The ones she found most disturbing were the string of copycat school shootings following the killing spree by two teenagers at Columbine High School—another horrendous mass murder in Colorado, and just around the corner in Littleton where she had lived briefly after college.

The number of copycat killers surprised her, cases she had forgotten about. There were the Tylenol killer copycats and the *Natural Born Killers* copycats. The list seemed endless.

She checked her phone and saw that nearly three hours had passed. She had to stop or she would go crazy.

She thumbed through the pages of her notes then closed her eyes and massaged them. It was like being a voyeur into the minds of the most demented psychopaths. She wanted to shower, to wash the heinous details of torture and murder from her memory.

After getting dressed and a quick lunch, Georgia decided an early afternoon run might help clear her head.

She pulled the map Jonathan had given her off the shelf in the sitting room and studied the trails he had circled. She quickly ruled out the ones marked 'Expert' and 'Difficult'. They would still have snow and ice this early in spring, and although she was an experienced climber, she wasn't sure if she was up to something that challenging yet—especially not alone.

She decided on Hunter Creek Trail, one of Jonathan's favorites and rated good for intermediates. It was just over a mile outside of town. Later, when more snow had melted and she had acclimatized to the altitude, she would try one of the more difficult hikes near Maroon Bells he had circled.

It was a clear cold day with only a few clouds. The snow-capped mountains were in crisp focus against a turquoise sky. Georgia ran for twenty minutes then stopped, put a hand on her hip to keep from doubling over and tried to catch her breath.

She sat on a boulder on the edge of an open meadow. The air was cold and smelled of pine. The altitude app on her phone showed she was over 8,500 feet above sea level—no wonder she was out of breath so soon.

She pulled a water bottle from her backpack and drank, then fished her phone out of the bag and was surprised to see she had service. There were two voice messages.

"Hi, Georgia, it's Jonathan. Call me back when you get a chance. There's something I want to talk to you about. No rush."

The second message was from Parker Randolph. "If you're not busy, I'd like to meet with you in Aspen on Sunday. Please call me back when you get this message so we can arrange a convenient time and place. I look forward to hearing from you."

What could be so urgent that Parker needed to come to Aspen to discuss it with her? Were they going to try renegotiating her salary? She would hold firm.

She remembered the first lunch she had had with Parker and his father. Malcolm had praised her story on the Paladinos, complimenting her on her investigative skills and hard-nosed style of journalism. Parker had been mostly quiet. She wasn't sure why, but she thought she had sensed disapproval, maybe even a touch of hostility.

She shook her head. Whatever his reason was for coming to Aspen, she wasn't going to let it ruin the rest of her run. Best to find out now and get it over with. She touched the redial button.

"Parker Randolph."

"Parker, it's Georgia Glass."

"Georgia, thank you for calling me back. I hope I'm not interrupting anything."

"No. Just taking a break from an afternoon run."

"Ah, that sounds awesome."

"It is. It's gorgeous here." She was anxious to get to the point of the call. "You mentioned you needed to come to Aspen. Is there anything wrong?"

Parker laughed. "No, not hardly. My father wants me to convince you to start work early."

"Okay, that's a relief. But as beautiful as it is today, I'm not sure I would want to leave early."

"Don't make any decisions yet. Let me come out and go over the details with you, then you can decide. Besides, it's an excuse for me to get out of the city for a day. Don't blow that for me." She heard the smile in his voice.

"I'd never do that."

"Great. I'll fly out Sunday morning on one of the company planes. Would lunch at The Monarch work? Or if you want something lighter—The Wild Fig? Coastal has an account at both."

Accounts at expensive restaurants, company planes, flying from L.A. to Aspen at the drop of a hat... she was going to love working at Coastal News. But she wasn't sure if she wanted to leave Aspen yet.

"Either place sounds wonderful," she answered. "I'll let you decide. Text me what time you'll land. I'm happy to drive out to the airport and pick you up."

Next, Georgia called Jonathan Kramer.

"Hi, Georgia. I talked to Harriet Winston. She said she'd like to meet you. She suggested tomorrow at their house, after the service for Rachel."

"That's very nice of her. I was considering attending the funeral."

"Then let me pick you up. We can go together. I'll introduce you to the Winstons myself."

"Thank you, Jonathan. I would really appreciate that."

"The service is at ten. I'll pick you up at nine-thirty."

On the run back to her car, Georgia wondered what it was going to be like meeting the parents of the murdered girl she found. She was apprehensive, but decided she would offer the Winstons her sincere condolences first, then ask a few questions about Rachel. She wanted to know more about the girl she found in her garage. Then hopefully, at a later date, she could have a conversation with them about the night Rachel went missing.

Sunday she would have dinner with Parker Randolph. Now

that she knew the Randolphs weren't trying to renegotiate her contract, she was surprised at how much she was looking forward to lunch with Parker.

She would see how things went with the Winstons on Saturday, then assess the traction of her investigation and make a decision about whether or not to leave for Los Angeles earlier than planned.

On the winding highway back to town, she noticed the sun had dropped below the mountains, the waning daylight casting long shadows across the road. She had forgotten how quickly it got dark in the Rockies.

As she turned onto her street and pulled to the curb in front of the house, a white van with a deep gash on its side passed her going in the opposite direction. It was traveling at a slow speed and for a moment she thought it was slowing to a stop but it didn't. As it crawled past, she caught a fleeting glimpse of the driver shrouded in shadows.

There was something unsettling about the encounter. Although the driver's face had been completely hidden in the dark void of a hooded jacket, she could tell he had turned to look at her.

CHAPTER 25

TOM MURPHY GLANCED across the living room at his wife who sat on the sofa like a bag of dry cement with the morning edition of *The Wall Street Journal* opened across her broad lap. She had already read *The Financial Times* and tossed it aside on the floor.

"I can't believe that even *The Journal* has a story on the Winston murder," she said. "I'm so tired of *Winston murder this, Moss murder that.* Surely there's got to be something more important in the news." She folded the newspaper and tossed it on top of the other.

She had been reading *The Wall Street Journal* for years. Tom supposed somewhere in her delusional mind she was keeping herself prepared for when she would be called upon by the Fairchilds to take over the family business.

It was no secret June loved regaling anyone who would listen to her stories of her exalted genealogy and the indispensable part she played in the family fortune. But what Tom knew, and what June always left out, was the fact that her own father and uncle had years ago banished her from the family firm. Despite a business degree from Wharton and a brief stint at one of the largest investment banking firms on Wall Street, June had been "too imperious" as former colleagues and subordinates had complained, many threatening to quit before June was summarily let go.

Tom had whisked her off her feet just before she was fired. He remembered how delighted he was to find out that despite being sacked from the family firm, she got to keep her trust fund.

"I'm sure *The Journal* is reporting it because of the Winstons' prominence on Wall Street," Tom said, not looking up from his own paper—*The Aspen Times*. Since they had left New York, Tom had quit reading everything except the local paper.

"Well of course I know that, Tom," June replied. "I'm not stupid. It's just that I'm sick of hearing about it. And now that nasty Detective Martin is harassing us again and going to line us up like a bunch of common criminals after the funeral."

Tom turned a page and without looking up and replied: "It's not a line-up, June. He just wants to question us again."

"All of us—at the same time? And the same place? What does that rude man expect? That with all of us there watching someone is going to blurt out a confession? It's nothing short of a formal inquisition."

June had been in a particularly foul mood since Jack Martin had called the day before. He had told them that following the funeral, everyone who'd been a guest at the Winstons the night Rachel went missing was to report to the conference room at the St. Regis.

"And I'm sick and tired of the jeans and those ridiculous cowboy boots he always wears," she continued. "He looks more like a Texas Ranger than an Aspen detective. I think that man fancies himself a modern-day Dirty Harry."

"Dirty Harry wore a coat and tie, dear."

She ignored the remark. "At least he had the decency not to organize it somewhere like the Holiday Inn. *That* would have been the last straw. I would have refused to go."

Too bad, Tom thought. He'd give anything to see what the police would do if June refused to show up. Issue her a ticket for not complying with a murder investigation? Arrest her and give her jail time? That was too much to ask for, but it was fun to consider.

Life before being shackled to the screeching harpy had been good. Tom thought of all the women who'd crossed his path over the years—still crossed his path when he could manage it. He couldn't believe his rotten luck at having to spend the rest of his life with June, even *with* her Fairchild trust fund. Their life together had been easier in the beginning—before June had morphed into Medusa. He might have loved her once, but that had been so long ago that he couldn't remember.

Living with her was hell. Thirty years earlier she had found out about his affair with a nurse at the hospital. She had helped him cover it up to save his job. Not out of altruism, Tom knew, but out of self-preservation. Tom had been on the fast track for promotion and she wanted to ensure her husband stayed at Mount Belvedere. Plus, there was no way she was going to be humiliated by having her husband's affair made public.

For whatever her reasons, Tom had been relieved by her unexpected support and discretion at the time. He had gone on to enjoy a stellar career at Mount Belvedere, publishing regularly in medical journals, guest lecturing at medical schools, and finally being promoted to Chief of Staff.

He was grateful no one knew why he had resigned so abruptly six years earlier. "Retiring early to move to the mountains," he had explained at the time. Although he suspected June had never really believed his story, she never questioned him. She was suspicious, but driven by self-preservation. Tom knew she wouldn't want to know the truth if it risked humiliation.

He had endured thirty years of wrath over the early affair and couldn't imagine the hell he would endure if she ever found out why he really left Mount Belvedere. In her mind, his status at the hospital had increased *her* status in New York society as well. She never forgave him for resigning.

He looked over the top of his paper to steal a quick glance and grimaced. She was particularly unappealing in the morning before she had time to smear on her daily war paint.

Although life with June hadn't started out bad, it quickly went to hell and was only getting worse. He gave it another five or ten years before he was sure it would become unbearable. The only thing worse than a nearly sixty-year-old June would be a seventy-year-old June.

Till death do us part, he remembered from his wedding vows. "Hmm, now *that's* an interesting possibility."

"Did you say something?"

Tom didn't realize he had said it aloud. "Nothing, sweetheart." He folded the paper and looked at his watch. "We should probably leave for the funeral in about an hour. After we meet with Detective Martin, I think I'll come home and take a nap. I didn't sleep well again."

"I'm sure you need a nap after being out all night," June said eyeing him suspiciously. He didn't reply. "I woke up around midnight and you weren't in bed. Where were you this time?"

"Uh, I did some research for that TV reporter Georgia Glass last night—I told you she stopped by while you were shopping Thursday—"

"Yes, you told me she was researching serial killers. How nice of you to help her, and how convenient she is so beautiful."

Ignoring the remark, Tom continued. "When I was done on the computer, I went for a walk to clear my head and wind down. Take my mind off things before going to bed."

"Murder, murder, murder. It's no wonder you don't sleep," June said in a tone that dripped with contempt. "So, do they help?"

"Does what help?" Tom asked.

"Your midnight strolls, when you think no one is watching."

CHAPTER 26

JONATHAN KRAMER HAD every intention of going for a run when he'd gotten out of bed and pulled on a pair of comfortable sweats and long-sleeve T-shirt, but now there wasn't time.

He shut his laptop, once again having been sucked into the internet black hole, only to pop out the other side disgusted at the futility of it all.

For two hours he had scanned business news, read celebrity gossip, checked weather forecasts for the mountains, and devoured all the stories online regarding the recent murders.

The weather forecasts all predicted a mild spring. Aside from a single storm the following week, no additional snow was expected. Under normal circumstances, this would have been great news for real estate, but the negative publicity surrounding the murders was going to hurt. Business had already started to taper off.

Who would want to lease a condo in Aspen, much less buy a house, with the possibility of a serial killer walking the streets? Thank God for the regular visitors. Maybe paparazzi photos of Heidi Klum and her children, or Goldie and Kurt would signal all was well and bring the real-estate-buying tourists back. He hoped it would.

He only had an hour until he picked up Georgia for the funeral. He made a quick breakfast of scrambled eggs, washed it down with a cup of coffee, and went upstairs.

He took a navy blue suit and a gray pinstriped one and held both up to the mirror, decided on the gray one and pulled a silk paisley tie from the rack.

He watched in the mirror as he looped the tie around his neck, tucking it under his shirt collar and began knotting it, taking extra care to make sure it was straight.

He ran through the pros and cons of asking Georgia to dinner. He wanted to get to know her better but didn't want to move too fast and scare her away. That had happened too many times in the past. This time would be different.

They had hit it off from the first telephone conversation, and since then, she hadn't mentioned seeing anyone since her breakup with the football player.

When he had finished dressing, Jonathan stepped back and studied himself in the full-length mirror. Not bad, he thought.

"Jimmy's," he said aloud, the idea having popped into his head. "It's perfect." American cuisine and a meticulous wine list, with just the right combination of atmosphere and good food. Not too casual, but not too stuffy—just like Georgia. She'd love it.

Jonathan studied his reflection a few more seconds until he was satisfied. Feeling confident, he decided he would ask Georgia to dinner.

As he reached for his keys and cell phone, his phone vibrated. He let out a heavy breath when he read the caller ID. For a moment he debated not answering, then did.

"Hello, Mother."

After a couple minutes talking about the weather and how fabulous her recent trip to San Francisco had been, she got right to the point. Jonathan expected nothing less.

"I need you to get the condo ready, Jonathan. I'll be in Aspen next Friday."

"That's great," he said. "Are you coming for any particular reason, or just to visit?"

It had been almost a year since her last visit. He needed to plan something. He ran through the possibilities in his head. The Commodores were playing at the opera house, she might like that, he thought. Maybe a day trip to Vail? They were debuting the new spring Wine and Cheese Festival. She might prefer a dinner out—the two of them, or he could invite Georgia. She would like Georgia.

He realized she had been talking—something about her condo.

"What were you saying, Mother?"

"The condo, darling. I was saying, what was the point in keeping it if I don't come use it every now and then."

Jonathan had often wondered the same thing. She owned one of the nicest condominiums in town—six thousand square feet of marble and glass overlooking Aspen Mountain. It had been featured in *Architectural Digest*. The framed cover hung on the wall of his office.

She was still talking. "You never come to Beverly Hills, darling, so I guess if I ever want to see my youngest child again, I need to come to you."

The guilt arrow hit its target. "I'm sorry, Mother. I've told you how busy I've been."

"I'm in New York this weekend but flying back to California Monday. I have a charity gala Wednesday evening. I'll pack Thursday and be in Aspen Friday afternoon. We will have dinner Friday night. Be a dear and call Cache Cache for me and reserve my table."

Jonathan knew it was pointless bringing up The Commodores or Vail. Marilyn Swanson wanted Cache Cache, and Marilyn Swanson *always* got what she wanted.

"I'll call them now," Jonathan said. "And I'll have the condo ready for when you get here."

After a couple minutes more, Marilyn said her goodbyes and Jonathan clicked off his phone.

He would call the restaurant, but first he needed to notify the management company she was coming. They would have to mobilize the housekeepers, schedule the butler. Jonathan needed to arrange for a driver and to have the refrigerator in her condo stocked.

He sat down at the kitchen table, started to scroll through his contacts but gave up. He set the phone on the table and dropped his throbbing head in his hands. With his eyes screwed shut, he massaged his temples.

CHAPTER 27

WHEN CARLO FERRARI finally got out of bed and made his way to the kitchen, Bridget was sitting at the table eating her daily breakfast—half of a wholegrain bagel with a dollop of mashed avocado spread across the top. It was something Carlo wouldn't offer his dog to eat, if he'd had one.

"How about bacon and eggs for a change?" he asked. "Maybe with a side of pancakes or waffles, drizzled with melted butter and soaked in maple syrup."

Bridget had lectured him for years on his weight and eating habits, but to no avail. Carlo had told her numerous times that no self-respecting Italian man would acquiesce to a diet of kale and quinoa, much less mashed avocado for breakfast.

He watched as Bridget got up and rinsed her plate, admiring her slender form under the pale silk pajamas. He knew what people whispered behind their backs, *how could someone like him*— a balding, overweight, struggling local businessman— *marry someone like her?* He still wondered sometimes himself.

Although life with Bridget wasn't easy, after seven years, he still enjoyed ogling her. She was forty-one with the body of a thirty-year-old. Carlo watched her bend over and slip the plate into the dishwasher.

She turned and looked at him. "You're up earlier than usual. I thought you would sleep in after being up most of the night."

Carlo felt his chest tighten, a cool bead of sweat formed above his upper lip. He remembered going to bed around midnight, which was typical for him after a night at the lounge, but he didn't remember anything after that. As far as he knew, he had come straight home and slept like a baby. Or that's what he had hoped.

"You really should call the doctor and go in for a checkup," Bridget said. "Your insomnia is getting worse. You can't afford that on top of your horrendous diet. You're snoring is getting worse, too. You need to lose weight, Carlo…"

She kept talking but he didn't listen.

As far as Bridget was concerned, he had insomnia. What she didn't know was that he had episodes of full-on blackouts, chunks of time he couldn't account for. Lately his blackouts seemed to come more frequently. Bridget thought it was just a night-time occurrence. She didn't know about the half a dozen or so that had happened during the day.

It terrified him, those empty periods of time dropped from his brain—an hour here, an hour there.

Last week it had happened on Tuesday night. He remembered leaving the lounge as usual around 11:30. The next thing he knew, he was getting into bed still fully dressed except for his shoes, and covered in sweat. He had glanced at the bedside clock. It was two in the morning. What had happened during the previous two and a half hours remained a mystery.

The episodes began a couple years earlier, not long after he and Bridget moved to Aspen. They began as bouts of sleepwalking, then had graduated to gaps of time he couldn't account for. Except for his doctor, no one knew the truth about what was happening to him, especially not Bridget.

But it was getting hard to conceal. Carlo had always been an insomniac, never sleeping more than four hours a night, getting up at all hours to work or read. For years, while he was building his private equity firm, not needing sleep had come in handy.

His current episodes weren't insomnia, but something more serious. He suspected the stress of running the lounge caused the recent increase in their frequency. He wouldn't let himself think it was early-onset Alzheimer's, the disease that had ravaged his father years earlier. He had also tuned out his doctor when he suggested it could be something called transient global amnesia. No, it was the cigar bar he told himself.

Carlo poured himself a cup of coffee and sat down at the table. "The funeral is this morning, remember?"

"How could I forget? That detective wants us at the St. Regis when it's over."

"Then we won't be going to the Winstons after the funeral to pay our respects." Carlo was relieved. He hadn't been back to the Winstons since the night Rachel disappeared. That night he had had one of his episodes. He vividly remembered certain details of the party—who was there, what they were wearing, the food. He even remembered speaking with Rachel early on in the evening. But he didn't remember anything after that. When he woke the next morning, it was all a blank.

He didn't know what a dire predicament that particular episode put him in until he and Bridget were called in for questioning by the police the next afternoon. Carlo didn't have an alibi, at least not one he could remember.

The whole situation left him overwhelmed with a feeling of dread he couldn't reconcile. He had avoided Walter and Harriet ever since.

Bridget was on her way out of the kitchen but turned back. "The detective said we had time to visit Walter and Harriet after the funeral. But to go to the St. Regis right after."

Carlo sat alone at the table drinking his coffee. He had told the police that after he left the party, he had gone home and gone to bed, that he hadn't gone anywhere else until he went to the lounge late the next morning.

He wasn't sure if that was really how the rest of his night had gone, but that's what he had told them, and that's what he would tell them again.

CHAPTER 28

JONATHAN SHOWED UP promptly at 9:30 to take Georgia to the funeral. She met him at the front door, stepped out onto the porch and locked the door behind her.

"You look beautiful," he said. "Too bad it's for a funeral and not for dinner or something more enjoyable."

"Thank you." Georgia was glad she had brought her favorite black sheath dress instead of sending it on to Los Angeles with the bulk of her clothes. At the last minute she had thrown it in a box bound for Aspen. You never know when you'll need that perfect black dress, she had thought at the time, but she never imagined she would need it for a funeral.

Jonathan opened the passenger door of his Range Rover and waited until she was seated, then shut it. Georgia watched him as he walked around the front of the car, handsome in his gray suit and tie, more formal than the jeans and sports coat he had worn that first morning at the cafe.

As they pulled away from the curb, he commented: "I see Karl has gotten started with your garage remodel. How's it going?"

"He's doing great. Such a nice guy. Thank you for the referral."

"I figured you'd like him. Most people do. Karl's a character, and a good contractor, too." There was a pause in the conversation before he continued. "So any regrets on the house? After finding a body, you had to have had second thoughts."

Georgia considered the question a moment. "No, not really," she said. "I mean… having *not* found a body would have been nice, obviously, but I can't say I regret owning the house. Does that make any sense?"

"It does. And I'm glad you don't regret it."

"I'll admit, it *has* been a rough few first days in town, but I already know I'm going to love it."

"You will," he said. "I've never regretted moving here. One thing I *will* regret, though, is if I don't take you to dinner sometime to thank you for the business."

"I'd love dinner," Georgia said and meant it. It had been a rough few days in Aspen, but being with Jonathan relaxed her. She was glad to have a friend.

"Jonathan, can I ask you something, but you have to promise to tell me the truth?"

He looked at her with both a smile and a frown. "Now I'm interested."

"I asked you to arrange an introduction with the Winstons, but since then I've been a little worried. I didn't even know Rachel. My only connection was that I found her, and she was in my garage. Do you think they're okay with meeting me? And with me being at the funeral?"

"I'm sure they're okay with it. I know they're devastated about losing their daughter, but they are very nice, gracious people. I wouldn't worry about it at all, if I were you."

"I'd like to ask them a couple questions sometime," Georgia said. "But I don't want them to think of me as someone from the media who's come to snoop."

"They won't think that about you," Jonathan assured her. "I told them how fabulous you were. Plus, they're fans of yours. Harriet told me they watched you almost every night on the news when you were in Denver."

Jonathan turned the corner and Georgia saw Crosstimbers Church. She imagined it was what Frank Lloyd Wright would have designed had he been commissioned to build a church in the mountains. A modern wood-planked design with a wainscoting of stacked rock, soaring wood beams and lots of glass. It was a beautiful building.

He turned down a side street looking for a place to park. Although they were early, there were already cars parked on both sides of the road and people were making their way into the church. He found a spot near the end of the block, pulled to the curb and shut off the engine.

Georgia watched several mourners walk past the car on the way to the service. "The murderer will be here."

Jonathan turned in his seat. "What? How do you know that?"

"Experience. Their ego usually keeps them close. They're curious. They want to watch the scenario they set into motion unfold. You've heard the old saying, *criminals always return to the scene of the crime.* They can't help themselves."

Jonathan shifted his gaze from Georgia to the people walking toward the church. "You're probably right."

"And think about it. The police think it's someone local, someone close to the family. Anyone close to the Winstons who doesn't show up to grieve with them might as well wave a flag that says *I did it.*"

"Huh," Jonathan said, still staring at the mourners who had passed. "So, guilt by *dis*-association."

"In a way… yes. But who knows, the police could be wrong. It could be someone they don't suspect, someone who doesn't know the family. I haven't met them yet, but it doesn't seem they'd be the type to befriend a sadistic sexual predator."

"They're not," Jonathan said. "But who said the motive was sexual? The police haven't reported that she was assaulted."

"Just a guess," Georgia replied. "From experience, again. Think about it—two beautiful, young girls kidnapped and murdered. What are the odds it's not sexually motivated?"

Inside, the church smelled of flowers and oiled wood. Large beams crisscrossed overhead in the open sanctuary built of stacked rock. A simple set of three stained glass windows behind the altar spilled sunlight of various colors across the floor and into the first couple rows. There were flowers everywhere.

Georgia asked Jonathan whether he would mind if they sat near the back. She told him it was out of respect for the family and friends—she didn't know the Winstons and felt more comfortable in the back. What she didn't tell Jonathan was that she wanted to watch the mourners during the service. Let's see who looks uncomfortable, she thought, who fidgets, or whose eyes dart around the sanctuary like they're planning an escape route just in case.

Jonathan took her elbow and guided her to two seats along the back wall on the far side of the sanctuary. He stopped several times along the way, greeting mourners that he knew and introducing Georgia. They had just reached their seats when the organ began to play.

Georgia scanned the crowd.

Where are you? she wondered as she studied row after row, scanning the faces she could see, and watching for suspicious behavior or body language.

The killer was there. She could feel it.

CHAPTER 29

AT TEN O'CLOCK on Saturday morning, Susan Taylor was on her way to work. It was late spring, and traffic at the museum would start to pick up soon. She liked it when it was busy. The days went by faster, but mainly she liked meeting new people and working closely with Brenda.

Half the year, when things were slow, Susan only worked part-time, mostly by herself at times when Brenda was traveling to conferences or other speaking engagements. But during the peak tourist seasons, winter and summer, she worked *with* Brenda almost every day. Those were her favorite days at the museum.

She loved working with Brenda, especially since the previous archivist had about as much personality as the large chunk of petrified wood on display in the front lobby. He had been a dull, little man. Short in stature, Susan had secretly referred to him as "Stumpy." She didn't miss Stumpy after the museum's board finally forced him out to pasture nearly three years earlier. Brenda had been hired right after that.

Her new boss's enthusiasm for history had been infectious. Susan soon grew to love a job she had previously considered mundane. She had also grown fond of Brenda, considering her a friend as well as a boss.

Before she reached the museum, Susan's cell phone rang. She dug through her giant purse until she found it.

It was Brenda's mother, who still lived in Durango where

Brenda had grown up. "Susan, have you seen or heard from Brenda today?" She sounded nervous.

"No, not yet, but I'm almost to the museum. We're both scheduled to work today."

"We always talk on Friday night. She lets me know how her week went and what her plans are for the weekend. But she didn't call last night. I waited until around eleven, then I called her to make sure everything was alright, but she didn't answer. She didn't answer this morning either."

Susan knew about Brenda's weekly phone calls with her mother, and knew she wouldn't miss one.

"I'll be at the museum in just a couple minutes," Susan said trying her best to hide her alarm. "I'm sure everything is fine. Maybe her cell phone isn't working, or she lost it."

"Maybe." Brenda's mother sounded skeptical. They both knew Brenda was too organized to have misplaced her phone for long.

Susan steadied her voice. "As soon as I get there, I'll have her call you."

"Thank you."

What Susan didn't tell Brenda's mother was that she had also tried calling Brenda that morning. An unexpected leak had sprung under the kitchen sink, and the plumber who told her he would be there at eight o'clock had shown up at nine. Knowing she would be late, Susan had called Brenda to let her know, but she hadn't answered, or even returned her call, which wasn't like her.

The museum was only four blocks away and Susan made it in record time. When she saw Brenda's car parked in the small lot behind the building, her heart caught in her chest. Susan remembered Brenda had parked her blue Honda Accord at an odd angle the previous day, blocking a portion of the second designated employee parking space. Brenda had apologized, telling her a UPS truck was blocking a portion of her spot when she parked.

Brenda's car was still parked at the unusual angle. She had never left.

Susan's hands were shaking as she inserted her key into the back-door lock. That's when she heard Crockett barking. When she turned the key and found the door already unlocked, she wanted to turn and run. Instead, she pushed it open slowly and stepped into the dark hallway.

Crockett continued to bark and whine.

"Brenda?" She called out in a weak voice.

No answer.

Her heart thumped in her chest as she eased down the hallway toward Brenda's office. She leaned around the doorframe and peered inside. Except for Crockett, barking and still tethered to Brenda's desk, the office was empty. She noticed Crockett had nearly chewed off the leg of the desk he was tethered to.

"Brenda?" Susan called out again as she made her way into the museum exhibit area. That's when she saw her.

Susan let out a guttural scream that sent shockwaves through her body. Her legs collapsed beneath her.

Brenda Pawloski was lying in a pool of congealed blood. Her head was twisted to the side at an odd angle; dead eyes bulged from their sockets and her mouth was frozen in an open gape from a scream that had been silenced forever.

CHAPTER 30

DETECTIVE JACK MARTIN sat in a back pew at Crosstimbers Church with his partner Luke McCray. The preacher had already spoken, offering words of comfort, and Rachel Winston's sister was giving the eulogy. Jack heard none of it.

He was certain Rachel's killer was among the mourners—shedding crocodile tears—so he scanned the crowd. The thought of the murderer being in the very room at that moment made his blood pressure rise.

When the eulogy was finished and the last of the hymns sung, the preacher approached the dais once again for a final prayer.

Yea, though I walk through the valley of the shadow of death,
I will fear no evil...

Jack scanned the crowd for the umpteenth time.

He had planned to go straight to the St. Regis after the funeral and prepare for the joint questioning. But as he and Luke walked out of the church, their phones pinged simultaneously with texts alerting them to the murder of Brenda Pawloski.

When he got to the crime scene Jack was relieved to find three local patrolmen already guarding the entrances to the museum, one in front and two at the back entrance.

They entered the building through the front and saw the

guys from forensics already dusting for fingerprints. Dr. Lester Gorman, the county coroner, was bent over studying the body. He heard them approach and looked up.

"Hey, fellas," he said with false cheeriness that failed to mask the weary expression on his face. "Here we go again."

Jack got to the point. "Time of death?"

"Best guess? Somewhere between eight o'clock and midnight last night."

Jack stood looking down at the remains of Brenda Pawloski. A small pool of blood had fanned out to one side of her body; a cell phone lay on the other side.

Jack fixed his hands on his hips, taking in the rest of the scene. "Cause of death?"

"Gunshot wound to the back," Lester replied, pointing to a small hole in the back of her shirt with his pen. "Can't tell if there are any more wounds without rolling the body over. But my guess is that the one shot I can see, and its proximity to her heart, was enough to kill her."

Luke was taking notes. "Any sign of a struggle? Skin under her fingernails?"

Jack was impressed. The kid was learning.

"Nothing I can see in a preliminary examination," Lester replied, "but I need to get the body back to the morgue."

"We need more than preliminary opinions, Lester." It was Police Chief Carl Rogan. Nobody had seen him come in through the back door. "Let's get the autopsy done ASAP. The media's going to be barking up our ass wondering if this is connected to the Winston and Moss murders. Let's at least throw them a bone and give them a cause of death."

"She doesn't appear to have been strangled," Luke pointed out. " No scarf."

"You're right," Gorman said, pushing his substantial weight to a standing position. "No ligature marks on the neck." He peeled off his latex gloves and stuck them into a coat pocket, then motioned to Jack. "Have a look."

After twenty years with the FBI, Jack had seen his share of death, but he never got used to it. He took a deep breath then bent down and studied the single wound to the back. From the size of the hole in her shirt and the surrounding stain, he guessed the weapon was something around the size of a .38, fired at close range. Not that powerful, but enough to get the job done.

Gorman moved in closer. "When you're finished, we can get her to the morgue."

Jack nodded and stood up, then glanced around. He walked carefully around the different exhibits and display cases, scanning the artwork, old photographs and maps on the walls. Although he had never set foot in the museum before, nothing appeared to be missing or broken. When he and Luke walked in, the officer stationed at the front door had told them no door latches, front or back, appeared to have been broken. He also told them the assistant who found the body confirmed they didn't keep cash in the museum.

Luke stood next to him. "What do you think?"

Jack dragged a hand down his face. "Not sure yet. But there's nothing to indicate the murder was committed during a robbery."

They watched as the coroner's assistants turned the body over. Lester examined the front of the corpse and motioned them over.

"No apparent wounds in the front. If you guys are done, we're going to get her out of here."

"Shot in the back," Luke remarked. "Fleeing her attacker?"

Jack nodded and looked down the hallway to the back door. "No forced entry. She either recognized her attacker and let him in, or he was waiting for her to unlock the door and surprised her when she was leaving. My bet is she let him in."

"She had her cell phone on her, but her purse and her dog were still in her office," Luke said.

Rogan had marched over to them. "I don't give a damn if she was coming or going, we gotta find this guy ASAP. We don't need any more damned publicity. I'm leaving this to you guys. Call me as soon as you've got something—anything."

Jack watched them bag the body. "The question is motive—it's always motive. *Why* would someone want Brenda Pawloski dead?" He was talking to Luke and thinking aloud at the same time. "No robbery. If she wasn't murdered for something she *had*, there's a good chance she was murdered for something she had done, or something she *knew*."

Jack sent Luke outside to interview the woman who found the body. He wanted to hang around inside a while longer. A young forensic technician with pimply skin pushed his glasses up his nose and spoke to him.

"There's not much to go on, sir. We got lots of prints, but it's a museum. We expected that. I'm not sure how much use they'll be."

Jack nodded to him, then to the other technician who was busy packing up their gear. "Thanks, guys. I'm guessing you took the prints of the assistant who found the body?"

"Yes, sir. She was in quite a state, too. Good luck with that one. Hopefully she'll calm down enough to be able to help you guys out."

Jack turned to walk outside but a uniformed officer stopped him, held out a leash. Jack looked down and saw that it was attached to a big brown dog that wagged its tail nervously. Jack frowned.

"Detective, could you take the victim's dog outside and give it to the woman who worked with her?"

Reluctantly, Jack took the leash and led the dog outside.

"Where's the woman who found the body?" Jack asked Luke.

"Still recovering. I haven't been able to talk to her yet. Her name's Susan Taylor."

She was sitting on the back bumper of an ambulance breathing oxygen through a mask, an EMT medic sat next to her. A police officer stood with them but walked toward the detectives when he saw Jack exit the museum.

"How's she doing?" Jack asked the officer

"They've got her calmed down and on oxygen. She suffered a few minor abrasions but the medic indicated it was nothing serious."

"How did she get those?"

"She said after she found the body, she exited the building and collapsed on the pavement in the parking lot."

Jack nodded. "Has she said anything else?"

"Only what she reported to 911."

"Alright, let me go talk to her. You guys stay here. At this point, we don't want to overwhelm her."

"No, I don't need to go to the hospital," Susan Taylor was saying through the mask to the medic, fogging it. "I'm going to be alright. It was just so horrible finding Brenda…" Her voice grew weak and she started to cry again. "It was horrible," she sobbed. "Who would do that to her?"

Jack put a hand on her quaking shoulder. "Ms. Taylor," he began, his tone compassionate. "I'm Detective Martin. Could I ask you a few questions that might help us find out what happened to Brenda?"

Susan lifted the oxygen mask off her face and drew a hand under her dripping nose. With bloodshot eyes swimming in tears she looked up. "Who would do this?" she asked starting to sob again.

After the first few questions, it became clear Susan Taylor had no idea who killed Brenda Pawloski, but she had a definite opinion on *why* she had been murdered.

"You think she *knew* her killer?" Jack wasn't sure he had heard her right.

"Yes," she said nodding her head. Then she shook it, "I mean no. She didn't *know* him, but she had *seen* him."

Jack kept his tone calm despite his growing frustration. "I'm confused, Ms. Taylor. Can you elaborate?"

"I'm sorry," she said, covering her face with her hands for a moment before looking back up at him. "Brenda had mentioned to me that a man had come to the museum several months ago, and she noticed he was researching Gerald Ray Toomey. She said he tried to hide what he was reading on the computer screen, but she saw it."

"Who's Gerald Ray Toomey?" Jack asked even though Georgia had mentioned him before. He wanted Susan to keep talking.

"A murderer in Aspen. A long time ago. Georgia Glass came to the museum and she and Brenda dug up some old articles on him. Georgia can tell you more."

"Georgia Glass?"

Susan nodded, wiped her nose with the back of her hand again.

Jack didn't see the connection between Brenda Pawloski's murder and Toomey, but he would question Georgia again, and soon.

"Did she know this guy who came to the museum? Give you a name?"

"No, she said she couldn't remember who he was, but if she saw him again, she would recognize his face."

Jack's felt his pulse quicken. "You said this was a few months ago?" Anyone researching a local serial killer just months before Rachel Winston and Greta Moss were abducted and murdered would be put on their list of suspects.

"Yes, she said she thought it was about six months ago because she remembered preparing for her lecture at the Aspen Environmental Conference last October." Susan wiped a hand across her nose again before continuing. "She said she didn't think anything of it at the time and had forgotten about it, but after Georgia Glass's visit, something jogged her memory."

"Did she describe the guy?"

"All she said was that something about him gave her the creeps."

"Did she mention his age or height?"

"No." Susan shook her head.

"Hair color?"

"No. I don't think so," she replied still shaking her head. "I can't remember."

She looked on the verge of sobbing again. Jack acted quickly to quell it. "The information you've provided is very helpful, Ms. Taylor. It's important that if you remember anything else—anything—call me."

She fought back tears. "No one who knew Brenda would want to hurt her, detective. If you had known her, you would understand."

Jack nodded.

She struggled to gain her composure. "It had to have been that guy—the one in the museum that day, the one researching Gerald Ray Toomey."

Jack didn't say it, but he had a growing feeling in his gut she might be right.

Although shooting his victims had not been his previous MO, and Brenda Pawloski didn't exactly fit the profile of his first two victims, Jack suspected the same killer had committed all three homicides. He felt his worst fears being confirmed. An indiscriminate killer, one who thought nothing of slaughtering innocent women, was walking among them on the streets of Aspen.

He knew they had to find this monster before he murdered again. And there was little doubt, he *would* murder again.

Before he left, Jack held out the leash to Susan. "I was asked to give you the victim's dog, Ms. Taylor."

Susan pulled her oxygen mask back down before replying. "I can't take him," she said through snot and tears. "I can't. It's too much. He's a good dog. Take him," she sobbed. She pulled the mask back up and leaned back into the ambulance.

Jack looked around. Luke was nowhere in sight, but he saw patrol officer Bobby McDonald and walked the dog over. "Bobby," he said holding out the leash. "Do you want a dog?"

The officer shook his head. "Sorry, detective, I have three already. My wife would kill me if I brought another one home."

Jack frowned. "What do I do with it?"

Bobby glanced at his watch. "The shelter is closing soon— and will be closed tomorrow since it's Sunday. But I'm sure they'd take him on Monday. Looks like he's yours until then."

Jack looked around, searching for a better solution. When he realized there wasn't one, he looked down. The dog sat patiently at his feet, watching him with dark, sad eyes.

Jack took in a deep breath, then released it slowly. "Shit."

CHAPTER 31

GEORGIA STEPPED THROUGH a set of tall wooden doors into a foyer that stretched to a large living area at the far end of the house, terminating in soaring floor-to-ceiling windows that perfectly framed the snow-capped mountain range beyond. Two giant chandeliers made of antlers hung from a vaulted wood ceiling. It was elegant, in a rustic sort of way, and exactly what she would want if she could afford a multi-million dollar mansion in the mountains.

On the drive up from town, Jonathan had told her the area was named Red Mountain. "Nicknamed Billionaires Mountain for all the celebrities and billionaires who have vacation homes up here. They sit empty most of the time. The Winstons are one of a few that live here year-round."

Walter and Harriet Winston stood just inside the doors receiving condolences. Georgia admired their attempt at cheerful hospitality despite being visibly distraught. They looked small in the cavernous foyer. She wished she was meeting them under different circumstances.

When Jonathan introduced her, they welcomed her warmly. "Walter and I are so sorry that you were the one to find Rachel," Harriet said taking Georgia's hand in her own. "It must have been very upsetting, especially since it was your first day in your new home."

Harriet Winston's concern for Georgia's feelings at a time

when most mothers would be too overwhelmed with their own grief to think of anyone else was touching.

Walter Winston reached out and shook her hand next. "Jonathan tells us you're doing some investigating of your own," he said. There was no animosity in his voice, only weariness. She was relieved.

"I'm looking into it," Georgia said. "I'm an investigative reporter by profession, but this is personal. I hope that's alright."

Harriet took Georgia's hand back from Walter and squeezed it gently. "It is. We're okay with anyone who wants to help us find out what happened to our baby."

"Thank you," Georgia said quietly. "Maybe another time, when it's more convenient, I could ask you a few questions?"

Walter Winston spoke first, "Anyone who is looking to find the monster who murdered our baby girl has our blessing, and we will do *anything* we can to help."

As Georgia and Jonathan walked the length of the foyer, they passed the dining room. Wait staff scurried around a buffet table, replacing empty trays of food with new ones. Outside, groups of tables and chairs were set up along an enormous patio that offered spectacular views of the mountain range in the distance.

"Jonathan," a voice called.

"That's Bridget Ferrari," Jonathan said as they made their way across the patio.

Georgia glanced at her. Bridget was striking. Jet-black hair pulled into a tight ponytail that spilled down the back of her white wool jacket. She was dressed in a pantsuit Georgia recognized from Ralph Lauren's latest collection. Her legs were crossed, exposing the red sole of one of her stiletto boots— Christian Louboutin. Next to her on the flagstone patio was a black alligator Birkin bag the size of a small suitcase.

"Come sit with the rest of the line-up," Bridget said

when they got closer. "We're going over our alibis before the interrogation."

Georgia cringed at her crassness.

A somber-faced woman sitting across from Bridget rebuked her sharply. "Bridget, this is *not* the time or place for flippancy."

Bridget Ferrari didn't skip a beat. "'Life's too short to be so uptight, June," she said, then turned her attention back to Jonathan and Georgia. "You must be Georgia Glass?"

"I am." Georgia managed a smile.

"I thought I was seeing things," Bridget said in an exaggerated hushed tone. "From a distance, it almost looked like Jonathan had walked in with Greta Moss."

The woman named June immediately shook her head in obvious disapproval of the tasteless comment.

Jonathan turned and looked at Georgia apologetically, then paused, staring at her. "There *is* a resemblance," he said faintly. "I hadn't noticed it before."

Georgia was surprised to see Dr. Thomas Murphy at the table. He greeted her, then introduced his wife June as well as Carlo Ferrari, Bridget's husband. Georgia was surprised by the two unlikely couples. Before she was introduced, she would have guessed Bridget was Tom's wife, and the somber-faced June was with the shorter barrel-chested man that was actually Bridget's husband, Carlo.

Never judge a book by its cover, she reminded herself.

After the introductions and they had been seated, Bridget Ferrari spoke next. "Jonathan says you're only in Aspen briefly before you start a new job in L.A."

"That's right. I have a few more weeks before I have to be there."

"And you have a house here?"

"I do. For a while anyway. I haven't decided if I'm going to sell it or keep it yet."

Jonathan smiled, looked at Bridget but leaned in Georgia's direction. "I think she'll keep it. I grew up in L.A., remember? It's way overrated. She's going to want somewhere to escape to."

"Well, let's hope next time you visit there are no surprises like a dead body waiting for you," Bridget added with a smile dripping with sarcasm.

Georgia's intuition was telling her to stay away from Bridget Ferrari. She knew the type. The perfumed monster who could manage an insult inside a shallow compliment. Superiority or inferiority complex? Probably a mix of both. They liked to stir the waters, leaving chaos in their wake. Georgia would steer clear of her in the future.

Later, on the way out, Jonathan introduced Georgia to several other people he knew. Everyone—except maybe Bridget Ferrari—had been kind and very welcoming.

Georgia had particularly liked an elderly couple, Bunny and Dr. Bart King. Georgia learned Bart was a retired pediatric oncologist, having retired after nearly fifty years spent working at St. Jude Children's Hospital in Memphis. She couldn't imagine a more comforting doctor for sick children than the happy and cherubic Dr. King.

Bunny King told Georgia how they had met Walter and Harriet Winston twenty years earlier, when the Winstons had brought their oldest daughter Sophie to St. Jude after she had been diagnosed with leukemia. The two couples had grown close during the three years the Winstons spent off and on in Memphis for Sophie's treatment. The Kings had vacationed several times over the years with Walter and Harriet in Aspen. Bunny told her that when Bart retired seven years earlier, they had moved to Aspen permanently.

Georgia thought Dr. King must have worked well into his seventies if he had retired only seven years earlier. She guessed they were both in their mid-eighties.

Bunny told her how Jonathan had helped them purchase their home in town.

"Bunny is being modest," Jonathan said to Georgia. "It's not just any home. The Kings bought the old Dublin Mansion. The three-story Victorian at the corner of Hopkins and Waugh. It's a registered National Historic Landmark."

"You live there?" Georgia exclaimed. She remembered seeing the old mansion perched high on an elevated lot near the center of town. "It's a beautiful home."

"Well, I'd love to have you over for lunch sometime and show it to you," Bunny said smiling and patting Georgia's arm. "I'll arrange something before you leave. I assume you're on Facebook—I'll find you and send you a message."

Georgia had never known her own grandparents. She liked to imagine they were something like the Kings. She looked forward to getting to know them better.

Everyone said their goodbyes, then just before they parted, Bunny King hesitated and looked back at Georgia. "I couldn't put my finger on it at first, but now my old brain is working again. Has anyone told you that you bear a striking resemblance to Greta Moss?"

It was intended as an innocent observation and Georgia was sure Bunny hadn't said it to upset her, but the comparison for a second time was unsettling.

"Yes, I've heard that once before," Georgia answered, forcing a small smile to hide her uneasiness.

"Well you do," Bunny said. "And it's a compliment. The dear girl was a real beauty." Then Bunny patted her arm again and left.

Georgia was glad she and Jonathan were leaving. She suddenly felt nauseous and wanted to lie down. She tried telling herself it was probably the Swedish meatballs from the buffet that had upset her stomach, but, deep down, knew it was from being compared to a murdered woman twice within the timespan of an hour.

At home and safely inside, Georgia turned and locked the door then peeked through closed blinds as Jonathan drove off. Just as she was about to turn away, she saw it. A white van.

She watched through the crack in the blinds as it got closer. When it passed her house, she was sure of it—the same van, the same driver. It was warm and the sun was out, but he was wearing a jacket. As before, the hood was pulled up, shrouding his face in darkness.

CHAPTER 32

EVER SINCE GEORGIA Glass had called him about the recent text, Mark Thurmond hadn't been able to think about much else. The visit with Tony Paladino in prison had made it worse. He had spent the day before going back over the original stalking files.

There was little doubt amongst the other detectives in the department that Tony Paladino was guilty of stalking her. Although he never admitted guilt, Paladino had been caught on camera trying to break into her townhouse, and was arrested carrying a throwaway cell phone and a switchblade. He also had an iPhone with dozens of incriminating photographs of Georgia he had downloaded from the internet.

Consensus was Paladino was the culprit and the stalking case was closed. The only thing left was to wait for the trial. But since the arrest, a seed of doubt had lingered in the back of Mark's mind. That seed had grown exponentially following his prison interview with Paladino the day before.

Mark had somewhat successfully talked himself into believing that, with Paladino behind bars, Georgia was safe. Now he knew she wasn't.

As he worked in the flower bed that stretched across the front lawn, he talked about the case with his wife Jeannie. Years ago they had discovered gardening was something they both liked to do, tilling the earth while hashing out the world's problems. Soon into their marriage, Mark had begun talking to her about cases he was working on. Jeannie had proved a discreet and capable sounding board.

Mark looked over at her as she dug, dirt up to her elbows. Despite the passing decades having turned her hair from brown to white and etched her face with laugh lines, he still saw the dewy-faced young girl he had married years earlier.

Mark returned his attention to the flower bed and talked while he dug. "When we arrested Tony Paladino on the stalking charges, I was happy to get the guy behind bars for *something*. We've investigated him for years— illegal gambling, loansharking—but couldn't get any charges to stick."

"Is he guilty of those other things?"

"Without a doubt." He told her about Paladino killing the county guard while in custody waiting for the stalking trial. "And with his mob ties, he's a flight risk. Too risky to keep him in the county jail. That's why he's in maximum security outside Pueblo now."

"Sounds like an upstanding citizen," Jeannie said removing bulbs from a plastic bag and setting them on the cold grass.

Mark harrumphed and nodded, then continued loosening the soil in the bed. "I had hoped he was guilty in some way of Georgia Glass's recent stalking incident in Aspen. Maybe he had someone on the outside take care of it for him. But after talking to him yesterday, I don't think he did it."

"So who do you think did?"

"That's what's bothering me—I don't know." Mark pulled off a dirty glove and rubbed his forehead with the back of his hand. "Then there's Sammy Garafano."

"He's the mobster from New York?"

"Yes, the one who beat up Paladino before we arrested him. He's a hired thug for the Romano family, and currently being investigated for a couple mob hits in New York."

"Did you ever figure out why he was in Denver?"

"We're not sure yet. Presumably to kill Angelo and Estelle Paladino, but we don't have enough evidence to arrest him for the murders yet, and unfortunately we couldn't hold him for the assault charges on Tony Paladino after Tony claimed it was all a misunderstanding and refused to press charges."

What bothered Mark was why Paladino would let the guy who beat him up—and likely murdered his parents—get away with it. Fear maybe?

Mark knew Paladino's type all too well. Talks a big game, dangerous, but underneath, just an arrogant coward.

"Then there's TJ Williams. He could be the one stalking her." Mark threw the name out there. He didn't think Williams was responsible but wanted Jeannie's input.

"TJ Williams?" Jeannie echoed, grabbing a bulb but stopping to look at him before she planted it. "No. He's not the type."

Mark watched her as she set the dahlia bulb in the ground and covered it with soil. "Why not? He had motive."

Jeannie shook her head. "A bad breakup is a weak stalking motive for a womanizer. Besides, I read on TMZ that he's already dated and broken up with some young B-list Hollywood type and has been partying in Las Vegas." She thought about it a moment, then shook her head and went back to planting. "He's moved on. It's not him."

Mark felt the same way about Williams. Most likely he wasn't their guy, but he'd keep Williams's file on his desk just in case.

When they had finished planting, both stood up and admired their work. Satisfaction from a job well done.

Mark turned and looked southwest, toward the white peaks of Front Range and Mount Evans. Aspen lay just a hundred miles beyond. He thought of Georgia, and her stalker. He would have to ask for time off from the department, investigate this on his own time.

Jeannie must have seen him staring into the distance and knew what he was thinking. "It's not your jurisdiction. It's a different case now, Mark. Not yours."

He knew she was right but it didn't matter. The stalking cases were somehow linked, whether they were committed by the same offender or not. And that likelihood was enough reason for him to feel responsible for making sure the case was solved and justice done.

Jeannie laid a hand on his arm and let out a heavy breath. "You're not going to leave this to the guys in Aspen, are you?"

He shook his head. "Somehow the cases are related, Jeannie. Someone is trying to get to Georgia Glass again, and I think whoever it is knows a lot about the first stalking case. And nobody knows that case better than I do."

"So you're going to help." Jeannie started gathering the dirty gardening tools. "Do you know anyone in the department there?"

"Not yet, but I'm calling first thing Monday morning."

"Okay then. But first, you can help me clean up this mess."

He turned his back to the mountains and gathered the tools from her outstretched arms. "I'll call Aspen PD Monday morning," he said. "But first, I'm going to call Georgia Glass and warn her she's in danger."

CHAPTER 33

IT WAS ALMOST two o'clock Saturday afternoon. Twenty-seven people, including the employees of the catering company, the DJ, and the Winston's housekeeper, had gathered in the conference room of the St. Regis Hotel. Twenty-seven chairs had been placed around four large round tables.

Detective Jack Martin had come straight from Brenda Pawloski's murder scene and stood in front of a small lectern near the center of the room and scanned the faces in the crowd. He thought of Brenda's body sprawled across the museum floor and suspected that whoever had murdered her was probably in the room. His gut told him the recent murders of all three women had been committed by the same perpetrator.

But the news of Brenda's death hadn't been made public yet. Jack knew that none of them in the room would know about it, *except* for the killer.

Two material clues that linked the Winston and Moss murders were the Hermes scarves. The scarf used to strangle Greta Moss was a well-known fact. Following the discovery of Moss's body, the media began referring to the killer as the Hermes Strangler.

But the police had intentionally kept the existence of the second scarf—the one found with Rachel Winston's body—a secret. Besides the police, the only people who knew about the second scarf were Georgia Glass, Karl Kamp, and the murderer; and Jack wanted to keep it that way.

Although her body was found a month after Greta Moss's, Rachel Winston had been the first victim—a fact confirmed by Lester following his autopsy. The stage of decomposition of Rachel's body, and the fact that she was found wearing the same clothes she had worn the night she disappeared, indicated she had been killed soon after her disappearance.

Jack had spent a lot of time wondering about the scarves and what significance they played in the murders. He had decided the one used on Rachel was either a weapon of chance, something that had been picked up at the Winstons' house the night of the kidnapping, or it was something deliberately worn or taken to the party in order to commit the murder. He kept coming back to the first theory—the scarf was an afterthought. It seemed the more plausible theory, but it was too early to rule anything out.

"Thank you all for coming today," Jack began, his tone direct and to the point. "I know this is probably the last thing anyone wants to do following the funeral. But, as you know, all of you were present at the Winstons' home the night Rachel Winston disappeared and—we now know—was murdered. And although I've already talked with each of you individually following her disappearance, we believe that by bringing all of you together now, there might be something someone remembers from that night. It might be something you saw or heard that you didn't think anything of at the time, something Rachel said to you in passing that didn't mean anything then, but does now.

"What I'd like you to do is search your memory for even the slightest irregularity or clue. No detail that gives you pause should be dismissed."

He hesitated a moment before continuing. "Then I want to

briefly meet with each one of you alone with Detective McCray. We can go over anything you might want to keep confidential, and confirm where each of you was later that night after the party, and the following morning."

Jack scanned the room for any sign of discomfort or nervousness. Carlo Ferrari looked visibly upset, a furrowed brow and pursed lips contorting his round face into something resembling an overcooked ham.

In his first interview, Carlo had sworn he had gone to the lounge early on the morning following Rachel's disappearance. No one else had shown up at the lounge for several hours, so no one could corroborate his alibi. Sitting next to Carlo Ferrari was his wife, Bridget. Bridget Ferrari had told them before that she had slept in the next morning, and didn't know what time Carlo had left the house. So neither one had a solid alibi.

Dr. Bart and Bunny King were listening intently. Both in their mid-80's, Bunny was as chatty as her husband was mute. They both seemed eager to help and although Jack seriously doubted either one had anything to do with the murders, he hoped maybe they would remember seeing or hearing something.

Dr. Thomas Murphy sat with his wife June. Now there was an unlikely coupling. Conducting his previous interviews, Jack heard bits and pieces of local gossip that indicated Dr. Murphy wasn't the innocent doting husband, but had a roving eye for other women. After Jack had interviewed June, he wasn't sure he could blame the doctor if he did. The doctor seemed nice enough, but June was a piece of work, reminding him of his grade school principal who had terrorized her students with a yardstick and a face that could sour milk.

Dr. Murphy's current expression was as emotionless as it had been during his previous interviews. He was on record as saying he'd gone for a walk the night Rachel Winston went missing.

There were five additional elderly couples. Jack had already interviewed all of them, and was fairly certain, given their age and lack of mobility, that none of them had anything to do with Rachel's disappearance.

Then there was Ida Caldwell, mid-70's and widowed. She reminded Jack of Robin Williams's character in *Mrs. Doubtfire*. Round and amiable, she was definitely at the bottom of his suspect list along with Bart and Bunny King. Ida sat knitting, but her perceptive expression indicated she was undoubtedly soaking in every detail of what was going on around her. Like the Kings, Jack hoped Ida might have remembered seeing or hearing something that night at the Winston's that would prove useful.

Jonathan Kramer was sitting next to the Kings. Successful local real estate broker; and single. Could he have used that to his advantage to lure Rachel Winston to her death?

And Stanley Lauren, the elderly owner of Lauren's, a pricey clothing boutique downtown. Jack had never been there, no reason to. He knew he couldn't afford anything Lauren sold in his store and probably wouldn't wear it if he could.

Then there was the catering staff of four: A chef the size of a manatee who was completely disinterested in everything but the bowl of pretzels set in the center of each table, two female servers who looked like they weighed a hundred pounds combined, and their supervisor, Ray Stewart. Stewart was single and attractive, and dressed with a flair reflective of the stylish clients he served. If Stewart wasn't so obviously infatuated with Jonathan Kramer, Jack might have had him closer to the top of his suspect list.

After a quick five-minute recap of the facts in the case that had already been made public, Jack opened up the gathering to group discussion hoping the participants would recount their memories of the evening and bounce differing versions off one another. It quickly became clear that no one had anything new to offer, or maybe they were afraid to discuss it in front of the group.

For the individual interviews, a small meeting room adjacent to the conference room had been set up with a single table and two chairs. Jack sat at the table with the person being interviewed. Luke sat in a third chair off to the side with the notes from all the previous interviews, and held the leash of the large brown dog Jack couldn't figure out yet how to get rid of.

The objective was to rattle their suspects, catch them trying to change their story or cover something up. Jack had used the technique before, but never on twenty-seven people in the same day for multiple homicides.

Jack had two new questions for each of the interviewees, questions he had not asked during the first round of interviews following Rachel Winston's disappearance. "The night of the reception, did you wear or notice anyone else wearing a brightly colored silk scarf?" The second question was, "Did you know, or have any recent contact with, Brenda Pawloski at the Aspen Historical Library and Museum?"

The interviews crept by. So far, no one had remembered anything more than what they had told Martin and McCray previously. No one's answers contradicted their previous statement. No one remembered anything about the scarf; and none knew, or had come into contact with, Brenda Pawloski except for Bunny King and Ida Caldwell who were both members of the museum's board of managers.

Several years earlier, Jonathan Kramer had been to a real estate convention that Pawloski had spoken at, but he never met her. His alibi the night of the reception was the same: he'd gone to Poacher's Pub after the party for a couple drinks then had gone home—alone. Luke had stopped in the bar and spoke with the manager who confirmed he had spoken with him that night. Jonathan's alibi had checked out.

Next it was June Murphy's turn to be interviewed. She barged into the small room like a battleship, oozing fury and indignation. Her answers were short and dismissive. She made it obvious she found the process of being questioned again very insulting.

After only a couple minutes she had had enough. "Are we about done here, detective? I'd like to go home and lie down."

Jack took a deep breath before answering. He was as ready to be rid of June Murphy as she was of him. "One more question, Mrs. Murphy. The night of the reception, did you notice anyone wearing a brightly colored scarf?"

"Yes," she declared. "I was wearing a Hermes—a *very* expensive scarf. I lost it. Did someone find it?"

Jack felt his heart rate speed up but kept his tone calm and unaffected. "If you were wearing the scarf, how did you lose it?"

"Well of course I didn't lose it *while* I was wearing it, detective. I took it off and handed it to my husband with my purse. He put them on a table in the foyer with several other purses— or he was *supposed* to anyway. Somehow the scarf was lost."

"Did either of you search the Winston house for it before you left?"

"Of course not, detective. That would be the height of rudeness to go rummaging through someone's home during a party. No, we did not search for it. We looked amongst the purses and handbags on the front table, but that was it. Tom called the Winstons the following day to see if it had been found, but it hadn't."

"Could you describe the scarf?"

June shook her head like it was a foolish question. "It was Hermes. Red and green with a bit of blue and yellow. It was very expensive."

"One last question, Mrs. Murphy."

"You insinuated the previous question would be the last one."

"One more," Jack said without apology. He wasn't about to apologize for any inconvenience the murder investigation might inflict on the pompous June Murphy. "Do you know Brenda Pawloski?"

"From the museum? Yes, I know her. I co-chaired a luncheon a couple years ago that she spoke at. It was a fundraiser to benefit the museum. We raised quite a lot of money, if I remember correctly. But then again, we always raise a lot of money when I chair an event."

"Have you seen her or spoken with her in the last week?"

"No, not at all since the luncheon a couple years ago. Why would I?"

When she was out of earshot, Jack told Luke, "We need Thomas Murphy in here before she has time to fill him in on what she told us."

Luke sprung from his chair.

A couple minutes later Dr. Thomas Murphy sat across the table, appearing relaxed. But sensing something amiss with the good doctor, Jack studied him closer. The quick rise and fall of his chest belied his calm demeanor. He was nervous. Then Jack noticed a small bead of sweat had formed just above the doctor's upper lip. He's not *nervous*, Jack thought to himself, he's petrified.

"Dr. Murphy, did your wife lose a scarf at the Winstons' home the night of the reception?"

Jack saw it immediately. Behind the cool indifferent expression he had worn since he walked in, Tom Murphy was stunned by the question. There was a moment of silence before he answered. "Yes, she did. Why?"

"Did she give it to you after the two of you arrived at the Winston home? Ask you to hold it for her?"

"Yes—uh, no. I mean she didn't ask me to hold it for her. She gave it to me, along with her purse, but asked me to place it on a table near the front door where there were already several other purses."

"And what did you do with it?"

"The scarf?"

"Yes, the scarf."

"I set it on the front table—with her purse."

"You're sure you placed it on the table?"

"Yes, I'm sure. But when we left, it wasn't there." He shifted in his chair.

"And the next day, did you call the Winstons to ask them if they had found it?"

"No, I didn't."

"Would it surprise you if I said your wife told us that you *did* call the Winstons the following day?"

"No, that wouldn't surprise me." When Jack looked at him quizzically, he continued, "The next morning, when June remembered she had lost it, it was already known that Rachel was missing. As much as I wanted June off my back about the ridiculous thing, there was no way I was going to call and bother Walter and Harriet about it. I told June I had called, but I hadn't."

So he readily admits to lying to his wife, Jack thought. Could he just as easily lie to the police? He was curious how the good doctor would answer the next question.

"Do you know or have you had any recent contact with a Brenda Pawloski at the Aspen Historical Library and Museum?"

Thomas Murphy frowned and shook his head. "I've never met her."

Jack studied the man sitting across the table from him, saw the veins in his neck constrict and his pupils dilate, and knew immediately that he was lying.

CHAPTER 34

GEORGIA CLICKED OFF her phone and massaged the bridge of her nose between her eyes trying to ease her stress. Detective Thurmond in Denver had just called to tell her he didn't think Tony Paladino was her stalker, and had again urged her to take extra precautions. It was only 9:30 in the morning but Georgia was already exhausted.

As she finished her second cup of coffee, her phone rang. What now? She looked at the caller ID and was relieved to see it was Parker.

"It's a two-hour flight and we're just about to take off."

"Perfect. I'll be at the airport when you get there."

"I made reservations for noon at The Wild Fig. They serve a mean brunch. I hope that's alright."

"That sounds great. I'll see you at the airport around 11:30."

After she hung up, Georgia decided to take a bath and read the morning newspaper, hoping it would ease her tension after the call from Detective Thurmond.

After the reception at the Winstons, she had spent the afternoon and long into the evening going over the notes she had taken from her online research and the materials Dr. Murphy had given her.

The funeral for Rachel had been heart-wrenching enough. Then hours of reading notes on the heinous motives and methods of serial killers had taken its toll. She had had enough strangulations and mutilations, shootings and stabbings. Enough psychotic women who hated men, and psychotic men who hated women. The estimated number of active serial murderers currently in the U.S. was overwhelming. She never imagined serial killing was as prolific as Dr. Murphy's information indicated.

Now she needed to organize the information in some way that would help her analyze it, but that could wait. She'd had enough death for twenty-four hours. A hot bath with the morning paper sounded infinitely more appealing.

She thought about lunch with Parker Randolph, and wanted to be rested—or at least *look* rested—when she picked him up at the airport.

In the kitchen, she grabbed her cup of coffee and *The Denver Post* and headed upstairs to draw a bath. Morning light flooded the small bathroom and Georgia decided to close only the bottom half of the shutters on the window. She'd have her privacy but still be able to enjoy the sunshine.

When the water level was just right, she slipped off her robe and stepped in. Settling back into the tub, Georgia opened *The Denver Post* and was immediately struck by the headline that stretched across the front page: HISTORIAN MURDERED IN ASPEN MUSEUM.

For a moment, her mind froze in disbelief. *Brenda Pawloski?* Georgia had just met with her. This couldn't be happening. When the initial shock wore off, she glanced at the accompanying photo of the victim, took a deep breath, and read the first paragraph.

"Brenda Pawloski, Chief Archivist at the Aspen Historical Library and Museum, was found shot in the back Saturday…"

She read each successive paragraph with increasing alarm. When she finished the article, she dropped the paper onto the bathroom floor and settled back into the tub, her mind swirling with the warm water.

She knew that before Rachel Winston and Greta Moss there hadn't been a murder in Aspen in decades. Now there had been three within two months. It was too coincidental, and she didn't believe in coincidence. All three murders were related. But how?

From the material Dr. Murphy had given her, Georgia knew serial killers typically displayed patterns of similarity—a particular victim type, a certain method of killing, common locations where the crimes were committed or bodies disposed of.

Georgia mindlessly pushed the water around in the tub as she contemplated the victims. The similarities were obvious. All three were women, all attractive. All three were single, and, as far as authorities could tell, murdered in or around Aspen. It was the differences in the cases that bothered her.

Although similar, Brenda Pawloski's murder seemed to be an outlier. Brenda had been shot, not strangled like Rachel Winston and Greta Moss. And Rachel and Greta were both in their early twenties. Brenda was two decades older.

The first two victims had been abducted, their bodies hidden, but Brenda was found where she had been killed—at the museum.

Although the differences were significant, she couldn't shake the feeling that all three were related. Rachel and Greta fit a pattern—Toomey's pattern—but Brenda didn't.

Georgia realized her skin was starting to prune and got out of the tub. As she dried off, her cell phone rang.

Detective Martin was calling to see if he could ask her a few more questions. Georgia got dressed and met him at the door when he showed up thirty minutes later.

He was alone. Dressed in jeans, a maroon flannel shirt, and the same well-worn boots he had been wearing the night he came to her door after she found Rachel's body. He didn't look like what she expected a detective to look like. He didn't wear a suit, or even a sports coat like Detective McCray. But he carried himself in a way that indicated competence and commanded respect.

They sat in her living room.

"I'd like for you to tell me what you know about Gerald Ray Toomey," Detective Martin said.

Georgia was surprised by the request, but told Detective Martin everything she had learned about Toomey and his crimes through her research online and at the museum with Brenda Pawloski.

"But I'm stuck on connecting her murder," he said when she had finished talking.

Georgia nodded. She shared his frustration in making sense of Brenda's murder. "There's a pattern between Toomey's murders and the murders of Rachel and Greta," Georgia told him. "It's almost like they're copycat killings."

"Someone copying Toomey?" He didn't sound shocked, just curious for more information.

"It seems that way. After you mentioned the possibility I could be dealing with a copycat stalker, I researched copycat crimes—murders mostly. But Brenda's murder doesn't fit the pattern."

Detective Martin shook his head and tapped a pen on his notepad. "There's got to be a connection. Somehow, Brenda Pawloski's murder is tied to the Winston and Moss cases. Virtually no violent crime in Aspen in decades, now three dead in two months. It's too coincidental, and I don't—"

"Believe in consequences," Georgia finished for him. "Neither do I."

He settled back into the couch. "I'm intrigued by your research on copycat crimes. We touched on profiling at the FBI Academy, but that was years ago. I'd like to hear more."

Georgia summarized the highlights that she had uncovered

in her research. When she was done, he asked her for a copy of her notes.

"Of course, detective. I want to help in any way I can," she said. "There's just one thing."

He looked at her skeptically.

"I'd like for you to keep me abreast of any developments in your investigation. I won't reveal anything without a closed case or consulting you first. In turn, I'm going to continue my research—"

"Investigation," he said eyeing her.

There was no sense in denying it. "I'm going to continue my *investigation*," she admitted. "And I will contact you in turn if I come across anything that I think could help you find the killer."

Detective Martin hesitated a long moment, then nodded in agreement.

After he left, Georgia reflected again on the crimes. She remembered that Toomey had killed five women, each a month apart. If the current killer was a copycat, the murder of Brenda Pawloski would not be his last.

CHAPTER 35

AT 11:15 GEORGIA pulled into the parking lot of Pitkin County Airport. The terminal was a small building sheathed in stacked rock and large tinted windows. She pulled into a parking spot off to one side, only feet from where sleek private jets sat lined up in rows like sentinels.

She lowered the window, unbuckled her seatbelt and turned off the engine. For a moment, everything was silent. It was an unseasonably warm spring day. Not a single cloud marred the turquoise sky. She took in a deep breath, redolent of pine, and let it out slowly.

After a few minutes, she noticed a plane bank on the horizon and turn toward the airport. It was slow and silent in the distance, but she could hear the faint whir of jet engines as it came closer. She watched it glide lower and finally touch down, its wheels screeching in protest as they met the runway.

The jet had a sleek silver-blue fuselage and long wings that turned up at the ends, its tail emblazoned with the Coastal News Corp logo. She watched as it taxied then rolled to a stop in front of her. After a minute or two a set of stairs unfurled from the fuselage like a spring flower opening to the sun.

She saw Parker emerge from the plane and got out of her car and waved. She was relieved to see he was wearing jeans and a casual shirt. After her bath, she had briefly debated wearing slacks or a skirt, but had opted for jeans and a light cashmere sweater instead.

It took Parker a couple minutes to make his way through the small terminal and back outside to her car.

"What a gorgeous day," he said greeting her with a broad smile. "It does *nothing* for my confidence in thinking I can talk you into leaving and starting work early."

Georgia had forgotten how attractive he was. Parker was tall, with a lanky build and dusty blond hair that curled up at his collar. He walked with an easy gait and looked more like a California surfer than an executive at a national news network.

"It's good to see you, Parker. But about this starting work early thing…"

"Never mind that," he said with a wave of his hand. "We'll talk about it over lunch." He tossed a jacket and a file folder onto the back seat then got in the front. "It's good to see you again, too."

"What has it been? A month, I think." She pulled out of the airport and onto the highway.

"It has. And not much of a vacation for you so far, I guess."

He was referring to the recent murders, but probably didn't know about Brenda Pawloski yet. For now, she wouldn't say anything. "So far, it hasn't been the relaxing stay in the mountains I had anticipated."

"Then all the more reason to start work early. This is beautiful," he said with a hand sweep toward the mountains, "but California has great weather, too."

She smiled, but didn't reply.

"But that's a discussion for lunch. Seriously though, how are you doing? The recent murders have to be unnerving. I knew Rachel Winston. Our parents know each other, and a fraternity buddy of mine is married to her older sister Sophie."

Georgia remembered seeing Rachel's sister at the funeral.

During the service, she had been comforted by a man she assumed was her husband. "I saw them at the funeral."

Parker looked surprised. "You went to the funeral?"

He didn't know. Georgia took a deep breath. "I was the one that found Rachel's body."

Parker stared at her in silence.

"She was in my garage." Still no response, so Georgia continued. "It was the day after I arrived from Denver. I had planned on renovating the garage and the contractor was at the house. We found her body. I—I didn't know her, but I felt a need to attend her funeral. My realtor knows the Winstons. He took me."

Parker finally spoke. "I heard she was found in some sort of abandoned building in town. I had no idea it was your garage."

"It was. I wish it was anywhere else," Georgia answered in a soft voice.

"Do the police have any idea why she was there?"

Georgia shook her head. "No—none that they've mentioned." *Why* was *she put there?* The question ate at her a little more each day. She drove, watching the highway stripes slide by one after another.

"Whoever murdered Rachel and Greta Moss did it for no apparent reason," Parker said. "There was no sexual assault, no robbery. This is obviously one sick psychopath."

Georgia nodded. The lack of a discernible motive bothered her, too.

"I don't want to alarm you," he continued, "but you fit the killer's profile."

She looked at him and frowned.

"Think about it—young, beautiful, single."

Georgia shook her head. "I appreciate your concern, but that's such a stretch."

"Is it?"

"Yes," she said with a clipped laugh. "It is. Do you know how many young single women there are in Aspen? They're a dime a dozen."

"Not just young and single, but *high profile*. A model. The daughter of a billionaire tech titan. Not one of the locals waiting tables or working in one of the hotels." He pointed at her.

"Parker—"

"I don't mean to scare you," he relaxed his tone. "Just be cautious. You *do* fit the profile."

She was already dealing with being stalked, now she had to worry about a murderer. The idea was at the same time ludicrous and terrifying.

"But there's been another murder. She *doesn't* fit the profile."

Parker whipped his gaze back to her. "Another one?"

Georgia filled him in on the few details she knew about Brenda Pawloski's murder, then pointed out the differences in the case, including throwing in some of the criminal psychology she had gleaned from her online research and the materials Dr. Murphy had given her.

"You've put a lot thought into this," he said. Then it dawned on him. "Georgia… are you investigating the murders?"

"It's what I do." She negotiated a sharp turn in the winding road. When he didn't reply, she continued. "I'm working on the story as a possible first show. I've got an outline with a few notes for you and your father to look at." She gestured toward a sheet of paper lying next to his jacket on the back seat. "It's back there. I'll email it to both of you, too, but I thought we could go over it at lunch first."

Parker settled back in the seat. "Georgia, this story could be dangerous. You're too close to it. For Pete's sake, one of the bodies was found in the house you're living in."

"My *garage*," she corrected, but he ignored her.

"It's dangerous. Does anyone know you're investigating this?"

Probably everyone in town by now, Georgia thought, but didn't say. Sensing his obvious disapproval, she picked her words carefully. "I'm here and I'm involved—indirectly, but still involved. It's what I do and why you and your father hired me." When he started to protest, she held up a hand. "Hear me out. I've thought it through and made up my mind. Plus, it's on my own time. I'm not on Coastal's payroll yet. I'm going to research it and see how it goes. If it pans out, it'll make a great first show, if it doesn't…" She shrugged.

He looked skeptical. "It's not just about the show though, is it?"

There were coming into town and she slowed down. "Not completely," she admitted.

"Would you be as interested in the story if her body had been found somewhere else?"

Georgia thought about it. "I don't know." She remembered the dark and dusty garage, the wooden toolbox, the shoe. "But I *did* find her," she said. "And I want to know what happened. I'm going to look into it and see what I can find out. I don't have any delusions about solving the cases—I'll let the police do that. But I can help. I want them to nail this guy and put him away."

Parker held up a hand in surrender. "Okay. Just please keep what I said in mind—you do fit the profile."

"Maybe, maybe not."

Having made her point, she decided against mentioning the stalking incident. That would be a conversation for another day.

Georgia took a deep breath, tightening then loosening her grip on the steering wheel. Parker had gotten to her. He was right, Rachel's murder *was* personal. She hadn't fully admitted it to herself until that moment.

The day was warm, and they were seated at an outside table

at The Wild Fig, a large blue umbrella providing shade in the spring sun. A waiter set glasses of water in front of them and offered menus.

Georgia took the menu and opened it. She didn't read it, but watched over the top as Parker studied his. In the four months since first meeting him and his father, she had dined with them three times, but never with Parker alone.

Her first impressions had been mixed. She had immediately assumed Parker was a rich man's spoiled son filling the obligatory board room chair at his father's side. Another undeserving heir apparent. But he was caring, and seemed genuinely concerned about her safety. She was beginning to think her early impressions of him were wrong.

He was intelligent, with a quirky sense of humor. Different from his father—more relaxed, easy-going. He almost reminded Georgia of her mother until she told herself that was ridiculous.

Georgia identified more with Malcolm—driven and ambitious. She had read multiple accounts of his rags-to-riches story in *Forbes* and *The Wall Street Journal*. She could relate to that, could understand that.

Parker was different. At first she had pegged him as aloof or lazy, now she wasn't sure.

He looked up and caught her watching him. She glanced down at her menu.

"There's something I need to tell you," he said.

As he told her his plans to leave the network, Georgia was surprised to find she was disappointed. "That's a big change. Is your father upset that you're leaving?"

"Yes and no. Deep down, he had to have known I wouldn't stay. I don't love it like he does, and I've told him that dozens of times over the years, but he would dismiss it. I think it did come as a surprise when I told him yesterday that I would be leaving. I told him I wouldn't quit until I talked you into starting work early, but something tells me that's not going to happen."

Georgia shook her head. "I'm afraid not."

"I didn't think so. Dad's not going to be happy, but I'll tell him you're already working on a story, that will appease him some—especially when I point out you're not on Coastal's payroll yet and working on your own time." An easy smile spread across his face. Parker put his menu down and relaxed back into his chair. "Now that business is done, what are you going to have?"

It was six o'clock by the time Georgia dropped Parker off at the airport and made it back home. It had been a wonderful afternoon. After lunch, they had spent almost three hours walking block after block, popping into a store now and then, all on the pretense of walking off lunch, but Georgia suspected Parker didn't believe that any more than she did.

Georgia smiled as she stepped through the front door, thinking about what a welcome respite the afternoon had been. As she shut the door, her phone vibrated with an incoming text. She assumed it would be Parker telling her what a fabulous afternoon he had had, or maybe reiterating his points for coming to Los Angeles and starting work early.

When Georgia looked down at her phone she felt the color drain from her face. The text wasn't from Parker, or from anyone else that showed up as a contact. It was anonymous, and included a photograph.

She read it slowly. "I was there. I'm always there."

Her fingers trembled as she touched the attached photo to enlarge it. She took in a quick breath. It was grainy, obviously taken from a distance and cropped, but she could clearly make out herself and Parker sitting at an outdoor table shaded by a blue umbrella.

CHAPTER 36

BY MONDAY MORNING, Jack Martin had finished writing his reports on the interviews following the funeral and Georgia Glass's second stalking incident. He had spent the night before reading through Georgia's notes on copycat criminals. At the FBI academy, he had training on profiling, but nothing specifically on copycats that he could remember. Her information had him thinking—not just about the stalker, but the recent murders.

It was just after eight o'clock when Jack and Luke walked into Chief Rogan's office to update him on the events of the busy weekend. Luke took a seat in front of the chief's desk, but Jack remained standing.

Rogan set aside the paperwork he had been working on and leaned back in his chair. "What's the report, boys?"

Jack answered first. "We've got a couple guys searching Georgia Glass's house this morning for any additional clues in the Winston investigation."

"*Additional* clues?" the chief barked. "I'm not sure we have *any* yet, do we?"

Jack ignored the remark. "I doubt the guys will find anything inside. The house has been locked up, and there aren't any signs of a previous forced entry, but we've got to check it off our list."

Rogan nodded. "Let me know if they find anything." He

then leaned forward and threw his meaty forearms onto the oak desk. "What about the interviews at the St. Regis? Tell me you've got something new."

Jack felt they had made progress in the investigation over the weekend and hoped Rogan would agree. "The scarf we found with Rachel's body belonged to June Murphy," he said.

The chief raised a bushy eyebrow but remained silent.

Jack continued. "After the Murphys arrived at the party, June Murphy stated she asked her husband, Thomas Murphy, to put it—along with her purse—on a table near the front door where other guests had placed their personal items. Thomas Murphy corroborated this and said he did in fact place the scarf along with the purse on a front table along with about a half a dozen others purses. They both claim June Murphy got home with the purse, but not the scarf."

Luke added, "With it on a table near the front door, it's possible anyone at the party that night could have taken it."

"Yes, anyone *could* have," Rogan said gruffly, drumming his fingers on his desk, "but who *did*?"

Jack spoke next. "He lied about calling the Winstons the next day to ask about it. He told his wife he had called them, but admitted to us he had not because it was already known their daughter had gone missing. But if he lied to his wife—"

"Is he lying to you?" Rogan finished.

"Maybe. But there's something else. I think he was lying when he denied knowing Brenda Pawloski."

Rogan raised a second eyebrow. "Any evidence that he knew her?"

"We're working on it."

The chief thought about it a moment. "So what else do we know about this Dr. Murphy?"

Luke flipped open a notebook. "Dr. Thomas Murphy, fifty-nine years old. No priors. Solid credentials. Retired former

Chief of Staff at Mount Belvedere Hospital in Manhattan. He's a forensic psychiatrist and has published several articles on criminology including at least one on serial killers."

Rogan's unruly eyebrow shot up again. "Is that so?"

Luke continued. "He abruptly retired from Mount Belvedere Hospital six years ago, at which time he and his wife moved here to Aspen. The circumstances surrounding his retirement weren't disclosed, but we're working on it."

Rogan nodded and turned his attention back to Jack. "And you think he knew Brenda Pawloski?"

"It's still just a hunch," Jack said. "We're looking into it."

Rogan leaned his substantial weight back in his chair and tented his fingers on his stomach. "I heard the rumors about your uncanny hunches while you were with the FBI. Let's hope they amount to something here. Anything more on the Greta Moss case?"

"Nothing significant," Jack answered. "We spoke with her parents in Munich who confirmed what her friends and agent had said—that she had no known enemies and no history of drug use. She was clean. NYPD is still questioning old boyfriends and neighbors for us, but they haven't come up with anything yet, and no one has come forward with any new information. We can't find any apparent reason why someone would want her dead. I think when we find who killed Rachel Winston we'll find who killed Greta Moss."

"I sure as hell hope you're right," Rogan said. "And I sure as hell hope that's soon."

Next, the detectives gave a report on Georgia Glass's stalking incident.

"She's a tough one," Jack said. "I got to her house and she was obviously upset, but composed. No emotion. She's been through this before."

Jack filled him in on the details of the previous stalking case in Denver.

Rogan's brows furrowed together, "So if there was an arrest, and the guy is locked up, who's stalking her now?"

"She thinks it could be someone related to her first stalker—an accomplice," Jack said, "But I spoke with the lead detective on the case in Denver—Mark Thurmond—and he doesn't think so."

"Denver PD?" Rogan asked. Jack nodded. "So what *does* he think?"

"He said he recently talked to the guy who's been charged with stalking her in Denver, but he doesn't think the guy did it. He believes they got the wrong perp and whoever stalked her in Denver is still out there."

"So after talking to both of them, what do *you* think is going on?"

"I think it's one of three scenarios. First—it's a copycat. Someone found out she was in town, heard about the previous stalking case, and just want to make some mischief. Second— Thurmond is right. They got the wrong guy locked up and the real stalker has followed her to Aspen. Third... It's just a hunch—"

"Spill it." Rogan was impatient.

"Third," Jack continued, "whoever killed Rachel Winston and Greta Moss is toying with her."

Rogan's face hardened, his eyes boring into Jack. "Now how in the hell do you link stalking Georgia Glass with the murder cases?"

"It's not a likely scenario, but we've got to throw it out there." When Rogan started to protest, Jack held up his hands. "Hear me out, Chief."

Jack went on to lay out the evidence Georgia had given him regarding the possibility of a copycat killer. All three men agreed the similarities between the recent murders and the Toomey cases were too coincidental to dismiss.

Jack paced the room with a hand on his hip as he talked. "Then along comes Georgia Glass who finds Rachel's body in her garage. It's not a stretch to assume someone who would copycat a murderer could also copycat a stalker."

Rogan brought his weight forward, putting his forearms on the desk again. "So if you had to say now, which scenario are we probably looking at?"

Jack thought before answering. "The first one—a copycat stalker. Someone who knows about her stalking case in Denver and who's got a sick way of getting off."

"That's the scenario you *hope* it is." Rogan's gaze revealed his skepticism. "Which scenario do you *really* think we're looking at?"

Jack took a deep breath. "I think Georgia Glass is in danger."

CHAPTER 37

EDDIE JENKINS WASN'T scheduled to work Monday morning, but he showed up at the television station anyway. He wanted to grab a set of tools that he would use to install the security system for Georgia at her home in Aspen later that day.

He parked his battered Subaru wagon in the employee parking lot and entered the building through the back door. As he made his way down the long corridor toward the small room where each of the station's cameramen had a desk, he overheard two reporters talking.

"Thank God they've got me working with Brian today and not Eddie again."

Eddie recognized the voice as that of Lisa Starks, the perky special assignment reporter hired by the station only a few months earlier. Eddie had worked with her regularly since she had been hired. Nobody could ever replace Georgia, but he thought he and Lisa had developed a mutual friendship. He had obviously thought wrong.

Lisa was talking to the early-morning traffic reporter, another twenty-something right out of school. "Eddie gives me the creeps. We drive around all day and I can feel him watching me. Creepy. Plus, it takes everything I have to not tell him to trim that nasty beard."

The weather girl laughed. "It's horrible. It's so bushy. I've wondered if there was something living in it."

"And the way it creeps down his neck. Can you imagine what his back must look like?"

"Eww."

They were laughing. Everyone except Eddie, who stood out of sight in the hallway and heard it all. He was overwhelmed by a familiar mix of anger and shame. He was stocky, barely average height, with a face pocked with acne scars—*moon face* his mother had called him since puberty. In high school, he was no stranger to insults. He knew he was ugly, but he liked to think he made up for it with his personality, winning people over with his jokes and self-deprecating humor. Still, over the years the insults had hurt, but he'd done a good job of not letting anyone know.

Then there was tech school and, later, the opportunity to work for a network affiliate. It was his dream job. For almost twelve years, he prided himself in being the hardest working and best special assignment cameraman at the station. The first reporter he worked with was friendly enough. When Eddie started with the network, Sarah Mitchel had been at the station several years and didn't mind giving him pointers on how to do the job. She was very efficient and hardworking like Eddie, but she had always been a bit distant and cold. But Eddie had learned a lot from Sarah and was disappointed when she took an anchor job at the affiliate station in Tulsa.

But then the station hired Georgia Glass. Right away Eddie loved working with Georgia. She was different than Sarah— warm and open. He could talk to her about anything and he in turn listened intently when she would confide in him. They quickly became close friends, and although Eddie would have liked to have taken the friendship to another level, it wasn't in the cards. He was devastated the night she had rebuffed him. As he had done in school, he bottled the hurt and buried it deep inside. He wasn't going to lose Georgia Glass.

He stood in the hallway and listened a while longer, then strolled past the doorway. "Good morning, ladies." He startled them. They looked first at Eddie then back at each other, their mouths frozen mid-chatter. His hurt had turned to anger. He would at least inflict a little humiliation.

On the road, Eddie sped through traffic, threading his way between slower moving cars at lightning speed, occasionally yelling obscenities and flipping off motorists who hadn't yielded to him soon enough. He had the Subaru's gas pedal pegged to the floor. As much as he fought it, the years of anger and humiliation pulsed through him. The old feelings of rejection and ridicule he'd known all too well in high school came crashing back with a vengeance.

His eyes welled, making the center stripes of the highway watery blurs as they whizzed past. With gritted teeth he pounded the steering wheel with a clenched fist and vowed to get back at them.

As the interstate veered west and climbed into the foothills outside Denver, Eddie's thoughts turned back to Georgia. Slowly, the muscles in his face relaxed and his heart rate slowed. There was always Georgia.

He'd think about those other girls later. He didn't have time for them now. He had a job to do.

He glanced back at the assortment of boxes on the back seat, a high-tech security system including cameras that he would install for her. The toolbox he had picked up at the station was resting on the floor. He had everything he needed to make her feel safe. It had worked the first time. He remembered how she had thanked him profusely when the police arrested Tony Paladino after the cameras he installed caught Paladino lingering outside her home. When Georgia called to tell him of the recent texts she had received and to ask for his help again, he had been elated. She needed him.

Eddie checked his phone. There would be plenty of time to get to Aspen and install the security system for Georgia before dark.

He eased off the gas, relaxed his grip on the steering wheel and turned on the radio. As he passed Genesee Park, the snow-capped mountains of Front Range came into view in the distance. He had two hours until he would reach Glenwood Springs, where he would turn off the interstate and head south toward Aspen.

He knew the route well. It was his fourth trip in a week.

CHAPTER 38

LIZ KELLY HATED the term paparazzi, but as an investigative reporter for *The National Tattler* she had been called that and worse. But she knew the truth. She was a journalist who just happened to cover the news of the rich and famous. She wasn't among the rabble who camped outside the homes of celebrities, swarming and heckling them in order to get a story or just the right photograph.

No, Liz Kelly was a journalist in the truest sense of the word. A professional who had checked into The Little Nell hotel in Aspen to investigate the recent murders. It was a juicy story she knew would sell thousands of magazines and bring even more visitors to *The National Tattler* website. Her name would be on the tip of tongues across the country. She would be interviewed on the biggest television magazine shows. But that would come later. First, she had to get the story.

It was mid-morning. She sat in the dining room of the hotel, on alert for someone she could strike up a conversation with. Some of her biggest tips in the past had come from the unlikeliest of sources. She considered it part of her job to talk with as many people as she could, delicately pumping them for information.

The waitress that morning had been more than willing to chat with her about the recent murders. The stories were the talk of the town, especially among the locals. But from what Liz could discern, the young girl didn't know any more than what she had learned from the press conference and social media. It wasn't a surprise that someone of her station wouldn't personally know any of those involved. Liz had quickly determined the young waitress wouldn't be of any help.

Liz had then turned her attention to the other patrons in the dining room that morning. There weren't many, but she chalked that up to it being a Monday.

One guest, however, did intrigue her. The hostess had greeted him by name when he walked in. A distinguished looking man in his mid- to late-seventies, white hair and a meticulously groomed matching white beard. His tailored suit and plaid pocket scarf made him look as though he had just stepped out of a Burberry catalogue. He walked with a limp and a silver-topped cane. Liz had been thrilled when the hostess sat him at an adjacent table.

She watched out of the corner of her eye as the same waitress who served her approached him. "Good morning, Mr. Lauren. Would you like your usual breakfast today?" She set a cup of black coffee in front of him.

"That sounds wonderful," the man replied in the cultured tones of someone with money. "Thank you, Abby."

Liz watched from the corner of her eye as he unfolded a newspaper. She touched up her lipstick and smoothed the sides of her hair. Time to go to work.

Only minutes later, Liz Kelly and Stanley Lauren were in deep conversation about the recent murders. She had eased a small notebook out of the canary yellow Birkin bag she had spent her life savings on and scribbled notes under the table as the old man talked.

To her astounding luck, Stanley Lauren was not only a friend of the Winston family, but had been a guest at a party the night their daughter went missing. And when he revealed that all the guests had been questioned by police in one giant interrogation, well, that was a juicy tidbit tabloid reporters prayed for but rarely got. She had struck gold.

With Liz's tactful probing, honed by years of experience, she got Stanley Lauren to tell her exactly how the police had gathered all the guests of the Winstons that fateful night at a hotel following Rachel Winston's funeral. He recalled how the police had called them in for questioning one by one, and went on to explain how the detectives had asked if anyone had seen a particular silk scarf.

"Hermes, they said," Stanley Lauren told her. "I thought it was quite odd at the time that they asked about a missing scarf... from a party... in a murder investigation. It was all quite boggling at the time, and then I remembered that poor Moss girl had been strangled with a Hermes scarf. Do you think Rachel Winston could have been as well?" he asked looking at Liz over the tops of his wire-rimmed glasses. "Also murdered with a scarf that is."

"It's possible," Liz said. "But the police haven't commented on the manner of death."

Stanley Lauren looked perturbed, or confused, Liz couldn't tell.

"No, they haven't," he said looking down at his manicured fingers spread across the white table cloth, then looked back up. "That's a bit odd, too, don't you think? Surely they know *something.*"

Liz knew darned well that the police knew how Rachel Winston was murdered, and they just weren't telling. The bit about the scarf had her heart pounding. Had Rachel Winston been strangled with a silk scarf like Greta Moss? Then it *would* undoubtedly be the work of a serial killer.

"Did you say it was a Hermes scarf that was missing from

the reception?" she asked. She thought of Greta Moss and her killer, the Hermes Strangler.

"Indeed, it was," he answered.

Liz's mind was racing. If her suspicions were correct, and they usually were, her story was now about a serial killer walking the streets of Aspen, maybe stalking his third victim that very moment.

"But then they informed us the owner of the scarf had been found," Mr. Lauren said.

"They found it?"

"Found what?"

"The scarf."

"No, no," Stanley Lauren said. "As far as I know, the police have not been successful in their search for the scarf. However, I dare say Dr. Murphy likely wishes they had."

Liz shook her head. She was losing her patience and took a moment to compose herself. "I'm confused, Mr. Lauren. They *didn't* find the scarf? And who is Dr. Murphy?"

Stanley Lauren took a slow sip of coffee before continuing. Liz sat on the edge of her seat, suppressing the urge to strangle the old guy if it would get the information out of him faster.

He cleared his throat. "You are correct. As far as I know they have not located the Hermes scarf in question; however, they did discover that it belonged to June Murphy. When they questioned her, Mrs. Murphy revealed she had misplaced the scarf at the party, and that it was her husband's fault—Dr. Murphy. She claims to have given it to him to place on a table with her handbag."

"Her name is June Murphy?" Liz asked, scribbling on the notepad hidden on her lap.

"Yes."

"I might know her," Liz lied. "What is her husband's full name again?"

"Dr. Thomas Murphy," he answered. "Nice fellow." He raised his coffee to his mouth but stopped short and shook his head. "Must be horrible living with that dreadful woman. In front of the whole lot of us after the questioning she reprimanded him harshly for having misplaced the bloody thing. It might have been a Hermes, but it did look quite worn and not worthy of making such a fuss."

"You saw the scarf?" Liz held her breath. From what she already knew, and what he was telling her, she had begun putting the pieces together. The police wouldn't have asked the assembled group of guests about the scarf if it wasn't a clue in the case. Rachel Winston had been murdered, probably strangled, and probably with the missing scarf.

Liz was excited at the thought of writing this story. And to think, there weren't any of her major competitors here—just a handful of network folks, a few online news guys, and someone from *The Denver Post*. If she could keep it quiet for a while, she'd have the whole story to herself.

"I was moving a bit slow that evening, the arthritis in my knees had been acting up. I was one of the last ones to arrive. When I walked in, I noticed it on a table in the foyer among several women's handbags. I own a boutique around the corner on East Cooper. I carry Burberry, Savile Row, Hermes, and the like. My memory is not what it used to be, but I am sure that is why I noticed the one on the table in the foyer that night. A shabby Hermes pattern from decades ago. I felt the owner needed to pop in and shop for a replacement."

Liz forced a smile and batted her mascara-caked lashes. She had found over the years that a little flirting could go a long way in getting what she wanted. She wanted to keep the old guy talking.

"Always marketing, Mr. Lauren?"

"Guilty," he said with a slight grin and gentle dip of his head. "It's in the blood, I'm afraid. I do hope you will come by the store while you are in town. Are you here on business or pleasure?"

"Uh..." Liz knew better than reveal her identity or motive. Stanley Lauren had been tremendously helpful. She would likely want to talk with him again. "Pleasure," she answered. "And I love to shop. I'll definitely come by sometime this week."

"I look forward to it," he said with another tip of his head, glancing at the inexpensive scarf Liz had knotted around her neck. "We just got a shipment in from Paris. Maybe I could interest you in one of the new Hermes patterns."

Liz self-consciously adjusted the knock-off at her neck. "I look forward to it."

"I haven't seen them yet. We'll put them on display today. We sold our last Hermes a few weeks ago. To a local fellow, I think." He placed a hand on his temple as if to massage the memory back into existence, then shook his head. "His face has slipped my mind. I'm sure it must have been a gift for a lady friend."

"Lucky girl," Liz said.

Then it dawned on her and she drew in a deep breath at the possibility. Someone had purchased a Hermes scarf from Stanley Lauren around the time Greta Moss went missing.

Could she really be this lucky?

CHAPTER 39

TWO POLICE OFFICERS had spent nearly an hour and a half searching Georgia's house that morning. When they were finished, they simply thanked her then left. As far as she knew, they hadn't found anything. She had been dreading the inconvenience, but now that the search was over, she was glad they had done it. She could have the peace of mind there wouldn't be any more surprises.

After they left, Georgia had spent the rest of the morning organizing her notes into a variety of lists and charts, bullet points and sub-points—a left-brain masterpiece, her mother would have called it.

Georgia was sitting at the kitchen table when she heard a loud bang. She jumped, then realized it was the mail slot in the front door. She walked into the foyer and scooped up the mail where it had fallen onto the rug.

Without looking at any of it, she carried it to the kitchen and placed it on the table. That's when she noticed it. A plain white envelope stuck between a postcard advertising a new restaurant and a circular for the local grocery store. It was addressed to her in a stilted handwritten print. There was no return address.

Georgia pulled the envelope from the stack and opened it. Inside was a single sheet of white paper. She unfolded it and saw that it was a black and white photocopy of a newspaper clipping—dark, like the original had aged. It appeared to be a page out of a scrapbook, the article cut from an edition of *The Denver Post* dated April 30, 1957. The headline read—"Third Woman Murdered in Aspen."

It wasn't the article or one of the accompanying photographs, all meticulously cut from the newspaper and glued onto an old scrapbook page that shocked her. It was the note scribbled at the bottom written in the same stilted handwriting that was on the envelope that drained the color from her face.

Kill them once, kill them twice, will killing the third one be as nice? Below it was scrawled, *You think you can find me? Ha!*

After recovering from the shock of the envelope's contents, Georgia had hurried upstairs to find her cell phone and called Detective Martin.

Twenty minutes later Georgia opened the front door. "Hello, detective. I'm sorry to have to call you twice in twenty-four hours."

"No apologies," Detective Martin insisted. "But I *am* surprised. How are you holding up?"

He was perceptive, and seemed genuinely concerned. She looked a wreck and knew that it was futile to put on a brave face.

"Fine, I guess. That text… knowing someone was across the street watching. Wondering if they followed me home? Were they already outside watching when I got here? It's the not knowing that's the worst."

He nodded. "That text would have rattled anyone."

Georgia took a deep breath. "I'm rattled—yes—but not scared. This is my home now, and whoever is doing this to me is not going to scare me out of it. I have a security system being installed later today. Cameras caught the stalker the first time this happened. I'm hoping they'll catch this guy, too."

"We've added extra patrols to your street, and everyone has been instructed to contact me immediately if anything unusual is observed."

"Thank you."

"The message you received today," he asked, "it was through the mail this time? A copy of a scrapbook page?"

"Yes, right before I called you." Georgia turned toward the kitchen. "It's in here. The only mail that I've received since I've been here has been either junk mail or a couple of things addressed to Ernest Galloway. But this was addressed to me." She pointed to the envelope that lay on the table. "There's no return address."

He put on the latex gloves he had in his pocket and picked up the photocopy lying next to the envelope and studied it. He then removed two plastic bags from his coat pocket and carefully dropped the envelope into one and the photocopy into the other.

"I'll get this to the guys in forensics. This might be a sick joke, but we have to assume it's a credible threat and treat it as such. But I can assure you we're going to find out who's behind all this."

Something about him reminded her of Detective Thurmond in Denver. For some reason, she instinctively trusted and liked both men.

"So which do you think it is, detective? A sick joke or a credible threat?" she asked. "Am I in danger?"

He looked at her a moment then nodded in the direction of her garage. "After what you found in your garage, and with the recent stalking incidents and what you got in the mail today, I think you need to take this very seriously. But until we can get more information, I'm asking you not to say anything to anyone about the texts or what you got in the mail today."

Georgia shook her head. "I won't. The only people who

know about the texts are Detective Thurmond in Denver and my friend Eddie who is installing a security system for me. He installed the one I had in Denver that caught my stalker there."

Detective Martin looked at her with concern. "Alright, but don't tell your friend about the scrapbook page. The fewer people that know, the better."

"Do you think whoever is sending the texts could have sent me the newspaper article?"

"Possibly, but we've got to treat this as two separate cases until we know for sure."

When he was done, she walked him to the door. He hesitated, his hand on the knob. "Georgia, you really do need to be careful. While this guy is still out on the street, you living here alone—even with a security system—is not a good idea."

She took in a deep breath. "I've been through this before. I'll get through it again."

His expression was grim. "The difference is, the guy before wasn't a possible murderer."

Georgia felt a knot tighten in her stomach and knew he was right. She was in danger, but had been working hard to clamp down the fear. She kept her expression frozen and hoped he couldn't see he had upset her.

"I've got your number, detective. I promise you'll be the first one I call if there's any trouble."

After he pulled away from the curb, she shut the door and leaned back on it. She had been putting on a brave face for everyone, but she knew the truth. Even with Eddie installing a state-of-the art security system, even with the police patrolling her street and actively searching for whoever it was threatening her, deep down, she was afraid.

She carried her cup of coffee to the kitchen table and sat down, opened the photos on her phone and selected the last one she had taken. It was of the scrapbook page. She had snapped a picture of it before Detective Martin had arrived, knowing he would take the original as evidence. Later, she would print a copy to keep.

Georgia used her fingers to zoom in on one of the photographs. A short, thin-boned man in a dark suit and fedora was bent over an opened trunk tossed alongside a gravel road. Inside the trunk were the remains of a woman, her stockings and shoes visible in the photograph. It was eerily similar to how she and Karl had found Rachel Winston's body.

Georgia looked closer at the man in the photo—there was no name. She then turned her attention to the second photograph that had been glued to the original scrapbook page. The same man stood in a row with three others. Two were dressed in similar dark suits and fedoras, but one on the end wore a policeman's uniform and held a rifle aloft against his hip. All had somber expressions.

Something nagged at her. She closed the photos app on her phone and dialed her mother's number.

Joni Glass confirmed that Uncle Ernest had in fact been a Pitkin County deputy sheriff. A quick check of the dates revealed he had been in Aspen during the time of the Toomey murders.

Joni mentioned she thought there was an old photograph of him somewhere around the house. She would find it and text Georgia a copy as soon as they hung up.

Later, when Georgia received the text from her mother, her suspicions were confirmed. The lawman peering into the trunk at Toomey's third victim was Ernest Galloway.

CHAPTER 40

DR. THOMAS MURPHY was lost in his internet research when he was startled by the doorbell. June had gone to Denver to scrutinize potential musicians for an upcoming charity event.

Tom was looking forward to a day of uninterrupted work. He had borne the brunt of June's wrath since the police interview at the St. Regis. June had been alternately angry with him for losing her scarf and resentful of the humiliation of it being a preoccupation of the detectives.

"If you hadn't lost it, they wouldn't be asking about it," she had told him several times.

Tom didn't have a response for her. He would never admit that she was right, and that he was becoming increasingly nervous that the lost scarf would be used to implicate him in the murder.

Tom answered the door. A short middle-aged woman with a bob of platinum hair had close-set blue eyes lasered in on him like he was prey. She was thin, wore a royal blue business suit, heels, and a strand of fake pearls the size of gumballs around her scrawny neck. In a town with plenty of well-dressed wealthy women, she stood out as trying too hard.

She wasted no time on introductions. "Dr. Murphy, your wife's scarf has been missing from the home of Rachel Winston's parents since the night she disappeared. Do you have any idea why the police are interested in the whereabouts of it?"

He kept an expressionless face, but tightened his grip on the door handle as if it were the foul little woman's throat.

She continued. "I'm Liz Kelly, investigative reporter for *The National Tattler*. I'm writing a story on the Moss and Winston murders, and for some reason the police are asking about your wife's Hermes scarf. Before I include that information in my article, I thought I would give you the opportunity to comment."

Tom considered closing the door on her but didn't. "I don't know why the police are interested in my wife's scarf. She had it at the party, then we couldn't find it when it was time to leave. It's as simple as that."

"I understand your wife asked you to put it on a table for safekeeping, and that it wasn't seen again."

"That's correct, with her purse. And I did put it on a table near the front door, but when it was time to leave, the purse was there but the scarf was gone."

She scribbled notes onto a small notepad—not looking up, not saying anything. Tom felt his blood pressure rise.

He filled the awkward silence. "There were a handful of other purses already on the table when I set June's scarf there. Someone must have picked it up by mistake on their way out."

"Do you know why the police are asking about it? Why is it important to the investigation?"

"I don't have any idea. But I am in the middle of research I need to finish."

"Research on criminal psychology, Dr. Murphy? On murder?"

"It's my work," he replied curtly.

But it didn't stop her. "Did you know Brenda Pawloski?"

He felt the blood drain from his face and shut the door on her.

Back at his computer, Tom stared at the monitor but saw nothing. Liz Kelly had obviously dug into his past, but how far back had she gone? What else did she know? Were the police doing the same thing? In any case, he knew she would write something salacious about the missing scarf that would make him look guilty.

Should he have admitted to the police that he knew Brenda Pawloski? Would they find out the truth? Or would Liz Kelly find out first?

His cell phone rang. Tom took a couple deep breaths to slow his heart rate.

"Dr. Murphy, it's Georgia Glass. I hope it's a good time for me to call."

His grip on the cell phone relaxed. He welcomed the distraction, especially one from someone so beautiful. "It's the perfect time."

"Great. I got your message about the additional material."

"Yes, I'm having the records storage company where I stored a lot of my research and files when I left the hospital send me some additional information I think you will find interesting. It should be in sometime tomorrow. I was wondering if I could drop it by on Wednesday."

"That sounds great, but I can pick it up. I hate for you to go to any more trouble."

"It's no trouble at all."

Tom clicked off his phone, closed his eyes and took a deep breath, imagining Georgia Glass. She slid into the house, closed the door behind her. She was dressed in something seductive... a knit dress that clung to her curves... black, he decided, the darkness setting off the loose blonde waves of her hair that fell to her shoulders.

He put his hands on either side of her, caressing the soft skin of her arms and shoulders before gently taking her head in his hands.

She closed her eyes and tilted her head back, parting her

CHAPTER 41

JONATHAN WAS AT his desk reading a contract for a six-million-dollar home he had listed only a week earlier. Life was good. Then the intercom on his desk phone buzzed.

"Mr. Kramer, your mother is here." Margie's voice sounded confused. For a moment, Jonathan was, too. He thought he hadn't heard her correctly, then his mother sailed through his door in a cloud of perfume and face powder.

Jonathan stood up and came around his desk. "Mother, what a surprise. I thought you weren't coming until Friday. It's good to see you." He put a hand on each bony shoulder and bent to give her a kiss.

Marilyn Swanson turned her head side to side receiving a brief kiss on each cheek from her youngest son. "Yes, yes it's a surprise for me, too, Jonathan."

Margie stood in the doorway, looking flustered. Jonathan looked at her and nodded. Satisfied everything was okay, Margie pulled the door closed.

"You should have called me. I could have picked you up at the airport."

"You know I don't know how to work those mobile telephone contraptions," she said waving him off and settling herself into a chair. "I had the pilot call ahead for a car. Besides, I know how busy you are, dear. At least I hope you are."

Jonathan took a seat in the chair next to her. "What brings you to Aspen early? I didn't expect you until Friday."

"I was on the way home from New York and had a stack of magazines to get me through the flight, and there it was. I had no idea!"

"There *what* was?" Jonathan asked. His mother's flair for the dramatics had tried his patience since childhood.

"A story about the murders—in Aspen! You didn't tell me," she said pointing a meticulously manicured fingernail at him.

"I didn't tell you because I didn't think it mattered."

"Well of course it matters, darling. You live here, don't you? If there is a madman running about murdering people, of course it matters. I wanted to come see for myself that you were alright. Plus, we were over Colorado and it was easy for the pilot to change the flight plan."

Jonathan was skeptical of the explanation for the early visit. With Marilyn Swanson, over-the-hill Hollywood star, once feted from Rio to Rome, the truth was never on the surface. If there was one thing he was certain of, it was that his mother had not altered her schedule and was now sitting in front of him unannounced because she was concerned for his safety.

"I'm sorry, Mother. I guess I should have told you," Jonathan said playing the game he had for years—appease her long enough to peel back the layers of pretense until the truth was revealed.

"Yes, you should have." She pursed her lips and frowned, her face taking on an odd contorted expression with a surprising lack of wrinkles for someone her age. That explains the trip to New York, Jonathan thought. Botox, fillers, surgery—there were endless possibilities. He knew his mother was addicted to her New York surgeon like a hooker addicted to crack.

"So what took you to New York this time?" he asked with a wry smile.

"Visiting friends." She waved a dismissive hand. "But I don't want to talk about that. I want to know more about what has been going on here."

After Jonathan filled her in on the questioning at the St. Regis, and what little news the police had released to the media, she stared at him incredulously. "So they don't know *anything*?" she asked. "Not even a clue as to who might have done it?"

"It seems that way."

"And Walter and Harriet? How are they holding up? I must see them while I'm in town. Walter had pledged a sizable donation to the Guild Ball I'm chairing in Los Angeles next fall, but that was before all this. I hope he's still planning to honor the donation."

There it was, the truth. The rotten core of the onion once the layers were peeled back. She still wanted to be the belle of the ball, despite her middle-aged movie roles drying up along with her over ten years ago.

He looked at her. Even though she was now seventy-two, most people would still consider his mother beautiful. In moments like these, he didn't see it.

For the next twenty minutes, she droned on about his brother Charles, saying something about a recent promotion, a raise, then something about his beautiful wife, the new house. After the first couple minutes, his thoughts wandered.

Charles Kramer had been born first and had always remained the favorite. He was "slightly older, slightly taller, and slightly better looking," Charles liked to tease Jonathan from time to time. Through the years, it became apparent their mother felt the same way.

Jonathan had tried his hand at acting years ago. Unsuccessful, he had moved to Aspen and worked tirelessly to build up his real estate business, courting even the most insufferable snobs and spoiled second and third wives. Anything to make a sale. Success hadn't come easy to him like it had his brother. And Jonathan was convinced his mother took every opportunity she could to point that out.

Marilyn prattled on, but he had sat back in his chair and let his mind drift to a million other things. There was the occasional head nod or "uh huh" to lead her to believe he was still listening. He stared at her without seeing.

He noticed the silk scarf around her neck and it reminded him of the recent murders. His years of hard work carefully cultivating clients. He was finally growing the business to a level he had hoped for, a level even his mother would eventually have to admit was a success. Then he thought about losing it all, about having to start over again with nothing but his name.

He remembered the nights and weekends he'd spent working, the hundreds of properties listed and shown. He thought of Charles—the job, the house, the wife. Then he noticed his mother's mouth yawning and closing like a fish sucking in air. He heard her, but it was muffled. Her voice droned on, a cacophony of barely decipherable sounds.

Something about her past movie rolls, future ones. Family legacy. Charles, this. Charles, that. Snide snippets about Jonathan leaving Los Angeles and moving to the mountains. If only he had been more patient, worked harder...

Why wouldn't she stop?

Jonathan stared at her—stared through her.

He wasn't sure how long it had been when he interrupted. "Mother, I'm very sorry, but I've got a showing I have to leave for soon."

Marilyn Swanson rose from her chair. "I'm sure you do," she said. "And I have a million things to do when I get back to Beverly Hills. Be a dear and cancel our dinner reservations for

Friday. I'm going to see Walter and Harriet Winston tomorrow, then I will be flying home. I hope you understand."

"Of course I do," he said.

On her way out, Marilyn pushed the door open and turned back. "Oh, and be a dear and put my condo on the market for me. I almost never get out here anymore and don't think I will need it any longer. I'll miss you. Do think about coming home more often."

"I will," Jonathan lied, but she had already sailed out the door.

CHAPTER 42

ON A HUNCH, Detective Mark Thurmond was back at the state prison outside Pueblo. He no longer thought Tony Paladino was guilty of stalking Georgia Glass, but he was certain the degenerate thug was guilty of something besides killing a prison guard, and had a good idea what it might be.

He had been waiting almost ten minutes when the heavy iron door to the small interrogation room swung open. Tony Paladino stood before him, again shackled in chains.

"Detective Thurmond," Paladino said with a wry smile as he dropped into the chair across the table. "The crime business must be slow if you're harassing me again." The two guards accompanying him each took a corner of the room.

"I told you I wasn't done with you yet, Tony."

"Lucky me."

"I've done some digging and it seems you might be smarter than I originally gave you credit for." After years of detective work, one thing he had learned was that criminal narcissists thrived on adulation.

Paladino leaned back in his chair and raised his chin. "And you came to this conclusion all by yourself?"

"I had some help," Mark said opening a file. He glanced through its contents. "It appears you were making quite a go of your old man's businesses before you got yourself busted for stalking Georgia Glass."

Paladino puffed up with self-satisfaction. "I'll withhold comment on the grounds of not wanting to incriminate myself."

"You're a shrewd one, Tony. I'll give you credit for that. Now tell me about Garafano."

"What about him?"

"Why wouldn't you press charges after the guy beat you to a pulp?"

"I told you then," Paladino huffed. "It was a simple misunderstanding."

Mark flipped through the pages in the file until he found what he was looking for. "Multiple lacerations, displaced rib fracture, bruised lung." He closed the file and looked back up at him. "And one chipped tooth."

Paladino's defiant expression didn't change. He cocked his head to one side. "My lawyer advised me against talking to you again today—afraid you'd trick me into making some mistake, say something I shouldn't—but I told him to go to hell. I handled you once and I can handle you again."

Mark nodded, pretending to agree. "Aside from killing that guard, you've played it pretty close to the vest. But you have to admit, that was one whopper of a screw-up, Tony. Not too bright."

Paladino lurched forward in his seat, clanking the chains, his self-satisfied smirk gone.

Time to reel him in, Mark thought. He slapped the file and looked up at Tony. "There are a couple things I don't get. Why risk it all by stalking Georgia Glass?"

The conversation came fast and furious.

"I didn't stalk—"

"Your father was out of the way. You had the family business to yourself. You were respected, could have made a real go at it. Why make a bone-head decision to throw it all away to stalk a woman?"

"I didn't."

Mark stabbed the file with his index finger. "From what I've read here, I would have put money on you being smarter than that."

Paladino's face turned crimson. "I *am* smarter than that. I didn't stalk her."

"Everyone thinks you did."

"I didn't!"

"You *didn't* stalk Georgia, Tony, because you're smarter than that, *aren't you?*"

"You're damn right I am."

"You didn't need her. Just like you didn't need your father, did you? He didn't give you credit for how smart you were, made you feel inferior. Didn't he, Tony?" Mark didn't wait for an answer. "I've heard how bad the old man treated you. He was over the hill, a has-been—"

"I'm better than my father ever was."

"But he didn't see it that way, did he? Humiliated you in front of the guys even though you were probably smarter than him."

"I *was* smarter than him."

"And you don't take shit from nobody!"

"Nobody—"

"So you killed the son of a bitch!"

"Damn right I did!" Tony Paladino's face froze.

The silence hung heavy. Mark noticed the guards exchange silent looks. Witnesses, he thought. Perfect.

Mark spoke first, his voice calm. "Just tell me one thing, Tony. Why'd you kill your mother?"

Paladino sat silent, clenching and unclenching his jaw. His eyes narrowed to slits radiating cold-steel hatred. His breathing came fast but shallow.

"Because she was there."

CHAPTER 43

GEORGIA TURNED ONTO Durango Avenue and saw Eddie Jenkins's brown Subaru parked at the curb in front of her house. He was sitting on a step to the porch.

"I'm so sorry I wasn't here when you got here," Georgia apologized as she walked up the sidewalk. "I had to return some research material to the man who loaned it to me."

"No problem, blondie. Traffic was light and I got here earlier than I expected."

Georgia gave him a hug.

In the kitchen, she saw Eddie eyeing the avocado monster skeptically. "Don't worry, it won't bite," she teased.

"Never seen one like this before." He shook his head and pulled open the door. "Lettuce, tomatoes, *more* lettuce? Still eating like a rabbit, I see."

Georgia slapped him with a dish towel. "How about the best Chinese takeout in town?"

"Sounds good to me." Eddie smiled and shut the refrigerator door.

Georgia dug her phone out of her purse and dialed the number for Little Ollie's. She didn't have to ask Eddie what he wanted. Over the years they had ordered Chinese takeout for each other dozens of times.

While they waited for the food to be delivered Eddie unpacked the boxes of security equipment.

"How's the new reporter you're working with," Georgia asked him. "Lisa, isn't it?"

He shrugged. "She's alright—still a work in progress. She won't be filling your shoes anytime soon, that's for sure."

"No, I heard they hired Jenna Thompson from the Albuquerque affiliate for that."

"Yeah. As far as I can tell, she's working out fine."

"And not bad to look at?" Georgia teased. "With that flaming auburn hair and green eyes. I know how you like red heads."

Eddie smiled briefly, then returned his attention to unpacking the boxes without a comment. His reaction seemed odd. Georgia hoped she hadn't offended him. It was possible Eddie had asked Jenna Thompson for a date and she turned him down. She remembered the night she and Eddie were stranded together on assignment years ago, the awkward tension when Eddie had asked her out. Georgia decided she wouldn't bring Jenna up again.

After they had eaten, Georgia cleaned up the kitchen. Eddie started to help, but she stopped him. "Don't worry about that. I've got it." She took his plate from him. "Since you're insisting on driving back tonight, you need to get started. I don't want you on the road too late. I really wish you would stay over."

He gave her a grudging smile. "Can't. I got to be at the station in the morning. The news doesn't wait, Georgia, you of all people know that."

"I don't want you on the road tired." She set a stack of files on the cleared table. "I'll be in here if you need me for anything, not that I have a clue about security systems."

Eddie glanced at the folders she had spread across the table. "Are you working on something for the new show?"

"Maybe." Georgia filled him in on the murders of Rachel Winston and Greta Moss. She told him about the ones committed decades earlier by Gerald Ray Toomey. "I'm convinced there's a connection. I've been researching possible motives, psychological issues with copycats. It's slow, but I think I'm getting somewhere."

"Profiling?" Eddie asked.

"Kind of," Georgia admitted. "If I find something, it might help the police. Plus, it's good material for a first show, don't you think?"

"Forget the show. Are you sure this is a good idea?" he asked. "Trying to out a murderer who's obviously spent time in your backyard? Maybe your *house*?"

"Investigative reporting is my job, Eddie. Why wouldn't it be a good idea?"

"Because you're too close to this story." He nodded in the direction of her garage, "Literally."

"That's a good reason *to* look into this. Another reason is—again—this is my job."

He pointed to the files on the table. "But this is a small town. What if the killer finds out you're investigating the case? It's not hard to figure out you're living here alone—and way down here at the end of the street by the river. Is it really a good idea to bait this guy? Piss him off by trying to figure out who he is? Not to mention the new stalking incidents? I just don't think this is the time to be helping the police find a murderer. You were going to spend a few weeks here relaxing, getting ready for the new job. I thought they were going to have the first few shows already lined up and ready for you, *then* you could start your own investigations."

Georgia let out a big sigh. "You sound like my mother."

"I like your mother."

Georgia smiled at him wearily, "Thank you for your concern, Eddie, but I've made up my mind. I'm looking into it. And you have to admit, if I can get a story out of this, it's going to make one heck of a first show."

He stared at her a couple beats then nodded his head grudgingly. "It will be one heck of a good show, blondie. Just promise me you'll watch your back."

She waved him off. "You know I can take care of myself. Especially when I've got *you* watching my back. Thanks again for driving all the way here and putting the security system in for me."

"Yeah, yeah." He threw up a hand and turned to leave the room. "But it's going to cost you."

"I know how it works, Eddie," Georgia said as he walked away. "The next meal on me will be a steak dinner—I promise."

"Now *that's* a date," he answered from the other room.

Georgia cringed at the word *date*.

She studied her notes and charts for over an hour, barely taking notice of the noise Eddie made as he went in and out of the house installing the outside cameras one by one. She was used to working in a loud news room, so the cutting open of boxes and whine of power tools hardly fazed her. Two or three times she had seen him out of her peripheral vision walk around the side of the house. Eddie was nothing if not thorough, she thought. He would make sure every door and window was contacted and covered by a camera.

She heard the front door open and close, then another box being opened.

"One more to go," he called out from the front room. "Then I'll be all done and out of your hair."

Just then Georgia's cell phone rang. Detective Mark Thurmond.

"Hello again, detective. Twice in one day—should I be nervous?" She tried sounding light-hearted, bolstering herself as much as trying to convince him.

He got right to the point. "Georgia, I know for a fact now Tony Paladino isn't your stalker. He never was."

Georgia sat motionless for five minutes as he filled her in on his conversation with Tony Paladino—how he had battled a lingering doubt that Paladino was her original stalker, and that Paladino had admitted to murdering his parents.

"So the one who stalked me in Denver…?" Georgia asked, hearing the tremble in her voice as it trailed off.

"Is more than likely the one stalking you now," he finished for her.

Eddie had heard the conversation and stood in the kitchen doorway watching her, listening to the rest of the conversation with concern etching his forehead.

When the call was finished, Georgia set her phone gently on the table in front of her and took a deep breath. She told Eddie what Detective Thurmond had said, that Tony Paladino was guilty of killing his parents, but wasn't her stalker.

"He said that he always had doubts about the case," she said. "Even though they charged Paladino with the crime, and the district attorney thought there was enough evidence to prosecute, he wasn't convinced Paladino was guilty."

"Why wouldn't he say something? Let them know he didn't think he was guilty?"

"He did. He said he brought up his concerns to the DA but no one wanted to hear it."

"What makes him so sure it's not Paladino?"

"Several things, but one thing he said always bothered him was that when they checked Paladino's phone after they arrested him, he had photographs of me on it, but they were photos downloaded from the internet. There weren't any that he had taken himself. None of the ones I had received."

Eddie shook his head. "You need to be careful, blondie. Even with a security system, you're vulnerable."

"I'll be fine," she said and managed a weak smile. "A little mystery in life is a good thing, don't you think?"

Eddie's repeated concerns about her living alone and investigating the murders again fell on deaf ears. Reluctantly he gave up his protest and finished installing the last camera.

When he left, Eddie had installed contacts on all the first-floor doors and windows, cameras on all four sides of Georgia's house, and a fifth camera at the front door. She would be able to see who was at the door if someone rang the bell. What Eddie hadn't told her was that he had also installed a sixth camera—inside the house.

As he maneuvered the mountain road north towards the interstate, he remembered Georgia's shaky voice as she talked to the detective. He grinned. She had assured Eddie that she was okay, that she wasn't nervous, but he knew the truth.

Georgia had rejected him romantically, humiliating him by refusing him then treating him like a kid brother. At first he had tried to settle for friendship, but it had been hard, especially watching while she dated that meat-head football player that didn't deserve her. But now she was moving half a continent away, leaving him behind... or so she thought.

He wasn't going to let her get away that easy.

CHAPTER 44

LUKE MCCRAY WOUND his car down the dirt road to where he hoped Jack's trailer was. He was twenty minutes from town and it was getting dark. The last thing he wanted was to get lost on one of the back roads in the mountains. The guys in the department would never let him live it down. Newly promoted junior detective gets himself lost in the woods and has to call for Pitkin County search and rescue.

Luke was still getting used to the mountains, having grown up in a small town in eastern Colorado where the landscape was flat and looked like scorched earth ten months out of the year. It was a far cry from the rugged peaks around Aspen.

The mountains still intimidated him, but in the six years he had been on the police force he had learned to love them. He had even taken up snowboarding his second year in town. He knew he was never going to be a contender for the X Games, but was satisfied he was getting better every year.

The road finally opened up in a clearing. Jack's trailer was small, set on a slight rise, its silver skin still shining in the waning daylight. Luke let out a sigh of relief that he had found it.

Jack had invited him over after work. It was the first time Jack had shown an interest in spending time together outside work. Luke wasn't about to refuse the invitation.

As Luke pulled his car off to the side and got out, Jack

emerged from the silver trailer with a beer bottle in each hand and the brown dog at his heels. He handed Luke a beer.

"You found me."

"I was beginning to get nervous." Luke looked around. He could just make out the dark silhouette of the mountains against an ink blue sky. "You're pretty far out. How did you find this place?"

"It wasn't easy," Jack laughed. He threw a couple logs into an iron burn pit and lit a fire. "Have a seat."

Luke sat in a folding chair next to a flimsy card table. He watched as Jack pulled another chair from a small compartment near the front of the trailer.

"I have another one," Jack said holding up the chair. "I've never used it, but they came as a pair when I bought them."

Jack opened the chair, sat down and leaned back, taking a long draw of his beer, the brown dog settling into a spot at his feet. Amid all the chaos, the media scrutiny, and the pressure put on him by Chief Rogan, he appeared steady, calm.

"I see you still got the dog."

Jack looked down. "Want him?"

Luke held up his beer and his free hand. "No, but thank you. Did you try the shelter?"

"I did. Took him in this morning."

Luke frowned. "But he's still here?" he said bending over and scratching the dog behind his ears.

"The woman at the shelter complained about being over-crowded. Then she looped a leash around his neck and the old guy started rearing and bucking like a bronc. I wasn't getting good vibes about leaving him, so I decided to look for another home for him myself."

The dog had laid its head on one of Jack's boots and was sleeping.

"He looks pretty comfortable here."

"Well he's not staying."

A gentle breeze caught the flames from the logs and made them dance. Luke stole a quick glance at his boss from the corner of his eye. He had often wondered about him. In the time they had worked together, Jack had never talked about his past, or his family. Luke wasn't sure he even *had* a family.

After almost a year, Jack was still an enigma. Luke had heard the stories—rumors, really—about his years with the FBI, about some incident in Houston. He knew Jack grew up in Baton Rouge and later moved to Texas to play college football, but the rest was a mystery. How did he come to work for the FBI? What happened in Houston that led to his resignation? Luke wanted to know, but had decided on the drive out that he wouldn't ask him about any of it. Jack Martin wasn't the kind of guy you felt comfortable asking personal questions.

They sat in silence a while longer. The only sound was the crackling of the dry logs in the burn pit. As the minutes passed, the sky got darker but the stars shone brighter. It was a clear night, the wind had died down, but it was cold.

Luke pulled his jacket closed and stuck his hands in his pockets.

Jack reached over and threw another log on the fire, the flames smoldering a moment before they grabbed the dry bark and crackled to life. It startled the dog to attention, but Jack ignored him.

Finally Jack broke the silence. "I thought it would be good to go over the cases in a different environment—get out of the office. Talk through what we know without any notes, or white boards, or phones ringing. I've found sometimes I need to get away from the office to think clearer. Kind of the 'not being able to see the forest for the trees' kind of thing."

Luke nodded. "That makes sense."

"So I thought we'd go over a few things. I'd give you my

theories on solving crime—for what it's worth. Maybe it will give you a different way of looking at the cases."

"Sounds good." Luke took a sip of beer.

"First off, I've found solving a murder isn't so much about figuring out what happened," Jack said. "But *why* it happened. At some point, a normal human emotion morphs into something hideous and then—bang!" He clapped his hands together, causing Luke and the brown dog to jump.

Jack took a drink, set the bottle back on the table. "That's the killer's motive. And there's *always* a motive. Whatever the motive is might not make any sense to you and me, but it will make perfect sense to the criminal. Often, the key to solving the case is not to think rationally, but to try thinking *irrationally*. Does that make sense?"

Luke nodded. "It does." This way of thinking was new to him. He was taking mental notes, hoping he'd remember everything in the morning.

"And if a murder isn't completely random—which it rarely is—and you don't have much in the way of forensics, witnesses, or some other evidence—which we don't—you have to look to the victim for clues."

Luke frowned, working hard to follow the logic. "Or victims, plural," he said.

Jack dipped his Shiner bottle at him. "Exactly."

They discussed the merits of Georgia Glass's theory about a copycat killer, comparing victims, murder weapons and timing. They talked about the scrapbook page mailed to Georgia, her stalking case, and the fact she lived where one of the bodies had been found.

They went over it all, Luke seeing everything in a different light, learning to think about everything in a different way. Just when Luke felt buoyed by his new understanding, Jack dropped the bombshell.

He set his third empty bottle on the table and swayed slightly in Luke's direction. Each breath a cloud of frozen air. "Of course, rehashing all of this could likely not mean a damn thing when it comes to catching this guy."

Confused, Luke was silent.

Jack continued. "A lot of serial killers are finally apprehended by patrol officers—not detectives. They're conducting their everyday duties, driving their rounds and it's a routine stop—a damn traffic violation—that finally gets em. That's why we regularly update the patrol guys. We can work our ass off, but they're just as likely to find them as we are."

After another hour or so, they stood up. Luke had drunk only one beer and that had been over an hour earlier. He assured Jack he would be fine making his way back to town in the dark.

Jack waved goodbye without looking back as he made his way to the trailer, not noticing the brown dog that trailed at his heels.

On the drive back to town Luke went over everything Jack had said. He was right; Jack's theories had given him a new way of approaching the cases. He was grateful for that. His only disappointment was that he hadn't learned any more about his boss than what he had known before.

He knew Jack was a good cop. He had heard he was an uncanny investigator. With all the pressure they had been under, all the crap thrown their way, Luke had never seen him flinch, never hesitate.

Jack was still a mystery, but Luke respected him, trusted him. Then again… you kind of wonder about a guy who won't pet a dog.

CHAPTER 45

THE *TODAY SHOW* segment didn't do his story justice. Only two minutes—it should have been longer; and they didn't even interview a single celebrity or expert. When he strangled his third victim, they'd have to give his story the time and respect it deserved.

No coverage at all on CNN or Coastal News. Until they reported his story with respect, he wouldn't watch either network.

The story on Fox News had been better. An interview with Detective Mark Fuhrman of O.J. Simpson trial fame, *and* a retired FBI criminal profiler. He almost never watched Fox, but kudos to them for acknowledging the story's significance.

But, damn the so-called experts. In the interview, the FBI profiler had been rocking along fine until he threw out his theory the killer could be a woman, citing the lack of blood and gore, and that neither victim had been sexually assaulted. At least the reporter had the brains to ask how probable it was a woman could have disposed of a body in a four-foot-high box in a vacant garage in town.

Not all great murderers are vulgar, or commit simple or crude crimes of passion or convenience. When he was finished, all the so-called experts would appreciate the fine-tuned intricacies of his achievements. Then he would enjoy his fame from the sidelines, keeping his identity a secret. It would make him one of the greats. They'd never catch him.

He just needed the perfect third victim, and he'd found her.

In a few days, Georgia Glass would be dead.

CHAPTER 46

"WHERE WERE YOU last night?"

The question caused Carlo Ferrari's chest to constrict.

Bridget Ferrari had been lying in wait in their living room when Carlo came down the stairs that morning. She was reclined on the sofa sipping what Carlo suspected was a Bloody Mary, her slender feet propped on the coffee table.

"What do you mean?" Carlo answered. "I was here with you last night."

"Not *all* night, you weren't."

Carlo looked at his wife. Long ink-black hair falling over a red silk robe. Her emerald green eyes today were fixed, staring accusingly at him. He remembered the feelings he had for her early on, pride and amazement that this gorgeous creature would be even remotely interested in *him*. He remembered how infatuated he was with her in the beginning. It was probably never love, he could admit that now, but he had loved being around her, being with her.

Not anymore.

She swung her feet from the coffee table and stood up. "I woke up around three," she said. "You weren't in bed."

Carlo thought quickly. "I couldn't sleep so I came downstairs for something to eat."

"You weren't downstairs. I checked. You weren't here, Carlo."

He felt his throat constrict. "You didn't let me finish," he said. "A snack didn't help, so I went for a walk." He struggled to find an excuse. "It's the stress from the lounge. Things aren't going as good as I'd hoped, but it will turn around. And you know I've never slept good."

"*Well*," she corrected. "You've never slept *well*."

He shook his head and started toward the kitchen.

"Wait a minute," Bridget called after him. "I'm not finished yet. I want out."

"Out of what?"

"Out of this marriage. Out of this town. I want half of the paltry amount you're still worth and I want to move back to San Francisco. You're a shell of the man I married, Carlo. I don't know who you are anymore and I want out!"

Blood rushed to his head causing it to throb furiously. "Calm down, Bridget," he said in an even tone that masked his growing anger. "Your facial contortions are ruining your Botox."

She stormed toward him with clenched fists. "How dare you. You're a pathetic excuse for a man and you're a liar." She stabbed a manicured nail in his chest with each sentence. "I think you've been lying to me for a long time. I think your insomnia is bullshit. You've been sneaking out. You snuck out last night, just like you snuck out the night Rachel Winston was murdered."

"You're crazy."

"I'm not the crazy one, Carlo—you are. But maybe you can use that as your defense." She stepped back from him and smirked. "Plead temporary insanity."

"I had nothing to do with Rachel Winston's murder, and you know it."

"Do I? How would I know that? What I *do* know is that you've been lying to me. I also know you had one of your *episodes* that night." She made the gesture for air quotes as she said it. "I think that detective would be very interested in hearing what you left out of your alibi."

The veins in his head and neck bulged. He grabbed Bridget's arm and squeezed until she winced from the pain.

"Don't even think about repeating your wild accusations to the police."

"Or what, Carlo?" She tried to sound defiant but he heard the flicker of fear in her voice.

"If you tell your wild stories to *anyone*," he tightened his grip on her arm, "you'll *never* see San Francisco again."

CHAPTER 47

THOMAS MURPHY WAS seated alone at a corner table in Starbucks when his cell phone vibrated. It was 8:30 a.m. and he had been there for over thirty minutes. June had been insufferable that morning and he had fled the house before he did something he would regret.

June had purchased a copy of *The National Tattler* at the market that morning. The cover story was about the murders. She had thrown the paper at him when she got home.

As he had feared, Liz Kelly had written a salacious story, including several paragraphs on the hunt for June's missing scarf, and mentioning his name and affiliation with the hospital in New York.

Staring at the vibrating cell phone on the table, Tom debated on whether or not to answer it. He didn't recognize the number, but from the area code, knew it would not be the Aspen police. He picked it up.

"Tom?"

"Who is this?" He was excited and intrigued by the breathy female voice.

"It's Tiffany."

He felt his blood pressure instantly rise. It had been nearly seven years since he'd last heard from her. "Tiffany, how are you?" he asked cupping the phone with his hand and turning away from an occupied adjacent table. Two women were laughing and talking in raised voices, but he didn't want to take any chances on someone overhearing his conversation.

"I heard about what's happening in Aspen and was concerned about you."

Tom took a deep breath and waited for what would come next.

When he didn't reply, she continued. "I read in *The National Tattler* that the police were looking for June's scarf. The article implied it might have been used to strangle a girl they found dead a couple days ago."

"That's tabloid speculation. The police haven't said how Rachel Winston was murdered."

"But that first girl was strangled with a scarf—the article said so. They call her killer the Hermes Strangler. So it's easy to assume that if the police are looking for another—"

"I wouldn't assume anything, Tiffany."

"The article said the police questioned everyone who was at a party the night she went missing. Said someone might have seen it or taken it, but so far, no one has come forward."

"Why did you call me?"

"Well, with everything going on and you back in the news, it made me think about what you did to me."

Tom talked through clenched teeth. "I didn't *do* anything to you."

"You did, and we both know it."

"Nothing happened to you that you didn't ask for at the time."

"Well I was thinking that I deserved more than what you gave me." Her voice had changed, it was deeper, edgy. "Listen, doctor. I could have caused a lot of problems for you, but I didn't. I've been a good girl. But times are tough, and looking back, I think you got off a little too easy."

"What do you want?"

"I'm betting I could get thousands for my story. I think ten thousand is worth keeping the real reason you resigned from Mount Belvedere a secret, don't you?"

"I can't get that kind of money right now."

"You were able to get five times that six years ago. Let's just put it this way, doctor, if I *don't* get it by next week, I'm calling Liz Kelly. I'm sure *The National Tattler* would love a juicy sexual harassment story about the disgraced former head of Mount Belvedere Hospital... *and* possible murder suspect." She let that last bit hang out there before she continued. "You have one week."

Thomas Murphy clicked off his phone and resisted the urge to hurl it across the coffee shop. Instead he set it down and smothered it with his palm, pushing it into the table with a controlled fury.

Women, he thought. *Not a single one has been worth a damn.*

CHAPTER 48

PARKER RANDOLPH SAT at his desk reading Liz Kelly's article in *The National Tattler*. When it mentioned the police were hunting for a missing scarf owned by June Murphy, and that her husband was Dr. Thomas Murphy, Parker set the tabloid down. It took him a second to remember why the name sounded familiar. Georgia had been in contact with a Dr. Murphy for information on criminal psychology.

He wanted to call her, but hesitated. He knew he had overstepped his bounds at lunch the Sunday before, insisting that she was in danger and pushing her to leave Aspen early. The last thing Parker wanted to do was pester her like some sort of overbearing parent.

He had enjoyed the afternoon with her—lunch at The Wild Fig, then strolling through town before he had to fly back. But the next morning he had faced his father's fury when he told him she wouldn't be coming to L.A. yet.

He didn't tell his father about the stalking incidents, but had called Georgia as soon as he heard.

"How did you find out?" she had asked.

"We're a news agency. We've got people covering the local police department. Of course we were going to find out."

"I'm sorry, I should have told you."

Parker thought she sounded more exasperated than apologetic.

He knew his father's reaction would be the same as his. *Get the hell out of that town.* But his father would have gotten the same response he had—a polite, but firm, mind-your-own-business.

With the flurry of media coverage surrounding the murders, including Liz Kelly's story that morning, Parker wasn't surprised when his father barged into his office.

"What the hell is going on in Aspen? There's a psycho walking the streets and he's already been to Georgia Glass's house at least once—to dump a body. Who's to say he won't go back?" Before Parker could respond, Malcolm shook a piece of paper and continued. "And she cited this Dr. Murphy in her show proposal you brought back. The same guy Liz Kelly mentioned had 'no comment' when she asked him about his wife's missing scarf—implying it could be the murder weapon."

Parker held up his hands trying to calm him down. "I expressed my concern when I was there. I called her again yesterday. She brushed me off both times. She wants to stay and try to get a story out of it. There's nothing more we can do."

"Idiot girl." Malcolm Randolph crumpled the paper in his hand and threw it on the floor. "I'll give her this," he said shaking his head and sticking his hands on his hips, "I admire her moxie. And if she wasn't so close to the damned story I'd tell her to stay—report on it. But give it another try, Parker. Call her one more time and see if you can get her to change her mind."

Parker let out a long sigh. He knew he should tell his father about the stalking incidents, but didn't. "She's a smart woman, Dad—stubborn, but smart. If she thinks she's getting in over her head, I'm sure she'll back off," he lied.

CHAPTER 49

JACK HAD BEEN at work since before dawn. He now stood with Luke in Chief Rogan's office to update him on the investigation. The chief's large oak desk was covered with newspapers and tabloids.

"These damn reporters seem to have more information on these cases than we do," Rogan barked. "Tell me that's not true, Jack."

"It's not true," Jack said without emotion. He dismissed the tabloids as merely a nuisance, regurgitated rumors, inflaming public speculation and his boss's temper.

Rogan nodded. "Then fill me in, damn it. Tell me everything you know so far on the doctor. Include what you might of told me before; refresh my memory. I'm getting too old for this."

Jack put both hands on his hips, flaring his Carhartt jacket, and began from memory: "Dr. Thomas Murphy. Only child, raised in the Midwest, attended the University of Nebraska then Johns Hopkins School of Medicine. Was at the top of his class both places. Bounced around until he landed at Mount Belvedere Hospital in Manhattan where he climbed the ladder with lightning speed and was eventually promoted to Chief of Staff. He had been at that position for eight years when he resigned unexpectedly and relocated here to Aspen six years ago."

Rogan frowned. "Do we know why?"

"No clue."

The chief leaned back in his chair and frowned. "Well that's not much new information."

"What's interesting," Jack continued, "is that there was an informal retirement party for him at Mount Belvedere, but none of the board members or administrators attended—only his staff and a few nurses. It points to there being more to the story of his resignation than anyone is letting on."

"Sounds like the good doctor is hiding something," Rogan said. "Keep digging into his background. Anything else?"

Jack looked at Luke and nodded.

The junior detective opened his notebook. "Yes, sir. Before becoming Chief of Staff, Dr. Murphy was a practicing psychiatrist who specialized in criminal forensic psychiatry—"

"I remember you mentioning something about it before, but what exactly does that mean?" Rogan interrupted.

"He diagnosed and treated mental disorders. In particular, the criminally insane," Luke answered. "Dr. Murphy has written several articles for medical and academic journals on criminal insanity and profiling, including a couple on serial killers."

Rogan raised an eyebrow. "*That* I remember." He looked at Jack. "So what do you think?"

Jack took a deep breath before he spoke. "The guy has done a ton of research on murderers—serial killers in particular. There's a good chance he's researched Toomey and was lying when he said he hadn't met Brenda Pawloski. The museum would have been the second place I would have gone to for research."

"Where would have been the first?"

"The internet. But the archived articles from the Aspen newspaper at the time of the Toomey murders haven't been digitized and aren't on the internet."

"They're at the museum," Rogan said dropping a fist on his desk.

Jack nodded. "I'm going to talk to the museum assistant—the woman who found Pawloski's body. I'll have her search for any evidence Pawloski might have known Thomas Murphy—emails, contact lists, everything. We might need to confiscate the computers, but aside from Thomas Murphy's name showing up, I thought her assistant would recognize anything that looked out of the ordinary before we did."

"Let me know what you find." Rogan stood up, indicating he considered the meeting over.

Outside, Jack paused and looked over the hood of his truck at his young partner. "There's something I didn't tell the chief," he said. "I came in early and finished going through all the old Toomey case files—the ones I promised to give Georgia Glass copies of. Whoever our guy is—and I'm not convinced it's Thomas Murphy—he *is* a copycat. I think Brenda Pawloski's murder is related, but she was killed for some other reason. I haven't figured it out yet, but she doesn't fit."

Luke nodded in agreement.

"Which means," Jack continued, "in a few days, this guy is going to kill again."

CHAPTER 50

DETECTIVE MARK THURMOND knew that when Tony Paladino refused to press charges against Sammy Garafano after his beating, the Denver police had no choice but to release Garafano. Soon after, Garafano had disappeared.

Just after midnight Wednesday morning, he was found. Garafano had been arrested while in the process of sneaking into the home of the late Angelo and Estelle Paladino.

Mark Thurmond walked into the interrogation room holding the arrest report. Sammy Garafano sat at a small square table. "Back again, Sammy? What's with you guys? Just can't seem to stay out of trouble, can you?"

The look on Sammy Garafano's face hardened. "You got nothing on me."

Mark Thurmond looked down at the report. "Trespassing, breaking and entering, attempting to flee the scene." He looked back up at Garafano. "It looks like we've got plenty on you this time."

Two-bit mob thug. Thirty-four years old and in and out of jail since he was fourteen. An eight-page rap sheet. Could have stepped right out of an episode of *The Sopranos*—short, muscular and balding, with a tattoo of a snub-nosed .38 on one forearm and the Virgin Mary on the other.

"What are you doing in Denver?" Mark asked.

"I thought I'd come try that snow skiing thing before all the snow melted."

"Why'd you break into the Paladino home?"

"I didn't break in. I was checking to make sure the place was locked up. Tony Paladino's a friend of mine. I was checking on his parents' place for him since he's in the slammer."

"Uh huh." Mark stood up abruptly, driving his chair back toward the wall. He braced both hands on the table and leaned forward. "Let me tell you why I think you were there, Sammy. You can tell me where I'm wrong."

"Shoot," Garafano said grinning. "Get it? *Shoot?*"

Mark ignored the remark. "We both know Tony Paladino murdered his old man to take over the business." Garafano's grin disappeared.

Paladino's confession hadn't been made public yet, and although Mark suspected Garafano and his bosses back in New York knew Tony was behind the murders, confirmation of it had caught the mobster by surprise.

Mark continued. "And we both know Tony is an idiot and was making a mess of things—attracting a lot of unwanted attention. I think you were sent here after Angelo and Estelle's murders to clean up that mess. I think that's why you were at the house. Your boss wanted you to come out here to Denver, rough up Tony, then break into Angelo's house to make sure there wasn't anything incriminating left behind that could tie Angelo to the family back East."

Mark watched the prisoner closely as he spoke—his eyes, his body language. Garafano remained silent, confirming what Mark said was the truth.

He continued, "We found a newspaper article on Tony's stalking trial folded in your wallet."

"Yeah, so what of it?"

Mark pulled the empty chair back into place and sat down. "Ever been to Aspen, Sammy?"

"What?" Garafano looked confused.

"Aspen—have you ever been there?"

"Too rich for my blood."

"By the looks of you, I don't doubt that, but I didn't ask you if you owned property there, I asked you if you've ever *been* there."

"No. I've never been there."

"Where were you last Sunday?"

"Sunday? Probably in church," Garafano said grinning again.

"Sure you were. Anyone see you there? Because you need an alibi."

The smirk faded. "An alibi? What are you guys trying to pin on me this time?"

"Where were you last Sunday?" Mark asked again, opening a small notebook he pulled from his pocket. "Between the hours of noon and three exactly?"

Garafano thought for a moment. "I was at Gino's—on Tejan Street."

"Anyone see you there?"

"Yeah, sure. Lots of people."

"Give me a name."

Garafano searched his memory. "Giorgio—the bartender," he said. "Start with him. The waiter's name was Luco or Diego or something. Ask him, too. I had the ravioli."

"Alright, Sammy." Mark scribbled the names into his notebook and closed it, pushed his chair back and stood up. He knew Garafano's alibi would check out. He had interviewed enough suspects over the years to sense when they were telling the truth and when they were lying.

Sammy Garafano was a two-bit enforcer sent to rough up

or take out Tony Paladino, but he wasn't the person stalking Georgia Glass.

Although he felt he was no closer to finding her stalker, when he got back to his office, Mark called Georgia to update her on the case.

"You haven't received anything else from this guy since Sunday's text?" Mark asked.

Georgia told him about the photocopy of the scrapbook page she had received through the mail, but Mark didn't think that fit the stalker's MO.

"I don't want to scare you, but I think you're dealing with two different guys here. I know you're getting tired of hearing it, but I'm going to say it again—you need to take extra precautions."

"I already have." She told him about the security system and cameras Eddie had installed for her. "In a way, I wish Tony Paladino *was* behind the stalking this time. At least I'd have the comfort in knowing he was behind bars. Now I don't have any idea who this guy is."

Mark heard the hint of fear in her voice, and was frustrated he didn't seem any closer to catching her stalker than he was before. And now someone had sent her an article on an old murder. What was going on?

He feared she was in danger, that her stalker, or the person behind the scrapbook page, would one day materialize and hurt her, or worse.

"You have to keep asking yourself who this might be. Someone from your past, from work, an old school chum, a previous friend or neighbor. Keep wracking your brain, and I'll keep working my end."

"I will, detective. Sometimes I feel like I can't see the forest for the trees. Maybe the clues are right in front of me, I'm just too close to notice."

"That happens all the time, but don't give up. Go over everything—consider everyone."

"I will," she reassured him again. "You might talk to my friend Eddie Jenkins. We're very close. I know he would be happy to talk to you. Maybe he will remember something I don't—maybe he saw or heard something strange, something he doesn't realize is important. We have lots of mutual friends and co-workers. We talk every few days; I'll let him know you might call."

Mark Thurmond made a note to follow up with Eddie Jenkins.

CHAPTER 51

BRIDGET FERRARI SAILED into Jonathan Kramer's office in a cloud of perfume and pretension. "I'm here to see Jonathan," she announced.

Twenty-nine-year-old Margie Berry, Jonathan's executive assistant, tucked an errant strand of unwashed hair behind her ear.

"Hello, Mrs. Ferrari. Mr. Kramer is on the phone, but if you'll have a seat, I'll slip him a note that you're here."

Margie scribbled on a yellow sticky pad and took it with her into Jonathan's office. On her way back to her desk she stole a sideways glance at Bridget, now sunk into an easy chair in the office's small reception area. She sat with her long legs stretched out and crossed in front of her. Tight-fitting jeans revealed a peek of black stiletto boots. With her fuzzy red sweater—probably cashmere—Margie thought she looked stunning. But then again, Bridget Ferrari always did look stunning.

"He'll be right out," Margie said, then sat down at her desk and smoothed the wrinkles from the top of her green pant-suit, painfully aware of her own lack of style. She watched as Bridget held out a hand and examined her long French-tipped fingernails.

"Well he better hurry," Bridget replied, now fondling a stack of gold bangles on her wrist. "I need a Bloody Mary. I stiff drink can cure just about everything."

"What are we curing today?" Jonathan asked coming out of his office.

Bridget stood up and kissed him on both cheeks. "I'll tell you all about it over lunch and a Bloody Mary. You're buying."

"I don't know," Jonathan checked his watch. "I've got to get a contract out this afternoon—"

"I won't take no for an answer. I need to talk to someone." Her voice shook. "Carlo is going crazy. *Look* what he did." She held out her arm and pulled up the sleeve to her sweater, revealing a faint purple bruise.

It was then Margie noticed Bridget's eyes were glassy, like she had been crying or drinking—maybe both, she thought. Then again it could all be an act. Margie had seen enough of Bridget Ferrari to know the woman had a flair for dramatics.

"Carlo did that?" Jonathan asked.

"Yes, and I'll tell you all about it, but I need that Bloody Mary first. Take me to J-Bar at Hotel Jerome."

Jonathan took in a deep breath and let it out slowly, "Okay, but we have to make it quick."

As Jonathan shut the door, Bridget said, "I'm really scared of Carlo. I don't know how much more I can take."

Outside, Jonathan guided Bridget by the elbow around the corner and toward the hotel. "Bridget, you have to watch what you say in earshot of Margie. She's a chronic gossip."

"I don't care, let her gossip. Carlo is dangerous and I'm scared."

After they had been seated and their orders taken, Bridget leaned across the table and took one of Jonathan's hands. "I want to thank you for being such a good friend." Her face was somber.

"You have lots of friends."

She shook her head and sat back, bringing her arms back to her side. "Not ones that I can trust like you."

Jonathan glanced around to make sure there weren't any diners within ear shot. He lowered his voice. "What's going on with Carlo? What happened?"

"I woke up last night and Carlo wasn't home."

"Where was he?"

"I don't know. It's happened several times. I'll wake up and he'll be gone. Sometimes he's somewhere in the house, piddling around like he's sleepwalking or something. But sometimes he's really gone. I mean he's left the house—nowhere to be found. He's always had insomnia, but I don't think that explains all of it. When I confronted him with it this morning, he said he had gone for a walk. But honestly, I don't think he knew where he had been." She shook her head. "I don't know what's happening. I think he's going crazy. Maybe it's that damned cigar bar."

"Have you told anyone else about this?"

"No. I told you—I don't trust anyone but you. But Jonathan, I keep thinking back to the night of the Winston's party, the night Rachel went missing." Her voice trailed off.

"What about it?"

"Carlo had one of his episodes that night. I woke up and he wasn't in bed, but I wasn't feeling good—too much to drink at the party—and didn't care enough to get up and look for him, so I went back to sleep. He told the police he was home all night with me, but he wasn't." Her eyes pleaded for an explanation.

"But Carlo wouldn't hurt Rachel. What reason would he have?"

"The money." Bridget's eyes were wide and wild. "What if he kidnapped her for the money and something went wrong?"

Jonathan shook his head. He was tiring of Bridget's habitual dramatics. He had known and played golf with Carlo for years, and there was no way he was responsible for Rachel's death. "I just don't think Carlo is capable of that."

Bridget laid her arm on the table and pulled her sleeve up just high enough to reveal the fresh bruise. "Well he's capable of *that*."

Jonathan was surprised by the bruise. He had heard rumors about Carlo's occasional temper flares at the lounge from a couple guys that worked for him that Jonathan knew. But other than a few tantrums because of missed shots on the golf course, Jonathan had never known Carlo to even raise his voice at anyone. "That does look bad, Bridget, but it's a long way from murder."

"But how do you explain his alibi—or lack of alibi? He told the police he was with me all night and I know for a fact he wasn't."

Jonathan took a deep breath, taking it all in, then let it out slowly. "Have you told the police?"

"No. Should I?" She looked and sounded weary, clearly not knowing what to do.

Jonathan felt the weight of her trust, but was also aware of the consequences of a misstep by telling the police. "No," he said in a low somber voice. "Not yet."

The waitress appeared and set their drinks in front of them.

Jonathan watched Bridget pick the celery out of her Bloody Mary, sit back in her chair, and take a long drink.

The fire had gone from her eyes. He knew it would be back, but for the moment she looked uncertain—defeated. It was the first time he had ever seen her this way. Did she really think Carlo was capable of murder?

CHAPTER 52

GEORGIA HAD JUST gotten back from a morning hike along the river when her cell phone rang. She pulled it from her jacket pocket, looked at the caller ID and hesitated. Thomas Murphy. She took a deep breath and answered.

"A box of my old research was delivered yesterday. There's more information for you on serial killers," Dr. Murphy told her. "I also found a book I had been looking for. It was buried under a stack of reports in a filing cabinet. I think you'll want to read it. I can drop it all off in an hour if that's convenient."

"Thank you, Dr. Murphy, but I don't want you to go out of your way. You've been so much help already. I would be happy to pick it up and save you the trouble."

"I wouldn't hear of it," he replied. "First of all, it's Tom, not Dr. Murphy. Second, I already told you it's no trouble at all. So I'll see you in about an hour?"

Georgia let the question hang unanswered until it felt awkward. "That would be great. Thank you."

She glanced at the papers spread across the table. Photocopies of the studies and articles Dr. Murphy had already lent her, her notes, lists and charts made in an attempt at profiling a suspect.

She gathered it all together in a neat stack at the corner of the table then placed her laptop on top of it all. Liz Kelly's article in *The National Tattler* had made it seem Thomas Murphy could be a possible suspect in Rachel's murder. Georgia wanted to keep him from seeing what she was working on.

She grabbed a folder from the kitchen counter and was going to hide it under the laptop but stopped. She sat down and flipped through its contents. She had read everything in it at least twice, but was compelled to look again.

It had taken a couple requests, but Jack Martin had finally let her into the museum to do more research on Gerald Ray Toomey and his murders. The folder contained the copies of additional newspaper articles she had dug up, stories about the victims and their lives before being murdered. Stories about Toomey, his life in and out of a succession of orphanages before settling on a life of crime.

There were articles mentioning her uncle, Ernest Galloway, referring to him as the lead investigator on the cases and finally, the arresting officer. He was quoted in the articles, but only making reference to the investigations and the arrest. Georgia couldn't find anything personal about Ernest Galloway and the newspapers treated him with a deference that made him seem more mysterious than the loquacious Toomey who gave several jail-house interviews after being caught. She made a mental note to visit the museum and dig further when it opened. She wanted to learn more about the enigmatic uncle whose house she had inherited. She was beginning to think the rumors of him being a crotchety old recluse were wrong. Maybe he was just married to his work. She could understand that.

Georgia was engrossed in an interview Toomey had given the night before he was put to death when the doorbell rang. Startled, she closed the folder and placed it under the laptop. In the foyer, she hesitated. The bell rang again.

Georgia opened the door and immediately took a step back. Dr. Murphy had been standing on his toes and leaning toward the door, trying to peer in the small glass window above it.

He laughed uncomfortably, "I'm sorry. I didn't mean to frighten you. I thought maybe you weren't home."

She forced a smile. "It's fine. I guess I'm just a bit jumpy."

"That's understandable with everything going on lately."

He was holding a small box that obviously contained the research he was bringing her. Georgia hoped he would just hand it to her and then go. Instead, he squeezed past her without waiting for an invitation and stood just inside the door.

"Cold front is coming," he said holding the box out to her.

Despite her reservations, she shut the door.

"It's just a cold front today," he said, "not too bad. But we're getting a monster storm Saturday night."

"I hadn't heard." Georgia took the box from him. "Thank you, Dr. Murphy—"

"Ah, ah, ah." He wagged a finger.

"Tom." Georgia smiled and nodded. "I'm just going to set this down," she said referring to the research he brought her.

He followed her into the kitchen. She saw him eye her laptop and stack of materials on the table. She set the box down in front of it, blocking it all from his view.

Without invitation, he sat down. "I've lived in Aspen for over six years now and I don't remember a single murder before the recent two—I mean three. It has the town jumpy. Not just you."

Georgia wasn't sure what to do. She sat down, smiled briefly and flashed her best poker face trying not to reveal her discomfort. She was shocked by what he said next.

"It seems I might be a suspect in Rachel Winston's murder."

"A what?" The words caught in her throat. She had read Liz Kelly's article and wasn't surprised he could possibly be a suspect, but was shocked that he admitted it so casually. She wasn't sure how to respond.

"A suspect," he repeated and shook his head. "I know, it's preposterous."

She stared at him, didn't know what to say.

"I might as well tell you," he continued. "It's only a matter of time before you find out anyway, but the police are fixated on my wife's missing scarf. She misplaced it at the Winstons' home the night of the party. It seems, since the missing scarf belonged to June, somehow I'm now a possible suspect. But the police haven't said how the damn thing figures into the murder. They've been very incompetent. I didn't want you to be surprised if you heard I was on their suspect list—as ridiculous as that is."

Georgia remembered the flash of color from inside the wooden box that had entombed Rachel Winston's body for so many days.

He leaned toward her. "Georgia?"

"Yes?" She startled back to attention. "Oh, sorry. I just can't think of why a missing scarf would matter." She wouldn't reveal what she knew.

"Neither can I," he said reaching toward her slowly. He pulled a book from inside the box, set it on the table and stabbed a finger on its cover. "Read this. It's good insight into the minds of violent criminals."

Georgia glanced at the title. *Offender Profiling: Theory, Research and Practice.*

"It's what the police should be reading," he added. "It might actually help them find the murderer if they had half a mind to think outside the box."

She felt his eyes probing her. His words *the box* echoed in her mind.

His expression was suddenly grave. "Be careful, Georgia. There is a murderer on the loose in Aspen and I don't think the police have a clue as to who it is." He stood up.

Georgia followed him into the foyer. She wanted him out of her house. Wanted to bolt the locks behind him.

CHAPTER 53

AFTER SEVERAL STRATEGIC purchases and conversations at Stanley Lauren's overpriced boutique, Liz Kelly had securely weaseled her way into the good graces of the old geezer. They sat together at a window table having lunch at a posh cafe.

"How long do you plan to stay in town, Ms. Kelly? I do enjoy a bit of east coast company in the wilds of our woolly state."

Liz had led him to believe she was a journalist from New York City. She hadn't lied, just hadn't corrected him when he assumed it. The old guy probably wouldn't give her the time of day if he suspected she worked for a tabloid in Hollywood. She felt no guilt in the deception.

"I'll be here probably another week or so. I love spring in the mountains and I'm not in any hurry to get back to work."

"How convenient that you have an employer that permits lengthy sabbaticals."

Liz picked nervously at her salad. She needed to redirect the conversation.

"What about you, Mr. Lauren? Do you live in Aspen year-round? A man of your education and sophistication must travel." Over the years, Liz had found that flattery was one of the best techniques to gain the trust of an unsuspecting source.

Stanley Lauren cleared his throat, dabbed at the corner of

his mouth with a white cloth napkin before laying it back on his lap.

"You're very intuitive, Ms. Kelly. In fact, I have a place in Naples, Florida that I spend most of the fall and winter at when I'm not traveling in Europe."

"Oh? What do you do about the boutique when you're not here?"

"Esther Granby—lovely woman and very capable—takes care of it when I'm not here."

Liz remembered meeting the chunky grumpy little woman. She looked more like a gnarled old Russian housemaid than the manager of an upscale women's boutique. "I met Esther when I was in the store yesterday," Liz said. "Lovely woman."

"I had intended to fly back to Naples this month," he said, mindlessly stroking his groomed white beard. "I am usually not in Aspen until May. I came earlier this year because of the Winstons' reception. Walter and Harriet are close friends of mine. I had intended to fly back to Naples immediately, but with all the commotion regarding the youngest daughter's disappearance—now murder—and the subsequent police investigation, I felt it prudent to delay my return trip. At this point, I should probably consider having my things shipped here that I will need for the summer and just stay. Traveling is very tedious at my age."

"That would make sense," Liz said stabbing at the arugula on her plate trying to hide her impatience. She knew she had to tread lightly. She needed to dig, but didn't want to scare him off before she could compile a list of guests the night Rachel went missing.

"I would imagine, being at the Winstons that night, that the police have pestered you mercilessly. It must be terribly inconvenient. Have you compared notes with any of the other guests?"

"We have to some extent, but only casually. Most of the others are acquaintances of mine. I am very fond of Bart and Bunny King—long-time friends. And Ida Caldwell. She is a close friend and very good customer at the boutique, if that doesn't sound too crass. And I do enjoy the company of Tom Murphy, but that wife of his…"

Once again, Liz took notes under the table. By the end of his second coffee she had the names of everyone at the Winstons' house that night.

She would continue to investigate the Tom Murphy angle, but it was possible the handsome doctor was telling the truth, and had no idea what happened to his wife's scarf. Liz was a seasoned reporter and knew not to get bogged down in following the obvious. The juicy stories were usually the ones she had to dig for.

For now, Stanley Lauren was providing a wealth of information. He told her about the gathering at the St. Regis. How the police had questioned all the guests at one time. How they had asked about the missing scarf. He bored her by talking at length about the food and the music the night of the party, then about the enormity of the Winstons' mountainside estate. Suddenly he stopped talking.

Liz watched him stare blankly out the cafe window, then a spark of recognition flashed across his face.

"That's funny," he said to himself.

Liz leaned in. "What is?"

"I remember something now…" He fell silent, stroking his beard.

"Remember what, Mr. Lauren?" He was still staring out of the window. She wanted to reach across the table and slap him out of his trance. "Mr. Lauren?" she repeated in an even tone.

"I may indeed have seen someone pick up the scarf that night—off the table in the foyer. I told you, I noticed it was a

Hermes pattern but a bit shabby…" His voice trailed off as he became lost in thought again.

"Yes, Mr. Lauren?"

"The gentleman… who picked it up…" He frowned, thinking.

"Yes?"

"I didn't think anything of it at the time, but I believe the same gentleman may have been the same one in the boutique a few weeks after the party." He looked up at her. "My memory isn't what it used to be, but I'm almost certain he was the one who purchased my last Hermes scarf."

Before Liz could ask him to elaborate, he continued.

"I don't pay much attention to the news, but wasn't that poor Moss girl strangled with a Hermes scarf? And now the police are asking about one missing from the party," he said still talking mostly to himself as he looked back out the window.

Liz watched in agitated silence as the wheels in the old man's brain creaked and turned.

"What a forgetful and absent-minded old fool I have been. Wouldn't that be odd if I had sold a similar scarf a few weeks later to the same man who might have taken the one from the party?" He looked out the window in astonishment. "Could that man possibly be the…?"

Liz couldn't take it any longer. "Who'd you see pick it up, Stanley?"

Stanley Lauren turned his head and looked at her. Liz knew immediately she had made a careless and damnable mistake by using his first name. His relaxed demeanor suddenly stiffened. His eyes flashed with suspicion.

"I think I've run on and told you well more than I should have, Ms. Kelly."

CHAPTER 54

SHE HAD BEEN snooping around, asking questions, thinking she could find him when even the incompetents in the local police department couldn't.

If she only knew what a fool she looked like running around pretending to be some great investigative reporter. She didn't deserve the paltry bit of fame she had, much less the glitzy new television job in Los Angeles. Some people are just lucky; success and fame are handed to them. But then they start to believe they've earned it—even deserve it—when clearly they don't. That's when they needed to be brought down a peg, or buried six feet under.

Who was she kidding? She was just a pretty face in front of a camera and couldn't come close to matching his wits. He had sent her the scrapbook page to prove it, and wished he could have seen her reaction when she opened the envelope. He had added the bit of poetry at the last minute. The additional touch of mystery had been brilliant.

If he let her, Georgia Glass would continue to make a fool of herself, exposing herself as the lightweight she was when the pretty mask was peeled back. He'd actually be doing her a favor when he killed her—save her further humiliation.

Some people were better off dead.

Georgia Glass was one of them.

CHAPTER 55

WHEN MARK THURMOND wasn't able to get ahold of Eddie Jenkins Wednesday night, he decided to pay him an unexpected visit Thursday morning.

It was eight fifteen when he pulled into the parking lot of the Hidden Manor Apartments on Denver's west side. He looked around. There wasn't a manor house in sight, but a cluster of two-story apartment buildings wrapped in lap siding with several layers of peeling paint.

Mark weaved between potholes in the parking lot until he found the building he was looking for. He double-checked the address in his notebook and parked his car next to a dumpster coated with a couple decades of graffiti. He got out and scanned the parking lot, surprised by the number of cars still there this late in the morning. He wondered how many residents of Hidden Manor had full-time employment.

Mark spotted the 1992 brown Subaru wagon registered to Eddie Jenkins parked next to an old, beat up white van. It was in front of a set of stairs that led to the second-floor landing of Jenkins's building. He took the low-rise concrete stairs two at a time.

He had met Eddie Jenkins face to face twice before. First, during the investigation into Georgia's stalking case, the second time during Tony Paladino's arraignment. Both times it was obvious Georgia considered Jenkins a close friend as well as a work colleague.

He knew it was a shot in the dark that Jenkins would know anything about who was stalking her, but Mark never left a stone unturned and wanted to check his visit with Jenkins off his list. Plus, he wanted to find out about the security system Jenkins had installed in her Aspen home. He hoped it was the same sophisticated setup that had helped nab Tony Paladino.

Mark had knocked several times on the door and was about to give up when Jenkins opened it. He was a mess, dressed in boxer shorts and a yellowed white T-shirt, with bed-head hair and squinted eyes.

"Detective Thurmond?"

"Were you sleeping, Eddie? Sorry about that."

"No, not a problem," he answered rubbing an eye. "Can I help you with something?"

"Do you mind if I ask you a few questions? Regarding Georgia Glass?"

Eddie stepped aside and gestured for him to come in. The living room was dark and small. A laptop computer sat on a round kitchen table along with other electronic gadgets Mark didn't recognize. Computer cables and wires ran everywhere, disappearing behind a dented two-drawer filing cabinet.

Eddie cleared some magazines off a tattered couch and offered the detective a seat.

"Eddie, I'll get right to it. I know Georgia has told you about the recent stalking incidents in Aspen, is that correct?"

"Yes, she did. In fact, I was there Monday and installed a security system and some cameras for her."

"She told me that. I was glad to hear it."

Mark got the details of what Eddie had installed and was satisfied it was the same type of setup that had caught Paladino on camera.

"One more thing, Eddie," Mark said before he left. "Do you have any idea who might be stalking Georgia? A former co-worker? Someone she hung out with after work? An old boyfriend maybe?"

Eddie scratched his head as he shook it. "I've thought and thought, detective, but Tony Paladino is still locked up—she told me that—and I can't think of anyone else who might want to mess with her. Maybe someone hired by Paladino?"

"I don't think so," Mark said. "I almost wish it was."

"What do you mean?" Eddie looked more alert.

"I'm worried this is more personal than a hired employee. This guy is a ticking time bomb. Did Georgia show you the pictures?"

"Yes, she did."

"Then you've seen they're similar to the ones taken when she was here in Denver. Same style, similar distances and angles. Same delivery method. Texted to her from a number registered to a throwaway phone."

Eddie looked concerned. "I hope the cameras I installed will help again."

"I hope so, too. I'm concerned that she's living by herself. It would make me feel better if she still had that linebacker boyfriend of hers around."

Mark expected Eddie to agree with him, but instead saw a momentary flash of anger.

"If that's it, detective, I need to shower and get dressed. I'm due at the station in an hour."

"Yes, that's all. Thank you for your time."

And now I'm going to spend a little time investigating *you*, Mark thought as he closed the door and started down the stairs.

CHAPTER 56

"THOMAS MURPHY IS a mystery," Jack said shaking his head. "I can't find a damn thing about why he resigned his position at Mount Belvedere so abruptly. No rumors. No hint. Nothing."

Chief Rogan frowned and jammed his hands on his wide hips. "That New York investigator didn't dig up *anything*?"

"Nothing—but not because he didn't try. I've tried, too. But every time I've talked to anyone even remotely associated with that hospital, they clam up, get all defensive at even the suggestion that something unseemly might have caused Murphy to resign. I think they're trying to avoid a scandal."

They were in Jack's office at the station. Jack knew Rogan wanted to hear first-hand what the investigator in New York had found out. They were both disappointed that so far, it was nothing.

"Luke and I are going to question Dr. Murphy again—unannounced. Hopefully catch him off guard."

"Good," Rogan replied. "Keep me posted."

Jack was anxious to interview Murphy, but first had to drop off the copies of the Toomey case files he had promised to Georgia Glass. He wasn't happy about it, but a promise was a promise. Besides, she had helped by pointing him in the direction of a copycat; it was a long shot, but maybe she could come up with something else.

In his truck, he turned to Luke. "Want to know what I think?"

Luke waited for his answer.

"I think someone has something on Murphy he doesn't want getting out. Something that would have hurt him or the hospital, or both."

"Blackmail?"

"That's my guess. And since blackmail more often than not involves something financial, I want to see Murphy's financial records—tax returns the years before and after he left New York, bank account records, asset sales or purchases."

Before they reached Georgia's house, Luke had already called the investigator in New York to have him look into Thomas Murphy's financial records.

"Murphy is hiding something," Jack said as Luke got out of the truck. "And we're going to find out what it is."

CHAPTER 57

"HOW LUCKY CAN a guy get? What brings *you* here?" Carlo asked as he sat down on a tufted leather sofa in a back corner of Ferrari's Cigar Bar & Lounge.

Bridget sat in a chair facing him. "Knock it off, Carlo. I'm not in the mood," she snapped.

"Alright then. What is it? I know you didn't come here to see how my day was going."

"I want out, Carlo."

A cocktail waitress swept past them with a tray of drinks.

"Out of what?"

Contempt flashed in her eyes. "I've told you already—out of here, this town, away from you. Out."

"Calm down, Bridget. Don't get overly dramatic. You just need a break. Take some time off. Go visit your girlfriends in San Francisco or Los Angeles. A little retail therapy always makes you feel better. We can talk about everything when you get back."

"I'm done talking, Carlo. Neither one of us has been happy for a long time. Don't try denying it. All your secrets, your weird midnight rendezvous. I don't care anymore."

"You're being ridiculous."

"Am I? No more talking, Carlo. I came by to tell you I was leaving. I've managed to get on the last flight to San Francisco tonight. Mother said I could stay with her until I found something of my own. I'm leaving."

Carlo reached across the small table between them and grabbed her wrist. "You can't do this." He felt the veins tighten in his neck. His breathing came fast and shallow.

Bridget wrenched her arm from his grasp. "You scare me, Carlo. It's over." She picked up her purse from the floor and stood up. Looking down at him she said, "And don't be stupid and blow what little you have left. Half of it is mine. My attorney will be in touch. In the meantime, stay away from me." She turned and marched for the door, nearly colliding with the hostess on her way out.

For several minutes, out of the corner of her eye, a cocktail waitress watched Carlo sit stone still and stare into space. A few moments later, she saw him get up and slowly walk out the door.

CHAPTER 58

GEORGIA HAD HER research separated into stacks across the kitchen table. Somewhere in her piles of notes and lists were clues to the killer's identity. Much of what she had read had been broad platitudes and academic mumbo-jumbo, but several articles had proved useful.

She had determined without a doubt the killer was someone intimately familiar with Gerald Ray Toomey. There were too many coincidences—the victims, the murder weapons, even the timing between the murders—a month apart.

Dr. Murphy's book *Offender Profiling: Theory, Research and Practice* had been intriguing. She had devoured it in a single day and had taken eight pages of notes.

She was sorting through it all when the doorbell rang—a welcome intrusion. She was feeling fatigued and needed a break.

At the door, Detective McCray held out a large manila folder. "As promised, Ms. Glass."

"Thank you," Georgia said taking the folder. She looked around him, saw Detective Martin behind the wheel of his truck and waved.

"Sorry about any inconvenience the search of your home might have caused."

"No, no problem at all," she said. "They didn't find anything, did they?"

"No, they didn't."

Georgia knew they probably wouldn't. The house was virtually empty when she bought it, except for the few pieces of old furniture that had been left behind. If something was there, she thought she would have found it. But she was glad they had checked, and enduring the police search was worth the inconvenience to get copies of the old case files. She hoped they would reveal more about the murders and Gerald Ray Toomey than what had been reported in the newspapers.

"Have any more ideas?" McCray asked.

"Not yet, but I'll let you know when I do. Thank you for this," she said indicating the folder.

"Well, the boss wasn't very happy about it," he nodded toward the truck parked at the curb. "But he'll get over it."

"Well, tell him how much I appreciate it. You can also tell him I won't share the reports or any of the information with anyone without asking him first."

After they left, Georgia settled into the worn couch in the living room, took a deep breath and began going through the old police records.

The first report she read was on the death of Barbara Hancock, Toomey's third victim. She read that Barbara had gone missing April 25, 1957 and was found four days later stuffed into a wooden trunk and left on the side of Highway 21. The report included the same black and white photograph that had been on the scrapbook page Georgia had received through the mail only a few days before. She recognized Ernest Galloway, short and thin in a dark suit and fedora, bent over the trunk that had been tossed alongside a gravel road. Inside the trunk were the remains of a woman, only her stockings and shoes visible in the photograph.

A second picture was a grainy close-up of Barbara still inside the trunk. The body was contorted at odd angles. She wore a heavy coat with a plaid dress underneath. Her face was partially covered by a knit scarf still wrapped around her neck.

The report went on to say that ligature marks on Barbara's neck indicated that she had been strangled with the scarf her mother later identified as belonging to the victim. She was only seventeen when she was abducted on her way to school and murdered. There were no indications of sexual assault.

The rest of the reports were much the same. Elaine Coolidge killed exactly one month before the murder of Barbara Hancock, Mary Lampshire one month before that. Next, Georgia read about Sissy White and Ruth English, victims four and five. All them were young, all strangled and dumped somewhere the killer must have known their bodies would be found.

The comparisons with the current murders were striking, both in their similarities and their differences. It was as if the current killer wanted to copy Toomey, but also wanted to one-up him—raise the profile of the victims, the murder weapon, and the publicity. Likely in his mind, he was raising the bar, the significance. Was he doing it for the notoriety? Obviously the current killer was familiar with Toomey, but how much did he know?

There were details in the police reports that hadn't been duplicated in the recent murders. It was unlikely the current murderer had seen the old police files. The only other places to learn about Toomey were online research and the archives at the museum. Now the head archivist at the museum was dead. Was this a coincidence? Again with the coincidences, Georgia thought.

Georgia's cell phone rang. Jonathan Kramer.

"I know it's short notice," he said, "but there's a great little seafood place that has all you can eat shrimp on Thursday nights. They'll be showing the Rockies game. Are you free later?"

"I am. I'll be ready for a distraction by then."

"You're still working?"

"Yes."

"But you're supposed to be on a sabbatical, remember?"

"I've got a couple more hours to spend in the 1950's and then I'll be done and ready for some company in the present day."

There was silence. "Okay, now I'm confused," Jonathan said with a chuckle.

"I've been reading," Georgia said squeezing her eyes shut and rubbing her temples with her free hand. "Going through old articles and reports on the murders committed in the 50's."

"Well, I'm still confused," Jonathan laughed. "But don't worry, I'll pull you back to the present. Six-thirty sound good?"

"Perfect."

Georgia clicked off and set her phone down on the coffee table in the living room. She hadn't realized she had been sitting so long. Time for a quick break, she thought.

She stood up and stretched, then tilted her head from side to side before heading into the kitchen for a fresh glass of iced tea.

She never saw the tiny camera hidden above the shelves in the sitting room.

CHAPTER 59

THE FIRST COUPLE days back at the museum had been difficult for Susan. Everything reminded her of Brenda. She imagined the terror Brenda must have felt the last few moments of her life, a life that had been cut violently short and left in a bloody heap on the museum floor. She tried forcing the images of that day from her mind but knew it was futile.

It would be impossible for Susan to forget what she saw that morning, and she knew she wouldn't be able to continue working there. The museum board had already started looking for a new chief archivist. She would stay long enough to help Brenda's replacement get settled in, then she would resign.

In the meantime, the board had asked Susan to prepare the museum to reopen the following Monday. Just ten days after Brenda's murder. It was hasty and callous to reopen so soon, but she had her orders. It's probably what Brenda would want anyway, Susan told herself.

Brenda had loved the museum. Susan wondered if she would have loved it so much if she had known that's where she would die.

Susan pushed the morbid thoughts from her mind and continued combing through the unopened mail on Brenda's desk. Next, she would check Brenda's email for any unanswered business, anything that needed to be addressed. Then she would wind up the email account.

She jumped when the telephone on the desk rang.

"Ms. Taylor?"

"Yes."

"This is Detective Martin. I'd like you to do something for me."

Talking to the police made her nervous. Her heart raced and her mouth went dry. She knew it was ridiculous, she hadn't done anything wrong. They were just trying to find out who killed Brenda. But it was that old scary feeling of getting called into the principal's office at school and not knowing why until they tell you that you forgot to give your mother the beginning of school year forms *again*.

Susan took a deep breath. "Sure, detective. I'll do what I can."

"Do you recall if Brenda knew a Dr. Thomas Murphy?"

Susan thought the name sounded familiar, but couldn't remember where she had heard it before. "I'm not sure."

"Unfortunately Brenda's cell phone shattered at some point during the murder. Our tech guys are working on it, but it's taking too long and I don't want to wait. Maybe she kept a synced record of contacts on her computer. Maybe emails, too."

"She did."

"Okay, good. And would you know if Brenda kept a calendar on her computer?"

"Yes, she kept it on both her phone *and* computer."

"Great. First check her emails and contacts for anything referencing a Thomas or Tom Murphy. Then check to see if he shows up anywhere on her calendar. Get back with me as soon as possible if you find something."

"I will."

"And don't let anyone else touch that computer. Depending on what you find, I may send someone to pick it up."

When she got off the phone, Susan finished going through the mail and returned a couple phone calls that had come in for Brenda. It was emotionally wrenching to have to tell people Brenda had died, but Susan got through it. She then turned on Brenda's computer and waited for it to boot up. There must be a reason the police were looking for information on a Thomas Murphy. She wanted more than anything for the police to catch and punish Brenda's killer. And if she could help them in finding him...

It was then she saw it. The name Thomas Murphy in the list of contacts. There was a cell phone number and an email address.

Susan was shaking as she next searched Brenda's calendar for any mention of a Thomas Murphy. She searched for several minutes. There was nothing in the current calendar year. She decided to go back further.

Bingo. Brenda had an appointment with a Dr. Thomas Murphy almost a year ago. Then she found another appointment only a month before that. She kept searching, going back to when Brenda had first started with the museum, but there were no other mentions of him.

Susan looked back at the two appointments. The first just listed Dr. Murphy's name and telephone number. But the second had a note attached. She clicked on it.

Her eyes grew wide as she read.

CHAPTER 60

LIZ KELLY'S STORY would go live later that night, and be on newsstands the next day. She knew it would send shockwaves through Aspen and pique the interest in the murders nationwide.

She read through it one more time.

Stanley Lauren, prominent Aspen merchant to the rich and famous, witnessed a potential suspect in the Rachel Winston murder case snatch the possible murder weapon from the Winston family's spacious mountainside estate.

"I may indeed have seen someone pick up the scarf," Lauren said. "I didn't think anything of it at the time, but I believe the same gentleman may have been the same one in the boutique a few weeks after the party."

Lauren went on to confirm the same man purchased a Hermes scarf from him similar to the one used in the murder of fashion model Greta Moss.

Lauren refused to give further information regarding witnessing the theft of the possible murder weapon, but revealed the guest list for the party the night Winston was abducted.

The story went on to list everyone at the party.

Dr. Thomas Murphy and his wife June. "A taxing woman," according to Lauren. "It was her scarf taken that night. She's an insufferable woman, sits on several local charity boards, but I dare say I don't know anyone who would admit to liking her."

Carlo and Bridget Ferrari. Carlo, a former hedge fund star, is

currently the proprietor of a local cigar bar. Bridget, according to Lauren,
"seems a bit on the flashy side."

Kelly went on to list the other guests, including any tawdry
details she had dug up, but was careful not to overstep the
legal limits. After years writing for the tabloid, she knew from
experience what she could get away with. There was a twinge
of guilt at throwing Stanley Lauren under the bus, but business
was business.

She made cursory mention of the elderly guests to complete the article, but didn't believe they were viable suspects.

She couldn't wait for the story to break. In the meantime,
there was more work to do. She attached the story to an email
to her editors and hit *Send.* That was tonight's story. It was time
to work on tomorrow's.

Liz had talked to Thomas Murphy. She had Carlo and
Bridget Ferrari on her interview list next. But first, she would
to talk to Jonathan Kramer.

She googled him, pulled up his website. He was handsome.
Interviewing Kramer would be tricky, but a lot more enjoyable
than pumping the dusty old Stanley Lauren for information. She
put Kramer's office address into the maps app on her phone.

The office was a remodeled storefront off Hyman Avenue.
When she opened the front door she was greeted by a young
receptionist. Probably late-20's. Even sitting behind the desk,
Kelly could size her up quickly—average height, dowdy, wearing some helplessly dated blouse and blazer. Mouse-brown hair
cut in a shapeless short style. Easy pickings, Liz thought. She
looked around, hoping they were alone.

"Hello, may I help you?" dowdy receptionist asked.

Liz smiled. "Yes. I'm here to see Jonathan Kramer. Is he
in?" She desperately hoped he wasn't.

"No, I'm afraid Mr. Kramer is out showing property at the
moment, but I expect him back shortly."

In an instant, Liz formulated her plan of attack. This wasn't her first rodeo. "I'd like to talk to him about a house," she said in the most innocuous voice she could muster. "I can wait a while, if that's alright. Unless it's an imposition, of course."

"Oh, not at all."

Liz settled into a chair in the small reception area. "So, it must be nice living in Aspen." She wanted to ease in slowly.

"It's okay," dowdy receptionist said. "I've lived here my whole life. It would be fun to live somewhere different sometime."

"How is it working here?" Liz asked looking around the office. "For Mr. Kramer? He's so handsome."

"Oh, it's great," she said. "He's a wonderful boss and a really good real estate agent—fair and honest. You can't say that about some of the other ones in town. But Jonathan—uh, Mr. Kramer—never rushes a buyer into anything. It's never the hard sell with him. He wants to make sure a house is just right for someone even before they put a deposit on it. He will tell buyers…"

"So he's one of the top agents in town? Large or small homes?"

"All of them—big and small. Yes, he's very well respected. He's always very busy."

"So he has lots of friends in town, then, I guess?"

"Oh, yes. Lots." Her smile was brief before it vanished. "Sometimes I think too many."

There's a story there, Liz thought. "Too nice for his own good sometimes?"

"Yes, sometimes. People will take advantage of a nice guy."

"Lots of people would take advantage of a nice person given the chance," Liz agreed shaking her head. "I've met plenty. Anyone in particular?" she asked fishing for a name.

Dowdy receptionist didn't hesitate. "Well, there's one in particular. Bridget Ferrari."

Bridget Ferrari, the woman Stanley Lauren found "flashy." She and her husband, Carlo, were both guests of the Winstons that night and the next ones on her interview list. This could be good.

"I've heard of her," Liz said, pretending to search her memory. "Has sort of a reputation, doesn't she?"

"That's putting it mildly. She's always flitting around town putting on airs, thinking she's better than everyone else. Tight clothes. Expensive jewelry. A real diva. Almost no one likes her."

"Except Mr. Kramer." Liz saw the girl's eyes flash.

"He does like Bridget," she said with a sigh. "But I think he gets tired of her. Sometimes she shows up unannounced, walks right in like she owns the place when everyone knows how busy Mr. Kramer is."

Liz nodded, letting her continue.

"She's always flirting, or crying on his shoulder about something. Just yesterday she was in here trying to make Jonathan—um, Mr. Kramer, feel sorry for her and take her to lunch."

"What would he feel sorry for her about?"

"She said her husband had abused her, was dangerous or something, and that she was scared of him. She showed him some bruise on her arm. A bruise," she snorted. "Big deal. She was just looking for attention and wanted Jonathan to take her to lunch even though he told her he was too busy."

So Carlo Ferrari might be violent, Liz wondered. Domestic violence could add another angle to her story. "*Did* she have a bruise? Did you see it?"

"Maybe," the girl said shaking her head. "I'm not sure. But

if it *was* a bruise, it wasn't much of one. But the point is she expected Jonathan to drop everything and take her to lunch."

She was now using her boss's first name and hadn't noticed. Dowdy receptionist had it *bad* for him.

"Does Mr. Kramer have a girlfriend?" Liz asked gently.

"No," she said then hesitated. "I mean he's *had* girlfriends, he's not gay or anything. They've actually been more like dates, not girlfriends really. But not many and never with anyone very long. He's just so busy, I guess."

"And family? Does he have family in Aspen?" The girl looked up at her, finally suspicious. Liz added, "I'm trying to find out as much as I can about Mr. Kramer before hiring him. He sounds like a wonderful man."

"He's great. You wouldn't regret hiring him. Are you looking for a home in Aspen?"

Liz needed to redirect the conversation. "Possibly. If I find just the right one. But I'm a little nervous about the process of making such a big purchase and need to find someone I can trust. That's why I'd like to find out as much about him as I can—before I meet him."

"Oh, you can trust Jonathan; he's really the best agent in town to have working for you."

There was a brief pause in the conversation. "So," Liz continued, "does he have family here?" she asked again, hoping she wasn't pushing her luck by asking too many questions, but dowdy receptionist continued.

"No, but he has lots of friends here. I believe his father passed away years ago. He never talks much about him, but he has a brother who lives somewhere in California, and his mother lives in Beverly Hills. She used to be in movies. In fact she showed up out of the blue on Monday." She frowned, thinking. "What was her name? Mary... Marilyn... Marilyn— that's it. Marilyn Swanson."

"*Marilyn Swanson* is Jonathan Kramer's mother?" Liz couldn't believe her luck. Idiot girl was too young or too stupid to know Marilyn Swanson was one of Hollywood's brightest stars in her day.

"Yes, she is. She came in Monday. She wasn't very friendly, not at all like Jonathan. Kind of a diva, you know?"

"What was she in town for?"

"I'm not sure, but she didn't stay long. I don't know what they talked about, but he was upset after she left." She sighed. "Poor Jonathan. He's really too busy for all the drama." She went silent, lost in her impossible schoolgirl crush.

Liz wanted to keep her talking. "Maybe they just had a temporary misunderstanding. Since Mr. Kramer is so nice, I'm sure his mother must be nice, too."

The receptionist looked at her suspiciously again, but quickly replaced it with a look of irritation. "I think it was more than that. He was in a terrible mood the rest of the day. In the three years I've worked for him, he's never been that short with me. Well, except maybe that time a seller backed out of large house on Red Mountain at the last minute—"

"So does Marilyn Swanson—his mother—come to Aspen often? I was wondering how close they are? And you mentioned a brother?"

Dowdy receptionist stared at her. Liz knew the look. Conversation over.

"Never mind," Liz said smiling again. "I know that's none of my business. It's just that I'm a huge fan of Ms. Swanson's. She was one of my mother's favorites growing up. It's just so exciting to talk to someone who has actually met her."

"I've probably told you too much already. But Jonathan spends a lot of his time out of the office, and it gets pretty lonely here all by myself, so when someone comes in, I tend to ramble."

"Well, it's been nice rambling with you," Liz said. "But I need to go. I'll call Mr. Kramer and set up an appointment. I probably should have done that in the first place."

"You don't want to wait?"

Liz pretended to look at her watch then stood up. "I can't. I wish I could." She walked to the door and turned back. "I didn't get your name."

"Margie. Margie Berry."

"It was nice visiting with you, Margie."

Poor little Margie Berry didn't know just *how* nice it was. Liz couldn't wait to get back to her computer to start writing. Tomorrow's story in *The National Tattler* would be about Bridget Ferrari and her stormy relationship with her volatile husband, Carlo. Liz wondered if there were any mafia connections. It was an unlikely stereotype, but she would cross her fingers and have the paper's research team look into it just in case.

But now she had a story for Saturday, too. Jonathan Kramer, Aspen's handsome bachelor real estate agent, was the son of aging movie star Marilyn Swanson. The suspect pool was getting more and more interesting.

The town was full of secrets, and she couldn't wait to find out more.

CHAPTER 61

AFTER THEY DROPPED off the old police records at Georgia Glass's house, Jack and Luke had gone straight to question Thomas Murphy again. They hadn't warned him they were coming, and Jack thought the look on his face when he opened the door revealed there was a secret the good doctor hadn't given up. Yet.

When questioned again, Murphy repeated his original story about laying the scarf on the table in the foyer with an assortment of purses. He hadn't seen the scarf since, and didn't know where it was. He said he hadn't even thought of it again until the next morning when his wife brought it up.

When asked again about Brenda Pawloski, Murphy admitted he recalled having gone to the museum a couple years ago, and might have met her, but he wasn't sure. "I remember meeting an attractive woman who was working at the museum," he said. "But I don't remember her name. It *might* have been Brenda Pawloski."

Jack pressed the issue. "What was the reason for your visit?"

"Curiosity. Nothing in particular. I'm a history buff and I hadn't been there since moving to Aspen."

"And you went only once?"

"Yes… I believe so."

"And how long ago was that, exactly?"

"I told you, probably a couple years ago. I can't remember exactly."

"You can't estimate the date any closer than that?"

Thomas Murphy appeared to think about the question then shook his head. "Maybe two and a half? I can't say for sure."

Jack wasn't buying it. He glanced at Luke and could tell by the look on his face that he wasn't buying it either. He hadn't heard back from Susan Taylor at the museum yet, but the probability of her finding Thomas Murphy's name among Brenda's contacts or emails just increased. Jack set a reminder on his phone to call Susan if he hadn't heard anything by mid-afternoon.

"Not much new information," Luke said after they left.

"Maybe, maybe not. I'm surprised he answered questions again without asking for the presence of an attorney. He's got to know he's on our suspect list—that damn story in *The National Tattler* would have tipped him off to that, if he hadn't figured it out already. If nothing else, we've got him rattled; and guilty and rattled is a good way to catch a criminal. They're bound to slip up, make a mistake, say the wrong thing to the wrong person."

"I hope you're right," Luke said.

"I am." Jack had decades of experience and intuition. He might not have the proof yet, but Thomas Murphy was guilty of something, and now they had him back on his heels.

Two things happened immediately following their visit to Tom Murphy that Jack thought could narrow their investigation. He might not have the smoking gun yet, but now it was close enough he could smell it.

The first came by way of a phone call from the investigator in New York.

"I've got a buddy who works in online security for the brokerage house where Thomas Murphy has an account. If it ever gets back that he was our source, he'd be fired on the spot.

But six years ago when Murphy retired from Mount Belvedere, he received two hundred thousand dollars as severance. It was deposited into his investment account at my friend's firm, but fifty thousand was immediately transferred to a bank in New Jersey—to an account in the name of Tiffany Rice."

"Who's Tiffany Rice?" Jack asked.

"You're not going to believe this," the investigator had replied. "Tiffany Rice was a nurse at Mount Belvedere. She abruptly resigned right around the time Thomas Murphy did."

"Where is she now?"

"Moved out of the city right after that. Give me 24 hours, I'll find her."

The second possible break in the case came by way of a phone call from Susan Taylor at the museum. Susan met him at the door and nervously ushered him into Brenda Pawloski's office. She sat down at the desk and tilted the computer screen so Jack could see it.

"Right there," she said pointing a shaking finger at the screen. "See—Dr. Thomas Murphy."

There it was—Thomas Murphy's email address and cell phone number listed among Brenda Pawloski's stored contacts. Yet Murphy had claimed he didn't remember meeting her.

"And look at this," Susan said jerking the computer mouse to the side and clicking it, bringing up a calendar. Several furious keystrokes later, Susan pointed again. "See, there. Dr. Thomas Murphy." She scrolled farther down the page. "And here he is again."

So Dr. Thomas Murphy had in fact visited the museum only a year earlier, not two years like he claimed. And although he had admitted going to the museum, he hadn't mentioned he had visited it *twice*.

"What's the shaded triangle at the top of the most recent one?"

"That means Brenda added a note to the entry in the calendar. This is what I *really* wanted you to see." Her voice shook as she clicked the mouse.

Jack leaned in for a better look.

No more appointments with Thomas Murphy. Creepy.

There were no additional notes, and Susan couldn't provide any further information. But it was a start. If anything, it proved Thomas Murphy was a liar. He *had* met Brenda Pawloski, and not just on one occasion, but two.

When he left, Jack called Chief Rogan, got his voice mail and left a message. "Carl, we're getting closer to some answers. Thomas Murphy has some explaining to do. I should know something more tomorrow, but the next time we visit the esteemed Dr. Murphy, it could be to arrest him."

CHAPTER 62

IT WAS A shame to kill Brenda Pawloski, but he'd had no choice. And just when his plans were back on track, there was another snag to take care of.

He checked the news several times a day—legit news, tabloids, everything. And there it was in *The National Tattler*. Somehow that horrid gossip reporter found old Stanley Lauren and triggered some foggy memory.

The story claimed Lauren had remembered seeing a man with a scarf the night of the Winstons' party. It also revealed he may have sold a similar scarf to the same man several weeks later.

How could he have been so stupid? Damn the old man. When he'd bought the scarf, he hadn't even decided to kill a second time. At least he paid for it with cash. There wouldn't be a credit card receipt with his name on it.

Thankfully the old guy hadn't revealed *everything* to the reporter. He probably didn't remember; everyone knew he was going senile and that frumpy manager woman was really the one who ran his store. Stanley obviously hadn't gone to the police or they would have paid him a visit by now.

But the old guy's memory could come back. He couldn't take the chance.

Stanley Lauren's boutique would close soon. He walked past it several times making sure the old guy was still there, watching as the woman working with him turned the sign in the window indicating the store had closed. She left, leaving Stanley alone.

He lingered in the darkened doorway of a closed shop across the street, pretending to look at his phone. He had darkened the screen so almost no light cast up into his face.

At 9:30 Stanley Lauren finally unlocked the store's front door, stepped outside and turned and locked it again. He was alone.

He followed him at a distance that wouldn't draw attention. The streets weren't crowded, but there were a handful of people from the night's dinner crowd still out. He pulled up the hood to his jacket and kept his head down. It was cold. His breath came out in thick clouds.

After a couple blocks, the old guy turned the corner. He followed him and realized the fates were aligning. They had walked out of the commercial district and onto a darkened residential street. He glanced around. They were alone.

They turned onto an even darker alley, and he knew it was his chance. He quickened his pace. Just as he reached him, the old man heard his footsteps and whirled around.

At first, Stanley Lauren looked confused, then his eyes widened.

He spoke his final words. "It was *you?*"

CHAPTER 63

IT WAS EARLY. Jack Martin sat at his desk drinking coffee and surfing the internet. As he always did, he had picked up the morning papers on the way to work, but had tossed them aside when he got to his office. He wanted to see what the tabloids were saying about the recent murders. In particular, he wanted to find out what Liz Kelly of *The National Tattler* was up to.

The department had gotten a couple calls complaining about her. He knew immediately after the press conference that she would be trouble.

When he found the web page he was looking for he swore under his breath. It took him less than a minute to scan the article.

He accessed the files in the police database and found Stanley Lauren's address and telephone number. When no one answered, Jack hung up and dialed the extension for dispatch.

"Get the nearest unit on patrol over to 239 Bitterroot ASAP. We're looking for Stanley Lauren. I'm headed there now."

He hung up the phone on his desk, grabbed his cell phone and truck keys. He called Chief Rogan on the way out.

"Carl, it's Jack. Liz Kelly from *The National Tattler* put out a story last night outing Stanley Lauren as a possible eyewitness to someone removing the murder weapon from the Winston home the night Rachel went missing. We've dispatched a patrol unit and I'm on my way to Lauren's house now. I sure as hell hope the killer hasn't seen the story yet. Lauren could be in danger."

At the same time, Bunny King was walking south on Sage Street with her toy poodle in tow. Unless the weather was bad, the octogenarian rarely skipped her morning ritual of strolling the tree-lined residential streets near her home. Rarely would she alter the route which she was convinced kept her on the town's few remaining level sidewalks. The last thing she wanted was to take another spill like the one she had suffered ten years earlier that resulted in a full hip replacement and confinement in a Denver hospital for nearly a week.

On most days Bunny never thought about her plastic hip, but this morning something didn't feel right. Maybe it was the cold weather, she thought. The front coming in. She stopped and took a couple deep breaths, rubbing her left side.

"Let's go this way today, Prissy," she said turning the poodle toward an alley that ran behind Sage and Bitterroot. It was a shortcut home. She picked her way between patches of black ice.

She had walked past several garages when Prissy started to pull and whine. "What is it, old girl?" Bunny asked. She looked up the street and squinted. There was something in the road. Prissy pulled her toward it.

It looked like a blanket discarded in the middle of the alley, but as Bunny got closer it became clear it was a long wool overcoat. Then she saw what looked like men's slacks and dress shoes sticking out from underneath. She quickened her pace, pulling Prissy close to her.

"Hello? Are you alright?" Her voice was nervous and shaky. When there was no answer, she slowed her approached until the man's face came into view, the staring eyes and open mouth, a trickle of blood crusted in the neatly trimmed white beard. Bunny screamed.

She turned at the sound of running feet. Detective Martin, thank God. She held her hand over her mouth suppressing the urge to cry out again and pointed down at the dead man.

The detective raced past her yelling something into his cell phone she couldn't make sense of. Then he squatted down and stared into the lifeless face of Stanley Lauren.

When he looked back up at Bunny, she couldn't hold back her tears. "Oh, detective," she cried, shaking her head. "Who would do this to Stanley? What is happening?"

When he didn't answer, she added in a weak cracking voice, "Which one of us is next?"

CHAPTER 64

BY THE TIME Georgia got out of bed Friday morning, it was almost nine o'clock. She couldn't remember the last time she had slept so late, and so soundly. She slipped on her robe and headed downstairs. In the kitchen, she popped an English muffin into the toaster.

It had been a wonderful evening. Jonathan Kramer was such good company. He had apologized again for all the chaos surrounding the recent murders.

"I don't know if you'll ever forgive me for selling you a house with a body hidden in the garage. How do we get past that?" he had asked only half joking.

He had been hesitant to bring it up, not wanting to draw the conversation into something dark, but it was obviously something that still bothered him.

Georgia had smiled at him reassuringly. "I'll admit, it hasn't been the quiet, relaxing first couple weeks in Aspen I had envisioned, but never once have I thought any of this was in any way your fault. So I'd say we're past it already."

He relaxed and sat back in his chair. "You don't know how glad I am to hear that. And I promise, if I ever sell you another house in the future, I'll inspect it *much* closer next time."

"I don't doubt it." Georgia laughed. "But it really hasn't been that bad. The worst of it—aside from finding the body—was the police searching the house. It felt invasive, but it was also a relief when they didn't turn up anything. There's been the looky-loos that walk by and stare. A couple media people have tried calling me, but that seems to have died down, too."

"And now you're lost somewhere in the 50's."

For a second, she was confused, then remembered she had told him about researching the Toomey murders.

"That's something to keep me busy," she shook her head to dismiss the subject. "I have time on my hands, and I thought if I could help the police in even some small way, I might as well."

"So you're reading articles on the old cases?"

"Yes, and some old police reports I was able to wrangle from Detective Martin."

Jonathan raised his eyebrows. "You got copies of official police reports? I'm impressed. I know they don't hand those things out to just anyone.

"Well, I had to do a little arm twisting."

"Pull out the familial connection, 'My uncle was in the department at the time' kind of thing?" he teased.

"No," Georgia laughed and shook her head. "Much worse. I told them if they wanted to search the house, I wanted the old reports."

"Blackmailing the police?" He laughed again. "Now I'm *really* impressed."

Georgia returned the smile. "Don't be. It's really one of my worst traits."

She was glad she had accepted the dinner invitation. It was good to get out, and Jonathan was easy to talk to.

After they had ordered, they touched on topics ranging from politics to sports. He feigned indignation when Georgia admitted she didn't know the NFL draft was the upcoming Sunday, and that the Broncos were anticipating drafting a star receiver from Texas A&M in the first round. In turn, she teased him when he admitted that he almost never watched the evening news, preferring to get his news online.

"Sports and business," he'd said with a grin. "I guess I'm a pretty dull date." It had been easy conversation.

Later, over their seafood dinner, Jonathan had opened up and revealed a part of his life Georgia hadn't known or expected.

"I have a brother," he had told her when she asked about his family. "But we're mostly estranged. I've only talked to him a handful of times since our father died. We used to be close. I guess a death in the family can do that sometimes. Some families grow closer, some grow apart. Ours grew apart."

Georgia could see the sadness in his eyes. He told her how close he had been with his father growing up—Aspen for skiing in the winter, hiking and camping in the summer.

"It was a happy childhood for the most part. But things changed when he died. My mother was devastated. He was such a large part of her life, even with having such different interests. She changed after he was gone—became more cynical, bitter. It's understandable, I guess. But then I got older and realized I didn't have much in common with my mother *or* my brother anymore. I was alone and missed my father. It was a harsh reality that I quite frankly didn't handle very well."

A different picture of Jonathan's life had emerged. From the first conversation they had had over the phone, Georgia had thought of Jonathan as the handsome, successful, well-adjusted bachelor that always had a smile on his face and a friendly word for a stranger. She never would have guessed the hardship and heartache he had endured. As he spoke, Georgia couldn't help but imagine the young boy after his adored father had died, turning his happy little world upside down.

Jonathan went on to tell her about his rebellious phase. "For full disclosure," he had said with a hesitant smile. He told her of charges of juvenile mischief, shoplifting, and even one aggravated assault when he had gotten into a bar fight in his early twenties. "I know now that I was lashing out. But I learned the hard way. Got my life together, worked in the entertainment business in California for a while, then moved out here and never looked back."

Georgia thought of the death of her own father and could understand the pain of his loss. She knew how the trajectory of life can change in a heartbeat. The nights she had spent crying until there was nothing left but the welcome escape into exhausted sleep. After her father was gone, it had been the string of first holidays and first birthdays that would reopen and magnify the pain.

But Georgia had been fortunate. Although she was an only child, she was close to her mother. If anything, their bond had grown stronger following her father's death. Jonathan didn't have that. As she looked across the table, she saw the lost little boy he must have been.

Then he shrugged. "There you have it," he said with a self-conscious smile. "I wanted you to know. Not many people know about my past... *indiscretions*, shall we say. But I would like to see you again sometime, and I want you to know what you're getting into—full disclosure. I hope it won't scare you away."

At first, Georgia didn't know how to respond. Her father, too, had died, leaving a gaping hole in her heart like the one Jonathan had in his. But unlike Jonathan, she hadn't responded with resentment and rebellion. That was never an option being raised by Joni Glass. There was grief, yes, but there was also a house always full of friends and music. There were parties and festivals, idyllic days spent outside filled with sun and laughter. And everywhere around her was her mother's wonderful and crazy art and writing which exuded her inherent happiness. Georgia might have shared a similar experience with Jonathan, but her life had been much different.

She looked across the table at him and laid her hand on top of his. "Thank you for telling me. And I won't say anything to anyone; your secrets are safe with me."

"I know they are." The warm smile again.

If she let herself, she could probably fall for him. Then from somewhere in the back of her mind, the image of Parker Randolph emerged. She realized there were now two men in her life that she could see herself with. But after the nasty breakup with TJ, she knew she had to take future relationships—if there were any—very slow. TJ had been a wolf in sheep's clothing, and she vowed not to make that same mistake twice.

Georgia broke from her reverie, from thinking about the night before. She didn't have time for that now. There were murders to help the police solve, and she only had a few weeks left in Aspen.

She drained the last of the coffee in her cup and re-read the notes she had taken from Ernest Galloway's interrogation of Gerald Ray Toomey.

One of Toomey's quotes made her shiver.

"There's a monster in all of us. You might not see the monster, but it's there."

CHAPTER 65

CARLO FERRARI WOKE the first time to the booming sounds of a garbage truck roaring down the street. He knew immediately he had a hangover. His head throbbed as the truck stopped in front of each house to empty large trash bins the neighbors had set out by the curb. He had gotten up and managed to down a single cup of coffee before deciding to go back to bed.

He woke a second time to the piercing ring of his cell phone. He rolled over and fumbled for the phone on the bedside table, cleared his throat, then answered it.

"Carlo, it's Sylvia. Where is Bridget? She was supposed to be here last night. Her flight was supposed to get in at ten, but I called United. She wasn't on it. Is she there? She's not answering her phone."

His mother-in-law's voice was hitting his brain in rapid-fire bursts. He pushed himself up and sat on the edge of the bed, dragging his free hand down his face. Bridget, he thought, his mind foggy. It was coming back in pieces. They had argued. She was at the lounge. She left.

"Carlo? Where's Bridget?" Sylvia asked again, irritated.

He searched his memory trying to remember everything Bridget had said. He could only grasp clipped pieces. She was leaving the lounge. Going home to pack. Then to San Francisco to stay with her mother. But she never got there. Why? Where was she?

Carlo stumbled to the window and pushed aside the curtain and squinted. The snow in the yard reflected the morning sun like a dagger; his head felt like it would burst. He checked the clock on the bedside table. It was already mid-morning. He tried to think but couldn't remember where he had been the night before. He let the curtain drop and sat back onto the bed.

"Carlo? Are you there? Where is she?"

"I don't know, Sylvia. She was at the lounge yesterday. Sometime around lunch. But she left. She said she was packing and going to stay with you. I didn't see her after that."

"Well, she's not here and never got on the flight. She must still be in Aspen."

"Hold on." Carlo stumbled into the bathroom, the cold marble on his feet hitting him like a slap in the face. He didn't remember drinking. Why would he have a hangover?

Bridget's cosmetics were still scattered across the counter. He opened the door to the large closet they shared and saw an open suitcase set on the large center island. It was empty. She hadn't packed.

He thought of the guest bedroom. She was always complaining of his incessant snoring and sometimes slept there. He checked, but it was empty. The bed was made as if it had not been slept in. Something else occurred to him. He ran barefoot downstairs and outside toward the garage, each footfall on the icy sidewalk shooting searing pain through his legs. He reached for the doorknob, took in a deep breath and held it before he opened the door. Bridget's car was there, but she wasn't.

Where could she be? He tried to think, but could only conjure staccato bits of memory. The lounge. Fighting. His car and patches of road. Trees. Then nothing. It was no use. He couldn't string together any significant amount of memory to make sense of it all.

"Carlo? What is it? Carlo?"

The distant sound of his mother-in-law's voice confused him until he realized he was still holding his phone. "I don't know, Sylvia. I saw her yesterday around lunch, but I didn't see her after that. I got home late last night—"

Sylvia had hung up.

He paced while he thought. Where could she have gone? What had he done yesterday after he saw her? Where did he go? But there was nothing. He remembered nothing. How could that be? This was his longest spell yet.

Twenty minutes later when the doorbell rang, he was ready. He told the uniformed officer he hadn't seen his wife since around noon the day before, then added, "Please, you have to help me find her. I don't know what I'll do if something has happened to her."

He said it with as much concern and worry he could muster, trying to convince the officer he was near panic. He worried he might have had something to do with Bridget's disappearance, and wondered what happened to her, where she was. But deep down, he wasn't sure if he really cared.

CHAPTER 66

JACK STUCK HIS hands on his hips, flaring his jacket, not noticing the bitter morning temperature. He was tired of playing defense and vowed to turn the tables on the son-of-a-bitch that did this to Stanley Lauren. He wasn't going to let this guy set the agenda any longer.

He remembered his interview with Stanley only a week earlier at the St. Regis. Nice old guy with a grandfatherly disposition. Now here he was lying in a woolen heap in an iced-over back alley, his eyes bulged and his mouth frozen in a hideous death gape.

At the interrogation at the St. Regis, Stanley had readily admitted he had seen the scarf that June Murphy had worn the night of the party laying on the table in the foyer. From Liz Kelly's article in *The National Tattler*, Jack thought Stanley must have later remembered seeing someone pick it up. Did he then remember who the person was?

It was possible the old guy mentioned something to the tabloids that had spooked the killer and got him murdered.

Jack was angry at himself for not seeing the article sooner and getting to Lauren first. He would have to put someone in the department on the job of constantly monitoring the media covering the case, especially the tabloids.

Jack stayed at the scene until the forensic team had finished up and the guys from Lester's office had bagged the body.

Luke approached him. "With all the ice, there's not a single decent footprint in the snow until you get nearly a block in each direction. And then there's so many they're worthless."

"Any fingerprints on the body?"

"None."

Jack shook his head. "Hopefully Lester will come up with something in the autopsy," he said knowing the likelihood of the coroner turning up anything of significance was wishful thinking.

"I'm heading back to the station unless you need something."

"No, go ahead," Jack said. "I'll hang around until things are done here."

Jack broke up the small crowd that had gathered at the end of the alley. Once Stanley Lauren's body was taken away, only a small contingent of reporters were left. Liz Kelly was noticeably absent. The reporters peppered Jack with questions he refused to answer.

Something about the murders of Stanley Lauren and Brenda Pawloski didn't fit the narrative. Jack was convinced Stanley and Brenda had gotten in the killer's way, weren't part of the master plan. But a murder of another high-profile attractive woman was. And it would likely happen soon, he reminded himself. Time was running out.

The phone in his pocket vibrated. It was Luke.

"Jack, Bridget Ferrari has been reported missing."

Jack took in a deep breath, then released it slowly. "What did her husband say when he reported it?"

"Carlo Ferrari wasn't the one who called it in," Luke replied. "Bridget's mother did."

Jack thought about it a moment. "Where is Carlo now?"

"At home. Dispatch sent a patrol officer to inform him and to take a statement. I'm headed over to question him now."

"I'll meet you there."

Jack was satisfied he had done what he could at the scene. He got into his truck and pulled away, turning south onto Sage Street.

Could it be possible the killer had abducted his third high-profile victim?

Was Bridget Ferrari already dead?

CHAPTER 67

JACK MARTIN AND Luke McCray arrived at Carlo Ferrari's house at the same time. Jack stopped the junior partner on the sidewalk near the street. "Fill me in."

Luke nodded. Jack had given him a list of things to check before they got there. "No bank account withdrawals on any of the known accounts. The last credit card charge was yesterday morning at Starbucks. The ticket was signed for by Carlo. And Bridget's cell phone has been offline since last night—no tower pings since then, and the ones earlier in the day were off the tower here in Aspen. She bought a ticket to San Francisco yesterday on United but didn't use it. Bobby McDonald was the one by here earlier and took Carlo's statement."

"What was his reaction when Bobby told him his mother-in-law had filed a report?"

"Bobby said: 'confused,' 'agitated.'"

"Guilty?"

"Possibly," Luke said. He turned his back to the Ferrari house and lowered his voice. "He told Bobby he didn't know anything about his wife's disappearance, but Bobby said he seemed nervous."

"Nervous about his wife being missing? Or nervous about getting caught?"

Luke shook his head once. "I don't know."

"Let's go find out."

Carlo Ferrari opened the front door. "I have no idea where she is," he said pushing stubby fingers through his black hair. "But come in." He turned and waved the detectives into the house.

Although Carlo appeared clean-shaven and wore starched khakis and a collared shirt, Jack noticed the room smelled of cigars and alcohol.

Carlo sat at one end of a long velvet sofa and gestured for the detectives to take a seat.

"I've been wracking my brain wondering where she could have gone," he said smoothing his pants over his thighs. "We were just talking about moving back to San Francisco, about me selling the lounge and us retiring somewhere in Pacific Heights with a view of the bay. A friend of hers lives there and is out of town. She offered the use of her apartment if Bridget wanted to look at houses. That must be where she's gone since she's not at her mother's."

Luke spoke next. "We've checked flights out of Aspen. Your wife's name showed up on one late yesterday but she never made it to the airport."

Jack watched Carlo for a response. He was silent. Calculating. Wondering where his wife had gone? Or what to say to cover up her disappearance?

Carlo shook his head and lifted his arms in a frustrated shrug. "I don't know what to tell you. My wife is impulsive. She could have changed her mind—gone somewhere else." He kneaded a creased forehead as he thought about it, then added, "New York or Los Angeles. She has friends all over and has been complaining about the long winter we've had here. She was sick of the snow and bugging me about taking a vacation, going somewhere warm.

Carlo squeezed and released his hands into fists, finally rested them on his knees. "I've tried her cell phone several times, but she could be in an area with no service. It's spotty in the mountains. Then there's the desert through Utah and Nevada—probably no service there either." He threw his arms up in frustration. "And the battery could be dead. She's forever letting it die and not having a charging cord with her."

Jack sat quiet, letting Carlo talk. His broad girth heaved up and down with each breath and hand gesture. He was getting agitated.

"We had an argument at the lounge," Carlo admitted. "Bridget came in for a drink but left early. I haven't seen her since."

"And you have no idea where she could be?" Jack asked.

"No. There's an infinite number of possibilities where she could be—gone to see friends, gone shopping." Carlo shook his head.

Jack watched him, taking it all in—what he was saying, his body language. There was no doubt Carlo Ferrari was nervous, but Jack wasn't convinced he was responsible for the disappearance of his wife. He looked confused.

Carlo continued. "It's not unusual for Bridget to throw a tantrum and leave without telling me. She's always been a bit... willful."

He talked a while longer—made excuses, threw out more theories. He was trying hard to convince someone Bridget could be anywhere. But convince who? Law enforcement or himself?

Jack couldn't tell—couldn't decide if Carlo Ferrari was a scared, frustrated husband concerned for his wife, or if he had something to hide. It might be both, he thought.

"Would you mind if we took a look around?" Jack asked.

"No. Of course not."

As soon as Carlo said it, Jack saw him break out into a cold sweat, his breathing become fast and shallow. "First I'd like to see the garage," Jack said, studying Carlo closely. "Mrs. Ferrari drives a black Range Rover, doesn't she?"

Carlo swallowed hard. "Detective Martin, I'm a patient man, but the way this investigation is going… I'm getting uncomfortable with your tone regarding my wife's disappearance. I'm sure she's somewhere with friends and I'll hear from her soon; and when I do, I'll let you know.

He took in another deep breath before he continued. "In the meantime, if you have any more questions for me, I think you'll need to talk to my attorney first. And if you want to search my house, you're going to need a warrant."

Outside, Jack turned to Luke. "I want you to do something for me. Nobody has CCTV video surveillance in this town because they don't need it—there's no crime."

Luke nodded.

"But I want you to pay another visit to the guys that run the webcams—the touristy ones they have set up around town and over at the ski slopes—but look at just the ones in town. See if we can catch Bridget on any of the cameras last night, and look to see if anyone was with her."

"Will do," Luke said opening his car door.

Jack hesitated. "And while you're at it, check the nights Rachel Winston went missing and Greta Moss was murdered. It's a long shot, but sometimes long shots pay off big."

CHAPTER 68

GEORGIA WENT OVER her lists and charts again. The killer would have some connection to Aspen. Maybe heard stories of the early murders. Maybe even lived in Aspen when Toomey had committed them. She almost immediately dismissed the last idea—that would make the killer too old. From the research studies Dr. Murphy had given her, she had learned that most serial killers were active in their 20's or 30's. Someone living in Aspen during the mid-50's would now be three to four times that old.

It would be someone familiar with the earlier cases. In small towns everywhere, locals talk. The murders would have been popular gossip in coffee shops, beauty parlors, and on front porches for many years. He could have heard the stories from locals.

But given the amount of time that had passed since then, it was more likely the current murderer would have researched the Toomey cases later, recently even.

It would be someone who blended in, someone who could mingle with the residents of Aspen without being noticed, who wouldn't raise any red flags—an edge-sitter. She remembered the term Dr. Murphy had used.

Georgia dug through a stack of papers until she found the Winstons' guest list the night Rachel went missing. She had read over the names at least a half a dozen times before, but decided to read them again.

The murderer would be on this list, or at least be someone close to them. It would be someone local. She had gotten half-way through the list when her phone rang.

"Hi, Parker, what's up?" she answered.

"I'm sure you've heard about Stanley Lauren."

"I did. It's terrible," Georgia replied.

"My guess is that it was *The National Tattler* article that did him in. Have you read it yet?"

"No, I haven't seen it."

"Poor guy didn't have a chance. You should read it, I'll text you the link. But you should think about keeping a low profile until this guy is caught. Murder has become rampant in that town."

"Parker—"

"I know, I know, you're a big girl and can take care of yourself. That's not why I'm calling." He hesitated before he continued. "I tried calling you a couple times last night, but you didn't answer."

"I went to dinner. I had my phone with me but forgot to charge it before I left and it died."

"Too engrossed in your research to remember to charge your phone?"

"Probably," Georgia admitted. "I plugged it in as soon as I got back but didn't have any messages. Just a couple texts from my mother and a friend from Denver."

"Yeah, I didn't want to bother you. It wasn't anything important. Just checking in to see if you had changed your mind about starting work early."

She laughed, but before she could reply he continued. "Don't worry, I haven't held out much hope you had changed your mind. I really was using it as an excuse to check in, hear for myself that you were okay."

She could see herself falling for Parker Randolph. Maybe someday, she thought, but it was too soon after TJ. She changed the subject.

"How's the book going?" she asked.

As he talked, she spread a small stack of photocopied newspaper articles across the table, mindlessly arranging them equal distance apart. She had nearly finished the stack when one of the articles caught her attention. She hadn't noticed it before. She pulled the page toward her, squinted at the grainy black and white photograph.

"Parker, can we talk later? Something's come up."

She read the caption below the picture. It was the boarding house where Gerald Ray Toomey had been living. Clapboard siding with a dozen same-sized windows, a small porch at the front door. It was similar to most of the old Victorian houses in town, including her own, just larger. But there was something different, something familiar.

She rifled through a drawer in the kitchen until she found her magnifying glass, sat back down and leaned over the photo. There was a window in the top of the gable, in an unusual starburst pattern. She had seen it before.

Then it came to her. Last week— the same starburst window, the same house. It belonged to Tom and June Murphy.

CHAPTER 69

SUSAN TAYLOR HAD sat at Brenda Pawloski's desk for nearly two hours, meticulously going through every file, notebook, loose document, and scrap of paper. It felt like she was invading the privacy of her deceased boss and friend, but Detective Martin had asked her to do it.

She had been told a uniformed officer would be there to assist her—probably to watch over her, she thought. She understood why Detective Martin had asked her to go through Brenda's things, and knew it needed to be done, but she didn't have to feel comfortable about it.

Susan carefully picked up the framed photograph of Brenda and her grandfather, the legendary Bernard Pawloski who had emigrated to the United States from Poland as a boy, and gone on to discover many of the fossilized dinosaur remains in the Colorado Rockies.

Susan assumed Brenda had inherited her grandfather's love of history, and that's why she had gone on to study archeology at the University of Colorado.

She pulled the photograph closer to get a better look at the bearded old man. Next to him was a young Brenda, brush in hand. They were standing over a dig somewhere in the mountains a long time ago. Susan wondered if the two kindred spirits were now somewhere together again. She wiped a tear away and forced herself back to work.

"Look for anything that catches your eye," Detective Martin had told her. "Anything that looks peculiar or out of place. Anything that might jog a memory or seem suspicious. Don't look for anything in particular, keep an open mind and just look."

She would notice anything out of the ordinary before someone from the police department would, he had told her. Somewhere there might be a letter, a contract, or a name or phone number that didn't feel right—that raised a red flag.

But so far, she hadn't found anything. Susan slipped the last stack of files back into the desk drawer and pushed it closed harder than she had intended.

Officer Bobby McDonald came in to check on her. "Need any help yet?"

Susan attempted a smile. "No, thank you."

"You alright?"

"I'm fine."

He looked at her with what she recognized as sympathy.

"Investigations can get to you," he said.

Susan nodded. It *had* gotten to her, she thought. But she had to get it done and get out of there.

The museum board wanted her to stay on, at least until they could hire a new chief archivist. But Susan had decided she wouldn't stay. She kept remembering the grisly sight of Brenda's body crumpled on the floor in a pool of blood. She wanted to finish here, find a new job.

"I'm just about done," Susan told Officer McDonald as she put the remaining files and notebooks back in their various drawers.

"I guess you didn't find anything?"

Susan shook her head.

He nodded. "I'll let Detective Martin know. Want me to stick around and walk you to your car?"

"No, but thank you. I'll be fine."

"Okay, then. Have a nice night." Officer McDonald left.

Rearranging the items on top of the desk to where they had been before, Susan realized she had overlooked the desk's shallow top drawer. There was no handle like on the side drawers, but was accessed from a hidden finger pull underneath. It would have been easy to miss. Probably nothing in there, Susan thought, but she decided to look anyway.

She pulled it open. There was an assortment of pens and mechanical pencils thrown in with a handful of paper clips. She pulled out several small Post-It notepads and shuffled through the blank pages. Nothing.

She was about to close the drawer when she noticed something shoved to the back. Pulling the drawer out further, she found a small stack of business cards wrapped in a rubber band.

The cards were for various contractors she knew had done work at the museum at one time or another. High Water Plumbing & Heating, Aspen Restoration Floorworks. There were also a couple cards of museum directors from across the state, names that were familiar to her.

But there was one card Susan didn't recognize. She turned it over in her hands trying to remember if she had heard the name before. She didn't. The name wasn't familiar to her and Susan didn't know why Brenda would have stored his card in her desk.

Susan rubbed a thumb along the edge and read the name again. She shrugged. It was probably nothing. But she would give it to Detective Martin and let him decide.

CHAPTER 70

"CARLO CLAMMED UP. Said he won't talk to us without his lawyer," Jack said.

Jack and Luke were in Chief Rogan's office briefing him on what they knew regarding Stanley Lauren's murder and the disappearance of Bridget Ferrari.

Rogan shook his head. "It doesn't sound like he's worried about his missing wife. What did you find in the house?"

"He wouldn't let us look. First, he agreed to it, then changed his mind."

"So let's get a warrant."

"That's in the works. We plan to be back over there this afternoon."

Satisfied, Rogan nodded.

Jack continued, "Before he stopped talking, he told us he thought his wife was probably in San Francisco visiting a friend. Then he threw out the possibility she could be visiting friends in Los Angeles or New York."

"So he doesn't even know what coast she could be on?" Rogan asked. "What about her car? Where is it?"

"We don't know yet. We've got an APB out on it to see if anyone spots it. But it could still be at the house. We'll know after we get inside."

"Get someone over there to watch the house so the

husband doesn't try to move it if it is there—or move *anything else* that might be in there."

"We're a step ahead of you, Chief," Jack said. "We had surveillance there before we left the premises."

"Did he say anything else before he started talking lawyers?"

"Only that he and his wife had argued the day before, at the cigar bar he owns. Luke spoke with a waitress there today."

Luke flipped open the notepad on his lap. "The waitress was working yesterday when the Ferrari's argued. It apparently was pretty heated. She said Mrs. Ferrari said something about being scared of Carlo then got up and left. That was the last time the waitress saw her—as far as we can tell, the last time anyone saw her."

Rogan raised a bushy eyebrow. "Get back to me after you search the house. It sounds like there's more to this story than Carlo Ferrari is letting on."

"There's something else," Jack said. "We need to consider Bridget Ferrari might be the third strangling victim."

There was a long silence. Rogan understood where Jack was coming from but wanted to know more. "What are you thinking?"

"She fits the profile. She's not in her 20's like Greta Moss or Rachel Winston, not by a long shot, but she's beautiful, high profile." Jack shrugged and shook his head. "Frankly I don't have a good feeling about finding her alive."

Rogan settled back in his chair and frowned. "It's a problem the husband isn't talking and, so far, looks damned guilty of *something*. But how does this connect to the recent murders?"

"It's a theory," Jack said. "I hope I'm wrong."

Luke spoke up. "Maybe she hasn't been murdered. The killer could be holding her somewhere."

Jack nodded. "Possibly." He turned his attention back to Rogan. "But not likely. She might have gone home after the argument with Carlo, been abducted from there. Maybe she got home, packed, but never made it out of town. Maybe she *is* out of town—California, New York."

Rogan leaned forward, lacing his fingers and laying his meaty forearms on the desk. "That's a lot of 'maybes,' Jack. Get me some answers."

The room was silent with mutual agreement and determination.

Jack spoke next. "We've got Thomas Murphy coming in any minute."

"How's that going?" Rogan asked.

"We'll see what he has to say when we confront him about his visits to the museum. He claimed he doesn't remember meeting Brenda Pawloski. Let's see his reaction and hear what he has to say when we tell him we have evidence that proves he did—twice."

Jack was at his desk when the department's receptionist buzzed him from the lobby. Thomas Murphy had arrived five minutes early. Detectives Martin and McCray showed him into the only interrogation room in the building and asked him to have a seat. The room was small and sterile, four white walls with a grey linoleum floor. A square table and four chairs where the only furnishings in the room.

Thomas Murphy took a seat and waited for the detectives to speak.

Jack got right to the point. "Dr. Murphy, we have evidence you did in fact visit the museum and met with Brenda Pawloski on two different occasions."

Tom Murphy kept his cool. Reiterated he didn't remember meeting Brenda Pawloski. He admitted again having gone to the museum out of curiosity—he was a history buff and had gone for recreation. He had simply forgotten he had gone

twice. Jack asked him a couple more questions but soon realized he wasn't getting anywhere. He changed the subject.

Jack asked him point blank: "Dr. Murphy, tell me why
at the height of your career, as the Chief of Staff at Mount
Belvedere Hospital in New York City, you would abruptly
resign and leave town?"

Tom Murphy sat silent a moment before he replied. "I
don't see how my previous employment has any bearing on the
ongoing investigation."

"It does. Please answer the question." Jack's tone was even.

"If you must know, I was sick of the stress of running one
of the world's largest hospitals."

"So leaving Mount Belvedere didn't have anything to do
with Tiffany Rice?"

Jack saw the color drain from the doctor's face. He had
to be careful; he needed to be direct, but not too harsh. He
had Murphy rattled, but he didn't want him to walk. He was
there voluntarily.

"Doctor, did Tiffany Rice have anything to do with why
you left New York? We know you paid her fifty thousand dollars right after you resigned."

The room was silent. The doctor looked from Luke back
to Jack, then took in a deep breath and shifted in his seat.
"Tiffany Rice was a nurse at Mount Belvedere—a conniving
vindictive young nurse."

"You had an affair." It was a guess. But Jack hit pay dirt.

"Yes, I had an affair. And I admit the relationship was
inappropriate. She was on my staff at the hospital."

"And you were married," Jack added.

Tom Murphy looked like he wanted to spit nails. "Yes. I
was married." He placed his hands palm down on the table and
took in another deep breath. "I eventually told Tiffany it was
a mistake—it was over. I think she had come to rely on the

dinners and the small gifts, and the cash I would leave her now and then. She didn't take it well and threatened to go public with the affair unless I gave her fifty thousand dollars."

"Which you paid her."

"I had no choice. She said she would swear I forced her into the relationship by threatening her job. She was ready to cry sexual harassment. Which would have been a lie," he said stabbing the air with his finger. "So I paid her."

"And then you resigned and left?"

"That happened just before I gave her the money. Somehow rumors reached the hospital board. I was approached by a couple of the board members who strongly suggested an early retirement to keep from having the hospital involved in a scandal. So I resigned. I wanted to place distance between myself and the whole mess, and my wife and I had been vacationing in Aspen for years, so we moved here."

"Leave the problems behind."

"Yes. Well, that was the idea initially. But it seems the publicity surrounding the recent murders got Tiffany's attention. She seems to think there would be renewed interest in her sexual harassment story since it's my wife's scarf the police are looking for and it appears I'm a potential suspect. She's threatening to sell her story to the highest bidder unless I pay her another $10,000."

"Were you planning on paying it?"

"No. Who's to say the blackmail would *ever* stop? I can't keep paying her indefinitely. I was going to tell her I wouldn't ever give her another dime, consequences be damned."

His belligerent posture long gone, Tom Murphy dragged his hands down his face and let out a long sigh. "I just really wish the whole thing would go away." He looked at his watch again and stood up. "I need to go."

Jack spoke up. "Just a couple more questions, doctor."

Tom Murphy reluctantly sat back down.

"Where were you between nine o'clock last night and six o'clock this morning?"

"At home, why?"

"You mentioned before that you walk at night. You didn't take a late-night walk last night?"

He stared at Jack a moment. "I did. I probably went out around ten."

Jack scribbled the time in his notebook then looked back up. "Did you happen to walk with someone?"

"No, I was alone. Sometimes my wife walks with me, but she is out of town."

"Where is she?"

"Denver. Looking for musicians to play at some charity function she's working on."

Jack thought about it a moment. The last thing he needed was another missing wife, but Thomas Murphy hadn't fidgeted, or shifted in his chair since coming clean on Tiffany Rice. Jack thought he was telling the truth. "You live in the same area of town as Stanley Lauren, don't you?"

"I do—just around the corner. I heard about his murder. It's horrible. He was a nice old guy."

Jack watched the doctor's body language closely, and listened for any unusual inflections or tone of voice. "Did you see Mr. Lauren on your walk last night?"

"No, I didn't," he answered without hesitation.

"Did you happen to see anyone you knew while you were out?"

"Not that I can recall. I wish I could be of more help, detective, but I really need to get going."

Jack got up, opened the door and stepped to the side. "We'll be in touch."

With nothing but a curt nod, Thomas Murphy walked out.

"So what do you think?" Luke asked after Jack shut the door.

"A few things. I think the doctor came clean on Tiffany Rice because he knew he had to—the cat was already out of the bag. If anything, the whole affair with the nurse shows he's attracted to younger women, but if you're going to kill one, why not the one who is blackmailing you?"

"And Tiffany Rice is still very much alive."

Jack blew out his breath. "Exactly," he said almost disappointed.

"But what about his alibi—or *lack* of an alibi?"

"That's a problem. Very inconvenient—or convenient—for the good doctor that he never runs into anyone he knows on the late-night walks of his. There's nobody who can confirm his alibi."

When Jack walked back into his office, there was a small envelope sitting on his desk. His name was written on the front along with the note: "I found this in Brenda's desk. I don't know where or when she got it, but you said to bring to your attention anything that stood out. I don't know why Brenda would have this man's card." It was signed Susan Taylor.

Jack opened the envelope and pulled out a business card. He read the name on the card and vividly remembered the person having denied ever meeting Brenda Pawloski.

Jack called Luke in and handed him the card. "This was just delivered. Susan Taylor found it in Brenda Pawloski's desk."

Luke read the name, looked back at Jack and raised his eyebrows.

CHAPTER 71

MARGIE BERRY KNEW Jonathan was angry with her when he sailed into the office without so much as a nod in her direction.

Margie couldn't blame him. She had been stupid to run her mouth. But she didn't know Liz Kelly was a reporter when she spoke with her. Surely that made a difference. She desperately hoped he would forget all about it.

The day before, when Jonathan returned to the office, Margie had told him a nice lady named Liz Kelly had come by to see him.

His face had gone white. "Liz Kelly?" he exclaimed. "The reporter for *The National Tattler?* Why would she come to see me?"

"She's a reporter?" Margie asked.

"The worst kind. Why was she here?"

"She said she wanted to talk to you about a house," Margie said, her voice growing shaky. "She seemed really nice."

"Good God, Margie, I hope you didn't say anything to her." He stared at her waiting for an answer.

Shocked by his unexpected response, Margie sat with her mouth open.

He leaned toward her. "Margie… you didn't talk to her, did you?"

Margie remembered the personal information she had

revealed and felt the familiar flush when her face turned a blotchy shade of crimson. "I—I—"

"I what? Spit it out! Whatever you said to her is going to be twisted and turned and will show up as vicious gossip on the internet. Do you read *The National Tattler?*"

Margie nodded. "Sometimes."

"Then you know Liz Kelly is a ruthless gossip and that rag she works for ruins lives. My mother and brother have been victims of their slander numerous times. They'll run trash stories without so much as a kernel of evidence. Twisted lies. You have to tell me *everything* you talked about."

Margie shook her head, trying to shake away the memory of the day before. It had been one of the worst days of her life. She would never forget the contempt and fury she saw on Jonathan's face when she recounted her conversation with Liz Kelly, even with leaving the most damning details out.

How could she have been so stupid? She had spent her life being stupid. But that reporter woman had been so cunning, and had seemed so nice. Margie was sure anyone would have been fooled by her.

She checked the time on her phone—10:30. She hesitated a moment, then opened the bottom drawer of her desk and pulled out the half-eaten package of Oreos. The familiar crunch and sweet goodness relaxed her. She ate until the last cookie was gone.

She was pushing the empty package to the bottom of the trash can when her cell phone rang. It was her roommate.

"Have you heard about the murder?"

"Which one?" Margie asked brushing crumbs from her mouth.

"The latest one," her roommate said breathless. "Stanley Lauren. That old man who owns the fancy boutique down the street from your office. He was found dead in the alley behind his house this morning. I saw it on Facebook."

Margie pushed her mouse to wake up the computer, her Facebook account was still logged in from earlier that morning. She found the article and skimmed it, then scrolled through the comments. Someone had posted a link to an article in *The National Tattler*. Margie clicked on it.

The article, written by Liz Kelly, had been posted the night before. She then scrolled through the comments to see if there was any updated information. As she read, her eyes grew wide. When she finished, Margie got up from her desk and stumbled into Jonathan's office.

Her voice quivered. "Mr. Kramer, there's been another murder. Stanley Lauren from the boutique down the street is dead."

"What?" Jonathan said as if he hadn't heard her correctly.

"That Ms. Kelly…" Margie said wide-eyed. "She reported last night that Mr. Lauren had seen someone take a scarf from the Winston house. She said it was probably the scarf used to kill Rachel Winston. She reported that—and now he's dead."

"That's terrible," Jonathan said and dropped his gaze in disbelief. "He was such a nice old guy."

"Do you think Dr. Murphy killed him?" Margie asked taking a step further into Jonathan's office.

He frowned at her. "Why would you think that?"

"The article said the scarf probably belonged to June Murphy. And she said she gave it to her husband then never saw it again."

"I've heard that story already," Jonathan said. "I'm sure the police are going to look at him closely, but you can't believe everything Liz Kelly writes. I told you that woman and her paper peddle gossip and lies. But let me know if you hear anything else."

Margie managed a nod and stood staring at her boss, thinking. Another murder. How many was that? She realized her mouth hung open and shut it.

Jonathan got up and came around his desk. Margie's knees grew weak. Just when she thought they would finally have an intimate moment, Jonathan gently turned her around and guided her toward the door. Her heart sank as he shut it behind her.

Before she got back to her desk, Jonathan opened the door again and leaned out. "Would you order lunch around noon? Get Chinese. And if you're not planning on getting out for lunch, go ahead and order something for yourself, too."

As Jonathan closed the door, Margie called out to him. "Do you want me to wait to make sure Mrs. Ferrari doesn't show up unexpectedly again?" She tried to say it casually but heard the wounded, sarcastic edge in her voice.

"No—Mrs. Ferrari won't be coming around. She's moving back to San Francisco."

"Moving? Permanently?"

"Yes," Jonathan answered and closed the door.

Jonathan thumped a pen on his desk. He had a million things to do. First, he needed to call a client about an offer he had just received for their condo. The offer was too low and he had already come up with a figure they would counter at, but would run it by his client first.

He reached for the phone on his desk but before he could dial the number, Margie announced over the intercom that he had a call.

"Jonathan Kramer," he answered.

"Mr. Kramer, this is Detective Martin."

"Yes, detective?"

"I need to talk to you."

CHAPTER 72

WHEN THE BARTENDER hollered *last call*, Eddie Jenkins waved a hand signaling for one more. The bar might be closing, but he had lost his job and wasn't done drinking yet, not by a long shot.

He had plenty of time on his hands, could stay out all night if he wanted. No need to go home since he wouldn't be going into work the next morning.

Eddie slammed back what remained of his fourth cheap whiskey on the rocks, and handed the empty glass to the bartender in exchange for a full one.

"You alright, buddy?" the bartender asked.

"Fine," Eddie said with a dismissive wave.

I am fine, Eddie thought. *And I'm going to be better than fine after tomorrow night.*

He would drive to Aspen the next day. But that was tomorrow. He had to get through tonight, first. He rubbed his temple with a sweaty hand, splashing whiskey onto the bar, then took another long draw of his drink to dull a rising rage that threatened to overtake him.

Everything was Georgia's fault. She shouldn't have left Denver—left him. But she had always thought she was too good for him. All the rejections she'd flung at him over the years, then pretending to be his friend. Maybe he could have handled it if she had stayed, but she left. He knew now that she had used him—used him to get ahead in her career, used him as a crutch when she dumped that meat-head boyfriend and when she thought she was being stalked by a fan.

And now he had been fired. That was Georgia's fault, too. The station told him it was because he had become unreliable—didn't show up to work on time, called in sick too many times, blah, blah, blah.

He stuck his fingers in his hair, grabbed chunks and squeezed, and let out a low growling sound. It was all her fault. If she hadn't left, he wouldn't have had to waste time driving back and forth to Aspen. All the hours on the road, the nights spent in the van, of course he was coming in late and having to take time off.

Then there was the new reporter, Lisa Starks. Maybe he would make *her* life miserable next. When he was let go, the HR director at the station hadn't mentioned Lisa, but Eddie knew the upstart wannabe must have complained about him. But that was Georgia's fault, too. If Georgia had stayed, he would have been promoted to a studio camera job by now.

The nightmare he now lived was all because of Georgia Glass. It was time to turn the tables. It would be *her* nightmare next.

CHAPTER 73

JACK MARTIN STROLLED into Jonathan Kramer's office, gave the nervous receptionist his name and asked to see her boss.

Jonathan immediately came out and greeted Jack, ushering him into his office.

"What can I do for you, detective?" Jonathan asked with a skeptical smile. "You in the market for a new house? Condo maybe?" His voice sounded hopeful that would be the reason for the visit.

Jack knew talking to the police made most people nervous. He saw that Jonathan Kramer was no exception. "Thank you, but no. I want to ask you a few more questions."

"Sure thing."

"You told us you had never met Brenda Pawloski."

"That's right, I haven't."

"We have a business card of yours that was found in her desk at the museum."

"Huh," he mumbled. He looked surprised, then pointed to a card holder on his desk. "I'm in real estate. I hand them out all the time without even thinking about it, sometimes I give people extras to give to friends and colleagues."

Jack saw there were at least a couple dozen cards in the holder on his desk.

Jonathan must have seen him looking. "I also keep them in

the reception area, in a holder on the table between the chairs. And in a small box outside for when the office is closed. You'll see them tacked on the cork board heading to the bathrooms at Poacher's Pub and a dozen other places around town."

Jack nodded. "Let me ask you something else. Have you ever heard of Gerald Ray Toomey?" Jack thought there was no indication on his face that he had.

Jonathan pursed his lips and shook his head. "No, should I?"

"He was a serial killer in Aspen back in the 50's. Strangled his victims with scarves—a month apart."

Jonathan thought about it a moment then his eyes grew large. "Is there a connection? With the Winston and Moss murders?"

"We think there might be."

While the detective was there, Margie had rolled her chair close to the door to Jonathan's office to find out what they were talking about. She had heard bits and pieces of the conversation. A copycat serial killer? In Aspen? The possibility was too terrifying—and exciting at the same time. When the detective left, Margie immediately started texting everyone she knew.

CHAPTER 74

JACK WAS AT the trailer when dispatch called him about a group of teenagers finding a body. There was no description yet. He didn't know who it was, but he had his suspicions. He pulled on his boots, grabbed his jacket and drove to the scene.

The property was a hundred or so yards off the highway, a couple miles outside of town—the other side of town. It had taken him over twenty minutes to get there. Next to the highway was a small wooden sign with faded and peeling paint. The words "For Sale" and a telephone number were still discernible.

Pulling off the highway onto a gravel road, Jack passed a couple news vans and a handful of reporters who had parked their cars just off the highway and stood gawking at the scene. He was glad to see Luke's car already there.

As he approached the group of reporters, he overheard one, microphone in hand, speaking into a camera. "Another murder in the tony mountain enclave will have residents reeling. When is the carnage going to end…?"

Jack noticed Liz Kelly standing a few feet away, furiously taking notes in a small spiral notepad. She was wearing dark glasses and a scarf that shadowed her face.

Jack ducked under yellow crime scene tape that had been woven between a handful of aspen and pine trees, and headed toward the house. It looked like it had been abandoned at least a decade before. Years of overgrowth choked the unpainted lap siding. The teenagers had probably gone there to drink.

A small outbuilding, probably an old smokehouse, sat off to one side near the back of the property. That's where Jack saw Luke with Bobby McDonald and a couple guys from the coroner's office. They were huddled around a dark heap sprawled on a patch of dead grass surrounded by snow. Puffs of fur blew with each icy gust of the spring wind.

The group stood their distance while Lester examined the body. One of the guys from forensics was already photographing the scene.

Luke turned to Jack as he walked up. "Nice Saturday off again."

"Any idea who the victim is?"

"Woman. Early- to mid-forties. Dark hair. They haven't located any ID and I haven't been close enough to get a look yet."

Jack nodded and glanced around. The abandoned home and outbuilding lay between the highway and a dense forest of tangled aspen and pine. He knew the limited patches of mud, dead grass and icy snow between the body and the road wouldn't yield many clues. A faint dusting of snow the night before blanketed everything.

He looked toward the dense forest and into the darkness beyond. There were no discernible footprints leading away from the body into the forest. The killer had to have entered the property from the highway.

"Any ideas how long she's been here?" Jack asked.

"Lester said she was probably left sometime early last night. Her body was covered with the snow we got just after sundown."

"Has he estimated a time of death?" Jack asked the question out of habit, a reflex, but he knew they wouldn't be able to tell the time of death in sub-freezing temperatures. Colorado in early spring wasn't like Houston. A body found outside in southeast Texas would just about pinpoint the time of death for you by its stench and bug activity.

"Lester said he'd have to get her to the morgue first because of the temperature," Luke replied. "It's the end of the month, Jack. Long hair, mink coat. Do you think this could be our guy's third victim?"

"Hard to say. Let's see who she is first."

Lester stood over the body, noticed Jack and Luke and motioned them over.

From a distance, Jack thought the mound of twisted fur and leather more closely resembled the corpse of a dead animal than a human. But as he got closer, it was clear it was a woman. As the guys from the coroner's office rolled the body over, Jack took a few seconds to bolster himself, then looked down at the dead woman's face. He recognized the frozen death mask immediately.

Bridget Ferrari. Her lifeless eyes were fixed in position like marbles set by a taxidermist. Her mouth frozen, lips pulled tight in an icy grimace.

Jack took in a deep breath and turned to Luke. "It looks like we're going to have to pay Carlo Ferrari another visit."

Lester cleared his throat and pulled his jacket tighter around his great mass trying to shield it from the biting wind. "Can't tell you much yet. We'll get her on the table and I'll get back with you in a few hours."

Luke looked to Jack. "If the killer is copying Toomey, and the victim has been strangled, this would be his third."

"You're going to need to rethink that theory, son," Lester said to Luke. He turned to Jack. "I can't tell you much yet, but I can tell you this victim wasn't strangled. She was shot."

CHAPTER 75

THE DAY HAD dawned clear and crisp, but it would soon change.

Georgia looked out the kitchen blinds, the early morning sun was casting a rosy glow over town, setting off the light snow from the night before in a purple shimmer. What was that old sailor's saying? Something about red sky in morning? She couldn't remember.

She showered and dressed, stuck her laptop in a bag with a few of her notes, and walked to Miner's Cafe. Enough solitude. She needed the background noise of the cafe.

It was windy, but a glorious spring morning in the Rockies. There wasn't any hint of the storm forecasters were predicting. She turned her face toward the warming sun.

It was less than a fifteen minute walk, and it was still early, but people were already milling about. She admired the eclectic mix—high-brow tourists, artsy hippies, native mountain types in jeans and flannel shirts. A group of millennials passed her on the sidewalk, probably still in town from the X Games.

She rounded the last corner before the cafe and saw them in the distance—dark clouds billowing just beyond the snow-capped peaks to the northwest. A sudden gust of chilled air made her shiver. She ducked inside the cafe. She knew the weather could turn on a dime in the mountains, but forecasters didn't predict the storm until later that night. She wondered if they were wrong.

Inside, Georgia ordered a breakfast of eggs and bacon with a side of pancakes. It was what Jonathan had ordered the morning she closed on the house.

An elderly couple sat at a table near her.

"I just don't believe it," the woman said in a low voice. "These kinds of things don't happen *here*. Do you think it could happen again?"

She then overheard two men talking at a different table.

"I know the police are doing everything they can, but it's not enough. I hate to say it, but I think another girl could go missing."

"You're probably right," the second man answered.

Georgia felt a pit form in her stomach and tried to focus on her reading. She read in fits and spurts for an hour or so, but finally gave up. She packed up her things and left a tip on the table.

Outside, the weather had turned overcast; dark clouds had rolled in from the mountains and settled over the town like a gloomy blanket.

She lowered her head against the wind that had started to blow harder and nearly bumped into someone as she rounded the first corner. "I'm so sorry—"

"Why are you in such a hurry, Georgia dear?" It was Bunny King. The elderly woman had a full-length black mink coat pulled tight around her ample middle, a black silk scarf wrapped around the sprayed helmet of blue hair, the ends billowing with the breeze.

"Hello, Mrs. King. I'm sorry I almost ran into you."

"Oh, it's quite alright. I'm actually in a hurry myself. We should all be staying in doors for a while." When Georgia didn't respond, Bunny leaned toward her. Georgia got a whiff of vanilla and rose perfume in the wind. "The murders, dear. Get yourself home and lock your doors. I told Bart I was going to the market to get what we needed for lunch and dinner today. When I got up this morning and heard the news, I decided right then and there. I told him we were going to stay home until the police find whoever is doing this. The Commodores are playing at the opera house tonight, and of course we have wonderful seats, but I told Bart a pack of wild dogs wouldn't be able to drag me out of the house tonight, not with a murderer running loose."

Georgia wasn't sure how to reply. Everyone in town seemed on edge because of the recent murders, but Bunny's fear seemed extreme.

Bunny must have sensed Georgia's confusion. She leaned in closer and wrapped a cold bony hand around Georgia's wrist. Her eyes were huge. "Honey, you haven't heard?"

Georgia watched her wrinkled powdered lips move, but could hardly hear her. It was as if her voice was caught up and carried away with the wind.

"Heard what?" Georgia asked. Her skin had grown cold, goosebumps sprung up under the sleeves of her cashmere sweater.

"Well, it's all over town. That murderer—the police think he's copying some old murders from long ago. And now someone else has gone missing—Bridget Ferrari!"

She still held Georgia's hand but patted the top of it with her free one, a jeweled black handbag swinging in the crux of her elbow. "Now you best get home. But you telephone us if you decide you don't want to stay in that house all by yourself. I'll have Bart go right over and get you. Nobody should be alone right now."

With that she was gone, like a foreboding specter that disappeared with the mountain wind.

Back at home Georgia sat in silence at the kitchen table. The sense of uneasiness in town had been contagious. For a day that started out glorious, she now just wanted it over.

She sat hugging herself, as if shielding herself from something. But what? Just the cold, probably. She grabbed a cardigan and pulled it on. There was work to do. She didn't have time to get sucked into the town's brooding suspicions.

Outside the wind had kicked up. She jumped at the sound of a loud bang, then realized it was the mail slot.

She got up and walked to the front door, then picked up the mail where it had fallen onto the rug. She shuffled through it—a smattering of junk mail, but there was something else. She pulled a white envelope from the stack. Her name and address were written in a stilted handwriting she had seen before. There was no return address.

Georgia's hands shook as she tentatively opened the envelope and pulled out a single sheet of paper. Another photocopy of a page from a scrapbook. Another newspaper story.

She read the handwriting at the bottom—

One and one and another make three.

Who do you think my next victim will be?

CHAPTER 76

DETECTIVE MARK THURMOND sat at his desk in the southwest station of the Denver Police Department. It was Saturday afternoon, and although he wasn't scheduled to be on duty, he thought a few hours of quiet would help clear his head. He needed to sort through the swirling tangle of suspects and theories that kept him from being able to enjoy a day off.

He'd never been one of those detectives who could go for a beer with a buddy or to dinner or a movie with the wife and let go of an investigation. Unsolved cases irritated him like an itch he couldn't scratch.

He knew there were cases that just wouldn't be solved no matter how hard they were worked. He didn't like it, but after exhausting all the leads, he eventually let those cases go, transferring them to the cold case vault.

But sometimes, even with pressure from the brass to call it quits, Mark would hold onto a case like a rabid dog. It was intuition, his gut telling him he was on the verge of a breakthrough. There would be one loose end he could still work or an errant clue out of sight, but not out of reach if he just kept digging. Those cases ate at him like worms on an elk carcass. The question of who was stalking Georgia Glass was one of them.

He sat staring out the small window in his office. One name kept popping into his head. Eddie Jenkins.

The day before, Mark had downloaded Jenkins's cell phone

records and gone through them with a fine tooth comb. There was nothing in them that showed Jenkins had been in Aspen at any time during the last couple of weeks, except for the day he had installed the security system. But the records also indicated there were large blocks of time Jenkins hadn't used his phone at all, not even during the middle of the day.

Most people didn't go more than a few hours before their phone pinged a tower somewhere, but on two occasions in the last couple of weeks, Eddie Jenkins had.

Mark pulled the phone records again from the case file and compared the blocks of empty time to the large paper calendar that covered his desk. He then scanned his notes for the dates Georgia Glass had received threatening texts with photos.

The blocks of time didn't match perfectly, but it was close—Jenkins's cell phone had gone black the day of, or the day before, each time Georgia had received an anonymous text.

Mark thought of the state's highway cameras, used to monitor traffic snarls near the larger cities and inclement weather on rural highways. Interstate 70 to Highway 82 was the only realistic way someone would travel from Denver to Aspen. There had been no sign of Jenkins's Subaru along Highway 82 leading into Aspen on either of the days in question.

Staring back out the window, Mark Thurmond frowned. His brow relaxed when the thought hit him. From his investigation, he knew Jenkins drove a beat-up brown Subaru wagon, but he could have used a different car to get to Aspen. A stalker wouldn't use something his victim would recognize.

He was angry at himself for not considering the possibility of another car. He reached for the phone on his desk. He would take advantage of it being a quiet Saturday. He asked a couple guys on desk duty to call rental agencies to see if Jenkins had rented any cars in the last couple weeks. If he had, Mark would have them check the cameras along Highway 82 again.

But there was another possibility, a theory that jolted that gnawing feeling in his gut that he decided to check out for himself.

Mark flipped on his computer and waited for it to boot up. He had a hunch, and hoped to God he was wrong.

CHAPTER 77

GEORGIA SAT AT the kitchen table studying the second scrapbook page she had just received. It was an article about Toomey's first murder, cut from an old newspaper and meticulously glued into a scrapbook along with a couple photographs. Again, she recognized Ernest Galloway in one of the photographs.

When her cell phone rang, she jumped. She hadn't realized she was so on edge. She took a deep breath and looked at the caller ID.

"Parker," she answered. "It's good to hear from you."

"Hey, I've been following the updates on Twitter."

"Updates?"

"The body they found. Bridget Ferrari?"

"Bridget Ferrari?" Georgia took in a deep breath. "She's dead?"

"You hadn't heard?"

"No. I—I've been busy. I heard she was missing, but I can't believe it…"

He must have heard the tension in her voice. "Did you know her?" he asked.

"Yes—no. I mean I met her once—at the Winstons—after the funeral. This is so horrible."

"I'm sorry. The tabloids are already making her out to be some sort of social-climbing diva."

"That's terrible," Georgia said then hesitated. "She was... beautiful. Maybe a bit flamboyant—lots of personality. We talked about California. She was interested in my job at Coastal and told me how much I was going to love Los Angeles. She said she had lived in the Silicon Valley area until several years ago when her husband sold his business and they moved to Aspen. Parker, I was sitting across the table from her just a week ago. So full of life. I can't believe she's dead."

"I'm sorry, Georgia. I didn't realize you knew her." He waited a moment to continue. "I hate to change the subject—"

"Please do." Georgia felt weary.

"Are you by chance free tomorrow? I wanted to come out, finalize a few things on the job, maybe try out that new brew pub that's getting rave reviews on TripAdvisor."

Georgia was suspicious. "Parker, it's not about finalizing a few things, is it? You're coming out to check on me."

He was silent a moment. "Maybe I just want another lunch date?"

She wasn't buying it. "No, don't fly. We're expecting a late-spring storm tonight. We got some snow last night, but this is supposed to be bad."

"If it's still bad in the morning, we can divert to Denver and I'll drive out."

She could tell he wasn't going to take no for an answer.

After he hung up, Parker sat at his desk in the glass and steel monument to his father's company. Another Saturday at work. He wished he was anywhere else at that moment. But most of all, he wished he was with Georgia Glass.

Despite her trying to cover it up, when he told her about Bridget Ferrari, she had sounded upset—even nervous. He was nervous, too. Georgia was in too deep, had gotten too close. It was likely she had already come into contact with the murderer.

CHAPTER 78

MARK THURMOND SCROLLED through the video from his dash cam, glad he had actually remembered to switch the thing on when he pulled into the parking lot of Eddie Jenkins's apartment complex a couple days earlier.

There it was—the early model white van with rusted gash down the passenger side panel. The angle wasn't right to read the faded logo, but Mark remembered it had been something to do with carpet—carpet cleaning, carpet installation. But because the van was in such bad shape, and the logo nearly unreadable in person, Mark thought it was improbable the van was still in commercial use, at least not for the company whose faded name was on the side.

He wasn't interested in the logo, but he zoomed into the plates. The characters were blurry, but he could make them out. He called downstairs.

"Hector, I need you to run a plate for me. Yeah, now."

It only took a couple minutes and Mark had the name and address of the owner of the van that had been parked next to Jenkins's brown Subaru the morning Mark had paid Jenkins a visit. The van was registered to Lief Rizzo. He lived in the apartment directly below Eddie.

Mark hit the number for his contact at Colorado Department of Transportation on his way out of the building. "It's Mark Thurmond," he said into his phone. "I need you to check the same highway cameras around Aspen, same dates, but for another vehicle."

He knew the guys at CDOT were fast, but he wasn't going to wait around for their answer. His gut told him that they might not have found Eddie Jenkins's brown Subaru on any of the highway footage, but they would find the scarred white van. He grabbed his coat and bolted from the office.

Mark pulled in the apartment parking lot. The same potholes pocked the crumbling asphalt, the same weeds choked the metal bars of a perimeter fence that had been ostensibly put in as a security deterrent at some time. To keep people out? Mark wondered. Or to keep some of these guys in?

Eddie Jenkins's brown Subaru was parked in the same spot it had been a few days earlier, but the scarred white van was gone.

Mark took the stairs to Jenkins's second-floor apartment two at a time. No one answered.

Then he knocked on the door of the ground-floor apartment closest to where the van had been parked before. A tall, lanky thirty-something with a bird's beak for a nose opened the door letting out a cloud of smoke. Mark immediately recognized the pungent smell of marijuana.

"Yeah, man, what's up?" the bird-man asked in drawn out speech, eyes half-closed slits.

"I'm Detective Mark Thurmond with the Denver Police Department. Are you Lief Rizzo?"

He had gotten the bird-man's attention. His drooped posture straightened, and trying to appear more alert, he fought a losing battle to force his eyes open wider. "Uh, yes, sir," he said, struggling to tuck his open Hawaiian print shirt into the front of his shorts. "What can I do for you?"

"Do you own a 1985 white Chevrolet van?"

"Uh, yeah?"

"It has a logo on it, doesn't it?"

"Yeah. Centennial Carpet Cleaning. I bought it off the guys when they went out of business a few years ago. Why?"

Mark took another quick look around the parking lot. "Where is the van now?"

"Uh, Eddie must have taken it again."

"Eddie?"

"Eddie Jenkins. Lives upstairs," he added with a nod toward the uncovered rusting metal and concrete staircase attached to the exterior of the building.

"Do you know where Eddie Jenkins is now?"

Bird-man scratched his matted unwashed hair and appeared to think. "No, I can't remember that he said anything to me. But Eddie's like that. He takes my van when he needs something bigger than his Subaru," he said pointing to the ugly brown car Mark knew was parked behind him. He didn't turn to look.

"He doesn't ask you first?"

"No, not always. Just leaves me his keys so I got something to drive."

"So you don't know where Eddie is now?"

"Uh…" Scratched his head again, thinking. "No."

Mark's cell phone rang. CDOT. He looked back at the bird-man. "I have to get this. I'll be in touch."

He turned and walked a distance away before answering. "This is Thurmond."

"We found your van. We got it on Interstate 70 just before Glenwood Springs, again on 82 between Snowmass and Aspen, then back. We got it to and from Aspen several times in the range of days you told us to look. We can't tell for sure, but it looks like the driver is the guy in the photo you sent over yesterday—when we checked for the Subaru." Mark heard the rustling of paper. "Here it is. The driver closely resembles the picture you sent of one Eddie Jenkins."

"I knew it," Mark said opening his car door. "Thank you. Can you send time-stamped photos of the van over to—?"

"One more thing, detective."

"Yes?" Mark asked, buckling his seatbelt with his free hand.

"On a hunch we ran back through today's tape. The same van…"

Mark was about to start his car, but waited.

"It passed both cameras several hours ago. Your guy is in Aspen now."

CHAPTER 79

GEORGIA LOOKED OUT her kitchen window toward the mountains. The highest peaks were swallowed in ghostly gray clouds that were turning dusk to night sooner than normal.

The weather forecasters were right. Aspen was in for a wicked spring storm and it looked like it would get there sooner than they had expected.

Georgia closed the window shades then pulled her cardigan tighter around her shoulders. Her cell phone rang. It was Detective Thurmond.

"Georgia, we've identified your stalker. It's Eddie Jenkins."

Georgia thought it must be a mistake, or a joke. "No, you're wrong."

"We're not wrong." His tone was sympathetic but firm. "We have him on camera making round trips to Aspen from Denver on or before the days you received your anonymous texts.

She shook her head. "It can't be true. Eddie would never do that."

"It *is* true, Georgia. Now listen to me. I've already notified the police in Aspen. They've put you on a regular surveillance rotation."

"What does that mean?"

"If it's like we do here, they'll probably have the uniformed guys on patrol swing by your house every ten or fifteen minutes or so. There's probably someone on the way now. They may throw in an unmarked car if they feel the need. But if Eddie Jenkins calls—don't answer your phone. Lock your doors and don't let him in if he shows up. Call the police."

"I just don't believe Eddie would—"

He cut her off. "We believe he's dangerous."

Tears welled in her eyes. Shock had morphed into a mixture of confusion and betrayal. How could he? He had been so concerned for her safety, installing the security cameras for her again. All the phone calls checking on her. The times she had called *him* after she had received anonymous photographs, photographs she was now being told *he* took.

Georgia sat down on the sofa in the living room, doubled over and buried her face in her free hand, and tried to focus on Detective Thurmond's instructions.

"Okay, detective," she said nodding, her head still in her hand. "Yes, I understand. Thank you."

After she hung up, Georgia sat staring into space. She felt numb. Then slowly the feelings of betrayal turned to anger.

"How *could* you, Eddie," she said out loud making fists in her lap.

Georgia heard a gentle thud on the porch. The wind had kicked up with the growing storm, but she knew it wasn't the wind. Her heart caught in her throat. She was sure it was a footstep. Eddie?

CHAPTER 80

THE VEINS IN Eddie Jenkins's neck bulged as he watched Georgia on the computer monitor. He couldn't believe they had figured out he was Georgia's stalker.

He had been so careful. He had watched hundreds of *Forensic Files* episodes and had done everything to ensure his plan was fail-safe. He knew to use throwaway phones so his personal cell phone wouldn't ping any towers around Aspen. And he had used Lief's van, not his Subaru.

How did they find out? He wondered.

He shook his head violently. It doesn't matter *how* they found out. They knew. And now they were looking for him. He would be arrested, but he would finish with Georgia first. He wasn't going to let her have the satisfaction of seeing him go to jail.

Out of the corner of his eye, he saw Georgia get up from the sofa. Eddie turned his attention back to the monitor and watched as she walked to the window and looked outside, then walked into the kitchen and out of view. He couldn't see her, but heard as she took something from the refrigerator and rustled around in a drawer.

It was quiet a moment, then she walked back into view of the sitting room camera. She was holding a glass of wine and disappeared upstairs.

Eddie could see a light at the top of the stairs switch on.

The shifting light of Georgia's shadow from upstairs was the only movement on the monitor. Then something caught his attention on another camera view. He clicked the controls and enlarged the feed covering the front door, and couldn't believe what he was seeing.

A dark hooded figure had crept onto the porch and was using a gloved hand to unscrew the bulb in the light fixture mounted next to the front door. The monitor instantly switched to the muted gray hues of the camera's night vision.

Eddie leaned in and watched as the figure stood outside the door looking in. Eddie's eyes widened; his breathing came faster. Whoever it was at Georgia's door wore a dark jacket and pants, even dark shoes.

Eddie watched as he pulled something from his pocket, looked at it, then shoved it back in. It was fabric—a shirt? A woman's blouse? What was it? His eyes widened when it dawned on him. He sat back into his chair and let out a strangled laugh.

CHAPTER 81

DETECTIVES JACK MARTIN and Luke McCray were still at the office Saturday evening. They had searched the Ferrari home and found Bridget's car still at the house. Carlo had refused their request for an interview until his attorney could get to Aspen from Denver.

"With or without his attorney, we'll get a warrant and pick up Carlo Ferrari Monday morning. He can wait for his attorney in the small holding cell at the station. One way or another he's going to talk to us." Jack felt the case coming together and wasn't going to let any suspect dictate the timing.

"We've got at least three possibilities," he told Luke. "One is that Carlo Ferrari is the serial killer and killed all of them." He ticked the names off his fingers as he spoke, "Rachel Winston, Greta Moss, Brenda Pawloski, Stanley Lauren and now his wife, Bridget. The second possibility is that he didn't kill any of the others but *did* kill his wife. And the third possibility, despite looking guilty as hell of at least killing his wife, he didn't kill any of them."

"Initial thoughts?" Luke asked.

"The manners of death are the sticking point. Rachel Winston and Greta Moss were strangled with scarves, and their murders are too similar to the Toomey ones in timing and manner of death to assume it's a coincidence. Then we have Stanley Lauren, strangled but not with a scarf. The autopsy report indicates the killer strangled him with his hands. Brenda Pawloski was shot. Now Bridget Ferrari is shot."

"No pattern. So there's a good chance we've got more than one killer."

Jack nodded once. "Possibly... but not likely." After a moment he added, "It's hard to believe that it's been decades since Aspen had a murder. Hell, it's one of the safest towns in America—statistically speaking. Now there might be *two killers* in town at the same time?" Jack shook his head.

"So you think we're dealing with *one*?"

"I do. We'll know more when we get ballistics back. If we find out Brenda Pawloski and Bridget Ferrari were killed with two different guns, we're looking at two murderers."

"Carlo Ferrari offed his wife, but someone else killed Brenda Pawloski."

Jack was still thinking. "Carlo could have killed his wife thinking we would mistakenly lump the case in with the other murders."

"But if they were killed with the same gun?"

"If the same gun was used in both instances, and we *can't* find a connection between Brenda Pawloski and Carlo Ferrari, then Carlo's probably *not* our guy."

Luke frowned. "Then we're back to one murderer. Except that doesn't explain why some were strangled and some were shot. There's still no pattern."

"Rachel Winston and Greta Moss are the pattern. I don't know how the others fit in. Maybe they were in the way or posed some sort of threat. Maybe they were in the wrong place at the wrong time, saw something they shouldn't have, but my gut tells me the key to solving this lies with the victims— Winston and Moss in particular."

Luke nodded. "The copycat murders."

"Right. And the problem I have with that is, if the killer is still mimicking Toomey, and needs five strangled victims, he's got at least three murders left. So he's going to kill again." Jack checked the date on his cell phone, "It's the end of the month. There's a good chance it will happen any day. Let's go back over our suspect list. Start at the top."

McCray looked at his notes. "Thomas Murphy."

"Who just today got us the audio tape he secretly recorded with Tiffany Rice. He's proved she was extorting money and that he was telling the truth, but I don't trust him."

"So he's still at the top of our suspect list."

They ran through the handful of other names.

Jack Martin leaned back in his chair and let out a long breath. "We can't just sit here. Let's start at the top of the list and pay each of our suspects a visit tonight. Check their whereabouts and activities, but also their reaction when we show up at their door. And let's start with Dr. Murphy."

"Oh, before I forget." Luke handed Jack a folder.

"What's this?"

"The webcam photos. From the cameras at each end of Main Street."

Jack remembered from reviewing the photos earlier in the case that the cameras took a new photograph every fifteen minutes.

They flipped through the dozens of photos and didn't recognize any of their suspects on the street the night Bridget went missing. They had almost made it through the stack the night Rachel Winston went missing when Jack stopped and looked closer.

"Wait a minute." He pointed to a man in the photo, took out a magnifying glass from his desk and leaned over the picture. He studied it a moment then sat back in his chair, handing the magnifying glass to Luke.

"What am I looking at?"

"Look at who it is, then look at the time."

Luke's eyes grew large. He looked up at Jack. "Let's go."

As they grabbed their coats, Jack's cell phone rang. It was Mark Thurmond in Denver relaying the message that Georgia Glass's stalker had been identified and was currently in Aspen. As Thurmond spoke, Jack wrote down Eddie Jenkins's name, physical description and the description of the van he was traveling in.

When the call ended, Jack looked at his partner. "Change of plans. We've got to check on Georgia Glass first."

CHAPTER 82

OUTSIDE, THE AIR was frozen and the temperature was still dropping. The sky had gone from purple to black.

He stood on the porch looking in.

The wind made high-pitched screams that he didn't hear, and the snow swirled in mad fits that he didn't notice. His razor-sharp focus was fixed on one thing.

He made sure the scarf was tucked deep in the pocket of his coat then knocked on the door. After a moment, Georgia glanced through the living-room blinds, saw him and smiled. He heard her turn off the alarm and unlock the deadbolt. His heart rate quickened as she opened the door.

"Jonathan. What a welcome surprise on such a scary night."

"Scary?" he asked, forcing a strained grin. He didn't notice the burst of snow swirling past him and into the house.

"The weather," she said ushering him in. "I'm glad you're here. Come inside, let me shut the door."

He stepped inside then turned and watched as she closed the door and locked the deadbolt.

She noticed him watching. "Habit," she said with a quick smile. "These days you don't know who's out there."

"No, you don't." Jonathan took off his gloves and jacket then laid them across the back of the sofa. "Better safe than sorry."

"Can I get you something to drink?"

"I'll have whatever you're having."

"Then Pinot Noir it is."

When Georgia returned from the kitchen with two wine glasses, Jonathan was sitting on the sofa, a stack of her research materials fanned across the coffee table in front of him. He had found the copied scrapbook pages clipped together and was looking at them. Something about him rifling uninvited through her things made her uneasy.

He looked up when she handed him his glass. "What are these?"

She felt nervous but didn't know why. She sat down in a chair facing the sofa. "They were sent to scare me."

He raised his eyebrows. "Did they?"

"What?"

"Did they scare you?"

"I guess a little," she said. "But it's probably just a prank, someone harmless."

"I don't know," he said. "I think you should take it seriously. You have to be careful about people. There's a monster in all of us."

It was a strange thing to say. Georgia knew she had heard it before. Or read it somewhere. Suddenly she remembered, but it was too late. In one swift motion he was on top of her, pulled her arms behind her and zip-tied her wrists together. She cried out at the pain in her shoulders and from the plastic ties cutting into her wrists.

She stood up and tried to kick at him, grazing his shin. He struck her, knocking her down. Before she could roll away, he was on top of her again. She tried to fight him off, but he was too strong. He flipped her onto her stomach and forced her ankles together then bound them with another zip tie.

Outside, the wind roared through the trees. She wanted to scream but knew it would be useless. No one would hear her.

Jonathan lifted her by her shoulders and threw her back into the chair.

She watched as he took his coat off the back of the sofa and pulled a brightly colored scarf from one of the pockets.

Her eyes widened when she saw it.

"*You?*" she asked. "You killed Rachel Winston and Greta Moss?" She heard the disbelief and fear in her own voice.

"You think?" He laughed at her, an eerie deep laugh she didn't recognize. "But that's not all. Keep going."

"What?" Georgia's head was swimming.

"Keep going," he insisted again. "Rachel Winston, Greta Moss—keep going."

Georgia thought for a moment. "The woman from the museum?"

"Bingo!" He stabbed the air with a finger. "And?"

Georgia sat watching him. He paced the floor, eyes wild and with a grin that held no humor. She shuddered when she realized how much he was enjoying it.

"And?" he repeated, stopping to look at her.

Georgia didn't know what to say.

He sighed and rolled his eyes. "Stanley Lauren."

"You killed Stanley Lauren?"

"Yes. Stanley Lauren—*and?*"

Georgia shook her head, then it came to her. "Bridget Ferrari?" Her voice shaking.

"There you go," he said smiling again. "Now you've finally got it."

"You killed all of them?" she asked in a stunned whisper.

Jonathan nodded with self-satisfaction. "And now it's your turn."

"What? Why, Jonathan? I don't understand." Fear caught in her throat.

"You don't understand? Well you're the great investigative reporter, you tell me."

She fought to control her mounting panic. One false move and it would be over. Keep him talking. The police were patrolling her house, Mark Thurmond had told her that. They would see his car. Somebody would come. And if they didn't, she would figure a way out. Just keep him talking.

"Jonathan, none of this makes sense. I thought we were friends—"

He snorted another laugh. "There's no such thing as friends. It's every man out for himself. I have to say how disappointed I am in you, Georgia. I thought you were smarter than this. Try again."

He was enjoying himself, enjoying toying with her, bragging. "Don't do this," she said, pulling against the zip-ties at her wrist, but it was useless. She looked up at him, tears welling in her eyes. "This isn't like you."

"What do you know about what I'm like?" he spat. "Nobody ever knows anyone. There's a monster in all of us, remember? You just might not have met it yet."

Toomey's quote again. It was then Georgia noticed the papers from her investigation scattered across the floor. Photos of the recent victims, yellowed newspapers articles and old police reports. She shuffled everything through her memory, combing it for clues. Then it dawned on her. The scrapbook.

She looked up at him, the fear in her eyes replaced by cold realization. "Toomey."

His smile faded, and she felt her confidence grow. A tense silence was broken only by the storm raging outside.

"It was Toomey, wasn't it?" she asked.

He didn't say anything.

"You knew about him, studied him, thought you could do the same thing."

She had figured something out and it had hit a nerve. But there was a fine line between keeping him talking and making him angry. She had to be careful.

"But better," he insisted. When she didn't reply, he added, "I could do the same thing, *but better*. I found out about Toomey thanks to good ol' Uncle Ernest. So I read about him. But Toomey was an idiot. He got caught. He didn't deserve all the attention he got. Do you know they still talk about his old murders?"

"Who does?"

"The media. Lots of people." He looked at her as though she was an idiot.

"No, I didn't know that."

"Well they do. I saw a documentary on serial killers a few months ago and they mentioned him, after all these years. But the guy was an idiot, left clues everywhere and got caught."

"So you thought you could do it better."

"Of course I could do it better, and I have!" He held out both arms, stretching the scarf in a sign of triumph before winding the ends around his fists again.

Georgia swallowed. "That explains Rachel and Greta, but why the others?"

"They got in the way." He unknotted a hand from one end and waved it dismissively. "Except for Bridget."

It was eerie hearing him say her name. Georgia thought he was friends with Bridget Ferrari, and yet he had murdered her. "Bridget was your friend," she said.

"I already told you there's no such thing. Everyone is out for themselves. Bridget was, too."

"So why did you kill her?"

"Bridget had a bad habit of showing up unannounced.

She came over at the wrong time when I wasn't home and saw the scrapbook. I had to kill her. And the timing was perfect. I didn't realize it at first, but her murder was the perfect distraction—a decoy."

Georgia frowned. "A decoy for what?"

He shook his head. "For a high-paid investigative reporter, you haven't figured out crap yet, have you?"

Georgia remembered the silky flash of color when she had discovered Rachel Winston's body. She remembered Greta Moss had died the same way. "How did you kill Bridget?"

He pointed a finger toward her and cocked an invisible hammer, then wound the scarf around his free hand again.

"You shot her?" He nodded once. "If you're copying Toomey—"

"I'm not *copying* Toomey." His jaw went rigid. "I *used* him… as inspiration. But I'm smarter than he was. I'm not making his mistakes. Toomey didn't get away with it, but I will."

Georgia needed to dial back the tension. She kept her tone slow and even. "But Toomey killed five victims. You've already killed five. Why me?"

He raised his hands in front of her and jerked the scarf taught, making her flinch, which made him laugh again.

Then she understood. "You need to strangle more victims," Georgia said in a soft voice. "Like Toomey."

"Now you're getting it." He took a step toward her.

Keep him talking, keep him talking. She noticed the scattered papers on the floor and thought of the scrapbook again.

"You mentioned Uncle Ernest?" she blurted. It worked. He stopped and waited for her to continue. "These are copies of *his* scrapbook pages that you sent me, aren't they? He's in the pictures, and the old articles." She motioned with her head toward the papers on the floor.

"Finally," he said clapping his hands slowly. "Brilliant work." He was mocking her.

She continued. "Tell me where you got it," she said. "The scrapbook. Did you find it here, in the house? Before I moved in?"

His crooked grin returned. "Huh? Maybe you could have made a decent investigative reporter after all. But we'll never know now, will we?"

He walked to the window, looked out at the raging storm. "This is perfect," he said. "No one will hear you scream."

Georgia took a deep breath and lowered a steady gaze on him. "I'm not going to scream."

CHAPTER 83

THEY WOUND THEIR way through the darkness, the street-lights casting wild shadows that danced with the trees in the increasing wind. They were still several blocks from Georgia's house when they saw it.

"Well, I'll be damned," Jack said, slowing the truck as they approached the white van.

Luke checked his notes from the conversation with Mark Thurmond, looked back up and squinted. The van was parked in the dark shadow of an old spruce, but the license plate was still visible. "That's it."

Lightning flashed and lit up the sky for an instant, revealing the van's hideous scar and empty front seats.

"Nobody's in it," Luke said.

Jack turned back, looking as they idled past. The van was dark—too dark, as if a barrier or curtain had been pulled shut behind the front seats and blocked the view of what was inside. "Let's check it out."

They circled the block and pulled into an empty spot several spaces behind the van. Both men got out.

"They're blacked out," Luke said about the rear windows.

Jack walked along the driver's side, squinted to read the faded logo sliced in half.

He peered in the front window then walked back to where Luke stood at the back of the van.

"Let's see if our guy is in there," Jack said, then rapped on one of the windows. "Aspen police," he called over the wind. "Open up!"

Nothing. He was about to knock again when they heard a latch release, then saw one of the back doors swing open.

"Eddie Jenkins?"

"Yeah. I thought maybe you guys would show up," he said before sitting back down on an overturned plastic bucket. In front of him was a narrow table made of plywood; on it were two large computer monitors and a keyboard.

Jack stepped forward, his hand on the butt of the pistol on his hip. "We'll need you to come with us," he said.

"Alright, alright," Eddie replied shaking his head, the muscles in his neck tensed, "I know the drill." He pulled a headset off his head. "But I want to finish watching this first."

That's when Jack saw it. For a second he stood stunned, watching the events unfold on the screen.

Eddie yanked the headset cord from the monitor. Suddenly the audio was projected into the van. "Here, listen for yourself," he said with a grin. "He's about to kill her."

Jack recognized Georgia Glass.

The audio reverberated through the hollow metal van.

"Why Stanley Lauren?" Georgia asked abruptly as Jonathan Kramer stepped closer to her. Jack knew instinctively that she was buying time.

Jack looked from the monitor to Luke. "Keep him here. I'll call for back up," he said as he turned and ran toward his truck.

CHAPTER 84

DESPITE GEORGIA'S WARNINGS, Parker Randolph had flown to Aspen that night, the pilot threading the needle between two storms to land.

Parker had a rental car waiting for him when he got there and decided that for his own peace of mind he would drive past Georgia's house before he checked into the hotel. He wanted to see for himself that she was okay, wanted to quiet that pesky feeling that something was wrong, that she was in danger.

As he approached Georgia's, a large pickup truck sped past him and parked directly across the street from her house. A man was getting out as Parker pulled alongside. He stopped and rolled down his window.

"Is there something wrong here?"

"Police business. Keep moving," was all the man said. He leapt around the hood of Parker's car and headed toward Georgia's house.

Parker pulled to the curb in front of the truck and got out. He followed the man claiming to be a police officer but not dressed like one. He knew it was a risky move, the man could be anyone, but Parker wasn't leaving until he saw Georgia and knew she was alright.

"Who are you?"

The man wheeled around on him. He replied in an impatient whisper, "Get out of here!"

Parker followed him to Georgia's front porch but stopped on the sidewalk when the man drew a pistol and took the steps in a single leap.

Jack peered through a sliver of an opening between the window frame and the blinds that covered it and saw Georgia still bound and sitting exactly as he had seen her on the monitor in the van. Kramer had moved closer and was now standing directly over her. She was looking up at him.

He saw Kramer loop the scarf around Georgia's neck and pull it tight. She struggled, immediately falling to the ground in front of the chair.

Jack knew that in a couple more seconds, she would be dead. He wrenched the doorknob but it was locked. Then in one fluid move, he kicked it in, splintering the wood door frame, took aim and fired.

The impact caused Jonathan Kramer to lurch headfirst onto Georgia.

Before Jack could reach her, she had rolled out from under him. She was coughing and gasping for air as Jack untangled the scarf from her neck.

CHAPTER 85

IT WAS SUNDAY. The morning was bright and cloudless, the sky a bluebird shade that seemed to reflect the new hope and optimism the town's residents felt at waking to the news that a murderer no longer walked among them.

Georgia sat at a back table at Miner's Cafe. Parker sat next to her. Jack Martin and Luke McCray sat across from them. Georgia realized the irony that Miner's Cafe was where she had met Jonathan for breakfast her first morning in Aspen. She kept it to herself, not mentioning anything when Parker had suggested the location for the group's late-morning breakfast.

Detective Martin sat directly across the table from her. "We had just figured out Jonathan Kramer had lied to us about his alibi. He said he went directly to a bar following the party that night. The bartender confirmed Kramer was there but couldn't pinpoint a time for us. We caught Kramer on the city's webcam on Main Street outside the bar two hours later than the time he said he was there."

"So there was a gap in his timeline," Detective McCray added. "It was during this time we believe he abducted and killed Rachel Winston."

Jack spoke up again. "We were on the way to pick Kramer up when we were alerted by Mark Thurmond that Eddie Jenkins was in town. It was on the way to your house that we saw Jenkins's van and apprehended him."

Georgia sat quiet, taking it all in.

"By the way," Detective Martin added, "you were right about Kramer having your uncle's scrapbook. We found it last night when we searched his house. He was in the process of putting together one of his own. He had cut out articles from newspapers and the tabloids, and had printed copies of online articles—not just about the Moss and Winston murders, but about Brenda Pawloski and Stanley Lauren, too. If he would've lived long enough, I'm sure he would have included articles about Bridget Ferrari."

And me, Georgia thought to herself. "Last night Jonathan told me he found the scrapbook in my uncle's house after he passed away. He had arranged for the house to be cleaned out but found it left on top of the bookshelves in the sitting room. That's where he first learned about Gerald Ray Toomey."

"And that was just the beginning," Detective Martin added. "We think he later went to the museum to research Toomey. That's where he came into contact with Brenda Pawloski."

"He killed her for the same reason he killed Stanley Lauren," Detective McCray added.

"Why was that?" Georgia asked.

"To tie up loose ends. Both could have possibly identified him."

Georgia shook her head in disbelief. She still couldn't believe that the Jonathan Kramer she had known—had dinner with—could have killed all those people.

"And Bridget Ferrari?" Parker asked the detectives. "Why did he kill *her*?"

Georgia answered. "She saw the scrapbook. He wasn't home and she came over and saw it. And as a side benefit, she was a distraction—her murder preoccupied law enforcement and the media while he made plans to kill me."

The group sat in silence. The gravity of what had occurred

the last couple weeks weighed heavily on everyone at the table, especially Georgia.

She was the first to break the silence. "Until Jonathan attacked me, I thought Dr. Murphy was the most likely suspect."

"He was at the top of our list," Detective Martin said. "It's not a secret any longer, so I can tell you—Tom Murphy is a womanizer, but he's not a murderer. We found evidence that he had made contact with Brenda at the museum. Probably first, because he's a history buff and would naturally—eventually—end up at the museum. But then he apparently became interested in her romantically. He lied about meeting her because he was nervous about becoming a suspect. He knew he was already a suspect in the Rachel Winston murder because of his wife's missing scarf."

"There was always something a bit off with him," Georgia said. "I never felt comfortable around him."

"With good reason." Luke McCray looked at her. "He's admitted to having an affair with a young nurse while he was director of Mount Belvedere Hospital in New York. The nurse accused him of sexual harassment and has been blackmailing him ever since. He got tired of it and came forward with the story. Liz Kelly got wind of it somehow and let us know it'll be in the news later today."

"But womanizing isn't murder," Parker said. "So I imagine Dr. Murphy is a very relieved man knowing he is no longer a murder suspect."

Detective Martin nodded. "But he still has the public humiliation of the coming scandal and the wrath of his wife to contend with."

Georgia remembered the starburst window. "I didn't get around to mentioning it, but I found out the Murphys lived in the old boarding house where Toomey lived in the 50's. I never put much faith in coincidence, but I guess you never know.

And Carlo Ferrari," she said, "he has to be devastated by his wife's murder, but relieved, too, that he is no longer a suspect."

"He was another one at the top of our list. He never had a solid alibi for the nights of the murders," Detective Martin said. "But on the advice of his attorney, he told us about a medical condition he suffers from. We confirmed it with his doctor. Legally, I can't give you any more details than that, but we know Carlo Ferrari had nothing to do with any of the murders. Jonathan Kramer was responsible for all of them."

The night before, after Jonathan's body had been removed from her house and the police department's forensic team was combing it for evidence, Georgia had packed a small duffle bag and check into a room adjoining Parker's at Hotel Jerome.

Even securely locked in her room at the hotel and with Parker asleep in the room next door, Georgia woke in the middle of the night trembling, sure that she had heard footsteps in the hallway and someone trying to turn the doorknob to her room.

Was it Jonathan? Then she remembered he was dead.

And then there was Eddie. With everything that had happened she had little time to digest the news that he had been the one stalking her all along. Looking back, there were signs. She should have known. But she didn't want to think about that now. She would confront Eddie someday, but not yet.

After a half-hour of reliving the nightmares, Georgia had gotten out of bed for a glass of water and a trip to the door to confirm what she already knew—that it was locked. She took a couple deep breaths then settled back into bed and vowed to once and for all not fall hostage to her fears ever again.

Earlier that morning, Detective Thurmond had called Georgia from Denver to check on her. Georgia had heard the shock and relief in his voice when she filled him in on how the night had unfolded after he called Detective Martin alerting him Eddie was her stalker.

"I can't say that I'm surprised," Detective Thurmond had told her. "More often than not, stalking cases are committed by someone the victim knows. I'm sorry Eddie Jenkins was a friend of yours, but I'm glad he's off the streets. And Tony Paladino might not be guilty of stalking, but he's going to spend a very long time in jail for killing a prison guard. You won't have to worry about him either."

Luke McCray was lifting his cup of coffee but stopped. "I forgot to mention they're cleaning your house as we speak. We finished the on-scene investigation last night and had the cleaning team go in first thing this morning. It'll probably be released to you in an hour or so. There won't be any evidence left of what occurred there."

"Except for in my memory," Georgia said with a long sigh. "But Jonathan Kramer isn't going to win. What he did is not going to scare me away from here."

"Good," Detective Martin said. "It is a good town. I wasn't sure about it when I moved here, but I've learned to like it."

Aspen might be a mishmash of the haves and the have-nots—of flannel and fur—but in the short time she had been there, Georgia realized how much she liked it.

"I've grown attached to my house," she said. "I talked to my contractor, Karl Kamp, this morning. He's going to give everything a fresh coat of paint—inside and out. Start new."

"Bravo," Parker said smiling. "Forget the old memories—you'll fill the house with new ones. Friends will come out of the woodwork wanting an invitation to come visit. In fact, I'd love to be one of the first ones. I could get some serious writing done here."

Georgia looked at Parker and saw the hope for a new beginning. She wouldn't let Jonathan or Eddie win. She would live and work in Los Angeles, but she had decided to make Aspen her second home. She would keep the house.

Georgia turned to Jack Martin. "So what's next for you, detective? I heard rumors this morning that you're leaving?"

He nodded. "After the last few months we've had, Detective McCray is more than ready for the promotion to senior detective."

"Will you go back to Texas?" Georgia asked.

He was silent a moment before he answered. "Maybe." He looked down at the brown dog asleep at his feet, his stoic expression softened a bit. "But I might try some hiking first."

Georgia leaned over and glanced under the table at his dog, then at his scuffed cowboy boots. "Well, you're going to need some new shoes."

ACKNOWLEDGMENT

Aspen is a beautiful town nestled in the Rocky Mountains of Colorado. Anything negatively portrayed in this novel is strictly for literary purposes and in no way based on real people or events.

I am hugely grateful to my editors extraordinaire.

To Kristen Weber for helping me learn today how to craft a better novel tomorrow. Your direction on how to tell an intriguing (and coherent) story was invaluable. You made this a much better book than I could have made it on my own.

To Jayne Lewis for your painstaking attention to detail in polishing the text, deleting all my unnecessary commas and catching the last few editing issues. I promise to brush up on punctuation before I send you the next manuscript.

To my three greatest creations—Jordan, Abby and Patrick. You are my endless source of pride and joy. Thank you for your encouragement and support. It means the world to me.

Finally, I'm forever grateful to my husband, Chris, for all of the "Are you finished yet?" queries. Yes, it's finally done. Sorry for all the takeout. Your support is what made this book possible. Now on to the next!

AUTHOR NOTE

Dear Reader,

Thank you for sharing this journey with me. I hope you enjoyed reading Now I See You. This is the first book in the Mountain Resort Mystery Series.

I'm a student working to learn a craft. I owe a huge debt of gratitude to three of my favorite authors—Mary Higgins Clark, PD James and Agatha Christie. I've spent years reading, enjoying and studying their novels, and have been significantly influenced by all three in writing Now I See You—particularly Mary Higgins Clark.

Writing Now I See You was a fun step in learning to write a traditional whodunit. I hope you will continue on this journey with me. Detective Jack Martin is investigating a murder case in Vail, Colorado next!

With gratitude,
Shannon Work